PRAISE FOR BOOK UNE IN
THE COMEBACK TRAIL SERIES, *KILLING ME SOFTLY*:

"Witty, with an intriguing concept that will
keep you hooked until the end."
Jonathan Whitelaw, *The Sun*

"Dark and very funny."
Jonathan Ray, BBC Radio Bristol

"Pulpy, wicked, and thoroughly entertaining."
Paul Burke, Crime Time FM

"Fantastic read and so funny.
It even makes you root for a serial killer."
Jodie Whitfield, Relish Books

"Captures the reader from the first page."
Quirky Book Reads

"Three hundred and sixty pages of dark deliciousness.
A book where I found myself rooting for a serial killer."
Kiren Parmar's Book Club, Radio Tamworth

ABOUT THE AUTHOR

Guy Hale lives in rural Worcestershire with his wife and son. He spent his early life avoiding serious employment as a professional golfer. He then spent several years trying to end it by racing motorcycles. Having failed, he then concentrated on business, which proved to be a safer and more suitable destination for his talents. He sold up and retired in 2018, and then started a record label in Texas. This led him to becoming a songwriter, and writing novels was a natural progression. He confesses to having a low boredom threshold.

BLOOD ON THE TRACKS

JIMMY WAYNE – THE COMEBACK TRAIL – BOOK 2

GUY HALE

Produced in United Kingdom.

For permission requests, please contact:
guyhale@hillside-global.com

Project management by whitefox

Typeset by seagulls.net

Cover design by Peter Adlington

Scan the QR code to hear Jimmy Wayne's record.

Find the author on Twitter, Facebook, Instagram
or Linktree under @HaleWrites

*To Alyson Hale, Clinton King, Dave Herbert
and Blair Kessler my beta readers.*

*They always tell me what works, and more
importantly, what doesn't. Thanks guys.*

THANK YOUS

Big thanks to Amelia Collins, my editor. Always full of constructive good advice and never lets me get away with anything, for which I'm grateful.

Thanks also to Chris Wold and Jess King at whitefox for all their hard work on this project and listening to my stream of consciousness without falling asleep.

To Laura Lees, PR Supremo and she who must be obeyed!

To Peter Adlington, for the fantastic covers.

And finally, to the Hillside Global crew: Oli Overton, James Dyble, Molly Allen and Jake Clarke, whose hard work and expertise help to make this happen.

CONTENTS

CHAPTER 1
LA BOUND

Jimmy Wayne stood on the parking lot of the Riviera Casino. As usual he was waiting for Kid Oscarson. The midmorning Nevada sun beat down on him like a blowtorch but he shivered as he gazed at the mountains to the south of town. He had secrets buried in those silent peaks. Within those towering stone walls was a valley enclosed by a sweep of sheer cliffs and there, like an altar set before a huge arena, was a rocky bluff. It was about forty feet high and a hundred feet wide, and lying in the warm desert sand that covered its surface was a crop that would never grow. Eight bodies, all dead by his hand. Wendy, the woman he loved, had been an accident but the others – they were no accident.

'You ready to go, Jimmy?'

Jimmy turned to see the giant form of Kid Oscarson approaching him. The sun was behind him and he cast a shadow like a breaking wave. He wasn't fat; he was just huge. A throwback to his Norwegian forbears, if Kid told you his father was Thor you would probably believe him. Jimmy sighed and took one last glance at the mountains, to the place where Wendy lay. The song cemetery! That's what she had called it. He used to go up there to try and write songs, but they never turned out right.

'This is the place where songs come to die,' she had said. 'We should call it the song cemetery.' Now Wendy lay there, a beacon of virtue, surrounded by seven assorted scumbags and criminals who had fallen at Jimmy's hand. Jimmy shuddered.

'Not sure I will ever be ready to go, Kid.'

Kid nodded. He knew about the Song Graveyard; he had helped to bury some of the bodies. He put his hand on Jimmy's shoulder and spoke with a gentleness that belied his physical size.

'Jimmy, Wendy will always be around wherever you are. She's still in your head, still in your heart.'

Jimmy nodded. 'I know Kid, we just said our goodbyes at the cemetery, even sung a duet I wrote.'

Kid smiled. 'You still seeing her then.'

'Yeah, just never know when she's going to turn up. She just appears, no warning no nothing.' Jimmy slowly shook his head. 'Do you think I'm going crazy?'

Kid shrugged. 'Define crazy, one man's ghost is another man's imaginary friend.'

Jimmy flinched. 'Oh man! Is that supposed to make me feel better?'

'No Jimmy, you killed your girlfriend, nothing's ever going to make you feel better.' He thought for a moment. 'It was an accident; it's left scars, some of which have been positive.' Jimmy didn't look convinced. Kid persisted. 'You discovered a gift for song writing, that was good, the only downside was that it only happens when you kill someone.'

'That's a pretty big downside.'

Kid thought for a moment. 'In Wendy's case, but all the others you killed were criminals and murderers. Killing them was a public service, and it got you some great songs and they got you a record deal and a way out of Blackjack. Wendy apart, I can't see a downside.'

Kid finished his joint and walked across to the nearest trash bin, rubbed it out and threw it in. Most people would just have dropped it and stubbed it out under their foot. Jimmy wondered if it was Kid's Nordic upbringing that made him so tidy. Kid stretched.

'You ready to hit the big time, Jimmy Wayne? I say we head for LA and make that record!'

Jimmy smiled sadly. 'You know there was a time when I would have given anything to get away from this dump. Now I'm finally leaving, it's hard to let go. I've been happy here, made friends. For the first time in my life I've put down some roots.'

Kid leaned towards Jimmy and whispered in his ear. 'You put down more than roots Jimmy, let's get going before the past catches up.'

Kid had a point. There was a whole new world waiting for him in LA. A big record deal based on the new songs he had written and then a major residency in Vegas. Jimmy Wayne and the Second Chance were standing on the edge of the big time. Jimmy nodded.

'You're right... let's hit the road.' They both took one final look at the Riviera Casino and Hotel. 'I been here six years you know, feels strange to be going.'

Kid shrugged. 'Jimmy, if we get it right in LA you can come back and buy the damn place!'

Jimmy laughed. 'I might just do that!' They both turned their backs on the past and climbed into the Dodge van. Kid fired up the motor.

'LA here we come! You thought of a name for the album yet, Jimmy?'

'Funny you should ask; it came to me this morning when I was up at the Song Cemetery.'

Kid nodded impatiently. 'Well come on, let's have it.'

'I thought *Killing Me Softly* would work!' Kid hit the brakes.

'Man, that's clever. "Killing Me Softly, with his song!"' Kid nodded enthusiastically. 'It could be our little in-joke.'

Jimmy sighed. 'It's going to have to be unless you like being strapped into an electric chair!' They both looked at each other and burst out laughing. You could still hear them laughing as they cleared the edge of Blackjack headed for LA.

As they headed out of town on the A93 they didn't notice the police car sitting on the forecourt of the gas station. Behind the wheel sat Sheriff Pence. He watched them go like a hawk watching a field mouse, his eyes intently fixed on the Dodge van until it disappeared over the horizon headed towards Vegas. He knew Jimmy Wayne was guilty, he just hadn't worked out what it was he was guilty of. Jimmy and Kid had been in Three Rivers when he and his deputies had been involved in the shootout with the Delta Biker gang at their clubhouse. There were three bikers missing, that bothered him. Pence had to investigate carefully, that was the only problem with being corrupt. He was Jack Lantern's bent cop, bought and paid for. To get Jimmy Wayne he had to be sure he had covered his own tracks first. The past always has a way of catching up with you and he had had a good run, this was no time to be careless. For now, he would close the case on the Three Rivers shoot-out and let the trail go cold. Bide his time until he could act.

CHAPTER 2

DRINKING, GOD AND HEAVY METAL

While Kid drove, Jimmy watched Nevada slip by his window, every mile taking him further away from the scene of his crimes. He began to relax. Jimmy fell asleep. Kid lit another joint and the soporific vapours floated across to Jimmy and eased him deeper. Slowly, through the fog of sleep, he fell into a dream. He was standing at a crossroad in the middle of nowhere, he looked into the distance and could see nothing for miles. The sign in front of him said, Give Way – to what, he wasn't sure, it didn't look like anything had ever passed this way. Jimmy stepped out into the middle of the deserted junction.

'Hey, watch where you are going sonny!' He jumped back just in time to see an old man on a bicycle skid to a halt.

'You going to get yourself killed.' Jimmy looked up and down the road again, nothing for miles.

'Where the hell did you come from.' The old man smiled, and it was a beautiful thing to see. Like the sun breaking through the clouds Jimmy felt himself being enveloped in a warm glow.

'I'm from your future Jimmy, we going to do great things together.' Jimmy looked at the old bicycle doubtfully.

'Not on that we're not!' The old man looked down at his rusty steed.

'Never take anything at face value Jimmy Wayne, the future is a story that is yet to be written!' He winked at Jimmy with his unusually deep blue eyes and then he just peddled into the distance and disappeared. Jimmy stood there staring at the cloud of dust that marked his departure. 'Who the hell was he and how did he know my name?'

———◆———

Jimmy woke with a start. Kid looked at him. 'You ok buddy, bad dream?' Jimmy wiped his eyes and sat up, trying to gather himself.

'Just a dream,' he smiled. 'I seem to have a lot these days.'

Kid frowned. 'Suppose those go with the territory,' he paused for a moment and then smiled broadly. 'Lucky for me I don't seem to get them.'

'Well, you don't actually do the dirty work do you, Kid? You're more like the Sorcerer's Apprentice.'

Kid acknowledged the barbed comment. 'True, but I don't need the songs. I just write the arrangements and help bury the bodies. I wonder how Rodgers and Hammerstein did it?'

Jimmy looked at Kid trying to work out how he arrived at his question. 'I guess I'm pretty unique in my song writing method.'

Kid didn't look so sure. 'I dunno Jimmy, there have been some pretty dark songs out there. Look at Leonard Cohen!'

'Leonard Cohen didn't kill people; he just wrote songs that made them wish he had!'

Kid smiled. 'Good point but I gotta be honest, I like Leonard Cohen.'

Jimmy smiled. 'Yeah, me too, what does that say about us?'

Kid thought for a moment. 'I guess that makes us thoughtful and enigmatic.' He thought for a further moment before adding, 'Also, eccentric and strange.'

Jimmy nodded. 'Eccentric and strange, that could be a review of the new album!'

Kid turned to Jimmy. 'Remind me, what is the title of the new album?'

'*Killing Me Softly.*' Kid nodded. 'So what you going to say when a journalist asks you about the title?'

Jimmy shrugged. 'I just tell them that I had to kill some people to write the songs so it made perfect sense as the album title.' Jimmy stared back at Kid and tried not to smile. Kid gave Jimmy a quizzical glance.

'Really, that could work if you said it just like that, but I wouldn't recommend it. What's the back-up plan?'

Jimmy looked disappointed. 'You don't like it, pity. I thought it would really give my interviews an edge.' Kid was still waiting for the correct answer.

'Well?'

'I could just say I have to wait for the muse to descend and the waiting is killing me softly.'

'Well, that's a load of pretentious artsy-fartsy crap. If that's your best answer I say go with option one and admit to murder!'

'What makes you think anyone will want to interview me? I'm just a one-hit-wonder trying to make a comeback. It's all very well being a star in Blackjack, but LA and Vegas are a different ballgame.'

Kid didn't share Jimmy's doubts. 'No, this stuff is good. We've got a great label and great contacts. We're going to get all the right promo and a great backstory, minus the murdering. It's great. Redemption, think about it Jimmy, climbing back out of the gutter to grasp the opportunity you threw away when you were younger. Hell, the media are going to love you!'

The miles rolled along under the Dodge's wheels; Jimmy stretched out.

'I need a pee; can we take a break?'

Kid looked at a sign coming up. 'Yeah, we gonna get to Pritchard in ten miles. There's a garage and a grocery store. I need to get some provisions for 3G!'

'What is 3G?'

Kid waggled his finger. 'Who, Jimmy, not what.' Now Jimmy was really confused. Kid elaborated. 'He used to be in the metal band I played in back in Norway.' Now this piqued Jimmy's interest.

'You were in a metal? Please tell me more.'

Kid smiled at the memory. 'Oh man, we were only kids when we started, nineteen, twenty maybe. Imagine Metallica but only heavier.'

Jimmy struggled to imagine that. 'What did you call yourselves... Base Metal, Led Balls?'

Kid shook his head. 'Nope, none of that metal stuff, we went for something far more esoteric.'

'Esoteric, that would have been a good name.'

'It would but we were only kids and such subtleties were way beyond us at that stage. No, we went for Soul Crusher, we felt it captured our vibe.'

'Soul Crusher,' Jimmy said it slowly trying to get a feel for it. 'Soul Crusher, and was the music reflective of the name?'

Kid winced. 'If anything it was too soft. We were like a ton of bricks being dropped from a great height.'

'Sounds like a Soul Crusher gig could be a tough evening. Any fans?'

Kid nodded enthusiastically. 'Yeah, we were quite big in Finland. Six months of darkness and snow does kind of crush the human soul. We were making music to embellish the misery of being cold and in the dark.'

'Sounds delightful.' Jimmy looked thoughtful. 'Don't suppose you had many crossover fans then?'

'Nah, we were pretty niche and the niche we were in wasn't pretty. We did get one crossover gig.'

Jimmy found this hard to believe. 'Really, please tell me it was Country and Western.'

Kid shook his head. 'Sorry to disappoint you but it was far worse. It must have been the name of the band. We got this booking for a festival in Telemark, Norway, quite a big fee, decent hotel and flights. We were over the moon, and also off our tits on booze and drugs so we failed to notice the type of festival it was. Naturally we were late and we missed our sound-check so we just had to plug in and go for it on the night. Well, we are backstage waiting to come on and there is this band like Sly and the Family Stone putting down some really funky, soulful stuff. We listened to them and then looked at each other and the penny started to drop. We glanced out into the audience and there were a lot of open shirts and medallions and some very sharp dressers. I nudged 3G in the ribs, he wasn't called 3G then, but I nudged him and suggested that whoever booked us had mistaken Soul Crusher for a soul band. In a state of rising panic I suggested we go and see the promotor but 3G stopped me. 'You may be right Kid, but we don't get our full fee unless we get on that stage and start playing. If we get bottled off it's not down to us. The promotor should have done his homework.' I wasn't happy. 'How do we play to this lot?' 3G just shrugged. 'Turn the amps up to max! They won't hear us over their screams!'

Jimmy winced. 'How did it go?'

Kid looked pained as if the memory had left a deep psychological scar. 'Well I managed to talk him out of the ear bursting plan, I didn't want to get sued. Unfortunately, my plan, although less painful to the eardrums, was not fully thought through.' Jimmy could see the memories were making Kid squirm in his seat.

'Oh man, this sounds like it's gonna be bad.'

Kid gritted his teeth. 'Superbad to be precise.'

Jimmy shook his head in disbelief. 'You didn't.'

Kid nodded. 'We did. You got to bear in mind we were only kids and we were doing a lot of drugs at the time.'

'So?' said Jimmy impatiently. 'What the fuck did you do?'

Kid sat silently gazing down the road and reliving the full horror of that long ago evening.

'Once I had talked 3G out of the ear exterminator option I suggested we play a soul number to get the audience on our side. Obviously, we didn't have one in our set so I told the guys to do a James Brown number. We had a quick chat, bear in mind there were eight thousand fans waiting, so we didn't really think it through. We picked a key and went for it. Back then me and 3G shared the vocals. The intro went better than expected. For a metal band we sounded pretty funky in a heavy metal way.'

'And then?' Jimmy could barely stand the tension. Kid sighed.

'Well, imagine how a soul crowd would react when four long haired, blonde Norwegians start singing, '*Say it loud, I'm black and I'm proud.*'

Jimmy sat there in stunned silence. Kid just looked forward his knuckles turning white as he gripped the steering wheel. Trying not to smile, Jimmy broke the silence.

'A clear case of cultural appropriation if ever I heard one. Was it well received?'

A muscle just below Kid's righteye began to twitch. 'At first, they just stood there in silence. Being youthful and still somewhat optimistic in my outlook I took this as a clear sign that they were awestruck.'

'That was optimistic.'

'Yeah, like I said I was young. Sadly, they weren't awestruck, more stunned. But still nowhere near rioting. The downside was that none of us knew the song apart from the '*Say it loud, I'm black and I'm proud*'. After about two minutes of repeating that the boos started, shortly followed by the bottles. Luckily for us we were in Norway so they were only plastic recyclable bottles, but the message is pretty much the same. After that we just sort of tailed off and stopped. I was about to suggest a tactical retreat but 3G, crazy bastard, shouts out "Zombie Apocalypse".'

Jimmy began to snigger. 'What the fuck was that?'

'That was our biggest hit, got into the charts in Finland and Iceland. It's a singalong number for the terminally depressed.'

'I'm guessing that went down a storm.'

Kid shook his head. 'I'd be lying if I said yes. Before we could reach the chorus, the promoter pulled the plug and we lost all amplification. He hooked us off the stage and told us to pack our gear and fuck off. I was upset, it was a big crowd but 3G was over the moon. As we drove off in the van he was singing. "Two songs for $10k... easy money!" We had been paid up front so financially we had done really well.'

Jimmy frowned. 'Press must have been bad.'

Kid nodded enthusiastically. 'Yeah, really terrible. "Metal band terrorise audience at Summer festival." That's great press in the Metal World. Bit like Ozzy eating a bat!'

CHAPTER 3

WEIRD SCENES INSIDE THE GOLDMINE

Jimmy sipped at his coffee as Kid continued to drive.

'How far to your friend's place.'

'About a hundred miles. He's in a valley about ten miles from Etna Station, do you know it?'

Jimmy shrugged. 'Never heard of it, is it famous?'

Kid thought for a moment. 'Don't think so. There was a station there during the gold rush but apart from some old cave paintings it's pretty much a forgotten community with nothing going on.'

'That why 3G moved there?'

Kid laughed. 'Hell no! Any people are too much for 3G. He's in the next canyon all on his own, just the way he likes it.'

'Bit of a change from being in a rock band. Any reason behind it?' Jimmy glanced at Kid and he could see a look of regret cross his features. He waited for Kid to answer in his own time. When he did it was a quieter more reflective Kid that spoke.

'We were friends from school when we started the band. He was the leader. He was confident back then but that all changed a few weeks after our concert at Telemark. We were both still nineteen and we got called up for National Service. Turns out that we both had special abilities and we got selected for a Special Service section. At first it was kind of exciting but then it got a bit serious and 3G just couldn't handle it. After about four years and some pretty heavy ops he had a bit of a breakdown and they discharged him. I stayed in the service for eight years and when I got out, he had disappeared off the map. I still had contacts in my special unit and they helped me track him down to Etna. That must be about four years ago, been calling in a couple of times a year and he's gradually getting better, but I've got to warn you, Aksel is not your average bunny.'

'Aksel, so 3G isn't his real name then?' Jimmy smirked.

'Strangely, no! I christened him that when I found him here in his little goldmine. Gal Gul Gruvearbeider.'

Jimmy was confused. 'I thought you said he was called Aksel.'

Kid smiled. 'He is, Gal Gul Gruvearbeider is Norwegian for Crazy Gold Miner... hence the 3G!'

'Sounds like a rapper, a rapper with his own gold mine. No problem sourcing his bling.'

'Wait till you meet him, Jimmy. Aksel isn't a bling sort of guy. Did you ever see any documentaries about the old prospectors in the original goldrush?' Jimmy nodded. 'Well, that's Aksel. Long hair, long beard but, reassuringly, all his own teeth.'

Jimmy had been listening carefully as Kid talked about Aksel and he had picked up on Kid's reference to National Service, especially the part about special skills. He always suspected that Kid had secrets in his past.

'When you say Special Service, what does that mean exactly?' Kid turned and gave Jimmy a cold hard stare, for a moment it was quite unnerving. Kid sighed.

'It's a long story Jimmy, if I told you everything I would probably have to kill you.' Jimmy went to interrupt but Kid raised a hand to silence him. 'I'll tell you this but nothing more, so when I've finished don't go pestering me for more information because it's not happening. You good with that?'

Jimmy nodded. 'Whatever you want to share buddy.'

'Ok.' Kid paused for a moment remembering back to his days of National Service. The long hair and vestigial beards that they had worn in the band were now gone. The jeans and t-shirts were replaced by uniforms. Their teenage world had changed so quickly. 'We had to sit a test when we were first called up. It was some kind of IQ test. Me and Aksel thought nothing of it but two days later we were called into a senior officers' meeting and there were two guys there who I hadn't seen before. They produced some forms; it was like an official secrets document. We had to sign it before they would tell us what the meeting was about. Well, we were nineteen and this shit seemed exciting so we signed. Turned out these guys were from the FS.' Jimmy looked puzzled. 'Forsvarets Spesialkommando to give it the full title. Kinda like your Navy Seals only more secret. Turns out we both had IQ's that were off the scale. Also turned out we were incredible shots. It was surreal. Ten weeks earlier we were drinking and smoking joints and playing in a metal band, now here we were being recruited into a Special Service corps in the Norwegian army.' Jimmy was hanging on Kid's every word.

'So, what did you do?'

Kid took a deep breath. 'Sadly, we accepted. Trouble was it wasn't the FS we were being recruited for; it was a new top secret off-shoot. Far more secret and far more deadly.'

'That doesn't sound like a good fit for the Kid I know,'

Kid frowned. 'I wasn't the Kid you know, by the time they had finished with me even my mother wouldn't have recognised me.'

'So, what happened to Aksel?'

A sad smile passed across Kid's features. 'He was too nice for the kind of work we had to do. Me, on the other hand, I turned out to be the stuff of nightmares. Took me eight years to realise it. That's when I quit and went back to the music.'

Jimmy couldn't believe what he was hearing. 'So were you like a hitman or something?'

Kid laughed. 'I wasn't a fucking gangster; I was Special Commando but I specialised in direct and collateral action. Black Ops!'

Jimmy slowly shook his head. 'That's unbelievable.'

'Just about as unbelievable as Jimmy Wayne being a serial killer?' Kid had a point.

'True, but I only killed scumbags.'

'Who do you think I was after? We went after terrorists, not florists. I guess we've both done things we ain't proud of but at least we did them for the right reasons.'

Jimmy leaned forwards. 'So, what happened to make you quit.'

Kid shook his head. 'That's all I'm saying. There were reasons I left but you never really leave Black Ops. We didn't part on good terms and the things I knew meant I'm a potential threat. The less you know the safer you are going to be.' Kid fixed his eyes on Jimmy. When he spoke it was in deadly earnest. 'This kinda thing is never over. There is a door to another world and it can be opened at a moment's notice. That's why 3G came to Nevada and dropped out. That's why I am a musician hiding in plain sight. I want them to know I am retired. I'm not that person anymore.'

The rest of the drive to Mesa Ridge they sat quietly. Jimmy was mulling over the information that Kid, as he suspected, had a very interesting past. Kid was remembering events from his past he had blocked out for years. These were demons he hadn't confronted since the last time he had visited Aksel. Like an open wound, it didn't take much to enflame them. Guilt weighs heavy on the mind of a decent person. Following orders can take you to some dark places. Any conscript soldier who has been in battle knows this. In these confrontational moments the thin veneer of humanity is shed and we either kill or we are killed. Jimmy knew now why Kid never wanted any part of the killing, even though these guys were murderers, rapists and dealers. Kid no longer had the stomach for it. Jimmy on the other hand still did, but only in the name of art and only to a deserving cause.

As the sun slowly began to drop behind the mountains, Kid slowed. They had turned off Highway 93 many miles back and these quiet sideroads were like a different, almost uninhabited, world.

'There it is.' Kid swung the Dodge off the road and down the dusty track that lay before them. It reminded Jimmy of the track that led to the Song Cemetery. They bumped along for about two minutes and then Jimmy saw the barn and beside it the small ranch style house. Kid turned off the motor and jumped from the van, keen to see his old friend. The door of the house swung open and there was Aksel. Jimmy did a double take. He was as big as Kid but thinner and more sinuous. He moved like a panther. Kid called out his name and they hurried to greet each other with a huge bear hug.

'Aksel, I've missed you, brother.'

Aksel leaned back. 'Let me look at you,' he nodded. 'Yep, you're getting fat.'

Kid just laughed. 'Compared to you maybe.' He turned to Jimmy who had climbed from the van and was waiting for them to finish their greetings. 'This is my good friend Jimmy Wayne.' Aksel nodded and gave Jimmy a warm smile.

'Good to meet you Jimmy, Kid has told me a lot about you. Reckons you're going to be a star.' Jimmy nodded and reached out to shake hands. He didn't fancy having a bear hug with these two giants. Jimmy was surprised by Aksel's appearance, it was nothing like Kid had described. His beard was trimmed short and his hair was clean, combed and only just shoulder length.

'Kid tends to exaggerate but we do have a shot at it. It's a bit like mining for gold. We're all just trying to strike it lucky. Nice to meet you.'

Kid had stood back while Jimmy and Aksel introduced themselves. He could see the change in his friend since his last visit seven months ago. He looked relaxed, confident.

'You doing ok, brother?'

Aksel nodded. 'Yeah, I think I'm doing ok. Seemed to have turned a corner since your last visit. Just like you said, I gave it some time.' He turned to Jimmy. 'You eat meat Jimmy?'

Jimmy smiled. 'Is the Pope a Catholic!'

'Yes, he is,' said Aksel, 'but tonight we are eating goat.'

'Hey I love goat, we used to eat it on the farm when I was a boy.'

Aksel ushered them over to the house. 'Let's go inside before it gets dark. It gets pretty cold up here in the evening.'

Jimmy was surprised by how comfortable it was inside. Utilitarian maybe, but everything you needed was there. From Kid's descriptions he had been expecting Aksel to live in a cave surrounded by the bones of animals he had hunted and eaten. There was an old but comfortable sofa and an armchair, that was clearly Aksel's, in front of a roaring wood burner. In the right corner of the open plan room was a big farmhouse table and six chairs and behind them was the kitchen. Again, open plan. A woodburning stove, a fridge and some cupboards below the worktop. The room was illuminated by electric lamps which Jimmy hadn't been expecting.

'Where does your power come from? You're miles off the grid.'

Aksel smiled. 'Back of the barn, I got a 6k solar farm set up with sixteen panels and a battery pack for storage just inside the barn. Gives me enough to run the place year-round. I got central heating too but I like a wood fire in the evenings.' The smell coming from the wood burning stove was delicious. Kid wandered over and took a look.

'Ahh, goat curry, rice and peas... my favourite.'

Aksel nodded. 'I know.'

'That's a Jamaican dish ain't it? Where'd you learn that?'

'Jamaica! Me and Kid were stationed there.'

Jimmy nodded. 'When you were in the FS?'

Aksel shot a look at Kid, surprised that Jimmy could know this. Kid smiled reassuringly.

'It's ok Aksel, you can trust Jimmy, he's one of us.' Aksel still seemed uneasy.

'He has served?'

Kid shook his head. 'No, but he has killed some bad people.'

Aksel turned to Jimmy. 'Freelance contract killer?'

Jimmy shook his head. 'Well, I guess you could say I killed for a contract.'

'Governmental?'

'No, record.'

Kid laughed out loud. 'Well, that was surreal. Why don't we wash up and settle down to dinner and then we can exchange notes about our dark pasts?'

Aksel nodded. 'Good idea.'

Surprisingly there were three bedrooms, all tidy and clean, and one bathroom with a shower and a bath. Aksel's little dwelling was turning out a lot better than Jimmy had expected. He said as much to Kid, 'I thought you told me Aksel lived in a dump, this place is nice.'

Kid agreed. 'Yeah, last time I was here it was, but something's changed. Aksel has finally got it together.' Kid leaned towards Jimmy and whispered, 'Don't ask Aksel about his past, if he wants to tell you he will.' Jimmy nodded. He didn't want to offend his host, not before the curry anyway.

The meal, when it arrived, was superb. Aksel had even baked a fresh loaf of bread to go with it. Jimmy couldn't remember the last time he had eaten a homemade meal and not a dish from one of Blackjack's non-gourmet restaurants. It was nice to eat something that wasn't chosen from a picture on a laminated menu. Finally, he cleared his plate and leaned back with that warm feeling of being pleasantly full. Kid was now on his second plate and he didn't look like he would ever be full. Aksel glanced across at Jimmy.

'He's always hungry, ever since we were kids. That's why our rucksacks were so heavy – we had to carry provisions for three!'

Jimmy smiled. 'Yeah, he does have an amazing capacity for putting it away. Was he like that with drink?'

Aksel nodded. 'Oh yes. The word that springs to mind is prodigious. Back in the days of the band the only time he would stop drinking was when he was asleep. He probably dreamed about drinking just to fill the void whilst he was sleeping.' Kid cleared his last spoonful and pushed his plate away. He leaned back in his chair and rubbed his stomach.

'Now then boys, you're making me sound like some kind of sideshow attraction. My drinking was done discreetly but it was done for several hours at a time. I was discreet, that's why nobody knew.'

Aksel shook his head. 'No, Kid, you were spectacular, everyone knew. You would pass out in the bar, the car, the supermarket – hell you even passed out on stage.'

Kid disagreed. 'No, I was merely resting my eyes, the stage lights were too bright.' Aksel seemed amused.

'Is that why you plunged headfirst off the stage into the orchestra pit?' Kid thought for a moment.

'That was for dramatic effect. I'm sure the audience appreciated it.'

Aksel nodded. 'Maybe, not so sure the ones who were standing in the orchestra pit would agree. A two-hundred-and-forty-pound Norwegian coming at you with terminal velocity is more dramatic an effect than you ever want.'

After the meal Aksel cleared the dishes. Jimmy offered to help but Aksel just smiled. 'Thanks, but I can load the dishwasher.'

Jimmy was surprised. 'You have a dishwasher for one.'

Aksel shrugged. 'I know it seems crazy but I hate washing up so I just bought more plates and I load it until its full and just do a wash every three days. It's a bit of luxury.' He paused for a moment. 'I can afford it so why not?' Both Jimmy and Kid nodded vigorously. 'Perhaps we could start a new movement. "Men against housework." Think it would catch on?'

Jimmy frowned. 'That's why you need a wife!' Kid and Aksel both groaned.

'You're on thin ice there, Jimmy, you sure you're not a Country singer?' asked Aksel.

'No, I'm not. Never been married either. Just judging by the way my dad used to be waited on by my mother, come to think about it, virtually every other married couple I have met, it's the woman does the washing.'

Kid looked at Aksel. 'So is Jimmy a male chauvinist pig or just too honest, how do we find him?' Aksel stroked his beard pretending to be giving the matter a great deal of thought.

'Can you be found guilty of stupidity?'

Jimmy nodded. 'Oh, I've been guilty of that all my life. Wendy told me I needed to work on my internal dialogue. I said, "What's an internal dialogue?" She just looked at me, pulled a face. "The opposite of that," she said.'

As Aksel loaded the dishes, Kid leaned across to Jimmy and spoke quietly. He was very happy with the progress his friend had made.

'This is the best I have seen him in years. Never thought he was going to get back to normal, whatever that is.' Kid looked into the distance, remembering how traumatised Aksel had been when he left the FS unit they had been attached to. 'He was gone, he couldn't communicate, couldn't look after himself. He saw things.'

Jimmy nodded. 'I see things too.'

Kid nodded. 'I know but you can't compare you seeing the ghost of your ex-lover with the things that Aksel saw. That's a happy memory for you.'

'Apart from the fact I accidently hanged her.'

Kid winced. 'Yeah, that was unfortunate, you got to be really careful with that autoerotic asphyxiation. Maybe they should put something on the rope like, "Don't Drink and Dive".'

'Don't go into advertising Kid, you suck.'

'That's why you write the songs Jimmy.' They were both laughing when Aksel returned from the dishwasher.

'You boys seem in good spirits.'

Kid shook his head. 'Let's not talk about spirits, bit of a delicate subject.' Jimmy and Kid both smiled and Aksel knew he was missing something.

'Fancy taking a look at my mine?'

Jimmy pointed to the window. 'It's pitch black out there, can't we do it in the morning.'

Kid glanced at Aksel and gave him a knowing smile. 'Can I tell him?'

Aksel nodded.

'The mine runs under the house. We can enter it from the workshop behind that door.' Kid pointed to a door to the right of the kitchen wall. 'Did you notice the rockface to the right of the place as we arrived.'

Jimmy thought about it for a moment. There was a wall of low rock that curved around the back of the barn. It was only about thirty-foot high by the barn but as it ran away from the barn it rose to over a hundred feet on the north side of the property. This protected Aksel's home from the cold northerly winds. Jimmy nodded.

'Yeah, I do remember the cliff now I come to think about it. What's that got to do with the mine?' Kid was about to explain but Aksel interrupted.

'Listen Jimmy, the entrance to the mine is in the barn, you won't even need to put your coat on.'

Kid jumped out of his chair. 'I would love to. You got a torch?'

Aksel smiled. 'We won't need one, follow me.'

Aksel walked over to the door at the side of the kitchen. They went out through the door which led into a workshop and from there another door opened onto the driveway. Jimmy could see in the starlight that the barn was only twenty feet away. He could also make out the dark brooding shape of the rockface as it rose off to the east. Aksel opened a small door on the left of the barn, clicked on the light, and suddenly the barn was bathed in a soft light. He waited for Jimmy and Kid to get inside and then shut the door behind them. Kid looked around.

'I don't remember this from last time.'

'That's because I didn't show you,' said Aksel. 'We took a walk down to the river at the bottom of the valley where I did my opencast dredging, but this place,' Aksel swept his hand around the barn, 'I kept secret.'

'So where is the mine?' asked Jimmy. Aksel raised a finger to his lips.

'Shhh, listen.' They all stood still and listened and there it was. The sound of running water across a stone riverbed. Aksel smiled. 'Welcome to the River of Fire, gentlemen.' He walked towards a wall full of shelving which had tools and boxes of screws and nails all neatly set out, and bent down and reached beneath the workbench. He looked up at Kid and Jimmy. 'What I am about to show you must never be talked about outside of these walls. Do I have your word?'

Jimmy sniggered. 'Sure, but I've seen a river before.' Aksel stood back up.

'You don't understand, Jimmy. This is the River of Fire.' Aksel words were intense, Jimmy stopped smiling.

'Can a river be on fire? Seems kinda counterintuitive.' Aksel closed his eyes, like a teacher trying to make a dense pupil understand an equation. He was about to explain when Kid spoke.

'By river of fire are you meaning the Phlegethon?'

Aksel's face broke into a broad grin. 'Exactly, Kid.'

Jimmy was confused. 'What are you guys on about?'

'Greek mythology, the Phlegethon was one of the five rivers of Hades, didn't you study it in school?'

Jimmy shook his head. 'I couldn't even point to Greece on a map.' Kid and Aksel both shook their heads.

'What about Homer, you must have studied Homer?'

Again, Jimmy shook his head. 'Only Simpson! Why don't you educate me?'

Kid smiled. 'Okie doakley Jimmy, where shall I begin?'

'You better take a seat,' said Aksel. 'This could take a while.' Kid allowed a look of mock offence to pass over his features for a moment and then began.

'Ok, Jimmy. Homer, the Greek Philosopher, was famous for two books. *The Iliad* and *The Odyssey*. In them he talks about the five rivers of Hades. The Phlegethon, the river of Fire. The Acheron, the river of Woe. Don't ever go for a cruise down that one, sounds like a real bummer.' Kid thought for a moment, trying to remember his Greek studies of twenty years before. 'Ah yes... then there was the Cocytus which was the river of Lamentation.'

'Man, this sounds like a terrible place to have a boat,' said Jimmy. 'Aren't there any happy rivers?' Kid shook his head.

'Sadly no, these rivers all flow into the Styx, and the Styx is the boundary between Earth and the Underworld. Or Hades, if you prefer.'

Jimmy was confused. 'I thought you said there were five rivers, what's the fifth?'

Kid nodded. 'There is Jimmy, but I can't remember the name of it.' Aksel sniggered and then Kid joined in.

'What's so funny?'

'Kid is playing with you Jimmy. The fifth river is the Lethe, the river of Forgetfulness.' Jimmy could see the joke but realised that from an educational point of view he was a million miles behind Kid and Aksel.

'How do you guys know all this stuff? We only did American History at my school.'

Aksel looked almost apologetic. 'It's not really history, its Philosophy and Literature. It was on our curriculum back in Norway. Most European countries teach it but I guess you're a long way from Europe in the US.'

'Shall I continue?' asked Kid. He was standing, peering down his nose like a teacher waiting for his class to pay attention.

'I think you're going to, whatever we say,' said Jimmy.

'He will,' agreed Aksel. 'Please continue, Kid.'

'Thank you, Lund. Wayne, see me after school.' Jimmy smiled; it had been a long time since he had been in detention, but he remembered it well. He looked across from Kid to Aksel. They were both from the other side of the Atlantic. It seemed like a different world. He had known Kid for a couple of years, but Aksel he had only met today, and here he was standing in a barn in the mountains of Nevada that led to an underground river and a goldmine. What a place to be receiving a lecture on Greek Mythology. His life really couldn't get any stranger.

'So, Jimmy are you familiar with the term Hades.'

Jimmy nodded. 'Yeah, another name for Hell.'

'It's also the name for the God that ruled the Underworld, not the criminal underworld but the land of the dead.'

'Let's get this straight,' interrupted Jimmy. 'Hades is the name of the underworld but also the name of the God in charge of it. That's like saying the God of God.'

Kid nodded. 'Correct, Jimmy. Hence the saying, "It's all Greek to me".' Jimmy turned to Aksel. 'Is that true?'

Aksel shrugged. 'It could be.'

Jimmy turned back to Kid. 'Is there a point to this story? Only I would quite like to take a look at this goldmine.'

Kid sighed. 'Does there have to be a point? Isn't the pursuit of knowledge enough in and of itself? I was just about to tell you about Pluto and Poseidon, and I'm not talking about the Disney dog or the sinking ship.'

Jimmy shook his head. 'Sounds fascinating but I would like to get a look at Aksel's river of fire.'

'Very well. Class dismissed.'

Aksel walked back over to the wall where the shelves and tools were mounted. He bent down and turned something beneath it and then stood back as the wall swung backwards to reveal a dimly lit passageway that appeared to go deeper into the mountain. For a moment it took Jimmy by surprise. It was like something from a spy film. Kid, however, was purring with delight. He walked around the fake shelving and admired the engineering.

'Nice secret entrance Aksel, I never spotted it.'

Aksel smiled. 'Yeah, you need to be careful when you own a goldmine.' They all walked through into the passageway and Aksel closed the secret doorway behind them. Kid watched him do it.

'Infra-red?'

Aksel nodded. 'Adapted it from an electric gate mechanism.' Kid approved.

'You always were a fine engineer.'

Aksel led the way down the pathway that was carved into the mountain. Its surface was smooth, too smooth to have been excavated by jackhammers.

'I'm guessing you didn't make this tunnel, Aksel.'

Aksel paused and rubbed his hand across the smooth contours of the rock.

'No, this was formed by another underground river that must have run dry many thousands of years ago. When I bought the place, the barn was there but it was pretty run down. I was using the forks on my tractor to move some old railway sleepers around and I got careless and put a fork through the back wall. When I turned off the engine I could hear the river. I'd never heard it before, so I decided to investigate. I kicked down the loose bricks and climbed into the tunnel where we are now. It wasn't like this then, there were boulders everywhere and no lighting. I think the previous owner had been afraid of exploring. Some of these underground rivers can suddenly dive hundreds of feet vertically. This one does, when we get to the mine you can hear the roar. I once floated an infra-red camera down it on a wire and after about 150 feet it just plunged into an abyss. I let out over 400 ft of wire and didn't reach the bottom.'

'Yeah, you don't ever want to fuck with gravity,' said Kid as he looked down the passageway. 'How far down there are we going?'

'About 160 yards,' said Aksel.

'Jeez, that's a long way.'

Aksel turned and smiled at Jimmy. 'You claustrophobic?'

Jimmy shook his head.

'Good, then let's get down to the river.' Aksel had rigged LED spotlights at regular intervals all down the tunnel and it gave the tunnel an eerily magical atmosphere. They followed his lead and their footsteps echoed around the walls. The sound of the river was getting nearer. Jimmy felt a sense of rising excitement, but nothing prepared him for what they saw as Aksel turned the last corner. The roof lights came to a halt and ahead of them lay only darkness. Jimmy could sense that they were on the edge of a much bigger space. When Aksel spoke the echo on his voice had changed.

'Stay here for a second. We are at the entrance to the mine. I have a separate lighting system down here with a hidden switch.'

'So, if somebody ever gets this far, they won't get to see what's down here.'

Aksel laughed. 'You know me so well, Kid.'

'I do,' said Kid. 'I'm assuming it's booby trapped!'

'Naturally. Stand still while I throw the switch, I've placed some pressure plates which you really don't want to stand on! Don't move until I have put on the lights and deactivated them.'

Kid chuckled. 'You always did like *Raiders of the Lost Ark*.'

Kid and Jimmy stood there and listened to Aksel's footsteps slowly move away into the darkness. Jimmy leaned over to Kid.

'How does he see where he's going?'

Kid knew. They had done the same training exercises together in the FS.

'He doesn't, he probably has his eyes closed. He has memorised the number of steps and he is touching the wall on the left.'

'How do you know?'

'Listen hard,' whispered Kid. 'You can hear that he is moving off to the left so the cave must be opening up. He's counting the steps and following the wall. My guess is he has his switches concealed down there somewhere.'

Jimmy thought about it for a moment. 'Why all the cloak and dagger stuff.'

'Well, it is a goldmine, Jimmy. Aksel is just protecting his investment.' He paused for a moment. 'Knowing Aksel, it's going to be very well protected so I suggest we don't move!' From the darkness they heard a call.

'You ready?'

'We're ready.' Suddenly the cave was bathed in soft light – but it wasn't a cave, it was a cathedral. They were in a huge cavern some forty yards long and just as wide and the roof was over a hundred feet in places. Aksel had used some red and yellow filters and the effect was stunning. Even Kid was rendered speechless for a moment. At the far side of the cavern the river appeared from a dark tunnel to the right and then meandered along the side of the cavern until it disappeared back into the darkness once again. Kid and Jimmy just stood there drinking in the stunning space that nature had created and Aksel had augmented.

'This is amazing Aksel, never seen anything quite like it.'

Aksel pointed down to the water. 'This is the River of Fire.'

'I can see why you call it Fire,' said Jimmy. 'It looks like the golden embers of a log fire. How do you get the effect, filtered LEDs?'

Aksel shook his head and smiled. 'No effects, just a white light.'

'But...'

'Don't say anything Jimmy, just come with me.' Aksel led them over to the edge of the river and as they approached, they suddenly understood the golden glow. The river was slowed by several small stone dams that Aksel had built and behind each one was a layer of gold particles reflecting the light from the LEDs and glittering through the ripples of the water.

'Oh my god, is that gold?'

'Yes, it is Jimmy.'

'But it's everywhere.' Aksel nodded. Jimmy turned to him. 'You've hit the Motherlode.'

Aksel shook his head. 'Technically no. Lode gold is embedded in rock. This is Placer gold.' Jimmy didn't understand.

'What's the difference, this stuff is real right?'

'Oh, it's real alright. You know how gold is formed, Jimmy?' Jimmy shook his head. He was still a little stunned by the sight before him. Aksel reached into the water and picked out a small nugget of gold. It was about the size of a frozen pea. 'This is worth about $250, Jimmy. Four of these would make up a gram and that's a $1000 right there.' Kid scanned the riverbed from one dam to the next.

'You got about $50,000 just in this bay.' He walked to the next one. There was less but still around $30,000 worth. He moved down the next two bays. The amount of gold reduced as he went down but there were still significant deposits. 'What am I seeing here?'

Aksel pointed to where the river entered the cave. 'The river arrives here at a good pace because there is a steady drop to this point. When the snows are melting I can't get in here because the cave floods back up the tunnel nearly fifty yards. That's why I put in this series of dams. Gold is a heavy metal, it sinks to the bottom and doesn't get washed over the dams as easily as stones. This time of year, it flows like this for months.'

Kid pointed at the glittering bays. 'And is this normal?'

Aksel nodded. 'Has been for the last year.' Jimmy couldn't believe what he was seeing and hearing.

'How long does it take to fill up like this, weeks, months?'

Aksel paused, he looked from Jimmy to Kid and back before replying. 'I emptied it yesterday!'

They stood there in stunned silence until Kid let out a low whistle.

'Wow, I did not expect this.'

Aksel shrugged. 'Nor did I. I set this up about three years back. I knew that the geology around here would give me a good chance of finding Placer gold in the flow and within a couple of weeks I was pulling out a $1000 a day.'

'That ain't bad, but what changed?' Aksel sat down on a rock at the side of the river and gestured that Kid and Jimmy do the same.

'Let me explain so you guys understand. Gold is formed on the site of old volcanos. This whole area of Nevada was once volcanic. Gold is formed when red hot magma burns into the rock ore and creates a seam. Once it cools it's stuck there and only mining or erosion will remove it. Gold mined from the rock is called Lode gold and that needs proper mining techniques. Placer gold on the other hand is gold that has been washed out of the seam by water erosion. That's what the panners were always dredging in the rivers for. It tends to be smaller but it can be just as pure, and easier to get at if you know where to look.'

'I never expected a Geology lesson today,' said Jimmy, still unable to tear his gaze away from the shimmering golden waters.

'Every day is a school day,' smiled Aksel.

'I should have gone to school more,' sighed Jimmy. 'Keep going, this shit is interesting.' Aksel pointed upstream.

'When I bought this place, I had studied the geology and I knew there was a high chance that there would be seams of gold in the mountain. The land runs down to the bottom of the valley and where the river slows there are a series of dredge bays. There was enough gold making its way down there to get about $50,000 a year. That's ok but its only subsistence mining. I was sure there had to be some filter between the seams, I believed it to be here. Gold is heavy so if there were some deep caverns chances were the gold would gather there. I knew the river ran through the mountain so I was intending to tunnel in and intercept it using bore holes, but then I got lucky with the tractor. So, I found the tunnel, cleared it. I put in lighting and built the bays using stones from the tunnel floor to build the dams. It started to work pretty much straight away.' Kid was shaking his head in wonder.

'This place is literally a goldmine!'

Aksel nodded at Kid. 'That's why I needed to protect it. I started off by rebuilding the barn and making a secret entrance to the tunnel. There's a keypad by the door. If you don't enter the code the door won't open. If it's forced it becomes live and will zap anyone that tries to gain entry.'

'Like a cattle fence,' offered Jimmy. Aksel scowled.

'More like an electric chair! I'm playing for keeps here, Jimmy. If you're in here without my permission you're never coming out.' By the tone in his voice, it was clear he wasn't fooling. Kid shifted uncomfortably.

'You don't think that's a bit over the top, buddy?'

Aksel shook his head. 'My mine, my gold. I took a load of gold, about ten grams to a buyer in Vegas eighteen months back. Kept it small to avoid causing a stir. He asked me loads of questions and I gave him nothing, but he bought the gold.

I had him do a transfer to an overseas account which couldn't be traced back to me or my location. Just like the old days, Kid, covering our tracks so nothing leads back.'

Kid nodded. 'Makes sense when you're dealing with something as valuable as this stuff.' Jimmy sensed there was more to the story so he stayed silent and waited for Aksel to continue.

'I was driving out of Vegas and I spotted this Chevy pulling out as I left the dealers. I went to the grocery store and then the hardware store to pick up some provisions and it was still there. It followed me up here and then it just pulled over at the end of the track and sat there... waiting.'

'Waiting for what?' asked Jimmy.

'For dark. That dealer had sent his muscle to find where I lived. They were going to try and steal my gold. I have surveillance cameras hidden all down the track, right to the road. I watched them until they got out as darkness fell. I got infrared so I could see them in the dark, loading their guns.' The mood in the cavern had started to darken, both Kid and Jimmy had a horrible feeling that they knew where this story was going.

'So, what did you do Aksel?' Kid asked. His voice was gentle but Jimmy could hear the concern in it. Aksel shook his head, his face filled with a mix of anger and regret.

'I relied on my training. I waited to see what they would do. I could have just gone out and terminated them before they could report back to their boss, but I wanted to give them a chance.'

Kid nodded. 'What happened?'

Jimmy realised he was holding his breath; the story was building to a climax and the tension was almost unbearable.

'They came for me at midnight, two of them. I saw they had handguns and one had a combat knife. I saw them glinting in the moonlight and I knew what I had to do. I had my sniper rifle and I put on the suppressor.'

'Still using the Steyr SSG 69?'

'Yeah, looks like a hunting rifle but it's super light. I'm too old to change horses now.' Both Kid and Jimmy said nothing and waited for Aksel to continue. 'Soon as I saw the weapons I knew what I had to do. I was over by the barn waiting for them to enter my kill zone. I put the first one straight through the head of the lead guy. Before he knew what was happening, I put another through the other guy's gun arm and another through his kneecap. He couldn't shoot or run so I grabbed his knife and interrogated him, didn't take long!'

Kid was looking serious. 'What did you ask him?'

Aksel shrugged. 'The usual – who sent you? Where are they?'

Kid nodded. 'The bodies?'

'I sent them down this river. I figure whatever comes out in the future won't be recognisable. I removed all clothing and jewellery first.'

'Anything appeared yet?'

Aksel shook his head. 'Nothing yet, let's see what next winter's melt brings.' Jimmy just sat there listening to Kid debrief Aksel. Clearly his friend had a past that he was not privy to. He wanted to say something but it was clear from Kid's face that the questioning was not yet finished.

'What about the intel you gained? Did you close the loop?'

Aksel nodded. 'Yeah, went down to the office in Vegas. The guy was a small-time mobster. Waited for him to be on his own and then used a syringe to put some air in his veins, he had a nice mole which hid the mark. Looks like he died of an embolism.' This seemed to relax Kid a little.

'You check for information about you and CCTV?'

'Yeah, all cleaned up and removed. No traces.'

Finally, Kid smiled. 'Good, you seem to have covered everything apart from the car.'

Aksel laughed. 'Well, that nice settee you sat on tonight was made from the back seats with a bit of alteration. All the panels and frame I cut up using an acetylene torch and then I melted it all down in my little foundry. The ingots are stacked in the corner of the barn for when I need to cast something.' Aksel turned to Jimmy. 'Can I trust you Jimmy?' Before Jimmy could assure Aksel that he could, Kid leaned forwards.

'Jimmy is a most prolific killer, to my knowledge he has killed at least eight people, deliberately. There have been a few accidents as well but nobody's perfect.' Jimmy could not believe that Kid had shared his secret with Aksel but he soon reconsidered when Aksel put his arm around him.

'I am so glad to hear that. I like you Jimmy – it would be a shame to have to silence you, seems you have secrets too.'

Jimmy smiled weakly. 'Yeah, us killers have got to stick together.'

Aksel laughed. 'I trust you only kill bad people.'

Jimmy nodded vigorously. 'Scumbags only Aksel, and only in the name of art.' Aksel seemed to approve.

'Yes, Kid told me a little about your song-writing technique.' They sat there for a few moments and then Kid spoke.

'So why do you think the amount of gold suddenly increased last year?' It was an unexpected comment but Kid was merely returning to the previous conversation. Aksel got up and walked to the river.

'Erosion. I think there are some big seams above here and the erosion from the river has uncovered them. All I have to do is sit here and catch them as they wash down. As a business model it's pretty much perfect.' Jimmy couldn't imagine having a river flowing through his property that delivered large amounts of gold every day. He couldn't even imagine what it was like to own a property.

'Do you mind me asking how much you have collected so far?'

Aksel grinned. 'Over twenty million so far.' Jimmy sat there in stunned silence. Twenty million in just over a year, no wonder Aksel was so protective.

'What have you done with it?'

Aksel let a slow grin spread across his features. 'Well, I have invested it in worthy projects. Children's homes. Green initiatives. Education for the poor.'

Jimmy was impressed. 'Very generous, how much have you invested?'

'All of it.' Aksel said it without drama. Jimmy couldn't get his head around it.

'All of it?'

'Yeah, all of it. I'm making reparations. I did some bad things in the past, Kid knows. I'm just trying to balance the scales. As long as the river keeps flowing, I'm going to keep giving. It's good for my soul. Good karma. You believe in Karma, Jimmy?'

Jimmy nodded. 'Suppose I do. What goes around comes around, do unto others. That kinda stuff.' Aksel slapped him on the back.

'Just remember that when you hit the big time, but just in case you don't I will put a few days harvest to one side for you and Kid!' It took a moment for the meaning of Aksel's words to sink in, whilst Jimmy was still weighing the implications Kid had already processed Aksel's offer.

'Really no need my friend. We are about to have a hit record and a very nice residency on the strip.' Aksel looked at them both and for the first time since they had come into the cavern, he looked truly happy.

'Kid, I've known you all my life. I trust you like a brother. Jimmy, I didn't know, but I knew if Kid vouched for you then you're ok.' He winked at Kid. 'You know me Kid, I had to do my background checks.'

'And did I check out?' Jimmy had tried to say it jokingly, but he still sounded a bit nervous.

Aksel smiled. 'You both did, no money and no attachments, especially you Jimmy, seems you killed all of those.'

Kid burst in laughter. 'Harsh but fair.'

Jimmy smiled weakly; the truth wasn't always a barrel of laughs. He wanted to defend himself but there was no point. Clearly both Aksel and Kid had done some dark deeds in the service of their country. They seemed to be as mired in blood as he was. He was sitting in a cave full of killers but, somehow, he didn't think any of them were bad people. That was a tough circle to square.

'The pursuit of money, wealth, call it what you will, has always been at the root of most evil. Once you have enough you should be incorruptible. I say "should" because for a few, there will never be enough. I want you and Kid to be free of that need. When you check your bank accounts you will find two million dollars has been invested in both. It's clean. It appears to come from recording and performing contracts for the next two years. It's also tax paid.' Even Kid had nothing to say to this revelation. Aksel continued. 'You are free of the everyday worries. There will always be cash in the account when you go to the bank. Use this freedom to be creative and if you are successful, share it around. Giving makes you feel good.'

'I don't know what to say,' said Jimmy, still slightly stunned at the news that he would soon be a millionaire. 'It's really kind of you Aksel, but it's just too much.' Aksel walked back to the edge of the river, turned back to face them and pointed upstream.

'I believe that the river has just eroded enough rock to access a new, huge seam of gold. I didn't tell you the full story when I said I had emptied the bays yesterday... I did it four times. Six today before you arrived. For the past month I have been pulling out over a million dollars of gold a day. In twenty days, I've pulled out more than I pulled out the whole of last year. Come see.'

He motioned for them to follow him as he walked down into the bottom of the cave. When he reached the end of the cavern near where the river disappeared into the dark on its descent to the bottom of the mountain he paused. There was a broom leaning up against the rockface and he picked it up and started to brush along the bottom of the rock face revealing a metal channel. He watched their faces as they tried to figure out what was going on. He dropped the broom behind him and grabbed an outcrop of rock. It was about the size of his hand. He pulled it downwards and the rockface slid open. Kid walked up and inspected it. The stone was only about two inches thick but it had been attached to the heavy plate door in such a way that it looked for all the world like a solid rockface.

'Man, that's some fancy engineering Aksel. I never would have known if you hadn't swept the sand away from the channel. What the hell is in there?'

'The river had started to erode another tunnel, but the rock was too hard and it followed another seam through weaker rock. Nature always finds the path of least resistance. It gave me a really nice store cave. I just made it a secret.'

'What's in it, my friend?'

'Oh, I think you know, but just in case.' Aksel threw a light switch inside the door. Jimmy gasped. It was like something from a Hollywood movie. Lined up along the left-hand wall were a series of old tin baths and each one was filled to the top with gold. It was like opening King Solomon's tomb, only this wasn't fiction; it was real. Kid stood there just looking at it, his face bathed in the golden reflection of light dancing off the gold.

'Fuck me Aksel, I wish I had paid more attention in those geology lessons. How do you process this much gold?'

'That's why I have a foundry. I melt it down into ingots and then I sell it through about twenty different bullion dealers. Nothing traces back to me. I have several shelf companies in Stockwood that do all the distribution for me. The gold gets collected from there by special courier. I'm only ever there to meet the courier and I always vary the pick-up point and it's never here, but in case anyone comes creeping around I have hidden CCTV which I check every day. Its all-online paperwork so that goes through several servers before it gets to me. Keeps me invisible and untraceable. I have two other pick-up points at old mines that I sometimes use to just cover my tracks.'

Kid was nodding approvingly. 'Looks like you've thought of everything. This is some operation, how long you planning on doing it for?'

'Until I have a billion saved up. When you have that kind of money it makes money so I can use the interest to fund my charities.'

'And then what?' asked Jimmy. 'If you're off in Europe running your charitable organisation, who collects the gold?' Aksel shrugged.

'Nature I guess. The dams will trap some of the gold and when they are full the rest will flow over the dams and into the abyss in the mountain. A little will make it to the river in the valley but I believe that most of it will be trapped in a deep lagoon further down the mountain. Someday we might find a way down there and if we did I think we would find the biggest gold hoard the world has ever seen.'

Half an hour later they were back in Aksel's lounge having a coffee. The last hour seemed like an incredible dream. Kid was smiling at Jimmy.

'Told you my friend here was a clever bastard, just never realised how clever.' Jimmy couldn't disagree. He was still trying to come to terms with the fact that he was a million-aire... twice over!

CHAPTER 4
ARTISTIC DIFFERENCES

As they turned back onto Highway 93 and headed south for Vegas, Jimmy finally broke the silence. They had waved their farewells to Aksel nearly an hour ago and driven down from above Etna station and back to the valley without speaking. They were both lost in their thoughts.

'Is it me or was that weird, even by our standards?'

Kid thought about it. 'Yeah, kinda weird, but our standards are pretty low when it comes to weird.'

Jimmy agreed. 'Well let's look at the positives first, we're gonna be millionaires!'

Kid gave a half-hearted, 'Whoo-hoo,' that Homer Simpson would have disavowed.

'And Aksel seems to be mended, apart from being a bit murdery.'

'That wasn't murder, those guys were coming to kill him for his gold. He had to kill their boss too or he would have been back with more men. They caused their own deaths, should have left him alone.'

Jimmy agreed. 'I take your point Kid but he seemed to switch into the role very easily, too easily. What exactly did you boys do when you were in the FS?' Kid drove on for a while without saying anything and then he seemed to reach a decision.

'If I tell you something you have to promise to never repeat it or ask me about it again. I closed that part of my life off years ago and I don't want to go back. Ever! This is a one-off deal Jimmy, take it or leave it.' Jimmy didn't hesitate. 'I'll take it.' Kid nodded gravely; it was clear this was a part of his past that he was uncomfortable revisiting.

'You have to understand that Aksel and I were barely twenty when we were called up. It soon became apparent, despite our very misspent youth, that we both had special talents. We both had seriously high IQ's, not something you normally associate with heavy metal. We both had a facility with language and were sniper-level marksmen. We were singled out for the FS. Aksel was a great technician and could make anything out of virtually nothing. You see what he has done with the workshop secret door and the rock wall door to his gold reserve. I guarantee you anyone who managed to get as far as the tunnel, and most wouldn't, would get either crushed, blown up, shot or electrocuted before they ever found where the lights were in the river cavern. Just like in *Indiana Jones and the Temple of Doom*, that place will be filled with so many traps that it's un-survivable. Aksel never leaves anything to chance. Now me, I could speak seven languages fluently. I also have a photographic memory. Cherry on the cake, turns out I was a stone-cold kill-ing machine. We formed an incredible team and were sent all over the world resolving situations for our government and on behalf of our NATO brethren. We really did just follow orders, my country right or wrong and all that shit. Now, I'm not proud of it but turned out we were pretty damn good. Killed a lot of terrorists and politicians, mainly from the Middle East, but we weren't fussy. Tell us where to go and who to eliminate, consider it done. To me, it wasn't a problem, but to Aksel the more we did the harder he found it. Final straw was a hit on a Russian mobster. He was running drugs and other stuff into Oslo and they wanted him stopped... permanently. Well, we got into his place and we killed him but just as we were doing it his little boy came running into the room. Aksel spun around and killed him stone dead. The Kid was only about six. He had long black hair. Aksel shot him straight through the heart and the little chap was dead before he hit the floor. Aksel never recovered from that. He had a breakdown and was invalided out of the force. Once they were sure he wouldn't talk they released him back into the wild a broken man. Took him a long time to turn it around but he did. I kept in touch with him while he was in counselling, and he kept on and on about mining for gold. He studied all these geological maps and one day he told me he had bought a mine in Nevada and he was going to work it and make reparations. I never understood what he meant until yesterday. Poor bastard is trying to absolve his sins by paying for them in gold.'

Kid continued to drive but the speech had finished.

'Is that it?' asked Jimmy.

Kid nodded. 'That's all I'm saying Jimmy. You do the math.'

'Not sure I want to but at least I understand why you didn't want to help me with the killing of the Deltas.'

Kid glanced across at Jimmy. 'Yeah, I had my fill of that. Now I just want to play my guitar and arrange your songs. Give some pleasure to the people instead of killing their loved ones. That's my way of making reparations.'

'How the hell did two musicians, three if we count Aksel, become killers.'

Kid shrugged. 'That's just life Jimmy. We don't write the script very often. We're just like logs floating downstream. Sometimes we float along serenely and then we get into turbulent waters and are tossed around by forces we have no control over. Every river eventually leads to the sea but sometimes it's best to stop paddling if you don't know which direction you're headed in. Meeting you gave me a chance to stop paddling, find some calmer waters. Right now it's getting a bit choppy, but I reckon we can keep out of the rapids if we are careful. What do you think?'

Jimmy thought for a moment. 'I think we should go and make this record. I also think we should buy some new clothes,' he glanced at Kid and winked. 'I think we can afford it.'

For the first time that morning Kid smiled back at him. 'Oh yes, I do believe we can.'

They drove on in silence for several minutes and then Jimmy spoke. 'Something else strange happened last night.'

Kid looked at Jimmy, one eyebrow was raised questioningly. 'Really, how much weird shit can you fit into one evening?'

'I had a dream.'

'Not too weird then.'

'Wait until you've heard the dream. You want to hear it?'

'Oh, I'm all ears, but nothing of a sexual nature. Not before I've had some breakfast.' Jimmy ignored Kid's assumption that his dreams were dominated by sex.

'I dreamed I was at the Song Cemetery and this old black guy dressed in a brown suit and trilby suddenly appeared from behind a rock.'

'You sure this ain't sexual?'

Jimmy shook his head. 'He was like really old but he seemed to be young – he had a vitality about him, y'know?'

Kid shook his head. 'Haven't got a clue.' Jimmy realised that what he was saying didn't make any sense.

'He moved like a dancer, graceful and lithe, but he's an old soul. When he looked at me I could just feel the knowledge and compassion flowing from him. It was weird.'

'Sounds weird, you sure this was a dream?' Kids eyebrow was raised again.

'Oh, it was a dream, but it felt real.'

'So, what happened?'

Jimmy stared out of the window as he tried to remember. 'He just appeared outta nowhere and came right up to me like he'd known me all my life. "Hey Jimmy Wayne," he said. "You wanna write a song?" Well I wasn't sure if this was a trick question because I didn't kill anybody yesterday, so I just said yes. He looked at me and then he smiled. "Without killing?" I didn't know what to say. He knew!'

Kid shrugged. 'Course he did Jimmy, it's a dream. Any old shit can happen in a dream.' Jimmy had to admit that Kid was right.

'Thing is, we wrote a song. We sat down and we wrote it together.'

'And you didn't kill anyone?'

'No-one.'

Kid winced. 'I'm guessing that it's pretty bad then.'

Jimmy shook his head. 'Actually, it's pretty good. You wanna hear it?'

Kid sighed and slowly let out a long slow breath. 'Must I?'

'I think you should.'

Kid nodded his acquiescence. 'If I must.' Jimmy pulled a folded sheet of notepaper from his pocket.

'It's called *Secrets*.' He held it out before him and began.

Late at night
When sleep won't come
I think of you
And the things I've done
Eyes wide open
Till the morning light
The Suns warm rays
My wrongs can't right

Kid nodded slowly. 'That's pretty damn good, Jimmy. You sure you didn't kill anybody?'

'Positive, we just sat down and wrote the song. When we finished, he read it through and then he turned to me. "Jimmy Wayne," he said. "You don't need to be killing all these people. There's another way, learn your craft and tap into your feelings and experience. I can help you." I didn't know what to say. Then he got up, looked at me, and said, "So long Jimmy, I'll be seeing you real soon." As he turned to go I called to him. "Who are you?" I asked. He just looked at me and smiled. "Everyone and no-one Jimmy".' Jimmy leaned back in his seat. 'It was the most real dream I ever had.'

Kid thought about it for a few moments and then slowly started nodding his head in a knowing fashion. 'Did he tell you his name?'

'John R. Deal.'

'Well, I think you need to dream about him again Jimmy because that's the best song you have written without death being involved!' Kid was right.

'He's coming back, I know he is.' Jimmy really hoped he would, there was too much blood on his hands.

———◆———

Jack Lantern picked up his mobile, he recognised the number. Sheriff Pence! What was he doing calling? He didn't like Pence much, but he did do his bidding when required and he was cheap to run. He picked up the call.

'What can I do for you Sheriff?' There was no enthusiasm in his voice, why would there be. He didn't care much for Pence and he was pretty sure the feeling was mutual.

'Wayne left yesterday with Oscarson.' This news brought a smile to Jack's reptilian features.

'Now that is good news, what time did they leave?'

'About ten a.m. They had all the gear loaded and they were headed for LA.'

'I know,' said Jack. 'They're headed to Small Print Records Studio up in Laurel Canyon.'

Sheriff Pence felt himself stiffen, just the name, Laurel Canyon, made him think of the late sixties and early seventies, when drug-taking hippies were always in the news. Declaring free love, dodging the draft and burning the flag. They would have all been shot if it had been left to him. Sadly he was still at school at the time and even with America's lax gun laws it would have been difficult.

'Laurel Canyon, that figures for a couple of deviants like Wayne and Oscarson.'

Jack laughed. 'Oh, it's nothing like that now Sheriff. All those hippies got priced out years ago. It's a place for the rich and the famous now. Hell, even you would like it.' Sheriff Pence didn't think so. He had seen the decadence and drug taking that those Californian liberal types went in for. Sounded like his idea of hell.

'I guess I will have to take your word for it because I have no intention of ever going there.'

Jack could hear the contempt in Pence's prudent, uptight voice, it amused him.

'You should transfer to the station on Laurel Canyon boulevard. You could shoot some of the local celebrities for fornicating.'

Pence didn't rise to Jack's baiting. 'Out of my jurisdiction,' was all he said. Deep inside he wished that he could give some of those liberal types a good ole fashioned beating. California! The day when the San Andreas fault tipped a load of them into the Pacific couldn't come soon enough.

'So why did you call me, Sheriff?'

'Well, there was something interesting last night.'

Jack's ears pricked up. 'Go on.'

Pence paused for a moment. He knew what he was going to say now would please Jack and that was always a good place to be. He hated Jack Lantern but he liked the money he paid him.

'I put a tracker on Oscarson's Dodge before they left Blackjack so I could keep an eye on him.'

'Hey, nice thinking, Sheriff. Where did they stop last night, Vegas?'

'No, that's the strange thing, they didn't get that far. They turned off the 93 and headed East up into the mountains and stopped in the middle of nowhere.'

Jack was intrigued. 'What like a little town?'

'No, literally in the middle of nowhere. No motel, no gas station, not even a ranch. I checked it out on Google Earth and the only thing I could find anywhere nearby was the site of an old open cast dredging mine.'

'What sort of mine.'

Pence's reply was short and to the point.

'Gold.'

Jack thought for a moment. Why would the boys be making a big detour to the middle of nowhere to stop at the site of an old gold mine?

'Could you send me the co-ordinates Sheriff? I may need to check it out. How far from Vegas is it?'

'About sixty miles. I already sent you the co-ordinates in an email.'

Jack smiled with satisfaction.

'You did good, Sheriff Pence, real good. You keep me posted on their little road trip.'

'Sure will, Jack.' Pence clicked off the call and breathed a deep sigh of relief. His decision to bug the van had paid off. He was back in Jack Lantern's good books.

As they drove down through the centre of Las Vegas the strip was just as Jimmy remembered it. They rolled past Carpenters Casino where they would soon have their residency. Originally Sam Estrin the owner had booked them for the much bigger Golden Flamingo but he and David had decided it would be too much pressure at this stage in Jimmy's comeback. Carpenters was a famous and respected venue and it was more of a music venue than any of the big casinos. When David had broken the news to them, much to his surprise, Jimmy and Kid had been delighted. Carpenters on the Strip was like playing the Fillmore East for a musician. A real music venue with real history.

'Hard to imagine our names are going to be up in lights on the strip in a couple of months ain't it?'

Kid smiled. 'Well, yours will be, I'm just one of the Second Chances.'

'You know what I mean, this is a band, we stand or fall together.'

Kid nodded in agreement. 'Don't get me wrong Jimmy, I wasn't complaining. If I play shit the fans will say, "Boy that Jimmy Wayne's Guitarist was shit." Then his friends are going to ask. "Who is he?" And they are just going to say, "Dunno, but he's in Jimmy Wayne's band." Sometimes a bit of anonymity can be a good thing. Just you remember that when it's bonus time.'

Jimmy looked at Kid. 'Is that a threat?'

Kid laughed. 'Of course. I gotta keep you honest!'

Jimmy shrugged. 'That's a pretty empty threat, Kid. You couldn't bear to play a bum note. Your standards are way higher than mine.'

Kid winced. 'Damn it, you've seen through my cunning plan. Now I'm just gonna have to toe the line and play well.' Jimmy took one last look at the billboard outside Carpenters and imagined his name up in lights.

'That's why I'm the boss Kid, and that's why you are driving.'

'Shall we stop and get some new clothes, boss?'

Jimmy shook his head. 'No, we can do that in LA, and don't call me boss.'

'Don't worry I'm not going to.' They cleared the outer limits of Vegas on Highway 15. Only about a hundred miles to LA. They spent most of it taking the piss out of each other and trying to imagine what fame would feel like.

———◆———

Michael Owen sat in the studio up in the hills off Laurel Canyon. His mobile was ringing and he knew the number. Jack Lantern. How he wished he had never met the man. It seemed like such a good idea at the time. His label had a great reputation, but he had suffered a few loss-making records as tastes had changed. He had been advised to realise some of the capital and sell some shares in the business. Small Print Records had a great reputation, and several investors were keen – that was until they looked at the books for the last couple of years. Jack Lantern, however, didn't seem bothered.

'Mikey, taste is subjective. You got an ear, won't be long until you get another hit.'

Although he hated being called Mikey, Jack had a point. Michael knew what he was doing, he still had a great reputation and plenty of fine artists wanting to work with him. Jack knew this. He also knew that Small Print Records would be a perfect vehicle to launder money through. Win, win for Jack Lantern. It had taken a while, but Michael had now worked this out for himself. He just had to accept that the four million dollars in his personal bank account was the price he had to pay to have Jack Lantern in his business. Up till now it had been a price worth paying.

———◆———

'Who you calling, Jack?'

Jack jumped. 'Jesus, Ma, don't creep up on me like that. You're gonna give me a heart attack.' Ma Lantern let out a cackle, she sounded like a Hyena that had been possessed by the Devil.

'Ha! You ain't got a heart Jackie, cus that's the way I raised ya! Nice boys get taken advantage of and that's not the game we are in.'

Jack looked at his mother. She was in her seventies but still wore her make-up the way she had when she was twenty. Her hair was still blonde and her neckline was low. She looked like a hooker who was a long way past her sell-by-date but beneath that *Whatever Happened to Baby Jane?* hooker-chic look, beat a heart as black as coal and a brain as brilliant as Einstein. She was crazy like a fox and was still one of the most feared mobsters in the West. Even now Jack could not hold her stare. He had thought about killing the bitch many times but he was too scared. If he failed, she would torture him to death. If he succeeded, she would come back and haunt him. It was easy to imagine Ma Lantern as a creature of the night, much easier than thinking of her as his mother.

'So, Jackie, what you got cooking?' His mother perched on the edge of his desk. She looked at him like a vampire waiting to feed.

'This and that Ma.'

'More specific, Jackie, I ain't fucking psychic.' He didn't want to tell her about Jimmy Wayne, but he knew she would find out. She always found out.

'You remember I bought a share of that record label in LA?'

'The one run by that English guy?'

'Yeah, that's the one.'

'He gay?'

Jack thought for a moment. 'I dunno, is it relevant?'

Ma snorted derisively. 'Course it's relevant. If you don't know and he is, it's probably because he is trying to hide it.'

'He lives in LA, Ma. People ain't bothered by that stuff anymore.'

'Did I raise you fucking stupid, Jackie?'

Jack shook his head. 'No Ma.'

'Then think! If he is and don't want it known it's a weakness we can exploit. If he's married but having an affair, it's a weakness. You need to know everything about this guy, we are going to launder a lot of cash through this business and there's going to come a point where he won't like it.'

Jack didn't agree. 'Mikey's cool, he won't be no trouble.'

Anger swelled in Ma's eyes. 'You don't know that, Jackie. You don't even know if he likes boys or girls. Do your fucking research like I taught you.' Ma sat on the edge of his desk glaring at him, he couldn't hold her stare. They say the eyes are the windows to the soul but the only thing to see in Ma's eyes was a long dark stairway that descended to hell. She forced a smile. The look didn't suit her. Her mouth contorted and she appeared to be in the throes of a stroke. Her smile was terrifying because it was so unnatural. Like a lion trying to eat a veggie burger. When Ma Lantern smiled the world was a frightening place, and somewhere was another agenda about to be opened. Slowly the rictus faded from her face replaced by her more natural scowl and the nature of the hidden agenda appeared from behind the mask.

'So, you still going to kill Jimmy Wayne?'

Jack had been dreading this moment. Ma wanted Jimmy dead from the moment she knew he had been screwing Lena, her daughter-in-law. She didn't care much for Lena but she was married to Jack and looked good on his arm. Jack should have killed him long before the bad debts had gone unpaid. It was principle. If anyone in her world found out he would be seen as weak, a cuckold. Disrespected. In her world these things mattered.

'Jack, you think you're tough, you think everyone's frightened of you and that may be true.' She leaned across the desk; her eyes fixed on his like a Cobra preparing to strike. 'But me Jackie, they're terrified of me. Even you are frightened of me. This business is tough, dog eat dog. But I'm the Queen Bitch and this is my town and I want Jimmy Wayne's head on a pole.'

Jack shifted uncomfortably in his chair. 'Ma, Jimmy alive is good business. He is on the verge of something big. This could be a major score for us.' Ma didn't seem convinced.

'So you say, Jackie, but I ain't convinced.' She slid smoothly off his desk with a litheness that denied her years. 'You got three months, if he hasn't covered his debt and put us into profit you bring him to me in the cellar.'

Jack shuddered. Just hearing his mother mention the cellar made him feel sick. Jack was a ruthless bastard but he always got other people to do his dirty work. He didn't want to be there or see it done. His mother, on the other hand, did all the dirty work herself. She enjoyed it.

He was ten the first time his mother had taken him down to the cellar. It was in the big house on the north side of Vegas. There was a man strapped to a chair. He had been badly beaten but he was still conscious and completely terrified. He had pointed at the man.

'He's bleeding, Mummy.'

Ma had grinned. 'Yes, he is Jackie. Do you know why he is bleeding?' Jack shook his head. She turned back to the bleeding man. 'Because he tried to take something from me, from us.' She turned back to Jack. 'You like this house Jackie; you like all the things we have?'

Jack had nodded too terrified to speak. His mother seemed to be filled with a dark brooding evil he had never witnessed before.

'Well, this is Aldo, and he is trying to take our business away. We can't let him do that, Jackie.' She walked behind the chair. The man called Aldo struggled to get free. Jack knew something terrible was about to happen but he just couldn't look away. There was a table behind the chair and Jimmy could see an assortment of knives and saws. He didn't know what they were for but there was something in his frightened ten-year-old brain that knew it was something terrible. He was almost relieved when his mother picked up a length of rope with a short piece of wood attached. Jack's mother put her hands-on Aldo's shoulders, he flinched at her touch and his breathing became louder and more rapid. She leaned forwards and whispered in his ear.

'That's right Aldo, get those breaths in while you still can.'

'Ma, we can sort this out.'

Ma punched him in the side of the head with a force that Jack had never seen his mother use.

'You don't have the right to be heard Aldo, you lost that right when you killed one of my dealers. You knew this was my district and you thought you could just take it from me because I'm a woman. Well, you were wrong.'

'I can pay, how much do you want?… We… we can do a deal.'

Ma smiled, that lopsided smile that opened like a crack in the entrance to hell.

'It's over Aldo.'

Aldo had started to sob.

'Can't we let him go, Mummy?'

Ma slowly shook her head. 'No darling, if we let Aldo go, he will come back and try to kill me and then you. Aldo here has got to die.' She held up the rope with the stick on the end. 'This is called a garrotte, Jackie. In Sicily, where Aldo comes from, they use these all the time.' With a speed that shocked Jack, his mother whipped the rope around Aldo's neck and looped it around the wooden handle and twisted it. Aldo straightened and he started to make a terrible gagging sound. His mother gave the handle another turn. Aldo's eyes seemed to bulge and his tongue came lolling out of his mouth. Jack had turned away.

'Don't you look away, Jackie.' Her voice was harsh, triumphal. 'This is what happens to people who try and take what is ours. Watch!' The last word was hissed and full of venom.

He opened his eyes; he couldn't look at Aldo's face but he watched his finger nails digging into the wooden arms of the chair. Scrabbling as if he was trying to gouge his way free. He watched until the fingers stopped moving and the awful rasping sounds had stopped. His mother calmly removed the Garrotte and dropped it onto the table. She walked around to her trembling son.

'Don't feel sorry for him, Jackie, he was a bad man and if I hadn't put him to sleep, he would have done it to me, and then maybe you.' She took him by the hand. 'You want some ice cream, Jackie?'

He had nodded. 'But what about Aldo?'

Ma waived her hand. 'Don't worry about Aldo, the boys will clear up the trash later!'

That had been over fifty years ago. What kind of a monster made her kid watch something like that? Ma had tried to breed her evil into him and, bad as he was, he was never going to reach the dark layers that his mother possessed.

'Trust me Ma, you're going to love Jimmy when you meet him, especially when he starts making us some real money.' Ma gave him a withering look.

'I don't even love you, Jackie, so I don't think I'm ever going to feel that way about a washed-up singer.'

'Just wait till the money comes, you know that will soften your heart,' Jack grinned at her. 'Assuming you have one.' Ma was already leaving the room.

'I don't,' she said, 'but I do have a cellar!' She shut the door behind her and Jack felt his whole body relax. Man! How had he grown up so nice with a role model like that. He picked up his mobile and punched in a number. It was answered on the first ring.

'Hi Boss.' It was Terry Moist, Jack's most trusted lieutenant.

'Never mind the social niceties, Terry, have you broken that fucker's legs yet?'

Terry held the phone away from his ear to avoid being deafened. 'No need boss, he paid up in full.'

Jack wasn't happy. 'I told you to break both his legs.'

'I know, boss, but he paid up in full and if he can't walk, he won't be able to make us any money.' Jack thought for a moment, Terry had a good point.

'Ok, kick him in the balls, hard!' Jack hung up. Yeah, he was a much nicer person than his mum, she would have cut them off!

———◆———

Kid swung a right off Laurel Canyon Boulevard and headed up Lookout Mountain Drive.

'Looks pretty swanky round here now, Jimmy. Hard to believe that only artists and musicians lived up here fifty years ago. Crosby, Stills, Nash and Young. Joni Mitchell, John Mayall. Must have been amazing back then. I guess we were just born too late.' Jimmy knew what Kid meant but he didn't buy into the nostalgia. Only the guys that lived it should feel nostalgic. That moment had come and gone. Now it was his turn.

'I kinda like the fact that we're coming here to make a record in the same place where all that stuff happened. Laurel Canyon may have changed but it's still here and so is the spirit of what it represents. I feel good about this place.' The

Dodge chugged on up the mountain road and then the voice of Samantha called out.

'Please slip into the entrance on the right in 200 feet, oh you're getting closer. One hundred feet – oh, you've reached your destination, big boy!' Kid pulled to a stop on the driveway of Small Print Records. Jimmy smiled at him.

'Man, it was funny at first but after five hundred miles Samantha the Porn Star Sat Nav gets a little tiresome.'

Kid shrugged as he turned off the engine. 'Each to his own, I just find being talked dirty to makes the miles fly by.'

'I could talk dirty to you,' smirked Jimmy.

'You could but I just wouldn't respect myself in the morning.' Kid slammed the door and turned to face the owner of the property.

Michael Owen was strolling towards them with a big smile on his face and his hand held out. 'Good to see you guys, welcome to Small Print Studio.'

Kid took his hand. 'This your house as well?'

Michael nodded. 'Yeah, I hate commuting into LA and I was lucky enough to buy a couple of acres up here. Bought the plot before the prices went crazy. I built the studio down the bottom of the garden with that little wood at the back of it. There's accommodation with sleeping for up to eight in the chalet that's attached. It's got a kitchen and dining room as well as en-suites in every bedroom.' Kid glanced down the gently sloping lawn to the studio. It was an idyllic spot. With the woods behind it felt like the old Laurel Canyon he had dreamed of.

'Nice set up Michael, keeps the musicians from having to go off site.'

Michael tapped the end of his nose with his index finger. 'You know what LA is like Kid. You let some musos from more sheltered backgrounds loose down there and we may never get them back.' Kid knew exactly what Michael meant. He had been one of those guys and his night out had lasted for three months! Jimmy appeared from the other side of the van. Michael hurried over to greet him.

'Hey Jimmy, good journey?'

Jimmy nodded. 'Very enriching.'

'Yes, travel broadens your horizons. You guys need something to eat or a coffee?'

'I could eat something,' said Kid. Jimmy shouldn't have been surprised but there were times when Kid's capacity for eating still shocked him. Only fifteen minutes before he had demolished a huge meal at the In and Out at the bottom of the Canyon.

'Just a coffee for me,' said Jimmy. 'I only just ate.'

Michael turned to Kid. 'What about you, Kid?'

Kid ignored the smile on Jimmy's face. 'Have you got any of that English Breakfast tea.'

'Well I am English, what do you want with it?'

'Food will be fine.'

Michael wrinkled his brow. 'Could you be more specific?'

'Whatever you have that's easy, I just have a void that needs filling.'

'Just bring him some milk and cereal, Michael, he'll probably eat the box as well.'

Michael led them around the back of the house and there, from the patio, lay Los Angeles. Sprawled across the valley in all directions.

'Wow, that's some view you got here, Michael.'

'Not bad, is it? I prefer to look at LA from a distance. Too much stuff going on down there for my liking.'

'Know what you mean,' said Kid. 'I'm from a little village in Norway and big American cities were a bit of a shock to me when I first arrived. So frantic and yet so lonely. You can be surrounded by a million people but not one of them is your friend.'

'That sounds like a great lyric for a song, you should write it.'

Kid pointed at Jimmy. 'He does the words I do the music.'

'Talking of words, do we have eleven songs?'

Jimmy smiled. 'We do, and arrangements.'

'Well, that's splendid, looks like this is going to be a doddle.'

'What's a doddle?'

'Sorry Jimmy, it's an English expression for easy. In England we would also say it's going to be a "piece of cake".'

Kid looked up. 'Have you got any cake?'

Michael laughed. 'Take a seat, gents, while I load the contents of the fridge into a wheelbarrow.'

They sat down at the table looking out across Laurel Canyon and down to LA just taking in the view and savouring the moment.

'Can you believe this? We're a long way from Blackjack.' Kid didn't answer Jimmy at first, he just gazed out at the view, 'What you thinking?'

'You know, I've dreamt about this place for years. When I was eleven years old my Dad gave me a copy of *Blues from Laurel Canyon* by John Mayall.' Kid turned to Jimmy. 'You ever looked at the cover on a vinyl edition?'

Jimmy nodded. 'I got that record for my fourteenth birthday.'

'You remember the photos of Mayall and the band just chilling amongst the trees. It was so peaceful, looked like some kind of Hippie commune.'

'Well, it was sixty-eight.'

Kid nodded. 'Look at it now, all built up, houses everywhere. There's no place now for the musicians and artists unless they are already wealthy and yet,' Kid paused, he seemed miles away, 'this is still the place. It may have changed but it's still the place. Can you feel it, Jimmy? We were meant to be here, even though we ain't rich and famous, we were meant to be here!' There was real conviction in Kid's voice.

'Well, we are kinda rich now.'

Kid smiled in acknowledgement. 'Yeah, we are, I'd forgotten about that.'

'How do you forget about having two million dollars in your account? What motivates you? Because it sure as hell ain't money.' To be fair it didn't motivate Jimmy but the idea of having his own home, a nice car and some money in the bank did sound appealing.

'You know Jimmy, a wise man once told me not to chase money. He told me once you have enough, the pursuit of more wealth was a waste of your life. He said one line that really left a mark.'

'What was that?'

'How many meals can you eat in a day?' Jimmy thought about it. It did make perfect sense.

'Yeah, I hear what he's saying there, Kid.' He paused for a moment. 'Out of interest, how many meals can you eat in a day?' Kid held up his hands in mock surrender.

'You know Jimmy, I never have found out.'

Michael returned with the drinks. 'There you go, coffee for you, Jimmy, and a pot of tea for me and Kid.' On the tray was a cake to which Kid was giving his undivided attention.

'What kind of cake is that?'

'Does it matter.'

'Not really, just idle curiosity.'

'It's a cherry madeira cake, very popular back in the UK.'

Kid picked up the knife. 'May I?' He held it above the cake like a surgeon about to make an incision.

Michael nodded. 'Take as much as you like, I have a couple more in the fridge, keeps them moist.' Kid cut the cake in half and then he just slid that half onto a plate. Michael and Jimmy stared in fascination.

'You sure you have enough there, Kid?' asked Jimmy.

Kid ignored the sarcasm in Jimmy's question. 'I'll let you know.'

Michael chuckled, quietly amused at Kid's dietary requirements. 'Remind me fellas, did you put cake down on your rider?'

A couple of hours later Kid and Jimmy had unpacked their luggage. They had taken the two best rooms with a panoramic view looking down towards LA. No Relation and Doug would be arriving shortly. When they had told Michael what time to expect the boys, he had seemed puzzled.

'No Relation, that's the drummer, isn't it?'

'Yeah, that's him,' said Jimmy.

'What's his real name?'

'No one knows, or cares Michael – all he has to do is keep time.'

'He seemed pretty good when I heard him back in Blackjack.'

Kid shrugged. 'He's like a broken watch, only on time a couple of times a day.'

Michael laughed. 'He's a lot better than that. Now come on fellas, what's his real name? I can't say, "Hi Doug, hi No Relation", when they get here. I'd feel like a total plonker!'

'What the hell is a plonker?'

Michael smiled apologetically. 'It's an English term for an idiot.'

Jimmy turned to Kid. 'Maybe we should call him Plonker.'

'Better than calling him Joe Rich.' Kid smiled at Michael as he watched the penny drop.

'Rich? That's an unfortunate name for a drummer, unless of course you were Buddy.'

Kid sighed. 'Sure is. Joe is definitely no relation!'

Two hours later Michael came walking down the garden path towards the guest house.

'You boys settled in?'

'Yeah, great place you got here.'

Michael nodded in agreement. 'I know, I'm a lucky guy.' He paused for a moment. 'You want to take a look at the studio?'

This was a question that didn't require an answer. Jimmy hadn't been in a proper studio since his first brush with fame twenty years ago. Before he could answer Kid appeared from the guest house.

'We would love to, Mikey.'

Michael Owen flinched slightly. 'Could you call me Mike or Michael, I know it sounds stupid but I hate being called Mikey.'

'Is that an English thing?'

'Maybe, but when I first came out here everyone called me Mikey and it made me feel really homesick. Made me realise I was a stranger in a strange land.'

Kid nodded. 'I know what you mean. When I came here from Norway nobody even tried to use my name. I remember the first recording session I played on the producer came across and asked me my name. Sigurd Lund Oscarson, I replied. He looked at me for a couple of moments then turned to the other musicians in the studio. 'This is Kid… he's from Norway.'

'Seems it stuck.'

Kid smiled. 'I've been called worse.'

'Let's go look at the studio.' Michael led them across the patio to the single-storey studio. From the outside it looked like a log cabin but, as they entered, they were greeted by a glazed wall which allowed you to look into the studio from behind the engineer's console. To Jimmy it looked like something from a *Star Wars* movie. The console was about sixteen feet long. There must have been eighty channels and forty inputs.

'What do all these buttons and sliders do?'

Michael laughed. 'I really don't know, never used half of them.' Kid had wandered over to the desk and was studying it intently.

'You know your way around a console, Kid?'

Kid looked at Michael. 'I know more than Jimmy – sliders!'

Jimmy shrugged. 'I'm a singer, I leave all that technical shit to people who can't sing.'

Kid didn't seem convinced. 'So, the proper name is?'

Jimmy smiled dismissively.

'It's a fader or, if you want to use a technical term, a potentiometer. Varies the resistance so you can set the signal level. Pretty simple really, Kid.'

Kid and Michael nodded approvingly.

'What do you think, Michael, should we get Jimmy to set up the input gain and balance it with the output faders.'

'We could but I thought you wanted this record to be a hit.'

Jimmy knew when he was beaten.

'Ok you tech-heads. Now we've established I'm not an engineer can we see the important stuff.' He paused for a moment.

'Sure, what do you want to see?' asked Michael.

'I want to see where the coffee machine is!'

'We may have to show him how to work it though.'

'Well why don't I kill two birds with one stone and make you a coffee?'

There were a couple of old leather sofas in the studio. Behind them were three glass booths. Michael pointed to the first. 'Obviously that's for drums.'

'Yeah, the kit was a bit of a giveaway.'

'The middle one is big enough to get a brass section in if we want to record them together. Or if we need a few backing singers.' Michael pointed to the third booth. 'That one's for you Kid.' Michael then indicated the room they were sat in. 'And this is the live room. It's got great acoustics so we use it quite a lot.' Kid and Jimmy were impressed. 'Quite some set up you got here Michael,' said Jimmy.

Michael looked around his studio, there was a sad smile playing across his face. 'Yes, it's what I dreamed of for years. The studio in LA was ok but this was my dream set up and after a few big records I had enough money to build what I wanted in the grounds here. Only wish it was all still mine.'

'Well, it is, isn't it?'

Michael nodded. 'Most of it but I sold some shares when things got a bit tight a couple of years back.'

Jimmy knew exactly why Michael seemed regretful. 'Jack Lantern?'

Michael seemed surprised. 'You know Jack Lantern?'

'Oh, we know Jack alright.'

Kid leaned forwards. 'Piece of shit, what the hell were you thinking?' Kid words sounded harsh, but Michael Owen showed no signs of being offended. He nodded in agreement.

'Can't disagree with you there. In my defence the crash of 2008 had made things tight and I then had a run of about six records without a hit. Suppose I went a bit out of fashion for a while. Sod's law though, just after I had taken Jack's money for fifty percent of the business I had a couple of major records and the studio and the label were flying high again.'

'Does he get involved much?'

'No, not really, apart from the demos he occasionally sends me of women he is obviously having affairs with, who think they can sing.' Michael laughed. 'He even brought one here last year and got me to record her… wow!'

'How bad was she?'

Michael smiled at Jimmy. 'Bad. Sounded like you had recorded her. Listen guys, now that we're talking about Jack Lantern I just need to warn you that Jack seems to be taking a real interest in this record. Any idea why?'

'Because Jack and I have a bit of a history. It's kind of a love-hate relationship but without the love element.'

'Is that going to cause us a problem?' Michael looked concerned.

'No. Jack is motivated by one thing. Money! He won't do anything that gets in the way of this record being a success.'

'That's reassuring because he was mentioning that it might be a good idea to use some of the girls from one of his strip clubs for the cover.'

'How like Jack,' said Kid. 'He thinks sex sells everything. Guess you gotta admire his consistency.'

'Let's just make the best record we can and ignore any suggestions that Jack makes.'

'You're right, Michael. Guess you're always going to have artistic differences when you're dealing with someone who thinks a pair of boobs is art.'

'Depends on the boobs,' said Kid thoughtfully.

CHAPTER 5

HEARD IT THROUGH THE GRAPEVINE

As Jimmy and the band were settling into the guest house, fate was gathering together the threads of Jimmy's past. Back in Blackjack, Sheriff Pence was waiting for Jimmy to return. He was sure that he had been involved in the disappearance of Jack Lantern's men and he planned to prove it. When Jimmy returned to Blackjack, he would give him a welcome he would never forget.

Jack Lantern was waiting for the moment when he could grab control of Jimmy's career, and Ma Lantern was waiting, like a black widow spider, for a chance to kill him. Fate is an intangible thing, a series of seemingly unconnected events that weave a web from which there is no escape. Like small moons being drawn into the gravitational pull of a dying planet. In an office in Las Vegas a few blocks and a million miles from the glamour of the strip a new player was being drawn into Jimmy's orbit.

Ronnie Reich, nickname Third, was looking at a readout that he was struggling to understand. As Jack Lantern's accountant he had his fingers in many pies. Most of them were other people's. Jack liked to know what was going on in his empire. Almost everyone on Jack's radar was being monitored. His reach was frightening. He even had hackers and corrupt officials working full time for him. That was why Ronnie Reich was looking at Jimmy Wayne's bank statement and wondering how the hell two million dollars had been paid into his account yesterday from an untraceable Swiss account. This made no sense. He knew he needed to call Jack and let him know.

Events that you have no control over. Jimmy hadn't asked Aksel for the money. Aksel had just done it as a kindness. Ronnie wasn't thinking about Jimmy Wayne until that icon on his screen had started flashing, and now – now he had to speak to Jack. Fate, just a series of events, they may seem unconnected, but eventually they gather together and when they do, they can shape your destiny.

'What is it, Ronnie? I'm very busy.' Jack wasn't lying. The scantily clad young lady sitting on his lap was demanding his full attention.

'Got something very interesting you need to know.'

Jack glanced at the young lady. 'How interesting?'

'Two million dollars!' Jack pushed the dancer off his lap unceremoniously. 'Now you got my attention.' She protested as she hit the floor, but Jack ignored her. She was pretty but money was beautiful. 'Where is it?'

'Just showed up in Jimmy Wayne's account.'

'What the fuck?' As Jack tried to absorb this information Tracy tried to slide back onto his lap. Jack pushed her away. 'Sorry darling, somethings come up.'

Tracy smiled. 'I was kinda hoping it would.'

Jack was no longer interested in Tracy's assets now he knew that Jimmy Wayne had two million of them.

'You're going to have to go, Tracy, I'll catch you later. Shut the door on your way out.' He waited until she had closed the door behind her. 'So, what do we know, Ronnie?'

'Nothing. It came from a Swiss account.'

'Do we know whose?'

'No. Untraceable. Must be some serious money behind it because it's virtually opaque. Whoever sent the money must have some serious wealth. Everything is hidden.' Jack thought for a moment. Who the hell would give Jimmy Wayne two million dollars, and why?

'This don't make any sense Ronnie.'

'Well, if you look at it in a positive light, boss, you know he is going to be able to repay his debt and the damages.' Jack wasn't bothered about that. His greedy little mind was focused on the fact that where there was two million dollars, there was bound to be a whole load more. And he wanted to get his grubby little hands on it.

'Do some digging Ronnie,' and then a thought occurred to him. 'Did Oscarson get any money?' There was a silence from Ronnie's end of the phone. 'Well, did he?' When Ronnie answered he sounded nervous.

'Afraid I don't know, boss.'

Jack exploded. 'What do you mean, you don't know? I pay you to know!'

Ronnie flinched and put the receiver back to his ear. 'I can't find an account for him. Everyone knows him as Kid Oscarson but nothing comes up under that name.'

'Jesus, Ronnie, Kid's a fucking nickname. Get a copy of his passport then go find him and check it out. I'm getting a funny feeling about this, and you know what happens when I get those funny feelings.'

Ronnie did and it usually involved someone's legs getting broken. 'Leave it with me boss, I'll have an answer for you in a couple of hours.'

'I know you will, Ronnie.' Jack put down the phone.

This was an unexpected and pleasant surprise. He knew that if Jimmy had money, he would find a way to get some of it. All he had to do now was find out why someone had transferred two million dollars into Jimmy Wayne's account. If Ma had been there, she would probably have said it was the Noise Abatement Society, trying to shut him up with a bribe. Ma didn't like any music after Sinatra, and not a lot before. Jack knew though. He had realised back in the Canyon Room at the Riviera in Blackjack that Jimmy had something. The way the crowd had reacted to the new songs and the sound. Jimmy Wayne was going to be a star; he was sure of that. But who would give Jimmy two million dollars? He picked up his phone to call David Parker. He was as close to Jimmy as anyone. Being the manager at the Riviera, he had known Jimmy for years. He scrolled through the P's and cursed when he went too far, but then he saw a name that made him think. Pence.

Sheriff Pence had called him this morning. Cunning old bastard had put a tracker on Kid's van. It was all coming back to him now. Pence had told him that the boys had spent the night in the middle of nowhere north east of Vegas. The only thing near there was an old gold mine. Jack Lantern's brain was adding two and two together and he was coming up with two million! There had to be a connection. He scrolled through his phone until he found the number for Terry Moist.

The Texan drawl was unmistakable.

'Hi Boss, what can I do for you?'

Jack was straight to the point. 'I'm gonna send you an email with some co-ordinates. It's an old gold mine up in the mountains sixty miles north east of Vegas. Go and take a look, see if there is anything there. Take Tony C with you.'

'Sure, any specific reason?'

'Yeah, Jimmy Wayne and his Viking sidekick went there last night and today somebody has put a couple of million in his bank account. Seems a bit of a coincidence to me.'

Terry let out a low whistle. 'Woah! Lucky bastard.'

Jack laughed. 'He ain't that lucky Terry, not now I know about it.'

Terry smiled. The boss had a point. 'Leave it with me boss, me and Tony will go up there tonight.'

'Ok, thanks Terry.'

Once again, the net was closing in on Jimmy. A random act of kindness caught in the lens of Jack Lantern's ever vigilant eye had drawn Terry Moist and Tony C back into Jimmy's orbit, and with it Aksel Lund.

Sixty miles away Aksel stood quietly harvesting his gold from the cold waters of the river of fire, unaware that Jack Lantern's thugs were loading weapons into their vehicle and preparing to head north to pay him a visit.

Back in Laurel Canyon, Jimmy lay on his bed in the guest house at Small Print Records. For the first time in a long time he felt truly happy. Everything finally seemed to be going his way. He hadn't killed anyone in weeks. It felt good. Nothing lasts forever though, and as he lay staring at the ceiling a familiar face, followed by a torso, came bustling through. It was Wendy.

'Jesus, Wendy, you gotta stop doing that. You're going to give me a heart attack.' Wendy smiled. He hadn't seen his dead girlfriend since the other morning at the Song Cemetery when they had sung the duet together. For a dead person she looked good. 'To what do I owe the pleasure?'

Wendy sat on the end of his bed. 'This ain't going to be a pleasure for you, Jimmy. I come bearing bad news.' Jimmy sat up; this didn't sound good.

'What's the problem?'

'Do you want the bad news or the good news?'

'I'll have the good news.'

Wendy pulled a face. 'There ain't no good news, you ready for the bad?' Jimmy didn't like the sound of this. 'Better make yourself comfortable Jimmy because there's a lot. Where shall I start?'

Jimmy thought for a moment. 'Just start, the suspense is killing me.'

'Ok then,' Wendy counted them off on her fingers. 'First, Pence bugged Kid's van and he knows you went to Aksel's gold mine last night.'

Jimmy groaned. 'Fuck!'

'Second. Lantern knows you had two million dollars paid into your account yesterday.'

Jimmy couldn't believe what he was hearing. 'Fuck!!'

Wendy looked at him disapprovingly. 'No need for language Jimmy. I'm just telling you what I know. Third! Jack has sent Terry Moist and Tony C out to Aksel's mine to check it out. Tonight.'

Jimmy put his head in his hands. 'God! Is that it, Wendy?'

She nodded. 'Yep, that's all the news for now.' Jimmy sat there trying to formulate a plan, they had to warn Aksel. 'Well?' Wendy was looking at him expectantly.

'Well, what?' he asked.

'Aren't you pleased to see me?'

Jimmy leaned over and gave her a big hug. 'Course I am Wendy it's just that you've dropped some pretty bad news here.'

Wendy looked indignant. 'Don't shoot the messenger Jimmy. I'm just doing my job.'

'I know, I know, it's just really bad news. I gotta phone Kid.' Before he could pick up his cell phone it rang. It was Kid.

'I just found a bug on the van, Jimmy. Someone's tracking us.'

'I know, it was Pence.'

'How do you know that?'

'Wendy's here, she just told me.' As a sign of just how weird their world had become in the past few weeks Kid didn't even flinch or question this revelation.

'I've warned Aksel and he has locked down the mine. He's going to hide his pickup down the valley and go back and see if anyone turns up.'

Jimmy sighed. 'They will. Jack has sent Terry and Tony C. Will Aksel be ok?'

Kid chuckled. 'Don't worry about Aksel. He'll be fine. It's Terry and Tony who are in danger.' He paused for a moment. 'You got more news for me, don't ya?'

'Afraid so,' he paused for a moment expecting Kid to say something. He didn't. Kid was caught in the same orbit and waiting for all the pieces to fall into place.

'Jack knows about the two million.'

'Of course he does. Trust Jack to have his spies everywhere.'

'What do we do, Kid?' Kid appeared at Jimmy's bedroom door. He was smiling wistfully.

'I guess we just have to sit tight and let this thing play out. Hopefully Aksel won't have to kill Jack's boys tonight and they'll have nothing to report to Jack.'

'But what about the two million?'

Kid just shrugged. 'Tell him it was a gift from one of the Waynette's, better still tell him to mind his own fucking business.'

'Yeah, that always works with Jack.'

Kid looked around the room. Apart from Jimmy the room was empty but as he turned to leave, he called back over his shoulder. 'Hi Wendy.'

Wendy smiled. 'Hi Kid.' She turned to Jimmy. 'He didn't see me, did he?'

Jimmy shook his head. 'No, only me Wendy. Guess he can just sense when you are around.' He turned to look at her but like a breeze she had slipped away unseen. Once more all the strands of fate were being inexorably drawn together. Wendy was in Laurel Canyon and, in Blackjack, David Parker was about to leave the Riviera.

He threw his suitcase into the back of his Jaguar convertible, smiling as he did so. The drive through the desert to Laurel Canyon was something he had been looking forward to. He had been couped up in Blackjack for too long. There was also a pleasant feeling of anticipation at seeing his old friend again. Michael Owen and he went back a long way. Private school in England over thirty years ago. Seeing Jimmy and the boys record the album would be something very special. Without him and his belief in Jimmy none of this would be happening. He jumped in and fired up the V6 engine. It purred into life and within seconds he was on Highway 93; another piece of the puzzle that made up the destiny of Jimmy Wayne and the Second Chance was falling into place.

———◆———

Jack pushed his dinner around his plate.

'What's the matter, Jackie, don't you like your Mama's cooking?' That was a joke, Ma had never cooked for him, not even when he was a kid. He supposed that was one of the benefits of being brought up in a brothel with a bar and a kitchen.

'No, Ma, dinner is fine. I just got a lot on my mind.'

Ma's ears pricked up. 'Problem shared is a problem halved, Jackie.'

Jack smiled. 'Not with you, Ma. It just becomes two problems.' Ma tried to look hurt but when you have no feelings it's not easy.

'Someone giving you grief.'

Jack shook his head. 'No, but someone's got a lot of money all of a sudden and I need to find out where they got it from.' The light in Ma's eyes seemed to dim and Jack felt the cold stare tingle on his face. How could he be scared of his own mother. He tried to look into her eyes, but the darkness was there. It was never far away. 'No, Ma, nobody's stealing from us, but somebody of interest has suddenly acquired a great deal of wealth and I need to find out from where.'

'Who is it?' Ma said it almost matter of factly, trying to get Jack to let it slip but he knew all of his mother's little tricks.

'I'm not telling you.'

'Why not?'

'Because you would kidnap them and torture them until you found out, and then you would kill them.' Ma held up her hands in protest but Jack wasn't buying it.

'So, what's wrong with that? You find out what you need to know and then I tidy up after you. It's just good housekeeping.'

Jack laughed out loud. 'And what the hell would you know about housekeeping?'

Ma grinned. 'I know enough to pay other people to do it.'

'All you need to know is that about $40k is coming our way. If I can get more, it's a bonus.'

Ma tutted. 'I raised you soft Jackie, way too soft.'

'Only compared to you, Ma, because you're the devil.'

She smiled. 'Do you think so, Jackie?'

'I know so, Ma. The boys are frightened of me, but they are terrified of you.'

This pleased Ma. In her seventies and she still had it. Truth is she still loved it. Loved the money, the excitement. Loved to see the fear in men's eyes when she looked at them. Weaker of the species? I don't think so.

———◆———

It was a lovely warm California evening and Michael had decided to throw a barbeque for the band. No Relation and Doug had arrived late afternoon and the boys had relaxed. Everybody was chilling and there was a sense of excitement when they talked about the start of recording the next day. The food had been great and they all sat around swapping stories about old bands and tours. No Relation was the oldest in the band. Like a true rock drummer, he still wore his hair long, only now it didn't grow in long flowing locks from the top of his head. Like the Amazon rainforest it was being denuded from all sides. His forehead had retreated so far only people behind him could see it. Like a scientific site of special interest, it was confined to an ever-decreasing area at the back of his head and funnelled down his back via a ponytail. Remarkably it was still jet black.

'Do you dye your hair, Joe?'

Joe looked at Kid with distain. ''Course not.'

'Then how come your chest hair is white? I thought the pubes always went grey first.' Joe smiled. Everyone knew he dyed his hair and he knew they knew but it was all part of the ritual.

'Talking about hair, did I ever tell you the story about the bass player in Stunner?'

'Stunner. Where the hell did that name come from?' Doug took a long look at Joe. 'I'm guessing it wasn't based on your looks!'

Joe ignored the laughter. 'No, we all worked in an Abattoir back in St Louis. Jeff, the lead singer, was a stunner and we thought it would make a good name for a hard-driving rock band. Anyway, we started to do quite well and got on a couple of decent tours. We were living in this dump in Philly, and Geezer our lead guitar boy had developed his heroin intake to

Olympian levels. It was the late seventies, maybe even the early eighties. We were all so stoned that we wouldn't have known what day, month, or year it was.'

'Is there a point to this story?'

'Yes Jimmy, there is. It involves death and voodoo and the disappearance of cheese in mysterious circumstances.'

Kid leaned in. 'Now there is a sentence you don't hear every day. Carry on Joe, I find that my interest has been piqued.'

'So, I wake up in the middle of the night to go for a pee and there, on the toilet, is Geezer. Needle in his arm and dead as a door nail.'

Michael shuddered. 'Wow, that got dark real quick.'

Joe nodded. 'It gets worse. We had a gig the next night, so we had to try and revive him. We tried everything. We shouted at him; we threw a bucket of cold water over him.'

'Maybe a bit of mouth to mouth would have helped,' observed Jimmy.

Joe nodded wistfully. 'Yeah, fair to say we were pretty shit in a crisis but in our defence, we were all stoners.'

'Excellent defence,' agreed Kid. 'Maybe call an ambulance?'

'Yeah, we should have but this was before mobiles and this place was a dump. It barely had electricity, let alone a phone.'

'They used to have phone booths in Philly. Why didn't you use a pay phone?'

'It was raining.'

Everyone looked appalled. Kid spoke for the audience.

'So, Geezer died because none of his mates wanted to get wet. That is shameful. I shall make a note to never die when your around.'

'We were young and stupid but we didn't let him go without a fight.'

'Is this where the cheese comes in?' asked Jimmy.

Ignoring the sarcasm in Jimmy's voice, Joe continued. 'You remember Jeff, our lead singer?'

'The stunner?'

'Yeah. Well, he had been to Haiti and apparently, he had had a fling with this girl who was into voodoo, so he says, "Let's bring him back from the dead." Now I wasn't sure. You could maybe get away with a zombie on bass. No offence Jeff.'

'Some taken.'

'But on lead I just didn't think a member of the undead could cut it.'

Michael just sat there shaking his head. 'Exactly how much drugs were you lot on?'

'The usual, too much and never enough. Anyway, we drag Geezer back into the lounge. We only called it the lounge because there was an old sofa in there. So, we lay him on his back and Jeff asks if any of us had got a chicken. I remembered that we had the remains of a KFC in the fridge, but Jeff says it has to be a live chicken. I thought he was being a bit picky but apparently, we need to swap a life for a life, so we needed to sacrifice it and then get it to take Geezer's place in the afterlife.'

'Guess the Colonel's special recipe isn't all it's cracked up to be,' observed Kid.

'Now how the hell are we going to find a live chicken at four in the morning in a downpour in Philly?'

'I can see how that would be tricky, but where does the cheese come in?'

'Wait for it, Kid, that comes later. So, Jeff is getting a bit annoyed. "How can you expect me to bring Geezer back from the dead if I don't have the tools for the job?" He was showing the same dedication that later took him through Med school. He became a doctor specialising in trauma a few years after.'

'Well, it's clear from your story that he obviously had a talent for it.' Jimmy's comment caused an outbreak of sniggering, even Joe allowed himself a little one.

'I suddenly remembered that we had trapped a mouse in the fridge and I say to Jeff, "Does it have to be a chicken or will any living animal do?" Jeff wasn't sure. "I've only seen it done with a chicken!" I had seen a documentary where they had put a pig's heart into a human, so I said, "If they use pigs I reckon a mouse would be fine." Jeff shrugged. "Don't see that we have a choice." "We could become a folk band," said Stevie. He was our bass player. "Bring me the mouse." I ran over to the fridge and there was Mickey tucking into the last of the KFC.'

'How do you know it was Mickey, could have been Minnie?'

Joe wagged his finger at Jimmy. 'Now that's a very good point, Jimmy. Jeff raised the same point when I gave Mickey to him. "Is it a girl mouse?" he asked. "Fucked if I know, I'm a drummer. I don't watch rodent porn." "Is that a thing?" We just ignored Stevie, like I said, he was just our bass player. Jeff looked unsure. "I think they use the chicken because it's a female. Females can give birth so maybe it's a fertility thing." So Stevie says, "Maybe Mickey's in touch with his feminine side." Jeff gave Stevie a withering look and then made the call. "Ok, we gotta go with what we got." He held Mickey in his right hand and knelt over Geezer. I thought he was praying but after about thirty seconds he looks up. "Anybody know the voodoo god I'm supposed to be praying too, I can't remember?" "What about the Pope?" "He's not a god, he's divine." Jeff gave Stevie a really harsh look.'

'Because he was a bass player?' asked Kid.

'No, because he was a moron.'

'Now Jeff was getting pretty desperate by this stage because ideally this sacrifice thing has to be done as close to the death of the deceased as possible so they can cross over. "Come on guys, think of a Caribbean God." I remembered seeing something on CBS about Papa Doc the ruler of Haiti. "Wasn't there a god that was something to do with Petrol?"' I asked.

'Oh, you mean Petro Loa,' said Kid. They all looked at him.

'How do you know all this shit?' asked Jimmy.

'I read; you really should try it.'

'Well, Kid wasn't there,' continued Joe. 'So, we had this debate about Petrol being a god. "That don't sound right," said Jeff. "The priestess blew into a conch shell, made this weird sound and then tried to summon the god."'

'"Well, Shell's a petrol."'

'The bass player?' asked Jimmy.

Joe nodded. 'So, Jeff gets us all to kneel down. He holds up Mickey and starts preying. "Oh, great god Petrol hear our prayer. Our brother Geezer has overdone it again and we need to get him back from the other-side. We offer you the life of Mickey the mouse in exchange."'

Joe looked at Michael. 'If you had known Geezer, that was a fair exchange! Anyway, Jeff was getting into it now. "Geezer is too young to die and we need a lead for tomorrow night's gig. Accept this life in return for his." Jeff looked at me. "You got a knife?" "No, I got a spoon. I offered it to him. Jeff didn't look impressed." "Come on Joe, how the hell do I sacrifice Mickey with a spoon? I don't think your taking this seriously!" "Boiled eggs!" We both turned to Stevie. "What the fuck are you on about?" Stevie leaned forward and took the spoon out of my hand.'

'Teaspoon?' asked Kid, barely able to supress a laugh.

'Dessert! He puts his hand around Jeff's and then smacks Mickey on the top of his head, just the way you would crack a boiled egg. Jeff understood. "Boiled egg. I get it." Clearly Mickey was no more. "Oh Petrol, take Mickey's life in exchange for Geezers".'

Everyone looked at Joe expectantly.

'So, what happened, did Geezer come back to life?' asked Michael.

Joe looked at the expectant faces around him and then shook his head. 'Nah, we had to cancel the gig! Funny things started happening though.'

'What, did Geezer come back and haunt you?'

'No, it was stranger. Whenever we were on tour after that we always stopped in mouse-infested dives and we would hear the mousetraps go off at night. When we looked in the morning there was nothing there, but the cheese was gone.'

'What the fuck does that mean?' asked Jimmy, unable to conceal his amusement. Joe turned to him, his face set in a thoughtful frown.

'I believe that Jeff somehow crossed the fates of Geezer and Mickey in the afterlife.'

Kid nodded. 'Sounds plausible, so basically you got a half-man half-rodent ghost stalking you.'

Joe nodded. 'That's what it seemed like at the time.'

Michael Owen patted Joe comfortingly on the shoulder. 'Hard to believe that you guys didn't make it. If only you'd had a chicken, you could have been stars!'

CHAPTER 6
ALL THAT GLITTERS

Terry Moist pulled up at the end of Aksel Lund's drive and turned off the engine. There was a steady humming but that was Tony C snoring in the passenger seat. For a man that could wrench an arm out of a socket with his bare hands he slept like a baby.

'Hey, sleeping beauty. Wake the fuck up!'

Tony snorted as if he had been shot. 'Whaa!' He rubbed his bald head and then scratched his balls. Terry didn't envy Tony's girlfriend.

'We're here Tony.'

Tony peered out of the window. The sun was going down and the sky was a burning fire that bathed the valley in a warm orange glow shimmering like the embers of a log fire.

'How can we be here, there's nothing to be here to!'

Terry looked at the beautiful glow from the fading sun and dreamed that one day NASA would find a rocket to reach it, with Tony inside.

'Come on Princess, we got to check this place out.'

Tony looked out of the window again. 'What place? There's literally nothing here.'

Terry pointed to the dusty track. 'That leads to a small ranch house about a mile down and it's on the site of an old gold mine. Jimmy Wayne came here last night and the boss wants to know why.' Terry checked the clip on his Colt. It was full, eight rounds. He tapped his jacket pocket and felt the reassuring shape of another two clips. Twenty-four rounds should be enough, he reached for the door. No, he thought, better take another couple, just in case. Terry had been in this game a long time and being prepared was the reason he still was. Tony looked at Terry's old Browning.

'Man, I cannot believe you are still using a 45? They been making those since 1911.'

'That's why they call it a Colt 1911, dummy.'

Tony pulled out a shiny new Beretta 9mm. 'This is what you want Terry.' Terry didn't seem impressed.

'How many people you shot with that gun?'

Tony looked at it. 'Well I ain't had it long.'

'Never mind that, how many?'

Tony shrugged. 'A couple.' He looked embarrassed. Terry laughed. 'A couple.' He brandished his old Colt. 'Two hundred and four.'

'You ain't never killed two hundred and four people, Terry.'

'Never said I had, just said shot. Done plenty of shooting in the arms and legs. You know what Jack's like when he's angry. "Shoot him in both legs, Terry!"'

Tony laughed. 'But how many people you actually killed? Take a guess.'

Terry didn't have to guess. He knew exactly how many people he had killed. On quiet nights when he couldn't sleep, he still saw their faces.

'Fifty-three.'

'Give or take?'

'Exactly!'

Tony nodded. 'Impressive. All with that museum piece?'

Terry smiled, a rare event and devoid of warmth. 'When I aim at something I hit it. That's pretty much all I want in a gun.' He stroked the barrel and re-holstered it. 'Let's go!'

On top of the rocky ridge, behind his workshop, Aksel Lund watched Jack Lantern's men on his phone. He had placed cameras all down the driveway and around his property and he could watch them from a mile away, unseen. They loaded their weapons and quietly climbed out of their pick-up. There was no slamming of doors or talking. The smaller man was clearly in charge and pointed to the other guy to circle around the back of the track. This amused Aksel because he knew there was no way to get behind his ranch. The man looked like he could play tight-end for the Rams; he was massive, but still athletic. Aksel made a mental note to shoot him; breaking his neck could be tricky. While the big man was scrabbling around the rocks, which would eventually bring him to a forty-foot cliff that would block his way, the smaller man walked up the track. He was trying to look nonchalant, but Aksel could see him scanning everything around him. He zoomed the camera in on his face. Soon he would be viewing him through the crosshairs of his scope. He would never hear the shot that killed him, but that was for another day. If these guys failed to return more would follow and his mine would no longer be safe. The big guy appeared at the side of the track and clambered down the rocks.

'No way round, there's a cliff that blocks the way.'

Terry took on this new information. He scanned the horizon and saw that a continuous wall of rock ran down either side of the track and the only way through was to follow the track. This place would be easy to defend. He climbed up the rocks on his right to try and get a look ahead. He could see the cliffs rising to the right.

'If I were defending this place that's where I would be.'

That's exactly where Aksel lay watching. He pointed his rifle directly at Terry Moist's protruding head.

'Guess we are just gonna have to walk right up to his front door.' Tony looked disappointed.

'Not really dressed for that are we.' They were both wearing suits. 'We should have changed before we came up here. The owner's going to be pretty suspicious when we show up looking like a pair of Insurance Salesmen.'

'We could pretend to be Mormons.'

'My God, Tony, we really would be looking for lost souls up here now, wouldn't we?' Terry tried the smile again but it just wasn't a good fit for his face.

'If we find anyone, we say we are looking for Etna, it's a little place in the next valley.'

Tony nodded. 'Yeah, that'll work.'

Aksel watched as they walked down the track, it was a long walk but eventually they came around the turn which opened up onto his property. Pausing, the smaller man scanned the area suspiciously. He pointed at the Ranch House.

'Let's go knock on his door.'

Tony nodded. 'Ok.'

They walked across the dusty driveway. Terry took in the fact that there were no vehicles except for the old John Deere by the barn. Looked like there was no-one home but he didn't relax. Expecting the unexpected was the reason he was still alive and fifty-three others weren't. He stepped up onto the veranda and called out.

'Hello, anybody home?' He waited for a few seconds and tried again. 'Hello, anybody home?' He pointed to Tony to go round the back and take a look. As Tony disappeared around the corner of the ranch, Terry leaned forwards and knocked on the door. He stepped back and waited, listening for any sound, any creak of floorboards that would reveal the presence of some-one inside. As he stood there listening intently, Tony reappeared from the other side of the building.

'Nothing doing, Terry. All locked up and nobody home.'

He leaned forwards and tried the door, it was locked. He turned around and surveyed the ranch buildings. There was an extension tacked on the side of the ranch house and then across the drive there was a big old barn built onto the side of the cliff.

'You know, Tony, if I was looking for a secret hideout this would be a good place. Easy to defend and virtually impossible to sneak up on.'

Tony shrugged. 'Man, if you lived out here you wouldn't have to hide. Who's gonna come looking? It's literally the middle of nowhere!'

Terry heard what Tony said but something wasn't right.

'So, why would you lock your door and shutter your windows? Like you said, there's nobody around here for miles.' Terry wandered over to the barn doors. 'Look at that padlock, you would need a blow torch to get that thing off. All the windows got security bars on. Two five lever locks and those doors are seriously heavy duty.'

Tony looked at the barn, he could see what Terry was talking about.

'Does seem a bit over the top, don't it?'

Terry looked back across the drive to the house. 'Something's off here. Middle of nowhere and locked up like Fort Knox. Somebody's got a secret they want to keep.'

Tony wandered over to the extension on the side of the building and tried the door, but it too was securely fastened. He looked above his head and there, concealed in the overhang of the roof joists, was a discreetly hidden security camera. Tony turned and walked away as casually as he could. He took Terry's arm and guided him down to the far side of the barn.

'Come and look at this, Terry.' Terry tried to pull his arm away, but Tony had it in a vice like grip. 'We are being watched,' he hissed under his breath. 'There's a surveillance camera on the underside of the roof joists above the door, in the extension. It's more like a covert op's camera than your normal security.'

Terry nodded. 'Something definitely wrong here. Whoever owns this place has got something to hide.'

'What do we do now, I'm on film.'

'We act natural. Let's put on a little show for the camera. Just go along with what I say.' Tony nodded and Terry strolled casually back to the back door. He tried the handle. 'You're right Steve, nobody home. Shame, because we could have picked Jimmy's wallet up for him.'

'He may not have dropped it here, Terry.'

Terry winced as Tony used his real name. 'Maybe, maybe not. But as we were passing it was worth a try – Steve!' Terry emphasised the Steve and Tony realised his mistake.

'Ok, let's go.' They turned and walked back down the long dusty drive to their pick-up. As they turned the corner and were obscured from the Ranch by the rocks Terry turned to Tony.

'Terry, Terry?? Fucking hell, what you got between your ears, sawdust?' Terry wasn't happy. 'So, this guy, whoever he is, speaks to Jimmy Wayne and says I had a Steve and a Terry over my place yesterday, do you know them? I know a Terry; he's a Texan enforcer works for Jack Lantern. Yeah, that's him says Jimmy.'

'Yeah, but I was Steve.'

Terry closed his eyes in exasperation. 'It's information you didn't need to give. Let's just hope this guy isn't reporting back to Jimmy Wayne.' Terry thought for a moment. 'We got one of those little solar-powered observation cameras in the cabinet?'

Tony nodded. 'We got a couple.'

'Go and get me one, we're going to do a bit of security filming as well.' Tony was about to complain but a quick look at Terry's face convinced him to undertake the long walk without protest.

As Tony strode back to the pick-up Terry climbed the rocks to get a look. He studied the approach to the ranch and the barn and could see no cameras aimed on the drive. Maybe the guy only had cameras over the doors so he could identify people who actually came up to the door. He was pretty sure there was no camera aimed at him now, but he was wrong.

Aksel was watching their every move as his array of hidden cameras' streamed pictures back to his phone. When Tony returned with the little solar-powered camera, he would aim it at the ranch and the barn. At this distance he could get them both in shot. Any pictures coming from the camera would come straight to his mobile. The cameras they used for covert observation were triggered by movement so they only filmed when something actually happened. Tony returned with the camera and a pair of binoculars.

'Thought you would want to make sure we were not being observed.'

Terry smiled. Finally, Tony was thinking again.

'Give 'em here.' He scanned the buildings very closely and could see no sign of surveillance. 'Ok, let's set it up here.' Tony clambered up beside him and skilfully positioned the camera and then weighted it with rocks which he also used to conceal the camera until there was only a small hole for the lens to poke through.

'Ok Terry, it's ready to roll.'

Terry signalled him to switch it on and Tony did.

High up in the rocks Aksel sighed. This was going to be a problem. Any movement he made would now be monitored by Jack Lantern's boys. If he threw the camera away, they would know he was onto them and be back the next day. He needed a plan.

He was still thinking about a solution to his problem long after 'Tony and Steve' had left. How the hell was he going to resolve this little conundrum? And then it came to him. What his visitors didn't know was that there was a way down the ridge to reach the back of his property unseen. If the big man had kept going when he went around the back of the ranch he would have seen it. Aksel had used it to circle round to their car via the foot of the cliff on the left, now he would circle round and set up his own camera right next to his visitors' camera and let it run for twenty-four hours. Then he would wait until it was the dead of night and place a monitor screen with his twenty-four-hour video in front of the spy camera. The spies could watch the same day happening over and over again. Groundhog Day for snoopers. He would put the monitor into a hood box to stop any potential reflection and would run a USB from his monitor into the spy camera and let their solar power keep his deception going. He smiled. This was a very elegant solution. He would keep out of sight whilst he was filming and then implement his plan the following day. All he had to do was place it smoothly and efficiently in the dark. If anyone was watching all they would see was a momentary flicker on the screen, not uncommon on a digital feed. He also had the added advantage of knowing when they would be coming back. He had their pick-up on film. Wouldn't be hard to find out where and who it was registered to and get a tracker on it, then he would know exactly when they were returning!

As they drove back to Vegas Terry had been thinking.

'You know what Tony, I reckon the guy that owns that place has found gold.'

'You think?'

Terry nodded slowly. 'Why else would you have all that security in the middle of nowhere?'

'But it was a drift mine in the river, down in the valley. That's where he would have his security.'

Terry shook his head. 'Nah, whatever he was panning out of the drift mine he would be bringing back home and be putting it somewhere secure.'

'Well, that place sure was secure.' Tony thought for a moment which wasn't easy for him. 'Maybe we could go to the river and see if we can find some gold.'

Terry sneered. 'I don't do manual labour. Let's just let this guy collect it while we keep an eye on him and just come and get it when we are ready.'

'Sounds a good plan, if he has any.'

Terry smiled. 'Oh, he has some, I can feel it in my bones!'

Terry drove on through the desert. It was night now, but a full moon cast an eerie glow. There were no streetlights out here.

'Where are we?' asked Tony.

'About twelve miles off Highway 93, only about sixty miles to Vegas.'

Tony gazed out onto the moonlit landscape.

'Man, we could be on another planet it's like…' Tony stopped mid-sentence. 'Hey, can you see him?'

Terry could. 'What the hell?'

As they approached a quiet crossroads, there on the corner, was an old black guy standing with his thumb out. He was dressed in an old suit and a trilby hat.

'Is this guy for real? He's never going to get a lift round here.'

'No, you're right,' drawled Terry. 'Unless we give him a lift.'

'Jack wouldn't like it.'

'Jack won't know, come on Tony. Let's do something nice for a change, what harm can it do?'

Tony frowned. 'Suppose it won't hurt.'

Terry slowed the truck down and came to a halt by the old man. He wound down his window. He could see the old man clearly now, his face illuminated by the moonlight. His suit was old, though sharply pressed, but it was his eyes that caught Terry's attention. They were the deepest blue he had ever seen.

'Evening sir, where you going?'

'Wherever you're going, son.' His voice was deep and sonorous.

Terry smiled. 'Well, we're headed for Vegas.'

'Then that's where I'm going.'

Terry looked to both sides of the old guy. 'You got any luggage?'

He shook his head. 'I travel light, usually find whatever I need.' He climbed up into the back of the cab with an agility that was surprising.

Tony turned round and smiled at him. 'I'm Tony.'

The old guy nodded 'I know.' Tony and Terry exchanged a glance. 'How'd you know that?' The old guy laughed. 'I'm shitting you, I'm John R. Deal, pleased to meet you fellas!'

'So where are you trying to get to John?' asked Terry.

'Wherever life takes me,' he leaned back in his seat and smiled. 'Today, it seems, life is taking me to Vegas.'

'You been to Vegas before?'

'Not since sixty-three, I expect the place has changed a bit since then.'

Tony and Terry looked at each other and shook their heads in disbelief.

'Where you from, John?'

John thought about it for a moment. 'That's hard to say Tony. I guess I'm from everywhere and nowhere. Always been a traveling man, lived my life on the road.'

Tony persisted. 'But you gotta be from somewhere.'

John smiled. 'I was born at a crossroads in the deep south. I just picked a direction and got moving.'

'Kind of a coincidence that we picked you up at a crossroads.'

'That weren't no coincidence, Terry, that was fate.' Terry glanced at John in the rear-view mirror.

'How'd you know my name?'

'Didn't you tell me.'

'No, Tony told his name, I never said mine.'

John chuckled. 'Oh, I must have got the Tony mixed up with Terry and the Terry mixed up with old Tony here.'

'How long were you waiting for a lift. It's pretty damn remote round here.'

'I couldn't say for sure. When I'm not doing, I'm thinking and when I'm thinking, I'm miles away.' John looked out the window at the moonlit desert. 'Maybe a day, give or take.'

Terry was starting to regret picking John up. The guy was strange. He didn't buy the fact that he accidently knew his name. Why hadn't he got any luggage, and why did he speak in riddles?

'So, what do you do, John?' Terry asked, using his kindly voice, he didn't use it very often and he was out of practice. 'You travel wherever you can get a lift to and you don't have no luggage.' Terry smiled, again, he looked a bit like a shark posing for a passport photo. 'You're a bit of a mystery John.'

John nodded. 'That I am Terry, that I am.' He closed his eyes and within a few seconds he was fast asleep.

'Well, that was strange,' said Tony.

'Disturbing is what I would say.'

'Nah, he's just a harmless old drifter. Maybe he's drunk too much, maybe he's just lost touch with reality. Kinda likable though.'

Terry didn't share Tony's opinion. He never took anything at face value and trust was not in his nature. There was something not quite right about John R. Deal.

Tony could tell that Terry was fretting.

'Hey, relax, you did a nice thing. The old guy could have died out there if we hadn't picked him up.' He gave Terry a big grin and nudged him in the ribs with his elbow. 'Are you getting soft in your old age, Terry?'

Terry turned and glared at Tony. His eyes were stone cold and even though Tony had worked with Terry for over six years he still felt a little chill run down his spine when he saw that look. 'You think I'm getting soft, Tony?'

Tony shook his head. 'No, Terry, you won't ever get soft, it's not in your nature, but I do think you're getting paranoid. John's just a harmless old drifter.'

'Did you see the way he hopped up into the back of the cab? He was like a panther.' Tony had to agree. 'Yeah, he moved pretty quick for an old guy.'

'How'd he know my name? Where's his luggage?' Terry shook his head. 'None of this adds up.'

'Stuff doesn't always have to add up, shit can happen for no reason.'

Terry wasn't buying it. Everything had to add up. In his world if he couldn't make sense of events, he couldn't control them.

'Look at his shoes and his suit, the guy is spotless and yet he told us he had been standing there at that dusty crossroads for hours.'

Tony turned and looked at John. He was fast asleep. A happy, contented smile played across his face. Terry was right, he was smarter than he had any right to be but despite this there was something about John that made Tony feel happy.

'Listen, Terry. We'll be in Vegas in an hour and we can drop John off on the strip and then he is out of our lives forever. Just a happy memory of a moment when we were actually nice to someone for a change.'

Terry nodded. 'Maybe.' He didn't share Tony's feelings. Something just wasn't right about this, and he had a horrible feeling that when he had opened the door for John R. Deal, he had let something into his life that he could not control.

John R. Deal sat in the back of the pick-up smiling as he pretended to sleep. Enjoying the doubt, he had sown in Terry Moist's mind. Yes, he knew who Terry was. He knew who everybody was.

An hour later John was woken by Tony prodding his knee. He still wasn't asleep but acted like he had been. 'Whoa, are we there?'

Tony nodded and smiled. 'Welcome back to Vegas, John.'

He looked out of the window at the huge hotels and streetlights and buildings as far as he could see.

'Man! It's changed since I was last here.'

Tony laughed. 'Over fifty years is a long time.' Tony pointed out the window. 'We're at the top end of the strip. Where do you want to be dropped?'

'Here will do fine thanks, fellas.'

Tony leaned forwards and pushed a fifty-dollar bill into John's hand. 'Get yourself a good breakfast.' John looked at the crisp fifty and smiled.

'There's no need for that, Tony.'

'I know, John, but I want to buy you breakfast.'

John reached out and squeezed Tony's shoulder and as he did so Tony felt a warmth radiating from John's touch and a deep feeling of calm spreading down through his entire body.

'You're a good man Tony, you may not know it yet but there is hope for you, son.' John glanced at Terry and gave him a wry smile. 'Thanks for the lift, Terry.' John flicked the handle and exited the pick-up in one smooth graceful movement. The door clicked shut behind him and Terry turned to Tony.

'Well, that was weird.'

Tony turned and watched John walking away and he felt a pang of loss. From the moment John had touched him he had been overcome by a feeling of serenity. He turned back to Terry.

'I liked the guy. There's something special about him.'

Terry shook his head in despair. 'Fifty dollars for breakfast, you're the one who's special.'

'Maybe,' said Tony, but he didn't care. Something wonderful had just happened. For the first time in his adult life, he didn't feel angry.

'Did you notice where we dropped him?' asked Terry. Tony turned back to see John's figure fading into the distance.

'Just outside Carpenters.'

Terry nodded. 'Yeah, just outside Carpenters, at the Crossroads!'

CHAPTER 7
STUDIO DAZE

Finally, the day that Jimmy had dreamed of for so long had arrived. He and the band were in Michael Owen's studio in Laurel Canyon to make his first album. It had been over twenty years coming and he wanted to savour the moment. He took a deep breath and looked across at his band. Kid and No Relation had been with him for years. Doug only a few weeks but already they were a tight unit. This was going to be fun.

Michael was sat behind the glass in the control booth. 'Ok guys, what I want to do today is to just record you playing each song straight through, the way you play them live. Once we've got them down, we can have a listen and see where we can improve, or just leave the arrangements as they are. Then we can record the drums and bass. Once those are nailed, we'll do lead and rhythm. When all that is in the can, we can let Jimmy do his vocals. You happy with that Jimmy?'

'Works for me Michael, what do you want to start with?'

'Let's take it in the order they will appear on the album.'

'"Vacant Stare".' Jimmy turned to the boys. 'You got that?' They had. Kid was tuning his guitar and No Relation was adjusting his cymbals. Doug stood there waiting for the others. He was ready to go.

Jimmy looked out through the window that looked down across the hillside towards LA. For a moment he could swear that he had seen Wendy standing at the edge of the woods at the bottom of the lawn. He looked closer but now there was just trees and flowers. He knew Wendy was around. She would always be around. Michael counted them in.

'One and two and three and...' he dropped his hand on the four and they were off. The journey had begun.

You look at me
With your vacant stare
I see you
But there's no-one there.

The band just flowed into the songs; they had become so comfortable with them that playing them felt as natural as breathing. In the control room Michael couldn't help but smile. This was going to be a great record!

———◆———

Just two hundred and seventy miles away Jack Lantern was having a conversation that would have wiped the smile off Michael Owen's face. Naturally, it was with his mother.

'Look Ma, let's give Michael a chance to record the album, then we can check out how it's looking. If you go up there and put the fear of God into Jimmy, he ain't gonna sing too good.'

'Might help him hit the higher notes when his balls tighten.'

Jack looked at his mother. She really was a mean woman, cruel didn't get close. Vicious got closer but it was only when you arrived at pure evil that you were using the right words to describe her.

'You really don't like Jimmy do you Ma!' It wasn't a question, but Ma answered it anyway.

'Nope, I think he needs to be dead, he's gonna be trouble. If this record turns out good, we should kill him just before the launch. Bound to triple sales at least.'

'Jesus Ma! If it's really good he will make a second and a third and we make a load of money off the back of it. Good long-term business.' Ma sneered.

'He slept with your wife Jackie, several times. Ain't you got no pride. If I was you I would have chopped off his balls myself by now and made him choke on them.'

'I think he's a vegetarian.'

Ma ignored Jack's attempt at a joke. 'Jackie, when are you going to learn that fear is the only thing that keeps you safe? The more terrified they are of you the less likely they are going to move against you.'

'Maybe, Ma, but you're too scary, we lose business because of it. Me, I'm just a bit menacing. People like me.'

Ma looked at him like he was crazy. 'People don't like you Jackie, they fear you. When you do what we have to do they have to fear you.'

'I know, I know but you just take it too far all the time.'

An evil little smile crossed Ma's lips. 'But I like my work Jackie, you know that.' Jack's phone rang, it was Terry Moist. 'Hi Terry, you find anything?'

'Yes and no, boss.'

'What the fuck does that mean?'

'No, we didn't find gold or the owner but we did find security levels that go way beyond what you would expect to find in the middle of nowhere on a worked-out panning spot.'

Jack liked the sound of this. 'Go on.'

'The place was like Fort Knox, he even had hidden cameras over the doorways to check on callers. Trust me boss, there's something off about this one.'

Jack did trust Terry's judgement and if he sniffed out something that he thought was off, he was usually right.

'So how did you leave it?'

'I set up an observation camera. Solar powered so it's going to keep filming for as long as we like.'

Jack was nodding happily. 'That's a very elegant solution. Stream it to me, better still, stream it to Ma's laptop. If I tell her that there's gold there, she'll watch it all day. That will keep the old bitch off my back for a while.'

Terry wondered what it must be like to have Ma Lantern as your mother. He had seen her do some terrible things in the past. He guessed that Jack didn't get too many bedtime cuddles when he was a kid. Come to think of it, neither had he!

Jack put down his phone and checked his emails, as always there was a queue of things waiting for his attention. Out of the corner of his eye he could see his mother smiling at herself in the lounge mirror, then she blew herself a kiss. He watched, fascinated by his mother's uncharacteristic behaviour. She winked at the mirror, but it hadn't worked. It looked more like a nervous tick. She took a deep breath and slowly blew it out puckering up her lips as if about to kiss, then smiled and gave a playful wink, which this time was disturbingly alluring. Jack tried to look away but now she was folding her arms across her chest and pushing her cleavage up and out. Ma caught him watching in the mirror. She turned and faced him.

'Do you think I'm sexy, Jackie?'

For once in his life Jack didn't know what to say.

'Come on, I know you Jackie, and you always have an opinion.'

'You're my mother for God's sake, how am I supposed to answer that?'

Ma wasn't fazed by Jack's discomfort or embarrassed. To feel that way you would need to feel shame, and Ma had no shame.

'Let me put a hypothetical to you.'

'I wish you wouldn't.'

'How old are you, Jackie?'

Jack stared at his mother. 'You're my mother, why don't you take a stab at it.'

Ma smiled dismissively. 'Come on Jackie, I'm not that kind of mum, just give me a ballpark figure.'

'I'm sixty, Ma.'

Ma looked surprised. 'You can't be sixty, that would make me...'

'Old!' Jack finished the sentence for her. Her eyes flashed anger for a moment and then, being the actress that she was, the alluring Ma returned.

'Imagine for a moment that you're not my son.'

'I don't have to imagine; I've dreamed of it for years.' He shook his head. 'Go on then, Ma.'

'Ok so, you're not my son and you're,' she thought for a moment, 'say sixty-seven or eight.'

Jack nodded. 'Ok, so I'm imagining that I'm not your son and I have just had seven or eight years without you being my mum.' A big smile spread across Jack face. 'Hey... this feels good!'

Ma looked impatient. 'Don't fuck around, Jackie. What if you were sixty-seven?'

'Or eight.'

Ma flashed Jack a look that made him shut up, and then continued. 'You're a man, in his late sixties, and I walk into the room and give you this look.' Ma smiled at him and placed her index finger provocatively between her lips. Jack winced but Ma took no notice. 'Well?'

'Well, what?'

'Would you?'

'Would I what?'

'Would you fancy me?' asked Ma, impatiently. Jack found it hard to believe what his mother was asking.

'You're my mother.'

'Not in this scenario.'

'But I'm your son, you can't ask me questions like that its, it's not right.'

Ma was irritated. 'Jesus Jackie, I just wanted your opinion as a man. Am I sexy or not?'

Jack stared down at his emails. He wasn't going to give his mother the satisfaction of calling her sexy. She did have a good figure and her boobs, thanks to some surgical help, were still defying gravity. Her legs were pretty great too, only the heavy makeup gave her that aging hooker look.

'Tell you what, Ma, go easy on the makeup and you would look pretty classy.'

Ma nodded. 'That's great Jack, but would you fuck me?'

Jack shook his head. Ma wasn't going to let this go.

'Ok,' he took a deep breath, 'if I wasn't your son, if I was single and nearly seventy then I,' he paused for a moment struggling to say the words that his mother wanted to hear, 'I would consider it.'

'Well, that's me damned with faint praise, ain't it?' Ma turned on her heels and headed out the door. She winked at herself in the mirror as she went past.

Jack waited for the door to close behind her before slumping back in his chair. That was pretty weird and disturbing but the really disturbing thing was that, for his mother, there had been nothing wrong with having that conversation with her only child. Jack consoled himself with the thought that she couldn't live forever, but then scowled at the knowledge that she probably would. He looked back at his emails and tried to pretend he was an orphan.

———◆———

Back in the studio Jimmy and the band had broken for lunch. Things had gone well and everyone was bubbling with enthusiasm.

'There's a buffet laid on outside,' said Michael. Kid looked up. 'Did somebody say buffet?'

'Nothing wrong with your hearing.'

'It's very selective. Kid only hears references to food and the voices in his head.' Jimmy was laughing as he followed Kid out onto the patio. There was a long table laid out with enough food for twice the number of people.

'Looks like you catered for Earth, Wind and Fire,' said Doug.

'No just us plus Kid.'

Kid looked at Jimmy reproachfully. 'It's comments like that, that make me want to comfort eat.' He turned and descended on the buffet like a biblical plague, devouring all before him but unlike locusts he would be coming back for seconds!

Michael took Jimmy to one side as the boys helped themselves. 'You know how good that was this morning, don't you?'

Jimmy nodded. 'Yeah, it was, wasn't it?'

'I've made a lot of big records, Jimmy, and this one has all the hallmarks. We got five demos in the can and all we need to do is just tweak them a bit. Just doesn't seem to be any area that's weak.'

Jimmy smiled; he felt the same too.

'Where did these songs come from. I checked back through your career.'

'I wasn't aware I'd had one, just one brush with fame and a whole load of missed chances.'

Michael shrugged. 'Maybe, but you always had something, Jimmy. That's why I was so keen to come and see you at the Riviera. When David called me up and said you had suddenly started performing your own songs I just had to come and take a listen.'

'David's a good friend.'

'He's also a shrewd judge. I knew if he thought you were special then you had to be worth a listen. David was right.'

No Relation called over to them. 'You better get over here before Kid eats everything.'

They watched as Kid walked past with his plate loaded like a multi-storey building.

'How do you get so much food on one plate?' asked Michael.

Kid shrugged. 'Pythagoras, he knew a thing or two about loading a plate!'

They all sat around the patio in the warm California sunshine. Kid looked at Jimmy and smiled.

'Laurel Canyon, baby.'

Jimmy smiled back. 'Laurel Canyon, Kid, does it get any better than this?'

It wasn't a question. Jimmy knew that he was fulfilling a lifelong ambition and they all had that delicious feeling that they were on the edge of something special. All the stars were aligning, and the fates were opening the doors of possibility.

In Vegas, Jack Lantern had persuaded Ma that killing Jimmy would be bad for business. Up in the Nevada mountains Aksel Lund had hidden his secret from Terry and Tony, and they had delivered John R. Deal from a crossroads in the middle of nowhere to the crossroads outside Carpenters on the Strip. Jimmy didn't know John, he had only seen him in his dreams, but John knew him. John knew everyone. He even knew where Jimmy was right now, but he could wait. Jimmy and the Second Chance would be at Carpenters in a few weeks. He and Jimmy would become acquainted then. For now, he would content himself with talking to Wendy. Yes! He knew Wendy too, only she didn't know it yet.

———◆———

After lunch, Michael got them back into the studio and by four thirty they had finished recording all the demos. Each track had been completed without anyone missing a beat, even No Relation. Behind the glass Michael Owen looked very happy;

this was going to be easy. He threw a switch on the deck which opened his studio mic.

'Ok fellas, that will do for today.'

Kid put down his guitar. 'Great, I was starting to feel a little hungry.'

Jimmy looked at Doug and shook his head. 'Do you believe this guy?'

'I do now, but if I hadn't seen it with my own eyes I wouldn't have believed it,' Doug turned to Kid. 'How can you eat so much and not be fat?'

'I worry a lot.'

Doug looked confused. 'What do you have to worry about?'

'I worry about where my next meal is coming from.'

Doug looked at Kid deadpan expression. 'Are you serious?'

The hint of a smile played across Kid's lips. 'All I will say is don't ever get trapped between me and my food, people have been injured!' Kid walked over to Doug and laid a massive hand on his shoulder. 'Feel the weight and size of these fingers, imagine having to play a solo with these. They suck all the calories outta my body and down my arms into my fingers. It ain't easy moving these mothers up and down the fretboard.'

Doug just stood there trying to work out if heavy fingers burnt calories.

Kid put his other hand on Doug's free shoulder so he could appreciate the weight of Kids fingers, hands and the arms that held them onto his body. He buckled slightly at the knees.

'It's not just the weight and size of my fingers that burn the calories Doug, I'm an athlete, so naturally I burn fast.'

No Relation had turned around when he heard Kid say, 'I'm an athlete.'

'I've never seen you exercise.'

Kid shrugged. 'I'm a natural athlete, that's why the Norwegian army put me in special commandos.'

'Yeah, you're special alright,' smiled No Relation.

Michael and Jimmy were watching the conversation develop.

'He does look pretty fit though,' said Michael.

'Oh, he is,' nodded Jimmy. 'He knows how to fight too, but only when he has to.' Jimmy lowered his voice. 'I think he did some pretty intense stuff in the army and now, unless forced, he's a pacifist!'

Michael gave Jimmy a knowing look. 'A couple of my friends were in the SAS and they are the same, still wouldn't want to cross them though.'

As they stood there chatting the sound of a sports car came growling up Lookout Mountain Drive. Michael turned his head to listen.

'Sounds like a V6. David's made good time.' They listened as he came growling up the mountain road towards them and then slowed. Michael reached into his pocket and pulled out a remote and aimed it up to where the gates were at the entrance to the house.

'Will it reach that far?' asked Jimmy.

Michael nodded. 'No problem.'

David Parker's F Type Jaguar convertible growled onto Michael Owen's drive and came to a stop next to Kid's van. They looked a bit incongruous next to each other, but the attention of the band was soon drawn to David. The roof was down but when he climbed out of the convertible not a hair on David's head was out of place. Despite the long drive his jeans and shirt still looked immaculately pressed. Jimmy turned to Michael.

'How does he do that?'

Michael smiled. 'He always was an elegant fucker, even when we were at school. He would finish a cross-country run and there wouldn't be a bead of sweat on his forehead or a hair out of place. That's where he got his nickname from.'

'He has a nickname?' asked Jimmy. 'You gotta tell me what it is.' Michael didn't seem sure.

'He wasn't keen on it.'

'All the more reason to tell me, you Brits love a bit of banter, don't you?'

'True, but he'd know that it was me who told it to you.'

Jimmy inclined his head and gave Michael a pleading look. 'Come on Mike, you told me I'm a pleasure to work with, I could change!'

Michael shrugged. 'Fuck it. We used to call him the Mannequin.'

Jimmy nodded. 'Good nickname.' They watched David walk towards them. He was wearing brown brogues that glinted in the sunshine and a pair of Aviator sunglasses. 'He does look like a male model.'

'Yes, he's like a mail-order catalogue model you see with the immaculate greying hair and the tan.' Jimmy nodded his agreement as Michael continued.

'Or one of those middle-aged lotharios that prowl the boulevards of the south of France looking for wealthy widows.' They both watched him walk across the lawn towards them. He moved so gracefully he almost seemed to float.

'How does he do that?'

'I really don't know, but he's done it ever since I've known him and we were only six then!'

Jimmy was surprised. 'I thought you got to know him at college.'

'English boarding school's system. Soon as we are off the breast, they pack us off to boarding school.' Michael took a bite from his sandwich trying not to remember the pain he had felt at being torn away from his family home and sent to a boarding school a hundred miles away.

'That must have been tough at six,' said Jimmy. Michael smiled sadly.

'Oh, it was Jimmy. Apparently, it was supposed to make a man of me.'

'And did it?'

'A damaged one maybe, but at least our parents didn't have to bother bringing us up. By then it was too late. When we got to college, we already had a stiff upper lip and were so emotionally dead you could have beaten our grannies to death with a shovel in front of us and the only response would have been, "Oh dear, that's made a mess of the carpet."' Michael turned to Jimmy. 'There's a reason why we like to live in detached and semi-detached houses, because we are semi-detached. Nothing like you Americans.'

Jimmy thought about his own childhood. 'I wouldn't be so sure Michael; we have other ways of fucking our kids up.'

Before they could develop their discussion about the various merits of English and American parenting, David arrived at the patio. He shook hands with Kid and Doug and waved to

No Relation, then turned his smile, perfect teeth on display, to them.

'Good evening gents, I trust all is well.'

Michael stepped forwards and gave him a big hug. 'Good to see you David, you made good time.'

David smiled. 'Well, the 93 can be a lovely empty road, it would have been a sin not to give the old girl a bit of stick.'

'Does that mean driving fast?' asked Jimmy. David turned to him and gave him a big hug.

'It certainly does, James.'

'Come up to the house – we can have some drinks on the patio up there. Sheila is going to do a barbeque later.'

'That sounds good. I'm starving. Only stopped for fuel and coffee.'

'What, no tea?' teased Jimmy.

David frowned. 'Harder to find since 1773.'

Jimmy looked puzzled.

'Boston Tea Party, James.'

Jimmy was always amazed at the spread of David's general knowledge. 'How do you know all this stuff?'

'I read; you really should try it sometime.'

Jimmy knew when he was beaten. 'Come on you old fucker, let's go and have a drink.'

They started up the path towards the house.

'I've got someone coming over to join us that I want you guys to meet.'

'Who's that then?' asked Jimmy.

'Probably the best agent in LA.'

'And who might that be?'

Michael looked at David. 'You don't know him, he doesn't advertise, he doesn't need to. He's a bit strange, one of those survivalist types, but he's good and he's loyal.'

'But also crazy,' suggested David.

Michael thought for a moment. 'Yes, a little, but they said Mozart was crazy and that turned out pretty good.'

'Right up until 1791.'

'What happened then?' asked Jimmy.

'He died, aged just 35 and was buried in a Pauper's grave.'

'Mozart, a pauper? He must have been loaded with all those hits.'

David shrugged. 'Sadly not.'

'Probably got robbed blind by Salieri,' said Michael.

'Was he in the mob?'

They both turned and looked at Jimmy sympathetically and he decided to never mention Mozart again.

The boys had all sat around drinking and chatting for an hour when they noticed some gorgeous aromas coming from the barbeque on the far side of the huge patio. Kid stood up like a blood hound and sniffed the air.

'I smell dinner! Where do we queue?'

'It's waitress service. Sheila will bring it over when it's ready.'

Kid looked concerned. 'What if she gives me a small portion?'

'Shelia doesn't do small portions; she's used to working with starving musicians.' David turned to Michael. 'I take it things went well today?'

Michael smiled. 'Very well. We got a demo of every song down and they sounded great. Nothing I really want to change in the arrangements or lyrics. All we got to do is record them properly and just get the mix and master right.'

'So, what's on the agenda for tomorrow?'

'Drums tomorrow.'

Joe's ears pricked up. 'You talking about me?'

Michael nodded. 'Yes, I want to track the drums tomorrow and maybe the day after.'

Joe smiled. 'I don't want to brag but you will only need a day. I have this lot nailed.'

'Maybe he is a relation after all,' said Jimmy.

'Probably a cousin,' suggested Kid. 'Married to a cousin, obviously!' Everyone laughed, even No Relation.

'The Rich name will be upheld tomorrow, I guarantee it!'

Before anyone else could come up with a smart ass crack the buzzer at the front gates went. Michael looked up.

'That must be Sonny.'

The gates opened and a blacked-out Hummer H3 rumbled onto the drive. Everyone looked up as the 5.3 litre V8 rumbled to a stop.

Jimmy summed up everyone's reactions best. 'What the fuck is that?'

It wasn't a standard Hummer it was clearly modified, it looked like something out of a Mad Max movie.

'Whose driving that thing, Rambo?'

The door opened and out climbed – fell would be a better description – a small dapper gent dressed as if auditioning for Miami Vice, Cuban Drug Dealer edition. As he landed, it was quite a drop, he toppled for a moment on his Cuban heels and then his years of tango training came to his rescue as he rebalanced and swung around to face them with a flourish.

'Did you order a clown with the barbeque?' asked David, barely able to suppress his laughter.

'Despite appearances to the contrary, this is no clown,' said Michael.

The small man raised his Panama to the assembled group in greeting. 'Gentlemen, good evening.' He hurried down the path towards them with the lythe grace of a dancer. Michael stepped up to him and shook his hand.

'This is Sonny Castiglia, the best music agent in LA.'

'The World, Michael, don't undersell me,' he turned to Jimmy. 'And you must be Jimmy Wayne.' He offered his outstretched hand to Jimmy.

Jimmy took it. 'Pleased to meet you, Mr Castiglia.'

'Call me Sonny.' He turned and looked up at Kid. 'You must be Kid, you're pretty big!'

Kid nodded. 'Not as big as your vehicle.'

Sonny smiled. 'Yes, it is pretty big.' No Relation gazed at the Hummer with interest. 'That ain't a standard H3 is it, Sonny?'

'No, it's a very special custom job. It's armour plated, has an onboard generator and water filter. There's a fridge, radar with a launchable pursuit drone. Gun cabinet with an assortment of automatic weapons including rifles and handguns. I even have a grenade launcher and an RPG 7 heat-seeking missile launcher.'

'You live in Compton?'

Sonny smiled at Joe's question. 'No, I just like to be prepared.'

'What the fuck needs that kind of preparation?'

Sonny looked at Kid. 'Bad times are coming Mister Kid.'

'Is Kid Rock making another album?'

Sonny grimaced. 'Hard to believe but it's worse than that.'

'Now that is hard to believe,' said Kid.

'And do you drive this vehicle around LA?'

Sonny turned to David. 'Of course. I have to be ready and able to get to my base in the mountains if something kicks off!'

David seemed surprised. 'What, you actually go to meetings in that?'

Sonny looked indignantly back at David as if it was the most stupid question he had ever been asked.

'Of course!'

David nodded slowly. 'Being so heavily armed must be pretty useful when you're in negotiations with major labels.'

Sonny smiled. 'You better believe it.'

As the evening progressed, they all came to realise that despite his somewhat unconventional outlook, Sonny Castiglia was a very switched-on agent. At one point David was listening to Joe talking to Sonny about his weaponry.

'So just how heat-seeking are those rockets you use on your RPG 7 Sonny?'

'Well, if you aim it at something hot, as long as nothing hotter gets in the way, it will seek it out and destroy it.'

Joe thought for a moment. 'So, say I was walking near a lake in winter and my brother-in-law, who is an absolute putz by the way, lights up one of his god-awful cheap cigars. Hypothetically the lake is frozen, and he has strolled three hundred yards out into the middle.'

'This is a pretty specific scenario, Joe,' said Sonny, looking a little suspicious.

'Bear with me, you ain't met my brother-in-law!'

Sonny nodded his agreement. 'Go on then, Joe.'

'So, he's out on the frozen lake and he has a cigar going, suppose someone, let's say three hundred yards away, had an RPG 7 with a heat-seeking rocket. Would it hit him?'

Sonny thought for a moment. He was aware that not only David but everyone else was now listening to the conversation.

'Like I said, Joe, provided no other, hotter heat source got in the way it would hit him.'

Joe nodded. 'Where can you buy these?'

'Lots of places, but could I suggest an alternative?'

Joe didn't seem keen. 'You could Sonny, but I think you need to meet the guy first before you try and protect him.' Sonny held up his hand.

'No Joe, I was thinking, if he is on a frozen lake, you would do better with a grenade launcher. That's going to blow him to pieces and blow a hole in the ice at the same time. Brother-in-law goes into the drink and the hole freezes over during the night. If it's a quiet place it's the perfect crime.'

'Remind me to never go skating with you guys,' said Michael. Everyone was chuckling, and Kid was looking at Joe and shaking his head slowly.

'Joe, you gotta stop saying things aloud. If your brother-in-law disappears this winter awkward questions are bound to be asked. You need to conceive the plan in your head and execute it without telling anyone. This kind of thing is strictly need-to-know stuff.'

Joe nodded thoughtfully. 'Maybe I should just mow him down with a stolen car and make it look like a hit and run then.'

Kid looked around the patio at the rest of the gang.

'What did I just say... Please tell me you all heard it!' They all nodded. David turned to Sonny.

'So, Sonny, apart from helping Joe here kill his brother-in-law, how else do you propose to help Jimmy and the band raise their profile and become stars?'

'He's an agent, not a miracle worker,' joked Jimmy.

'Actually, I'm both,' said Sonny. 'I just need to hear the demos first so I can make up my mind how and where to market you. You've been out of the spotlight for a while now Jimmy, I need to see how you have developed.'

'I've got the rough mixes of every track. I can put them on a stick for you or just stick them in a file to you. We recorded them today,' said Michael.

'Sounds good. Email them to me and I will get on them tomorrow.'

'As long as the world don't end and you're stuck in your underground shelter.'

Sonny looked at Kid with pity. 'Well, if that happens it won't be a problem. I have a full studio in my underground bunker and you ain't going to be touring so it really doesn't matter. I will be safe and snug in my shelter while you lot will be dead; suppose we could do a postmortem release.'

'It's a nice thought,' said Kid, 'but who would buy it?'

Sonny gave this some thought. 'Well, it's a long-term strategy but future generations of survivalists may want to hear music from the before time.'

Jimmy didn't look convinced.

'This ain't a happy clappy album, we've gone a bit Leonard Coen meets Jonny Cash on a dark day with it.'

This didn't faze Sonny. 'These folks have just been through an end of civilisation as we know it situation, so they're bound to be depressed. This could be perfect for them!'

David turned to Michael. 'He's good!' He smiled and turned to Jimmy. 'I think we should hire Sonny.'

Jimmy nodded. 'I agree.'

David offered his outstretched hand to Sonny. 'Welcome to Wayne's World!' Sonny smiled and shook David's hand.

'Thanks, but if I am on-board let's not have any more references to Wayne's World. I don't want Mike Myers and Dana Garvey suing my ass!'

CHAPTER 8
INTERNET SENSATION

The next week flew by. The recording had gone well, and they were ahead of schedule. Today had been earmarked for Kid's guitar solos and Jimmy had decided to sit in and listen but Sonny Castiglia had other ideas. He arrived as the band were finishing breakfast on the patio. He didn't need to ring the buzzer at the gates. They heard the deep rumble of the Hummer as it wound up Lookout Mountain Drive.

'He really does use that as his everyday vehicle then,' observed Jimmy.

'Crazy as a box of frogs, but really good at what he does,' said Michael.

'What's he doing back up here?'

'He's come to pick you up,' said David, desperately trying not to smile.

Sonny rumbled through the gates. Jimmy looked at the armour-plated Hummer.

'In that?'

'What else Jimmy? It's his daily commuter.'

'What's he use at the weekends, a tank?' mused Joe. Jimmy looked questioningly at David.

'Why's he picking me up?'

'He's arranged a TV interview for you.'

'He has?'

David pulled a face. 'He has. It's a big one too.' Jimmy looked up with interest. 'How big?'

'I'll let Sonny tell you himself.' David turned to greet Sonny and was just in time to see him freefall from the cab. He tried not to laugh. 'Sonny really should consider something more height appropriate.'

'Or get a step ladder,' suggested Michael. They were all still sniggering when he reached the patio. Sonny looked around at the laughing faces.

'Did I miss something?'

'Legs!' suggested Kid and everyone tried desperately not to laugh. Sonny was very self-aware, and he cottoned on quick. He looked back at his Hummer.

'I know it's a bit on the high side, but I'll be the one laughing when I am miles off-road up in the mountains headed for safety while you guys are stuck on the highway facing the zombie apocalypse!'

'Great name for a band,' said Doug.

'Already been done,' said Kid. 'New Jersey Thrash Metal, I believe.'

Doug nodded. 'Makes sense.'

'Yeah, but it would suck for Country,' observed Jimmy. 'Would have enjoyed seeing Conway Twitty tour with them as a backing band.'

'Twitty Apocalypse, got a ring to it,' said Michael. '"I see the decay in your eyes" would be the obvious first single, although

"Goodbye Darlin'" would be more appropriate given the zombified nature of the situation.'

Jimmy nodded approvingly. 'You know your country then, Sonny.'

Sonny shrugged. 'I'm in the music business, I try to make sure I know everything. That's why people want me to be their agent and only a few get me. If you're shit, I will know it. Lucky for you, Jimmy, you're not.' He looked at his watch. 'You ready to go?'

'Right now?' he asked.

'Right now. I ain't here for breakfast.' As Sonny said this as he poured himself a coffee and put some apricot jam on a croissant. He looked Jimmy up and down. 'You're good to go, just grab that black leather jacket you were wearing on the "Vacant Stare" video. That will look cool on the TV.'

Jimmy didn't argue. It was clear that Sonny had done his research.

'Who are we seeing?'

'Ron Blazer!'

Jimmy stopped. '*The* Ron Blazer, I thought he was dead.'

'Well if he is, it won't be much of a conversation,' growled Sonny, impatient to get moving.

'Wasn't he involved in some major sex scandal?' asked David.

Sonny shrugged. 'More an occupational hazard than a scandal. He had sex with a couple of the staff on his show, *What's Going Down Tonight*.'

'Unfortunate name for the show given the circumstances,' said Michael.

'I heard it was about six of the women who worked for him.' They all turned to David and he continued. 'Six that they could get to talk that is. Ron was powerful then and had plenty of apologists. They reckon the true number was nearer ten.'

Sonny looked around to make sure none of Michael's staff where within ear shot.

'Try twenty-two!'

'Bloody hell!' said Kid. 'He was old then, how the hell did he manage it?'

'Ambition, but mainly Viagra.'

'So how did he get away with it?' asked David.

'They asked him to resign, and they would keep it quiet, say he left for personal reasons. He knew the game was up, but he put a caveat in the severance deal that they give him. He wanted a show on one of their cable channels after taking a year's break, with a contract for the cable show to start straight after his sabbatical. Two years with an option to renew.'

'I suppose they thought he would just fade away,' said Joe. Sonny shook his head.

'Well, if they thought that they certainly didn't know him very well. He kept in the limelight for the next year. Showed up at all the right parties and every new book and film launch.'

'What about the girls he molested?' asked Doug.

'Paid off with an NDA. You gotta remember he's still a very rich guy.'

'Do you think he's gonna sexually assault Jimmy?' asked Joe, a big stupid grin on his face. Sonny shook his head.

'He prefers them younger,' he looked up and saw Jimmy returning with his coat. 'And slimmer!' Jimmy couldn't work out why they were all laughing when he returned.

'Did I miss something?'

'Not dinner!' said Kid.

As they rumbled down Laurel Canyon Boulevard towards LA, Sonny briefed Jimmy.

'Now don't go thinking that this is a chat with some old has-been. Ron Blazer models himself on Ron Burgundy.'

'But Ron Burgundy is crazy, and fictional!'

Sonny laughed. 'That don't matter to Ron Blazer. He says a lot of inappropriate stuff but that's why the kids love him, they tune in just to see what crazy shit he is going to come out with today. He's become a bit of a cult figure with younger viewers and still retained a lot of his older audience from when he was on National TV. He's a genuine double threat.' Sonny gave Jimmy a wink. 'Especially if you're female!'

'How big is his audience?' asked Jimmy. 'Two hundred thousand?' That would be pretty good for a cable show, he thought. Wasn't to be sneered at.

'Try three million on a good show!' Sonny let Jimmy think about that for a moment. Suddenly Jimmy felt nervous; three million was a lot.

'So, what are we going to talk about.'

Sonny stared at Jimmy. 'You're kidding me?'

Jimmy looked back at him blankly.

'Maybe you might want to mention you're making your first record in twenty years and it's on the Small Print Label and the fact that it will be produced by multi-Grammy, award-winning

Michael Owen! You might also want to mention that you are booked in to headline at Carpenters in Vegas in six weeks' time.' Sonny seemed irritated. Jimmy just nodded.

'Anything else?'

Sonny slapped his fist hard down on the dash. 'For fuck's sake Jimmy, the clues in the title of Ron's show.'

'What's it called?'

Sonny took a couple of deep breaths.

'Look Jimmy, I know you have been stuck out in the middle of nowhere Nevada for a few years, but this is LA. Michael Owen is a big deal in this town. Ron Blazer is a big deal in this town. Not up there with the Hollywood crowd but they are certainly in the B-Listers. Ron's show is called *Back from Oblivion*. It's about comeback stories, second chances. Just tell your story, it's a great story and it's headed for a happy ending. Everyone loves a happy ending!'

'Ain't that what got Ron into trouble?'

Sonny grinned. 'That and a whole load of other stuff.' Jimmy looked out of the Hummer's window. *Back from Oblivion* seemed to sum up his situation quite nicely. He couldn't tell all his story, best to leave out the killy bits, just in case Sheriff Pence was watching.

'Ok, Sonny, you've convinced me, I'll go for it.'

This seemed to please Sonny. He decided that he wouldn't mention Ron's little party trick of dropping a big surprise on his guests live on air. He would let Jimmy discover that on his own. Good or bad, the exposure was what he needed to get Jimmy Wayne back in the public's consciousness, and with Ron Blazer he was certainly going to get it!

The Hummer rumbled into Studio City and Sonny took a left onto Ventura.

'Nearly there Jimmy. Ron's studio is just over the back of the old CBS lot.' Sonny pulled down a tight one-way street. There was only a couple of feet either side of the Hummer as they rumbled towards the Studio.

'Where you gonna park?'

Sonny smiled at Jimmy's question. 'In this? Anywhere I bloody like!' He gave Jimmy the maniacal grin of a Monster Truck driver in a traffic jam and Jimmy knew that parking wouldn't be a problem. As it turned out, it wasn't. Ron Blazer's Studio was a smallish unit situated on an old estate behind the CBS lot and there was parking for about sixty cars and there were still three spaces left for Blazer Channel guests. The Hummer took two. Jimmy stared at the poster in front of the studio. It was Ron Blazer, appropriately in a blazer, looking for all the world like Ron Burgundy's estranged brother. The message beneath was unambiguous. Welcome To the Blazer Channel! Sonny turned off the engine and Jimmy just stared at the sign.

'This is a parody, right?'

Sonny frowned. 'With Ron, probably not. In his mind Ron Burgundy is real, he's probably trying to book him for the show.' Sonny glanced around the car park. 'We better get moving, looks like the audience are already here.'

'Audience, you never told me there was an audience.' Jimmy's nerves were starting to twitch.

'Relax, it's only about forty people. Ron likes to have some-thing to feed off. Makes the interview more real when you can hear some laughter or applause. Besides, it's live TV so you kinda need them.'

'Live!' Now Jimmy could feel cold knots twisting in his stomach. 'You never told me it was live.'

Sonny shrugged. 'Didn't think I needed to. You play to live audiences every night.'

'Yeah, but not three million.'

'For fuck's sake Jimmy, it's just talking. You know how to talk, don't ya?' Sonny opened the door and fell out of the cab. 'Come on, Jimmy, your public awaits.'

Jimmy lowered himself carefully out of the Hummer. He felt like the condemned man going to the gallows.

'Welcome to the Blazer Channel!'

Jimmy turned round as Ron Blazer hurried through the door towards him, his hand outstretched.

'Great to meet you, Jimmy.'

Jimmy stared at his moustache. It was a real Magnum PI of a moustache. He wondered if it had escaped from the CBS lot and made itself at home on Ron Blazer's top lip. Ron turned and headed back towards the door he had just come from.

'Follow me gents, the studio is through here.'

Jimmy turned to Sonny. 'Is it me or has that moustache got bigger since he was on Primetime.'

'Bigger,' said Sonny. 'He's clearly compensating.'

As he followed Ron through the door, he realised they had entered straight onto the set and an audience, obscured from Jimmy by the glare of the studio lights, started to applaud.

'Hey, Jimmy.'

'Jimmy, we love you!' He was momentarily taken aback but his old showbiz reflexes saved him, and he smiled and waved instinctively.

Ron walked up to the mic.

'Hold it down folks, this isn't Jimmy's proper entrance. We are just going to familiarise him with the studio, get him mic'd up and then we will be good to go.' There was an outbreak of whooping from the audience.

Ron turned to Jimmy. 'You will sit here, Jimmy, and I will sit opposite you. You will be talking into camera two when you're talking to me and camera three if you address the audience.' He pointed to the cameras. 'There are two other cameras which we will be cutting in and out of during the filming but two and three are the only ones that need to concern you.'

Jimmy nodded. 'No problem, Ron.' Jimmy pointed at the two other chairs set out next to his. 'Who else is on tonight.'

Ron smiled. 'Nobody important Jimmy, this show is all about you!'

Jimmy heard Sonny snigger behind him and the knot in his stomach gave another twist. The stage lights dimmed, and he was able to see out into the audience. Like Sonny had said, there were only about forty people there, but leaning against the studio wall on the left-hand side of the stage was Wendy. She winked at him. And now Jimmy was really nervous, something was definitely going on!

Five minutes later Jimmy was in the green room waiting to be called to the set. He watched the live feed on the TV. Suddenly 'Back in Black' by AC/DC came pounding through the speakers and Ron Blazer entered the set to as much applause as forty people can make. It sounded pretty good in the small studio. Ron appealed for the applause to die down.

'Welcome to another edition of *Back from Oblivion*.'

Jimmy turned to look at Sonny. '*Back from Oblivion*?'

Sonny shrugged. 'Does what it says on the label, Jimmy.'

Jimmy turned back to the TV and Ron Blazer was getting into his opening monologue.

'This programme is about second chances. It's about redemption. It's about never giving up and coming back against all odds.' Whoops from the audience. 'Tonight's guest has been on the edge of the precipice we call Fame, but he slipped as he neared the summit. For twenty years he slid down its unforgiving slopes but now, like a mountain goat, he has sprung back to the edge of that mountain top.'

Jimmy turned to Sonny, a look of horror on his face.

'Mountain fucking goat?'

'Interesting metaphor, don't ya think!?'

Jimmy did not think. 'Fuck this Sonny, I'm outta here.' Jimmy went for the door, but Sonny barred his way.

'Can't let you do that Jimmy. I got skin in the game here and I'm telling you this will be good for you.'

'I don't need to do this shit. The songs are good enough to sell without this!'

Sonny stayed by the door. 'Get your head out of your ass, Jimmy. Nobody's heard from you in fifteen years unless they've been gambling at a third-rate Casino in Nevada. It's no good making a great record if nobody knows about it. This will get you some great publicity.'

Jimmy wasn't convinced. 'What kind of publicity, this looks like a freak show.'

'No such thing as bad publicity Jimmy, now get your ass out there and sparkle!'

The door opened behind Sonny and the floor manager appeared.

'Ok, Jimmy, let's go.'

Jimmy looked back in desperation, but Sonny was ushering him into the studio.

'Eyes and teeth, Jimmy, eyes and teeth!'

Reluctantly, Jimmy followed the floor manager. Sonny walked beside Jimmy, keeping himself between Jimmy and the exit, just in case he made a run for it. As they waited for his introduction Jimmy was aware of someone standing beside him on the auditorium side. He turned slowly and there was Wendy.

'Hi Jimmy, you excited?' She seemed to be.

'What's happening Wendy, why are you here?'

He was whispering but Sonny could hear his muttering. He just assumed Jimmy was talking to himself. Trying to compose himself before he went on.

Wendy squeezed his arm. 'Don't worry it's going to be fine,' she paused. 'Ron's got a nice surprise for you.'

'Surprise?' He didn't like the sound of that.

'Ladies and gentlemen, Jimmy Wayne.' The floor manager pushed Jimmy forwards and he turned to Wendy, but she was gone. The studio lights blinded him for a moment, and he was blinking as Ron Blazer stood on the stage applauding. 'Jimmy Wayne, everyone.' He took Jimmy's hand and gave him a very firm handshake. 'Welcome to *Back from Oblivion*.'

Jimmy nodded. 'Good to be back.'

That bought a nice round of laughter. They both sat down. Ron had a clipboard with about twenty questions on. Jimmy tried to read them, but the first question was coming at him before he could.

'So, Jimmy, where did it all go so wrong?'

Jimmy thought for a moment, where did it all go wrong?

'Being young I guess. I was just twenty-three and I had a top twenty hit. People were saying that I was the next Jonny Cash and I started to believe it.'

Ron nodded. 'Easily done. I suppose you had no real management.'

'Well, the label did assign me a manager, but he was there to look after the label's interests, not mine.'

'A familiar story, especially back then, can you remember the name of the manager?'

Jimmy couldn't, but even if he could he wasn't sure it would be a good idea to name him. Libel tends to end up in court.

'No, I can't. It was a long time ago Ron.'

'And a lot of drinks ago?' He asked it as a question but there was a hint of accusation in his voice. Jimmy could have been offended but he decided to just run with it. Like Sonny had said, 'Three million viewers.'

'Too many to count. You're famous Ron, you know what the adulation and recognition is like. Sometimes it's a pain but it's also a drug. When it's gone you miss it. One day my face was on billboards, in magazines. I was being interviewed almost every other day and then in less than a year I couldn't get arrested.' Jimmy paused for a moment. 'That's not actually true, I did get arrested, several times.' This bought a nice outbreak of laughter. Jimmy let it subside and then continued. 'My morals were not all they should have been.'

Ron pulled a stern fatherly face. 'Yes, we know Jimmy. You made quite a few headlines for your partying back then. Even so your fans never deserted you.'

Jimmy smiled. 'I was very lucky. My fans were, still are, very loyal.'

'The Waynettes, that was it, wasn't it?'

Jimmy grinned in embarrassment. 'Sure was, though I didn't give them that title.'

'Was that your manager, Steve Bender?' Ron raised an eyebrow and Jimmy knew that Ron knew something he didn't.

'How did I forget a name like that?' Jimmy hadn't forgotten, he would never forget that snake and how he had stitched him up contractually. He nodded. 'Yep, that was one of Steve's ideas. To be fair it stuck.'

'So did the outfit.'

On a large screen on the backdrop behind them an old photo of Jimmy flanked by four Waynettes appeared. They were all dressed like Dallas Cowboy cheerleaders but across their chests was the legend, Waynettes.

'That was pretty racy stuff!'

Jimmy nodded and smiled. 'Yeah, that was the nineties.'

'But I understand they still dress like that today.' Ron leaned forwards conspiratorially. 'A little bird told me that when you started to attract attention again your fans started coming to the Riviera in Blackjack to hear you play.'

'They did.'

'And they still had their Waynette outfits.'

'They certainly did, Ron.'

Ron turned to the picture. 'How long since you saw those four girls, Jimmy?'

With a growing sense of foreboding Jimmy looked at the photo.

'Well Jenny and Sue came up to see me at the Riviera last month.'

'What about Elaine.' Ron looked searchingly at Jimmy and Jimmy knew he was walking into a trap. He nodded weakly.

'Elaine, haven't seen her for years.'

Ron's eyes hooded beneath his caterpillar like eyebrows. 'But you two were close, very close!'

Jimmy peered out into the audience, through the glare of the lights and he saw Wendy. She was pulling a face, almost laughing and her expression was saying, 'Let's see you get out of this one, Jimmy.' She really seemed to be enjoying his discomfort.

'You were close weren't you, Jimmy?' Ron's insistent questioning bought him back into the interview. Truth, he decided, was the best option.

'Yeah, we were close. We were young and free, everything seemed possible,' he trailed off. 'Sometimes the possible just becomes too hard. My career started to slide and I guess I started drinking.'

'And became a pain in the ass?'

Jimmy laughed. 'Oh, I was a pain in the ass before that!' The audience laughed. Ron let the laughter die down and then dropped his voice.

'You were going to marry Elaine, weren't you?' He delivered the line like a prosecution lawyer. Jimmy knew the trap was closing.

'It had been mentioned, but then we drifted apart.'

'A sad story of young love that was doomed to fail.'

'Isn't most young love doomed to fail Ron?'

Ron looked down at his notes and then back at Jimmy. 'I suppose you have a point Jimmy, but Elaine was smitten with you.'

Elaine was actually a borderline nut job, thought Jimmy, but he didn't want to say it out loud on TV. Crazy as she was, he couldn't be that unkind to her.

'She was more smitten with you than you ever knew, Jimmy.'

Here it comes, he thought.

'Elaine went home to small town Texas and changed her name to Wayne!' There was a gasp from the audience, Jimmy sat there. 'What do you say to that?' asked Ron.

Told you she was a nut job, was what he wanted to say, instead he just frowned.

'Elaine Wayne, I suppose it's got a ring to it.' There were a few sniggers from the audience.

'Why do you think Elaine would do that, Jimmy?'

'Psychological problems.' He said it before he could stop himself. Some of the audience laughed but others gasped at his callousness. 'I didn't mean it in a nasty way,' he tried to win them back. 'It's just that it's pretty unusual behaviour to break up with a boyfriend and then change your name to his. Let's be honest Ron, if we took the name of every girl we went out with our names would be too long for the phone book, not that anyone has a phone book anymore.' That got a little laugh.

'There is another reason, Jimmy.'

Jimmy didn't respond, he knew Ron Blazer had more cards to play, all he could do was wait for him to reveal them.

'What if you were pregnant and you wanted your son to bear his father's name?' There was a gasp from the audience. Jimmy felt the ground shift beneath him. In the green room Sonny Castiglia was chuckling away to himself. This was a shit show of epic proportions. If this didn't go viral his name wasn't Sonny Castiglia. To be fair it wasn't but who wants to be called Bert?

Ron Blazer rose from his chair. 'Ladies and gentlemen please welcome, Elaine Wayne!'

There was another gasp from the audience and then hesitant applause that grew as Elaine Wayne walked onto the stage. She was just in her forties and still looked good in her Waynettes Cheerleader outfit. She sashayed onto the stage. Jimmy, ever the gentleman, stood up to greet her. He held out his hand but she grasped him in a bearhug. As she pulled away, she planted a kiss on his cheek that left the imprint of her ruby-red lip-sticked lips.

'Hi Jimmy.' She acknowledged the applause from the audience and sat down.

Ron was still on his feet and then Jimmy understood why. 'Elaine Wayne, and her son. Jimmy's son!'

Sonny nearly fell off his chair in the green room. 'This is unbelievable shit!' It made him very, very happy.

Jimmy turned to the side of the stage and there was a young man standing just off-stage. The floor manager pushed him on. As the lights hit him, he winced. Jimmy looked at him. It was like looking in a mirror at his younger self.

He sat down next to his mum and nodded at Jimmy. The audience was in a state of shock.

'Jimmy Wayne, meet your son!'

Jimmy shot Ron a look that could kill and for a moment entered him on a potential song list. He turned to the young man and reached his hand out.

'Pleased to meet you son, what's your name?'

He took Jimmy's hand, clearly, he was as uncomfortable as Jimmy. 'It's Wayne, sir,' he said respectfully.

'No son, what's your Christian name?'

'It's Wayne, sir,' he repeated. Jimmy turned to Elaine.

'Wayne Wayne! What is he, a fucking panda?!' This bought a round of laughter from the audience which he instantly regretted. He turned back to his son. 'I take that back son, it's not your fault your mother is obsessed. I reckon you need to change one or the other. I would prefer that you kept one of them because, looking at you son, I have no doubt that I am your father. I only wish to God your mother had told me.'

Elaine shifted uncomfortably. 'How could I do that Jimmy; you had already climbed into a bottle before we split up.'

'I know, I am ashamed of my young self, but I've been clean for years. I had a right to know, and Wayne had a right to know me.'

Elaine smiled. 'Well now he does.' Her eyes gleamed with the same old intense madness that had made her so exciting, and alas, so disturbing. Jimmy looked past her at Wayne.

'Let's meet up after the show.'

Wayne nodded. 'I'd like that.'

Ron Blazer turned to the audience. 'More from Jimmy Wayne after the break folks!'

As soon as the red light went off Jimmy turned to Ron. 'What the fuck was that?'

'Great TV, that's what that was, Jimmy.' Ron looked over to Elaine. 'That was great, thanks Elaine, see you in the green room after the show.'

Elaine smiled. 'Ok Ron, we'll see you both in the green room after the show.' She squeezed Jimmy's hand and gave him that look she used to give him. He shuddered, still crazy after all these years. He looked past her to Wayne who looked slightly embarrassed by his mother. He looked up and for a second their eyes met, and Wayne gave Jimmy a knowing look. At that moment Jimmy felt that they were going to get on. He understood what his mother was like, and he didn't blame Jimmy for not being there because now he knew that Jimmy had known nothing about him until five minutes ago.

Jimmy and Ron were now alone on the set.

'Better sit down Jimmy, we are going to be live in a minute.'

Jimmy sat down and glared at Ron. 'Hope you don't ever want to interview me again Ron, because after that stitch up it ain't gonna happen.'

Ron laughed. 'You may hate me now Jimmy but trust me, that story is going to be all over the media tomorrow. People will feel sorry for you, not for that crazy cow Elaine.' He leaned close to Jimmy and whispered, 'She's fucking whacko!'

For once Ron was saying something Jimmy could agree with. 'You got any more surprises for me, Ron?'

Ron gave him an apologetic shrug. 'Just a small one.'

Jimmy felt the knot in his stomach tighten once more but this time it wasn't quite as bad. 'I gotta warn you Ron, if I don't like the shit you pull I'm going to lose it and burn your ratings.'

Ron looked delighted. 'Please do, Jimmy. The bigger the meltdown the better. The media sucks up stuff like that. It's good for you and it's even better for me!'

Jimmy saw the crazed look in Ron's eyes, the guy was enjoying himself. Ok, Ron Blazer, he thought. You bring whatever you want. The thought set him free.

'What's your policy on fighting?'

Ron considered Jimmy's question for a moment. 'Well, as long as you don't attack the host, and maybe don't hit women or children, that should be fine. Other men, feel free!'

Jimmy smiled. 'Thanks Ron, I will.'

Apart from the floor manager only one other person heard the exchange. Sonny, watching in the green room, heard every word. This is going to be good, he thought. Just then the green room door swung open, and Elaine and Wayne walked in. Sonny gave them a big smile.

'Hey, come on in and take a seat, the big fight starts in a couple of minutes.'

Elaine turned and looked at the set monitor. 'What fight?'

'The one between Jimmy and the next guest.'

'What makes you think there's going to be one?' asked Elaine. Sonny gave her a knowing smile.

'Trust me, it's going to happen, so you might as well get comfortable and take a ringside seat.'

'You know something we don't, Sonny?'

Sonny smiled mischievously. 'I certainly do Elaine; I most certainly do!'

'Back in Black' came blasting over the airwaves and Ron Blazer smiled at the camera.

'Welcome back to *Back from Oblivion*. Tonight's guest is Jimmy Wayne.' He turned to Jimmy. 'Hey, Jimmy.'

Jimmy nodded. 'Hey, Ron.' His demeanour had become very calm.

'So, Jimmy, over twenty years after your last hit, in fact, your only hit, things are really taking off for you again. Signed to Small Print Records.'

'That's right, Ron. I've been very lucky. Seems like I have a second chance at having a big career.'

'And what would you put that down to?'

Murder, thought Jimmy but went instead with something more mundane.

'Great songs, it's always about the songs.'

Ron nodded. 'You've never been noted as a songwriter before, Jimmy, how have you managed to develop those skills later in your career?'

Murder, he thought again.

'I guess I've matured,' he smiled. 'Got old, and that gives you a deeper perspective.' Ron was nodding.

'You obviously have some good people around you as well, like David Parker and Michael Owen.' Jimmy wasn't sure how Ron had known about David.

'You have good researchers, Ron.'

Ron gave him an 'I know something you don't know' look.

'I do, Jimmy,' he paused. 'David Parker manages the Riviera where you had a residency, doesn't he?'

'He does.'

'He realised you were suddenly coming up with some great stuff and made the call to Michael Owen. That must have been a big surprise when the owner of Small Print Records turned up.'

Jimmy shook his head. 'I couldn't believe it when David introduced me. We were playing in the Canyon Room at the Riviera by then and filling it twice some evenings.'

'How big is it?'

'It's only a three-hundred-seater Ron, but we were selling it out every night.'

'So suddenly you're on the up again and it's all because of these great new songs.'

Jimmy held up his hand. 'That's not strictly true, Ron. None of this would be working if I didn't have such a great band around me. Joe, Doug and Kid are awesome musicians. It's Kid Oscarson who has put together all the musical arrangements. He's a real genius.' Ron looked down at his notes.

'So, Jimmy, you have great songs, a great band. One of the best labels in LA with a world-famous producer and David Parker, not only a great friend but seemingly a great manager.' He paused for a moment as Jimmy nodded his agreement and then his eyes narrowed.

Here it comes, thought Jimmy.

'That hasn't always been the case though, has it?'

Jimmy laughed nervously. 'It has never been the case!' There was a ripple of laughter from the audience.

'When you had your first, and only hit, you didn't have a manager?'

Jimmy didn't know where this was leading but he didn't like it.

'Well I was signed to a label called Dude Ranch.'

Ron's eyebrows narrowed. 'Interesting name.'

Jimmy smiled. 'It was an in-joke. They were pretending to be a Country label but everyone on the label and all the artists were city boys. Just like the dude ranches where city boys can go and play at being cowboys for a month.'

'Actually, that's quite a clever little joke.'

'Yeah, it was. Looks a bit weird now if you don't have it explained to you, especially after *Brokeback Mountain*.'

There was a spattering of laughter from the audience and Ron forgot himself for a moment.

'Could have called it Queer Ranch.' He had been hoping for a burst of laughter but Ron had once again put his foot straight into the not-politically-correct hole he had fallen down several times before. He looked to Jimmy and saw the look of surprise on Jimmy's face. He turned to the audience, but all he heard from them was the tell-tale end of a sharp intake of breath. Ron glanced back to Jimmy for help, but Jimmy was just sitting blank-faced, unwilling or unable to jump in and try and dig him out. In his ear the floor manager was screaming.

'Move it on, Ron, move it on!'

Ron tried to move it on. 'F****t Farm, that would have been a good title.'

The floor manager started banging his head against the nearest wall and, apart from the rhythmical echo of a skull being thumped against a partition wall, the studio fell deathly quiet. So quiet you could almost hear the beads of sweat on Ron Blazer's forehead as they ran down his face.

Jimmy now realised what Sonny had been on about and why old Ron Blazer was so popular with a younger generation. He was an accident waiting to happen. It was like watching a car crash in slow-motion. Ron had put Jimmy in a tough situation in the first half of the show and now Jimmy decided to return the favour.

'Interesting fact about Dude Ranch, Ron. There was no front entrance.'

Ron, in his panicked state, grasped for the life line Jimmy had seemingly thrown him.

'What, you had to go in the back door?'

There was a huge burst of laughter from the audience which Ron mistook for laughter with him, not at him. Jimmy decided to throw Ron another lifeline, made of stone.

'Yeah, it was really strange. You could only get in the back door because there was no...' Jimmy pretended to reach for the right word and twisted his hand with a turning motion. Ron took the bait.

'A knob. You got in the back door with a knob!'

The place went into meltdown. The floor manager was shouting into his mic. 'Go to break, go to break!'

In the green room Sonny Castiglia was laughing so hard he fell off his stool. As always it was a long way down for him.

Jimmy leaned back, unable to keep the smirk off his face.

Ron still hadn't worked out what was going on. The audience were laughing but it didn't feel right. Were they laughing at him? The floor manager came marching up to Jimmy.

'What the fuck was that, you clever bastard.'

Jimmy played dumb. 'What? I didn't say anything. Your boy did all the talking.'

'And you just gave him more bullets to shoot himself with, you sneaky little has-been.' The studio manager had lost it but Jimmy stayed calm. He gestured towards the auditorium.

'The audience can still hear you know.' Jimmy smiled at him and then spoke quietly. 'Not nice being stitched up, is it?'

Rage flashed in the floor manager's eyes. 'Well, you'll be able to let me know soon enough, Jimmy, we got some more surprises planned for you.'

Jimmy was expecting it, but now he was ready and he couldn't care less.

The make-up lady had mopped Ron Blazer's dripping forehead and given him a touch of powder just to remove the sweaty shine. She rushed off the stage as 'Back in Black' came pulsing back through the speakers. Like a punch-drunk boxer getting back off the canvass Ron looked at the camera and tried to continue as if nothing had happened.

'Welcome back to the final part of our interview with our star on the comeback trail, Jimmy Wayne!' Big round of applause from the audience. Ron gathered himself. 'Let me take you back to Dude,' he hesitated for a second. 'Your old label.' The audience tittered and Jimmy smirked.

'Dude Ranch, you mean?' asked Jimmy innocently. Again, the audience sniggered. Ron wasn't getting caught a second time.

'Yes, that one.' Nicely done thought Jimmy. 'What happened when the second and the third record didn't chart?'

Jimmy shrugged. 'Like a lot of the big labels do, they cut me loose.'

'Didn't you have a contract?'

'I did, but it was only on a song-to-song basis. Have a hit, they keep you. Have two misses and you're gone.'

'You never saw any royalties on that first hit?'

Jimmy laughed. 'Dream on, Ron. They piled so many costs onto it that I would have had to sell a million copies to break even!' Jimmy shrugged. 'That's just the way it goes. The big labels always did have a habit of stitching up their new artists. Unless you're a big brand and move a lot of records you won't get any help, it's a business!'

'So where did Steve Bender come into this?'

Jimmy knew straight away that this question was the ticking bomb.

'Steve worked for the label, and he was appointed as my A&R guy.'

'Wasn't he more than that?'

Jimmy thought for a moment. 'When the label cut me, Steve acted as a sort of a booking agent for me. He got me on some TV shows as a guest, and a few gigs.'

Ron nodded. 'Like a manager?'

'No, like an agent.'

'Made you some money though, with all the bookings.'

Jimmy laughed. 'Allegedly, but damned if I ever saw any. Once he realised that I wasn't going to make it, he disappeared looking for the next meal-ticket.' He looked straight down the camera. 'I don't blame him though. We were all just trying to make a living and at that time, being my agent was like being the Captain of the Titanic!' There was laughter from the audience. Ron let it die down.

'Would it surprise you to know that Steve is still in the business?'

'Nothing surprises me in this business.' There was laughter from the audience. Out of the corner of his eye Jimmy saw the floor manager open the door that came onto the set from the green room. Here it comes, he thought.

In his ear mic Ron heard his floor manager's voice. 'And cue Steve Bender!'

'Not only is he still in the business, Jimmy, but he says he is still in contract with you!' Ron turned to the audience. 'Ladies and Gentlemen, Steve Bender!'

Jimmy noted with satisfaction that the applause was muted. Nobody knew who Steve Bender was. He looked up and there, twenty years older, was Steve. Jimmy nodded at him and accepted his outstretched hand.

'Good to see you, Jimmy.'

Jimmy frowned. 'Well, that remains to be seen Steve, don't it?'

Ron leaned in. 'Looks like there is bad feeling between you boys.'

'There ain't no feeling. I haven't seen this dude for twenty years,' said Jimmy. He leaned back in his chair and waited for either Ron or Steve to make the play. Ron made the first move.

'So, Steve, I believe you have something to show Jimmy.'

Steve nodded. 'Yes, I do!' He pulled a folded A4 document from his pocket and held it up. 'Do you remember this, Jimmy?'

Jimmy shrugged. 'Steve, I barely remember you!' The audience laughed. He had them on his side, he was determined to keep them there.

'It's a contract, Jimmy. You signed it.' Steve held it up to the camera.

'When did I sign it, Steve?' asked Jimmy casually. He knew exactly where this was going now, and he knew how he was going to play it.

Steve looked at the document. '1998, October 2nd.'

Jimmy nodded as Ron leaned forwards and looked at the document. 'Is that your signature Jimmy?'

Jimmy didn't even bother looking at it. 'It could be, what difference would it make?'

Steve smiled. 'Well Jimmy, you signed me as your manager and that gave me an option on the next three records.'

'That's unfortunate, Jimmy,' interrupted Ron. 'Aren't you signed to Small Print Records and have David Parker as your manager?'

Jimmy nodded. 'You know I am. Ron.'

Ron smiled like a crocodile going in for the kill.

'Well, that means you are in breach of contract with Steve here.' Steve nodded with approval. Jimmy ignored them both and looked straight down the camera.

'I signed with Steve when I was a young man with one hit behind me. He got me some gigs and TV but I never saw a penny, as my tax returns will prove. Where has he been for the last twenty years?' Jimmy stood up and addressed the studio audience. 'Steve is a shyster. Sees I am on the way back up, no thanks to him, and is now trying to jump on and grab a piece of the action. Ron here is trying to set me up on live TV to improve his ratings. What a pair of losers!' The crowd cheered. He turned to Ron. 'You are a homophobic moron.' He then turned to Steve Bender. 'And you are a conman and a bloodsucking leech.' Jimmy turned back to the camera. 'As far as I'm concerned, they can both kiss my ass, I'm outta here. That's all folks!' He blew a kiss down the camera, and he blew kisses to the audience. They went wild and he left the stage to cheering and applause.

In the green room, Sonny was whooping with delight. That was some of the best TV he had seen in years, and he knew Jimmy would be an internet sensation in a matter of hours.

CHAPTER 9
CAST A LONG SHADOW

Ma Lantern checked that she had recorded *Back from Oblivion* properly. It had been the usual Ron Blazer shit show. Ron had, as he often did, proved himself to be totally out of touch with the requirements of the modern world. He wasn't ever going to be 'woke', forever stuck in the coma he had entered in the seventies. The bastard had laid some nasty traps for Jimmy Wayne and Jimmy had handled them really well. The way he had turned the tables on Ron without him realising would make him very popular with the kids and the woke brigade. Ma was reluctantly warming to the idea of not having him killed, maybe Jack was right. Steve Bender was another matter. He was trying to take money from her investment. That wasn't going to be good for his health. She didn't like the look of him, slicked back hair and botoxed cheeks. A delicious thought occurred to her. It had been a while since she had entertained anyone in the cellar.

Jack turned off the TV in his office, he too had been watching *Back from Oblivion* just to see how Jimmy had gone, he had done well but that creep Steve Bender, he was a problem he didn't need. The creep clearly had a contract that he was going to try and enforce. It was a complication, and Jack didn't like complications. He reached for the phone to call Ma, but it rang before he picked it up. He answered.

'Hi Jackie.' It was Ma.

'Hi Ma, did you see it?'

'Oh, I saw it, Jackie. Jimmy did well.'

Jack smiled with satisfaction. 'Yeah, he did, but that little cocksucker with a contract, he's gotta go.'

This was music to Ma's ears.

'Can I have him, Jack?'

For a moment Jack was confused. 'What do you mean?'

Ma put on her appealing voice, husky and soft. 'Jackie, you know what I mean. I haven't entertained in the cellar for over a year now. Momma needs some fun time.'

Jack felt a shudder run down his spine. By fun time his mother meant torturing someone to death. He tried to dissuade her.

'Easier if I get Terry to whack him and bury him out in the desert.'

'Jackie, Momma needs some fun.' The playful tone was gone from her voice now. 'Get him picked up and bring him to the cellar!' She hung up and Jack sat there feeling the horror he had felt as a ten-year-old boy watching his mother garrotte Aldo. His mother really was a monster. He grabbed his mobile and pulled up Terry Moist's number. Terry answered on the second ring.

'Yes boss.'

'There is a guy called Steve Bender, he's just been on Ron Blazer's show in Studio City. I need him picking up, now!'

Terry didn't need to ask what kind of a pick-up it was, when Jack asked like that there would be no refusing the offer of a lift. 'No problem boss. Me and Tony are just on Ventura now.'

'You know what he looks like?'

Tony C held up his phone.

'Got him here, Terry, show's already going viral on YouTube.'

'Tony's got a clip from the show, we know what he looks like. Where are we taking him?'

Jack paused for a moment deciding Steve Bender's fate and then he thought about the contract he was waving on the show that might take money out of his pocket.

'Ma wants him delivered to the cellar.'

Terry and Tony turned and looked at each other. The cellar! What had this guy done to deserve that. Terry nodded slowly. 'Ok boss, we're on it.'

Jack rang off and stared at his phone for a moment. In just a few brief sentences he had condemned a total stranger to a horrible death at the hands of his psychopath of a mother. He almost felt sorry for him, but then he thought about how much money they could make out of Jimmy Wayne's success and any sympathy he may have felt faded. The life he lived had been distilled into acquiring power and wealth. Whatever got in the way got trampled underfoot. No question, no hesitation, no regret. He was what his mother had made him, but he could never stoop to the depths of pure evil that she enjoyed. To Jack, violence was transactional. It was used when required. For Ma, it was a pleasure to be savoured. He put down his phone and shuddered. He would eat out tonight with Lena and leave Ma some time to herself. Although the screams would not be heard in the house – the cellar was soundproofed – he preferred to not be around when it happened.

———◆———

Aksel climbed up the rocks to check on Terry Moist's camera. It was still in place and so was the monitor he had placed in front of it a week ago. Whoever was watching it had been watching the same twenty-four-hour loop for the whole week. He smiled to himself. All he had had to do was stay out of sight of the camera for one whole day and then drop the film onto the monitor placed in front of the camera. He did it late at night so if anyone had been watching they might have seen a momentary shudder as the monitor was placed in front of the camera. Could have been a bird or any creature of the night.

The river had continued to produce gold at an alarming rate. There was clearly a large seam that the river had exposed and erosion washed it down river and into his collection beds. Soon he would need to distribute some of his reserves out though the dealers and turn it into more liquid assets. But for now, he would just keep stockpiling. Maybe he could send some more to Kid and Jimmy. Kid had been his best friend all his life, like a brother from another mother and Jimmy – he had liked him from the first few moments. He was an open book, if you knew how to read him. Clearly, he had a secret, but he just felt that he was a decent man. Somebody he could trust. There weren't many people in this world he felt that way about.

He had been into the cavern this morning and the night's harvest had been bountiful. The bays in the riverbed were full, and when he had turned on the lights in the cavern the river had glowed gold. Like the golden embers of a log fire the river truly seemed to shimmer with refracted light from the precious metal.

As they drove up Lookout Mountain Drive, Sonny was still laughing.

'Oh, Jimmy, you knocked it outta the park today. The way you set Blazer up with the back door and the knob gags.' He started laughing again. Jimmy smiled too; he was happy about how it had gone, but not the surprise in the first half of the show.

'How much of that did you know, Sonny?' Sonny stopped laughing. His silence confirmed Jimmy's suspicions. 'I thought as much.' He paused for a moment to think. 'So now I have a son who is twenty-two and I didn't know existed until an hour ago. Don't you think you should have warned me?'

Sonny tried to placate him. 'Look, Jimmy, I thought you would be pleased.'

'Jesus, Sonny, I just had a family handed to me on live TV. Not really the place for it is it?' Jimmy was angry. Sonny opted for silence and drove on for a while. But only about thirty seconds.

'It's cable, not the same.'

'Three million people, you said.'

'Probably double that with social media from today's offering. Man, you handed that creep his ass!' He turned to Jimmy and smiled his best sympathetic smile. It looked as real as a Hollywood wife's breasts. 'Talking of ass, that Elaine is still packing.'

'She's a psycho,' snapped Jimmy.

'True, but she's got a nice ass, just saying.'

'Don't say. Apparently, she's the mother of my child so a little bit of respect would be nice.'

Sonny gave him a smirk. 'Listen to Dad of the year.'

Jimmy shrugged. 'The boy seems a nice kid, I gave him my phone number, told him to give me a call.'

'That's nice.' Sonny thought for a moment. 'You going to persuade him to change his name?' They both smiled.

'Wayne or Wayne?' asked Jimmy.

'Wayne,' replied Sonny. Confident but unspecific.

'Which one?'

'The one which makes him sound like a fucking panda!'

'That'll be the first one.' They both laughed.

'Wayne Wayne, what the hell was she thinking?'

'You never met me in my prime, Sonny. I drove women crazy. They did irrational things.'

'What, like buying your records? Sorry, record.'

Jimmy winced. 'Harsh.'

'Yeah, but meant with love brother, you know that right?' Sonny pulled into the driveway of the studio; the gates were already opening. 'How'd they know I was here?'

'Sonny, the whole mountain knows. You can hear this thing from the moment it turns off Laurel Canyon Boulevard all the way up the mountain.' Sonny looked genuinely surprised.

'Really, I was hoping it was a bit stealthier than that.' Sonny pulled into the corner of the drive and killed the engine. Jimmy went to climb down but Sonny caught his arm. 'That Steve Bender character, do we need to worry about him?'

Jimmy shook his head. 'That contract is over twenty years old and he has been nowhere for all that time.' Sonny didn't look convinced.

'That may be so, Jimmy, but you don't want to get caught up in a court case. Maybe be better to pay him off. If he's desperate you could probably get rid of him for $20k.'

Jimmy wasn't doing that.

'Forget it, the SOB never did a thing for me and he took all my fees in expenses. I would rather shoot him than give him a dime!'

Jimmy climbed down from the Hummer. He heard a thump from the other side of the vehicle as Sonny fell to Earth. As they reached the studio David and Michael were standing with the band and they all started applauding. David waited for the applause to die down.

'Congratulations, Jimmy. Or should I call you Daddy?'

'Thanks, I think.'

Kid came forwards and gave him a big hug. 'Man, you made old man Blazer look like a fool.'

'He is a fool!'

'I know, but you nailed his tired old carcass to the studio floor.' David turned to Michael.

'That has to be the worst idea for a rug I've ever heard!'

Michael flinched. 'Would you leave the head on like those terrible old tiger skin rugs?'

'Of course,' replied David as if it was the most obvious thing in the world. 'That moustache would be wonderful for buffing your shoes on!'

Michael nodded. 'Good point, if you had his mouth open you could use the upper teeth for levering your shoes off, save a lot of bending.'

Kid stood there shaking his head. 'Bloody English aristocracy, no wonder you're an endangered species. You're all stark raving mad.'

'We prefer eccentric,' said David. He and Michael both started laughing. When they stopped David turned back to Jimmy. 'Don't suppose you have checked on social media Jimmy, but you've gone viral. There's been over a million hits on your webpage in the last hour.' He raised his glass. 'Here's to you Jimmy, your profile has just gone through the roof!'

Jimmy smiled. He had certainly moved his career forwards, but at what cost? 'Aren't you worried about Steve Bender; I did sign a contract with him.'

David didn't seem concerned. 'Twenty years ago, where has he been since then. Whatever he comes at you with we can counter it. We'll offer him some cash to disappear.'

———◆———

Down at the Blazer channel parking lot Terry and Tony were waiting for Steve Bender to come out the Studios. They had plans to make him disappear permanently. They sat quietly, waiting.

'I hate doing this.'

Tony C nodded in agreement. 'I know what you mean, don't seem right giving anyone to that evil monster.'

Terry shrugged. 'We could snap his neck and say he struggled; accidents do happen.'

'When did we ever kill anyone accidently? We're good at what we do. Ma would rumble us and then we could end up in the cellar.'

They both sat there quietly contemplating being on the end of Ma Lantern's sadistic tendencies.

'I feel bad about it, but this guy has got to go to Ma because I'm not taking his place.' Terry knew they had no alternative but then a thought occurred to him. 'What if we talked him out of pressing his claim on Jimmy's contract. If we get him to back off, we could call Jack. Jack don't like it when Ma is torturing. Apparently, it ruins the Feng Shui in the house.'

Tony seemed impressed. 'That could work... What's Feng Shui?'

Terry looked at Tony with mild surprise. 'You're joking, right?'

Tony shook his head. 'Nah, is it like a Cantonese stir fry?'

'It's not food, you dummy. It's all about placing things in the right place in your home to give it a flow. Like a natural harmony.'

Tony gave Terry a sidelong glance. He had never seen the home décor and design side of Terry before. 'I suppose when Ma is finished with him, she could leave his head in the hall and a leg on the landing and maybe a foot in the bathroom.'

They both laughed. At the end of the day, they were both professional killers and the day you start getting sympathy for your victims is the day you become a victim.

Terry looked up. 'Here comes our boy now. Let's take him to the lock-up and see if we can persuade him to change his mind!'

Steve Bender emerged from Ron Blazer's studio. He looked up into the sun and felt the warmth wash over his face. Today was going to be a good day. He had five grand in his account from Ron Blazer and a contract with a soon to be resurgent Jimmy Wayne. He felt confident that the tide of his luck was turning. He couldn't believe it when he saw the reviews of one of Jimmy's gigs at the Riviera and he was stunned to hear the news that Jimmy had a record deal with Small Print. With Michael Owen producing, this record had every chance of doing very well. When Jimmy was young, he was naïve and he had managed to milk a living off the back of Jimmy's brush with fame. Even better, he had neglected to pass any onto Jimmy. As far as Steve Bender was concerned, if an artist was gullible enough to get taken advantage of, it was his social duty to do so. He had done it many times which was why, with his reputation going before him, he had been unable to sign any new talent for over two years. Jimmy resurfacing at the top was an unexpected bonus. The fact that Jimmy had just slagged him off on live TV didn't faze him at all. When you have no feelings it's hard to get them hurt. Jimmy's outburst had just raised his profile even further. With a skip in his step, he headed for his beat-up Ford. I'll be upgrading that soon, he thought.

Before he could reach his car an Escalade with blacked out windows rolled across his path. The passenger door swung open and a bald-headed man the size of a line backer jumped out. Tony C looked intimidating, but he was the owner of a lovely smile. He beamed at Steve Bender.

'Hi, Mr Bender?'

Steve paused, unsure whether to confirm or deny. The man was a monster, but he did have a nice smile. 'Who are you?'

Tony smiled again. 'I work for Jimmy Wayne's management. My boss would like to negotiate a deal with you to relinquish your contract with Jimmy Wayne.' Steve smiled. He had hoped this would happen, maybe he could make a quick killing and out. Unfortunately, for Steve Bender, Ma Lantern wasn't one for a quick killing, she preferred it slow, real slow.

'Sorry fellas, Jimmy Wayne ain't for sale.'

'You don't know how much my boss is willing to pay yet, Mr Bender.' Steve thought about it for a moment and Tony added. 'Can't do any harm to find out, can it?'

That was true he thought, maybe he should go and find out what the opening offer was. If it was in the ballpark of what he wanted he could always negotiate.

'Ok, I got my car over there, I'll follow you.'

Tony smiled again. 'No need, it's not far from here and we will bring you back afterwards.'

That much was true. If he accepted their offer, they would bring him back. Sadly for Steve Bender, the overriding emotion in his life was greed. It had ruined most of his friendships and had made it impossible for him to form any meaningful relationships. Maybe, he had thought, when I do have enough, I will be able to settle down. But no amount would ever be enough for him. Greed was like a drug, when he had money, he wanted more and when he didn't, getting some was all consuming. Falling prey to his weaker instincts he agreed to Tony C's kind offer.

'Can't do any harm, can it?'

Terry nodded to him as he climbed into the back of the Escalade. Whether he lived or died was up to him now.

'Hi there Mister Bender, my name's Terry, we're going to take you to meet Mister Lantern.'

Steve nodded. 'He Jimmy's manager?'

'He's more of an investor and a shareholder in the label. He's invested a lot in Jimmy's comeback, as you can imagine, he was unaware of Jimmy being in contract with anyone so he is keen to find an accommodation with you.'

This was music to Steve Bender's ears. This Jack Lantern must have sunk a fair amount of money into Jimmy's relaunch.

'Oh, I'm sure we can do that, gonna cost him a lot of money though.'

Terry looked over at Tony. 'Mister Lantern has a lot of money, Mister Bender, but I would advise you not to push him too hard, he's a very tough negotiator!'

Tony shook his head; it didn't look like this guy was going to listen to reason.

'Is this going to take long?' Steve was impatient to find out what the offer was so that he could find someone to make a better offer. This guy Lantern sounded desperate. Way too eager, this would be like taking candy from kids.

Terry shook his head. 'No, the office is only ten minutes away, it's between Ventura Boulevard and the LA River.'

'Ok then, put your foot down.'

Terry frowned. This clown was starting to get on his nerves, maybe he should just take him straight to Ma. He remembered the last time he had been in the dungeon when Ma was doing her thing. He shuddered; this guy was a prick but maybe he deserved a chance.

They pulled up in front of Jack's unit. It was in a quiet commercial street. There was a gym on the corner and a sushi take-away kitchen next door.

'This way, Mister Bender.'

Steve looked at Tony. 'This his head office? Don't look much.'

It wasn't Jack's office at all. His name appeared nowhere on the deeds. It was his undercover place where he could hide stolen goods. It was also where he could bring potential problems to be resolved. Once through the small entrance foyer there was an open plan office space. It had been soundproofed and all the doors locked automatically when you entered. Once in you could only open them with the key card.

'This is a subsidiary office; we got some storage space here as well and Mister Lantern uses it for an overflow area when we have products that need long-term storage.'

'Your boss isn't just in showbusiness then?' said Steve, looking around.

'He's into everything, as long as it makes money.'

'So where is he then?'

Terry switched on a forty-eight-inch screen that was on the wall in front of them.

'Take a seat Mister Bender, Mister Lantern is in Las Vegas so we are going to do a video call.'

'Oh, ok.' Steve was slightly disappointed at this; he was hoping to be able to negotiate in person.

The connection rang and then the screen was filled with a vison of Jack Lantern at his Las Vegas desk. He saw that Terry and Tony were with Steve Bender and waited for Terry to give him his lead.

'We got Mister Bender with us, Mister Lantern, as you requested. I was telling him that you wanted to come to an arrangement with him over the Jimmy Wayne contract.'

Jack understood immediately. Terry was trying to set up a situation where they could make this go away to avoid Ma getting involved. Jack turned on the charm, not something that came naturally to him.

'Hi there, Mister Bender, it's a pleasure to meet you.' It wasn't, but Jack was being pragmatic, for now.

'Nice to meet you too, Jack. I believe I have something that you want.'

Boy this guy was pretty cocksure, thought Jack but he kept on smiling.

'To be fair Mister Bender, I think we already have what we want but it seems to me that you did have a contract with Jimmy over twenty years ago, and I would like to give you some recompense, being as Jimmy is about to become very active again.'

Terry and Tony looked at each other, surprised at how delicately Jack was handling the matter.

Steve Bender smiled smugly. 'Well, that's very nice of you Mister Lantern but I think you will find that my contract supersedes yours and Jimmy is in breach of his contract. It wasn't defined over any set period.'

Jack wanted to step through the screen and batter this guy to death with his bare fists, but he kept the smile on his face. He spoke slowly.

'Look Steve, can I call you Steve?' Steve nodded. 'We have acted in good faith and invested a lot of money in Jimmy's comeback. Twenty years is a long time and we could very easily dispute the validity of the contract but we don't want to do that.' He smiled. 'Let's do a deal and move on.'

Steve Bender thought he could smell money. This Jack Lantern seemed to have it, and he wanted it. He was obviously worried because his investment was in jeopardy. Steve Bender was arrogant enough to believe that he was in a strong position.

'Look Jack, you seem like a nice guy.' Terry and Tony were behind Steve and were both shaking their heads. Jack could see them and had to try hard to suppress a smile. 'But you got no cards. Let me tell you how this thing plays out. You need Jimmy because you have invested heavily in him. I have him contractually tied to me so unless you pay me a lot of money, I think I will be calling the shots.'

Behind Steve Bender, Terry mimed a scream of horror. Jack tried to supress a smile once more. This Bender guy really thought he had all the cards. Jack knew he had none. It was the only reason he hadn't exploded with anger. He was such an arrogant ass.

'Well, that's not the way I would have put it Steve, sounds a bit uncivil.' Jack paused for a moment and punched some numbers into a calculator. 'What if I was to offer you twenty thousand dollars in cash to rip that contract up?'

Terry and Tony were surprised by this, they thought Jack would only go half that. Seems he really wasn't keen on letting his Momma have some fun in the cellar. Steve Bender didn't think much of Jack's offer. He laughed in Jack's face, never a wise move.

'You're kidding me. This contract is worth a fortune. Jimmy's going to make millions over the next couple of years.'

'Are you sure, Steve? Music is a very subjective business. We have put a lot into this new album but there are no guarantees, apart from the one I have just offered you.'

Steve sneered. 'You're gonna have to do better than that. I know this business and I have a pretty good idea of what is good and what is bad, and this is definitely good – very good. You need to be looking at around the million mark.'

Jack smiled and chuckled quietly to himself. 'Look Steve, you're playing way out of your depth here. We can go to court and tie you up for years. We have the money and we will. My guess is that you haven't got a pot to piss in, so you're going to lose.'

Jack had a point, but Steve wasn't in the mood to be intimidated.

'If we get tied up in court, how are you going to re-launch Jimmy's career?'

Jack nodded. 'You have a point Steve, so I'm going to give you my final, very generous, offer.' Jack paused for a moment and

Terry and Tony hung on his words. They knew that Steve Bender's life now hung in the balance. If he didn't accept the offer Jack was about to make, he would be condemning himself to death, a slow and painful death. 'I'm going to double that offer Steve. Forty thousand dollars to rip up the contract and walk away.'

Terry and Tony were surprised, that was a very generous offer. The boss must be getting squeamish in his old age. All Steve heard was weakness. Jack had just doubled his offer; this guy was desperate. He shook his head.

'You are kidding, Jack. Two hundred and fifty thousand minimum; to make that happen.'

Terry winced, expecting Jack to erupt. Instead he just picked up his cigar from the ashtray and lit it. He then drew deeply, very deeply, on it. The tip turned red and then molten red as he sucked harder. By the time he had stopped drawing it in there was a white-hot glow. It looked like a furnace; Jack was a lot angrier than he was letting on.

'Steve, I think I should warn you that if you don't take my offer I will be forced to hand this matter over to my mother.'

Steve hesitated for a moment. Had he heard Jack correctly? He laughed in Jack's face.

'Huh, did you just threaten me with your mother?'

Jack nodded. 'Trust me, Steve. My mother is the toughest negotiator you will ever meet. Imagine Josef Mengele in a dress.'

History wasn't Steve Bender's strong point. 'Who's he, some cross-dressing dude?'

'No, Steve, he was a Nazi torturer.' Jack spoke quietly. 'My mother is the devil in a dress. You really don't want to have to negotiate with her. Take the forty thousand dollars in cash, plus the money you made from the interview. For a man with a contract that has sat doing nothing for over twenty years I would say that this is a golden pay day. An unexpected and unearned windfall.'

Terry leaned forwards. 'Take the money Mister Bender, you really don't want to meet Jack's momma.'

Tony chimed in. 'Terry's right, take the money.'

Jack found it quite amusing to see two of the hardest thugs he had ever had working for him trying to talk this guy out of going to see his mother. He was even mildly amused at himself offering so much to make him go away. He really didn't want his Ma to go back to her murdering ways. It gave the house a nasty vibe and it made her crazy for weeks afterwards. He wished he could just get Terry to break Steve Bender's neck right here and now, but his mother would get the truth out of him – she always did. She just sensed if someone was lying to her. If it wasn't him, it would be Terry or Steve that were broken down by her questioning. Steve's only chance was to take the deal.

'Take the deal Steve, the boys are right.'

Steve just sat there. He was momentarily confused. Three grown men were telling him that if he didn't agree to the deal on offer, he was going to have to go and see the boss's mother. He had been in many negotiations, many heated, but never had he been in one this strange. There was a small voice in the back of his head warning him that something was very wrong here. The way they spoke about Jack's mother. They seemed genuinely afraid. These boys were crazy to think he could be intimidated. He looked at Jack.

'How old is your mother, Jack?'

'She's seventy-four, but don't ever tell her I told you.'

Steve laughed again. 'Seventy-four! I think I can handle a seventy-four-year-old woman in a negotiation.'

'How old do you think the devil is Steve? Because my mother is the devil. Don't tell me I didn't try and warn you.'

Steve laughed nervously. 'I knew LA was crazy and I know Vegas is crazier still, but do you really think I am going to fall for this crock of shit?'

Nobody said a word. For a few silent moments the fate of Steve Bender hung in the balance. The little voice in the back of his head was shouting louder now. 'Take the money, take the money.' He ignored it but it didn't stop. 'There is something wrong here. Take the money.'

They say a leopard can never change its spots, and Steve Bender was a creature driven by greed. He could have forty thousand in cash and walk away but he wasn't built that way. It was never enough. If they were offering that now he could double it, treble it. It was there and he could taste it.

The voice in his head was screaming now. 'For God's sake, take the money!' But greed makes a lot of noise and for some it drowns out everything else, even the voice of reason. He smiled.

'Let's go and meet your momma.'

Behind him Terry and Tony let out a sigh.

'Now you've gone and done it, Steve.'

He ignored both of them and looked at Jack in his Vegas office. 'Guess I will be seeing you in Vegas then, Jack.' He was cocky and self-assured.

Jack slowly shook his head. 'No, you won't, Steve. Goodbye!' Jack broke the connection.

That was a strange way to end the conversation, he thought. He turned to speak to Terry just in time to see Tony's fist come pounding into the side of his head.

———◆———

When he came around some four hours later, he was in a darkened room. There were no windows. He felt like he had been drugged and beaten. Then he remembered being hit by Tony. He tried to get up from the chair he was in, but his feet and his wrists were fastened to the chair. With rising panic, he tried to move the chair, but it was bolted to the floor. The voice in the back of his head was moaning now, quietly, but it was terrified. Something was very wrong here. To his left he heard the sound of a key in a lock and a door swung open. A light switch was thrown, and there in the door was a woman. He glanced around the room; it had a stone floor with a drain in the middle. He looked back to the woman. She couldn't be Jack Lantern's mother, she had long blond hair and a very tidy figure. She moved slowly and sinuously like a big cat stalking its prey. He was about to speak but she beat him to it.

'You must be Mister Bender, I'm Jackie's momma.' She smiled but there was no warmth in it.

'You can't be, you're not old enough.'

She smiled and moved over to him and ran her hand across his cheek. 'Oh, flattery won't get you anywhere Stevie.'

'You don't look seventy-four,' he blurted out. He saw the momentary flash of rage in her eyes but then she smiled.

'Thank you, Stevie, but I think you're trying to flatter me again. I'm not even wearing any make up.' She wasn't, and just like Jack had told her, losing the hooker-chic had taken years off her. Now she looked a very attractive woman in her late fifties. She was mesmerising.

'Why am I tied up? You have no right to kidnap me.'

She stepped back from him. 'But the boys said you insisted on coming to see me.'

Steve Bender was confused. 'To negotiate the sale of Jimmy Wayne's contract, not to be knocked out and tied to a chair.'

Ma smiled. 'The boys obviously didn't tell you I like my negotiating rough.' Her voice purred. Ma stepped back and looked at him. 'You're not a bad-looking fella.'

'What kind of negotiation is this? I'm gonna sue your ass when I get out of here.'

Ma laughed and then slowly started to remove her clothes. She was only wearing cotton sweatpants and a zipped cotton top. She undid the top and revealed breasts that had no right to be that perky. Steve tried to look away, but he couldn't. For a moment he thought that this was some weird game that they were playing on him. Ma Lantern dropped her sweatpants and stood naked before him. Steve smiled.

'You didn't need to tie me up. Let me loose so we can have some proper fun,' he said it with a bravado he didn't feel. Ma laughed and for a moment he thought all would be well.

'Oh, we're not fooling around, Stevie. I just didn't want to get any blood on my clothes!' She leaned past him and brushed his face with her breast. She picked something up from a table behind him; when she leaned back and stood in front of him he could see she was holding a small pair of bolt cutters. She took the little finger of his left hand firmly in her grip.

'This little piggy went to market.'

———————◆———————

When Jack came down for breakfast the next morning, he could hear his mother singing in the kitchen. She sounded happy, energised. He knew what had made her so happy. Stan, his bin man, had been down to the cellar and cleaned up after Ma. Stan cleared up all Jack's bodies. He never killed anyone, but he certainly knew where all the bodies were buried, except most of them weren't buried. They were fed to pigs or encased in a steel box courtesy of a car crusher. Jack owned a string of undertakers and two of them had their own cremation facilities which Jack had made use of on many occasions. He had told Stan to get in early and clear up after Ma.

'Call me when it's done.'

Jack's phone had rung at 7 a.m. 'All done boss.'

'Where did you take him?'

'Blue Diamond.'

Jack nodded to himself. He had an undertakers with a crematorium there. Steve Bender would be nothing but ashes now.

'Boss?' Stan sounded nervous. Jack knew what was coming.

'What is it, Stan?'

Stan hesitated for a moment. 'Ma is getting worse.'

Jack had been expecting this, she was like a vampire that had gone too long between feeds. He didn't want to know the answer but he asked anyway. 'How bad was it?'

'It was bad boss. She snipped off all his fingers and toes.' Jack shuddered but there was more. 'She put tourniquets round them so he didn't bleed out. She took her time boss...' Stan didn't finish his sentence. He had seen a lot in his time but this, it was bad. 'She chopped off his Johnson, boss!' There was horror in Stan's normally unshockable voice.

Jack stood there; he knew his mother was a monster, but she was his mother. He tried to lighten the mood.

'Girls will be girls, Stan.' Stan didn't answer. 'I'll sort you a nice extra bonus for sorting this one for me.'

'Ok boss, thanks.' He rang off.

Jack walked into the kitchen and his mother smiled happily at him.

'Morning, Jackie.' She sang the words happily. 'Sit down, I got some bacon and scrambled eggs on the go.' She looked ten years younger. The heavy make-up had been replaced by a subtler tone, it suited her. 'You and Lena have a good night?'

He nodded; it had been a good night. 'Yeah, we went to Gordon Ramsay's new place, food was great.'

'Oh, that's nice,' she smiled angelically. 'Did Lena enjoy herself?'

'Yeah, she did Ma, we both did.'

'I had a good night too, Jackie.'

'So I heard.'

For a moment she was confused and then she realised that Jackie was talking about Stan. She almost blushed.

'Yeah, I got a bit carried away last night. That Steve Bender was a real asshole.'

'Did you get anything out of him or did you just kill him for fun.'

She flicked Jack a playful look. 'Oh, come on Jackie, you know me, business before pleasure.' She came over to the table and pushed a manilla envelope towards him. Jack looked down at it.

'What's this, a finger?'

She gave him a playful tap on the back of his head. 'Don't be silly Jack, it's the contract he had with Jimmy Wayne. Dumb bastard was carrying the original in his jacket pocket.'

Jack opened it and sure enough it was just as his mother had said. Young Jimmy Wayne had signed an open-ended contract with the late Mister Bender.

'Well done, Ma. I'll shred this after breakfast.' He paused for a moment. 'You get anything else out of him?'

Ma smiled. 'Yes, he said I didn't look my age. For some reason he thought I was seventy-four.'

Jack shrugged. 'Lucky guess?'

'Never mind that, Jackie, there is something you need to see after breakfast.'

Jack winced. 'Please don't tell me you took photos.'

'Don't be stupid, I don't do stuff that could be used against me.'

Jack sighed inwardly with relief. 'What is it then?'

Ma moved the eggs off the stove.

'You know that camera up at the goldmine that Terry left.' Jack nodded. 'I've been watching the feed. The sun has cast the same length shadow every day at exactly the same time.'

'So?' Jack didn't see her point.

Ma sat down opposite Jack. 'This time of year, the days are getting longer by three minutes a day. Those shadows should have moved over the course of a week or more.'

Jack wasn't sure. 'That's hard to spot for sure, Ma.'

'Maybe, but I spotted it. There's something else.'

'What's that?'

'The sun has been out every day.'

'That ain't unusual this time of year.' He was hungry and getting bored of this conversation.

'But it rained up there last week, for two days. I checked!'

Now Jack was interested. 'What are you saying, Ma?'

Ma smiled thoughtfully. 'We are being played Jackie; somebody is showing us a film of the same day every day so that they can go on with their business without us seeing.'

Jack knew his mother was right. She never missed a thing. Looks like he was going to have to get the boys up there to pay another visit.

Ma went back to the stove and dished up Jack's bacon and eggs and placed it before him. He realised he was hungry, but before he ate he had one quick job to do. He picked up his phone and punched in Jimmy Wayne's number. After three rings Jimmy answered.

'Morning, Jack,' he said cautiously.

'Morning, Jimmy. I come bearing good tidings.'

'You emigrating?'

He smiled at Jimmy's cheek. 'That's funny, Jimmy. No, the good news is that Steve Bender has decided not to enforce his contract with you.'

This was good and unexpected news.

'How the hell did you manage that?'

Jack chuckled. 'Well, you know Ma, Jimmy. She casts a long shadow!'

CHAPTER 10

NEW SONGS FOR ANOTHER DAY

Jimmy put his mobile down. Now he knew what the piece of folded writing paper on his bedside table was. He had seen it when he got up for a shower. For a brief moment it had reminded him of all the mornings, after a killing, that he had woken to find a new song waiting for him. That couldn't be the case because he hadn't killed anyone in weeks but Jack's phone call had raised a cloud of doubt in his mind. If Jack had tried to persuade Steve Bender to tear up Jimmy's contract it was doubtful he would have offered the kind of money that Steve Bender would have wanted. There was that last comment as well about his mother casting a long shadow. He had heard many stories about Ma Lantern, but he had never met her. From what he had heard he never wanted to.

Jimmy went over to the bedside table and opened the folded piece of paper. He saw a song, written in his own handwriting. He dropped as if it was electrified. Steve Bender was dead. Jack or Ma had killed him and now he was free from the contract. He picked up the song and read the title. 'Breaking Chains', it was a strong title and summed the situation up quite nicely. Although he hadn't killed Steve Bender personally, he was dead because of Jimmy. He was a threat to Jimmy's success. Jimmy knew from personal experience that he didn't have to actually kill someone to get a new song. As long as the death was linked to Jimmy in some way that was all that was required. The car crash of Sleazy Petersen, the heart attack of Sammy and the death of Davy Digbeth had proved this to be true, and now Steve Bender. Dead because he had dared to challenge Jack Lantern and his mother about Jimmy's old contract. Seemed to Jimmy that to many who crossed his path he had become an angel of death. On the upside the song looked pretty good.

He read the song and it was good. He felt a pang of regret over the death of Steve. He tried to remember the good times they shared when he was trying to break into the big time. But he had none, Steve had only ever used and exploited Jimmy. Wendy floated gently through the wall.

'Hi Jimmy.'

He looked up and smiled. 'I wondered when you would show up.'

'Did you like my entrance? I know you don't like my sudden appearances.'

He smiled. 'Yeah, that was nice Wendy, subtle even.'

She feigned shyness and spoke with a Southern belle accent. 'I do declare, Mister Wayne, are you flirting with me?'

He shrugged. 'No.'

Her smile faded. 'Well, fuck you then.'

This was the Wendy he knew and loved. He held up the song. 'You seen this?'

Wendy shook her head. 'No, but I knew you were going to be writing one.' She shivered. 'I followed Steve Bender yesterday after the show.' She paused for a moment and smiled. 'Congratulations by the way, Daddy Jimmy.' She rubbed her chin thoughtfully. 'Does that make me an Auntie?'

'Well, if you rule out the fact that we ain't married and you're dead, suppose it does!'

'She does have a nice ass though Jimmy. I can see why you went for her. She's hot now, but she must have been smoking twenty years ago.'

Jimmy nodded and smiled at the recollection of the young Elaine.

'We had some fun but then she wanted something more than I was offering. I was looking for the big career and it was slipping through my fingers. She actually loved me for me. The more I backed away, the harder she chased me.' Jimmy sighed. 'It all got a bit crazy and then it was over. She just upped and went home to Texas, taking our unborn son with her. She should have told me.' Wendy put an arm around him.

'Would you have been interested then?' They both knew the answer to that one. 'So, what you going to do?'

Jimmy took a deep breath. 'Well, if he'll let me, I'd like to get to know him and maybe persuade him to change his name.'

'You should do that Jimmy.'

They sat for a moment thinking about Jimmy actually being a father. To Jimmy's surprise the idea did not fill him with horror.

'You said you followed Steve.' Wendy nodded.

'Wish I hadn't.'

'What happened?'

'Terry and Tony picked him up and took him to an office warehouse set up just between the LA River and Ventura. They hooked up with Jack via a video link in his Vegas office.'

This sounded all too familiar to Jimmy. 'Let me guess. Jack lost his temper and got Terry to beat him to death with a baseball bat.'

Wendy shook her head. 'Surprisingly, no. Jack actually went out of his way to try and talk Steve out of pressing his claim. He even offered him forty thousand dollars in cash to tear up the contract.' Jimmy couldn't believe what he was hearing.

'Wow! I knew the guy was greedy, but you would have thought he would have grabbed the money and ran.'

'You should have seen it, Jimmy. Jack and Terry, even Tony, were trying to persuade him not to try and push his claim. But despite them all telling him that Ma was evil he seemed to think he could walk all over a seventy-four-year-old woman.'

'So, what happened?'

Wendy pulled a face. 'Aww, it was pretty disgusting. She has a cellar under the house on the north side of Vegas – it's like her own personal torture chamber.'

Jimmy winced. 'Did you see it?'

'See it? I was there in the cellar. She had him tied to a chair and the chair was bolted to the floor. She stripped off and—'

Jimmy interrupted her. 'Stripped off? She's in her seventies.'

'Seventy-four,' agreed Wendy, adding, 'she still looks pretty good though.' Jimmy was thankful that he had never met Ma Lantern because that was an image he really didn't want in his head.

'What did she do then?' Wendy shook her head as she remembered the terrible scene.

'She got a pair of bolt cutters and started chopping his fingers off one at a time.'

Jimmy remembered how Jack had threatened to do the same to him the time that Vinny and Carmine had kidnapped him. 'Must be a family trait because Jack was going to chop off all my fingers that night in the quarry.'

'Well, Jack's Ma took it a step further. She chopped them all off and then did the same with all his toes.'

'Must have ruined his pedicure.'

Wendy looked at Jimmy disapprovingly. 'It wasn't funny Jimmy. He screamed like a wild animal caught in a trap. She made it last over an hour.'

'I heard she enjoyed her work.'

'Yes, she enjoys it all right. Her final act was to chop his Johnson off and put it in front of him surrounded by his fingers and toes. She wanted him to look at them as he bled out. It was pretty damn horrific.'

'So why did you stay and watch?'

Wendy shrugged and then smiled brightly. 'Well, the guy was a mean-hearted conman so he kinda had it coming. I wanted to hang around and see if I could see his soul leave his body.'

'Steve Bender didn't have a soul!'

Wendy nodded. 'Apparently not, all I saw leave his body was blood, lots of it.' She thought for a moment. 'And fingers.'

'And toes,' prompted Jimmy.

'How could I forget? Toes and,' a look of distaste spread across her features, 'and his Johnson. Yuck!'

Jimmy sat there contemplating what Steve Bender must have gone through in the last hour of his life. Then he looked at the song. It was pretty good, seemed like a fair exchange to him!

They both sat there lost in their own thoughts. Jimmy was thinking about the recording session today. He was tracking lead vocals. Wendy was still reliving the sights she had seen in Ma Lantern's cellar. Then she remembered what she had been talking about before they had got into the demise of the late Steve Bender.

'That Ron Blazer is a sneaky bastard ain't he?'

Jimmy smiled. 'He sure is, but I reckon I came out ok. The socials have gone crazy, and David was telling me that they have had over ten thousand pre-orders for the album. Like Sonny said, ain't no such thing as bad publicity.'

'Tell that to OJ.'

'Harsh Wendy, very harsh!'

'True but you killed a lot more people than OJ!'

Jimmy frowned.

'Allegedly. OJ was found innocent, and I never killed innocent people.'

'Hello!!'

Jimmy held up a hand of apology. 'Yeah, sorry about that. More manslaughter than murder though.'

Wendy shrugged. 'I'm still just as dead though.'

There was a knock on his bedroom door.

'You coming to breakfast, Jimmy?' It was Kid.

'Yeah, be there in a minute.' He turned back to Wendy, but she had gone. That was Wendy, she blew in and out of his life like an unexpected breeze. He would miss her if she ever stopped coming.

As Jimmy walked out onto the patio, the California sunshine wrapped him in its warm embrace. Far below he could see the madness that was Los Angeles. Home to nearly four million souls. From this viewpoint it seemed like another world. Above the madness, Laurel Canyon was a place he felt safe. Today he would track the final vocals and the album would be done. It was hard to believe that after so many years of being lost in the wilderness he was getting another shot. Great label, great producer, a great band and the best songs he had ever sung. It was a bittersweet feeling. Without the accidental killing of Wendy none of this would be happening. Every track on the record was forged in blood, most of it bad, but blood nonetheless. How could he justify success that was built on death? Jimmy felt sad but he had no regrets. Most of those who died had been total scumbags. As for Wendy and Sammy – Wendy was an accident, and Sammy died laughing. Sleazy Petersen had been forced off the road by Sheriff Pence, he was sure of it. He just couldn't prove it. There was only one piece of the jigsaw that he couldn't place. The body in Ted Baker's pick-up. He needed to find out who it was. The last loose end in the song cycle.

As he stood there mulling over the events that had brought him to this point an idea came to him. 'Blood on The Tracks' would be a great title for a song. Dylan had already been there, but his blood and his tracks would be different. He pulled the notebook he had started carrying from his back pocket and scribbled the title down. He underlined it and had an overwhelming feeling he could write this song unaided by death, and then another idea came to him. 'No Regrets.' He had no regrets. He scribbled it down and then closed the book and noticed Kid had been watching him from his seat on the patio.

'You writing, Jimmy?'

'Kinda.'

Kid looked around but they were alone on the patio. 'You planning on killing someone?' He was only half joking.

Jimmy walked over and sat down opposite him. He pulled out his notebook and carefully removed the song that had appeared this morning. He handed it to Kid.

Kid took it, handling it gently as if it was an unexploded bomb. He opened it and read out loud. 'Breaking Chains.' He read the song and looked up. 'This is good. Who'd you kill?'

'I didn't kill anyone.'

Kid gave him a sidelong glance. 'But this is good.'

Jimmy shrugged. 'Thanks for the vote of confidence but I don't have to kill someone to write a decent song anymore.'

Kid smirked. 'In my experience, you do!' It was a fair comment and Jimmy smiled.

'I wrote "Déjà Vu" without killing anyone, didn't I?'

Kid had to concede that one. 'Yeah, but it's not on the album because it's a duet you wrote for you and Wendy, and Wendy is,' he paused for a moment searching for the right words to convey his point, 'unavailable for touring.'

'But it's still a good song,' he could hear the defensive tone in his voice, 'isn't it?'

Kid held up his hands. 'Ok, I surrender, it's a good song. Is this one completely yours?'

He had to come clean.

'No, it was there on my bedside table when I woke up this morning.'

'I knew it!' Kid seemed pleased as well as vindicated in his assumption. 'Who did you kill?'

Jimmy kept his voice calm and he spoke slowly.

'*I* didn't kill anyone. Ma Lantern killed Steve Bender.'

Understanding flickered in Kids eyes. 'Got it, she killed him because he was after most of your earnings via the contract he had. Jack and Ma would have seen that as a threat to the profitability of their investment, makes sense!'

Jimmy didn't know whether to be impressed by how quickly Kid put it together or shocked by the matter-of-fact way he accepted murder in exchange for decent songs.

'Steve is only dead because he was trying to move in on me, so his death is directly attributable to me, hence the song. He won't be pressing his claim on the contract.'

'Excellent news. Never liked the guy from what I saw on the TV. Pretty sure being dead has improved him!' It was a harsh assessment but Kid never minced his words. He turned back to Jimmy. 'How do you know he's dead?'

'Wendy told me.'

'So, we have it on good authority – from a ghost, that only you can see?'

Jimmy nodded. 'Yep.'

'Well hold the front page!' Kid looked amused. 'I think that maybe you should just say nothing until we get some official comment from the powers that be. Say something now and you are going look guilty when the news breaks. What you going to say to David and Michael if they bring it up?'

Jimmy guessed he would cross that bridge when he came to it. Jack and Ma would quietly dispose of what was left of Steve Bender, but David and Michael were probably already prepping for a legal battle they were never going to have.

'I got it covered,' he said with a confidence he didn't possess. Kid nodded towards the house.

'Now's your chance, the English aristocracy are coming to join us peasants for breakfast.'

Jimmy followed Kid's gaze and walking down the lawn towards them were David and Michael. It occurred to him that Michael also seemed to float gracefully.

'How do they do that?'

'Deportment classes. The English upper classes have their children balancing books on their heads from the moment they can walk.'

Jimmy stared at Kid. 'Why would they do that?'

'I would imagine it's something to do with marrying your cousin.'

Jimmy smiled. 'That's rich coming from a Norwegian.'

Kid looked at him with distain. 'I think you're confusing me with someone from Sweden... it's something of a prerequisite there.' As they bantered back and forth laying waste the reputations of the English upper classes and every living Swede, David and Michael reached them.

'Morning gents,' said David. 'How are we this morning?'

They looked at each other.

'*We* are fine,' said Jimmy.

Michael looked slightly concerned. 'Can we have a chat about this old contract situation over breakfast? I don't like the look of that Bender character.'

'Ah,' said Jimmy, 'I have good news for you. Mister Bender had an offer he couldn't refuse from Jack Lantern and agreed to tear up the contract for a large sum of cash.' They all knew Jack Lantern, David spoke first.

'Do you think he is still alive or is he swimming with the fishes?'

Jimmy thought about it. 'Normally I would say swimming, but Jack seems to think we are going to do very well… Maybe he just bought him off.' They all murmured agreement although none of them believed it.

'Well, that's a problem solved then,' said Michael brightly. 'Shall we eat?'

The possible demise of Steve Bender did not have an effect on their appetites and soon they were all tucking into breakfast.

Joe and Doug had left early to do some sightseeing in Hollywood. All the drum and bass parts had been tracked. They had asked Kid if he wanted to join them – all his guitar parts were done. He declined, preferring to chill out around the studio and take the opportunity to relax, and more to the point, enjoy the excellent catering facilities supplied by Michael.

As they finished breakfast, David poured himself another cup of tea and cleared his throat.

'I think we need to go to Vegas when you've finished tracking the vocals.' He saw the questioning look on Jimmy's face. 'I want you to meet the owner of Carpenters. It's important. We can get some pre-publicity done there and I have arranged some local press.'

'Can't I just stay here and help with the master?' Jimmy wasn't keen to leave.

'I don't think an eight-time Grammy winner needs any help on the mixing desk. Leave Michael to get on with it and you and I can go and get the next phase of the plan into operation.'

'Plan!' Exclaimed Jimmy. 'I've never had a plan before.'

David smiled.

'That much is obvious. Too much at stake now to leave anything to chance.'

There was a lot at stake. Michael and the label would be sixty thousand dollars in the hole by the time the album was made. He had persuaded an old friend to take a chance on Jimmy filling the theatre at Carpenters. Carpenters was at the northern end of the strip. It was a small hotel with a casino but it was most famous as a music venue. The exposure at a place like that would be great for Jimmy, but it had come at a price. Sam Estrin, the owner, had been fair. Jimmy was an unknown commodity. That's why he had moved Jimmy down from the Golden Flamingo, but if he was going to take a chance, he wanted David to share the risk.

'It's going to cost me forty thousand a week to put him on. You underwrite half of it and we gotta deal.'

He had asked what the break-even point was, and Rick had told him two hundred seats. The place held six hundred. Rick would give him a month of doing five nights a week and, if he was hitting the numbers, would renew him. David had the cash and decided to take the risk. He wanted to help his friend, but he also had this feeling they were going to do really well.

'So how much are we getting for playing Carpenters?' Jimmy's question cut through his reverie.

'Twenty K a week and room and board at the hotel thrown in, but that's only if we are filling 60% of the seats.'

Jimmy nodded his approval. 'Not bad, do we get all merch revenue?'

David nodded. 'We do, all vinyl and CD sales as well. They just want the box office and the drinks and food.'

'That sounds like a decent deal.'

'It is, Jimmy.'

'How much are we risking in underwriting?'

David didn't say anything at first. He hadn't expected Jimmy to think about such things. 'You offering to help?'

Jimmy's face slowly formed into a satisfied smile.

'As it happens, I'm offering to underwrite everything.'

David couldn't help it, he laughed. 'With what?'

Jimmy looked over at Kid and he nodded. David noticed the exchange.

'What's occurring boys, last I knew you two hadn't got a pot to piss in!'

'Just so happens that Kid and I made an investment a few years ago and it's done very well.'

'Very well,' smiled Kid.

'Is it legal?' David was smiling but he did wonder what the boys had invested in that appeared to have given such a return.

'Really, David, how long have you known me, seven years?'

'Give or take.'

'Have you ever known me do anything illegal?'

'Obviously!'

'Really, like what?'

'Picking up chips that customers have dropped in the casino.'

Jimmy winced. 'Oh, you seen me do that?'

David nodded. 'It's amazing how much gets dropped.' David was staring at him like a teacher would to a naughty schoolboy.

'Ok! But they were a trip hazard.'

David continued. 'As I was saying, apart from picking up chips in the casino, filling your pick-up on the casino account at the gas station, and charging drinks to guests' rooms.'

Jimmy looked surprised. 'How did you know it was me?'

'The barmen used to make a note of every drink you ordered on guest tabs!'

Kid looked disapprovingly at Jimmy.

'Bad error, Jimmy. What you should have done is ordered room service to their room number and asked the waiter to just knock the door and leave it outside. Then you could have just strolled by and picked it up!' Kid smirked like a master criminal.

Jimmy held up his hands. 'Ok, apart from those three things, have you ever known me to be dishonest.'

David thought about it for a moment. 'Not in a major criminal sense. Are you and Kid talking about a substantial amount of money?' Kid and Jimmy looked at each other and then nodded to David.

'Very substantial.'

'Can I ask how you came by it?'

'Does it matter David? If we are prepared to take the risk of underwriting away from you, why would that bother you?'

David leaned back in his chair.

'It's not that I doubt you boys,' he shot them a smile, 'which of course I do! It's just that this is a deal I have set up. If you have dirty money and I use it to pay then should anything go wrong it's going to reflect very badly on me, and I can't have that. I still have a good reputation in Vegas.'

'Apart from the shagging,' said Jimmy. Kid pricked up his ears.

'What have you been up to David?'

David ignored the suggestive look on Kid's face. 'Well apart from making the mistake of telling Jimmy a secret, very little. All concerned parties are no longer involved in the Las Vegas scene.'

'Did you have them killed?'

'Really, Kid, a gentleman never tells, but, and it's a big but... I do have something of a reputation in Vegas amongst some very powerful players and I am not going to risk it by using money without provenance!'

Jimmy didn't understand. 'This is American money. Ain't nothing from France.'

For a moment David didn't understand what Jimmy was trying to say, he looked over to Kid for a clue.

'I think Jimmy thought you were talking about Provence.' They looked at each other and shook their heads. David turned back to Jimmy.

'Provenance means proof of where the money comes from. We have to know its bona fide!' He saw Jimmy's brow knitting in confusion. 'No, I'm not talking about Argentina.'

'What?' Jimmy was looking more confused than ever.

The conversation was becoming a jigsaw with missing pieces. David clarified the situation.

'I need to know that your money is legitimate. It has to be legal. I – we – can't afford any comebacks.'

'It's legitimate David, I promise you that.'

'Can you, Kid? Because that's what I am going to need.'

'It's in our bank accounts, all accounted for and all tax paid. It's been set up to look like payments from touring and advances against sales. It won't be an issue.'

David looked back and forth between them. 'What the hell have you boys been up to?'

'All that glitters, David – sometimes it is gold!'

Jimmy's words didn't explain a thing. If anything they made it more complicated. Talking to Jimmy and Kid was clearly going to get him precisely nowhere.

'Let me see the accounts and then, if I'm happy, we can proceed.' Jimmy and Kid smiled.

'Now that wasn't so hard, was it?' said Jimmy.

David was suddenly feeling very tired, despite the fact that it was only 9.45 a.m. Talking to Jimmy and Kid was like trying to knit spaghetti. He could feel the distant throb of a headache beginning to beat behind his temples. His saviour appeared in the shape of Michael as he poked his head through the studio door.

'Hey Jimmy! Ready for you.' His head disappeared back into the studio.

Jimmy got up. 'Time to track the final vocals.' He smiled, took a final sip of coffee and walked briskly across the patio to the studio.

CHAPTER 11
AKSEL'S GOLD

Aksel watched the little dot winking on the map displayed on his laptop and it was clear that the trip he had made to Vegas two nights before had been time well spent. The tracker he had placed on Terry Moist's pick-up was working and it was clear that he was headed to Aksel's ranch. He knew they would be back; having spoken to Kid, he also knew exactly who they were and what they were coming for. He tried to think of the best way to play it. He could be dealing with anything from two to five thugs, unless of course there was another pick-up in tow. He could kill them all very easily the second they pulled up. They would be dead before they knew what hit them. The idea was attractive, spoilt only by the fact that the man who had sent them would not be there. For his preferred option to work Aksel needed to chop the head off the dragon, but Jack Lantern would not be there with his men.

Option two would be to confront them, demand to know why they had been spying on him. No point in avoiding it, Jack Lantern's men had obviously worked out that he had discovered their camera and fooled them. These were not people you could just tell to go away. These were hardened criminals who would demand to know what he was hiding, even though it was none of their damn business. Aksel breathed deeply. He needed to be calm, stay focused. There would be questions asked about Jimmy and Kid. How would he explain that away? He thought for a moment. He and Kid had been friends since childhood, played in the same band and served in the SB together. All this was traceable. He had to assume that Jack Lantern would be able to discover this. His organisation had its fingers in many pies. The truth, or a version of it, was the best defence. Just a case of an old friend dropping in to see his best mate as he was passing. It was plausible and would explain Jimmy being with him. If that didn't work, he would just kill them all!

————◆————

Back in Vegas, Jack was feeling disgruntled. There were things happening that he couldn't explain. Jack was a creature of certainty. If he didn't understand a situation, he couldn't control it. Why had Jimmy and Kid diverted miles from their route to go to the remote ranch? Was it a co-incidence that two million dollars had shown up in Jimmy's bank account? He suspected it was related to his visit to the ranch. It had been a goldmine once. What if the owner had found a new seam?

Greed can play havoc with a man's mind. For all his wealth, Jack had a horrible feeling he was missing out on something. He just hadn't worked out what that something was yet!

'Who you sent up to the goldmine, Jackie?' Ma's voice broke his chain of thought.

'Terry and Tony with Danny and the new guy.'

Ma nodded approvingly. 'The one that strangled his fiancée?'

Jack nodded. 'Yeah, he was keen to go. I guess after ten years in prison he needs to make some dough.'

'That one's mean,' Ma smiled appreciatively. 'I like him!'

Jack shrugged. 'He strangled his girlfriend, what's not to like?'

'No, no, Jackie, he strangled his fiancée. That shows real commitment.'

'It might also show that he's a bit dumb.' Jack slurped the last of his coffee. 'But he's violent and he's cheap, which makes him employee of the month material in my book.'

Ma nodded approvingly. Her son had turned out better than she had expected. By her standards he was soft, but she did set a very high bar where violence and intimidation were concerned.

'You going into the office?'

Jack nodded. 'Yeah, I've got a meeting. Can you keep an eye on the goldmine situation? I asked Terry to report to you.'

'No problem,' she replied. 'Be my pleasure.'

————◆————

Aksel placed the Glock 19 semi-automatic in a crack in the rocks halfway down his drive. It had an extended mag with thirty-three rounds. He believed in planning. Across his property he had hidden six other Glocks and an array of grenades; he was nothing if not thorough. He had prepared meticulously. He didn't want this confrontation to turn violent but if it did, he was going to be ready. Once he was sure all his bases were covered, he went back into the house and waited. The flashing dot on the map was getting very near.

Terry Moist turned onto the track that led to Aksel Lund's ranch and pulled the pick-up over. He turned off the ignition.

'Keep an eye on the drive, let me know if you see anyone.'

Tony nodded and Terry climbed out of the cab and walked briskly down the track until he came to the point where it started to curve. He scrambled across the rocks to where his camera still stood as he left it, only now it had a new screen in front of it playing the same day on repeat. Not only had he been rumbled but he had been played. For once in his life, he felt fear. Whoever he was dealing with was clever. Suddenly a voice spoke right by his ear.

'Looking for something?'

Terry spun around and reached for his gun. Before he could, a hand darted inside his jacket and removed it. When he realised exactly what had happened, he was staring down the barrel of his own gun.

'This what you looking for?' Aksel Lund was a striking man. Tall, muscular and blonde with his hair pulled back in a long pony-tail, he looked every inch the Viking. Terry held up his hands.

'Easy now, I ain't looking for trouble.'

Aksel smiled an easy smile. He seemed totally relaxed. This made Terry tense.

'Come to pick up your spy camera?'

Terry wasn't sure how best to answer that question. 'Yeah, I guess you're wondering why I left it.'

Aksel nodded. 'It had crossed my mind.'

Terry lowered his hands but Aksel kept the gun aimed at him.

'You had visitors here the day before I came here, didn't you?'

'What's that to do with you?' Aksel stepped towards Terry. His physique was intimidating. 'I think you owe me an explanation, now!'

Aksel never raised his voice but as Terry looked into his cold, unblinking stare he knew he was in the presence of someone he could not intimidate.

'Your friend, Mister Oscarson, was with an employee of my boss. He was late getting to LA for an important recording and when we checked his phone records, we noticed he had been up here, and my boss wanted to know why.'

Aksel nodded thoughtfully. 'Your boss normally leave spy cameras at every place his employees go?'

When he thought about it, Terry realised the answer was yes.

'He's a cautious man!'

Aksel emptied the mag from Terry's gun and laid it on the rock. He stretched over and picked up Terry's spy camera.

'Yours, I believe.' He offered it to Terry who took it with an embarrassed smile.

'Thanks... Can I have my gun back too?'

'If you take out the two mags in your pocket.'

For a moment Terry considered lying but a quick glance at the cool hard eyes of Aksel Lund made him reconsider. He smiled. 'Let's just leave it there for now while we resolve this little misunderstanding.'

In the car Tony was wondering what was taking Terry so long.

'Go take a look what's keeping Terry.' He had meant for Danny Minx to go but, before he could stop him, Brian McCumber was out of the door and climbing the rocks.

'He's a keen one,' observed Danny wryly. 'Must be all that time banged up in prison, needs all the fresh air he can get!'

Tony hadn't been involved in the hiring of Brian. 'He the one that strangled his girlfriend?'

'Fiancée!'

Tony shook his head. 'What a dumb fuck, why not just dump her and then kill her later when you're not linked to her. Swear to God, crime is not attracting the right class of people these days.'

Danny leaned forwards. 'Brian ain't no criminal, he's crazy. You know where he strangled his fiancée?'

Tony shrugged. 'Does it matter?'

Danny snorted. 'Kinda, he strangled her at the hotel the night before the wedding.'

Tony raised his eyebrows. 'That's crazy. No way he would get his deposit back for that.'

Brian McCumber had jogged down the track until, approaching the curve, he heard the voices of Terry and another man. He climbed up the rocks and peered over. Terry was standing opposite what appeared to be a Viking.

'Who the fuck are you?' His less than diplomatic question brought a broad smile to the Viking's face. Brian was disconcerted, usually people were afraid of him.

'The owner of the property on which you are trespassing. Why don't you just close that dumb mouth of yours and crawl back down where you came from so your boss and I can discuss things.'

The red mist descended and what little rational thought that Brian McCumber possessed was consumed by an overwhelming desire to batter this tall, blond stranger. He reached for his gun but, before he got there, Aksel had deftly picked up the magazine, reloaded it and cocked Terry's gun. It was pointed directly at his heart.

'Leave it, Brian!' barked Terry. But Brian didn't want to leave it. He sprung up on top of the rock.

'One more step, son,' Aksel didn't need to finish the sentence. Brian paused for a moment and Terry barked out a direct order.

'Get back in the pick-up NOW!'

Brian stood there confused. A stranger was pointing his boss's gun at him and his boss was ordering him back into the pick-up.

'Now, Brian, me and—' he looked at Aksel but Aksel didn't offer his name. He turned back to Brian. 'We are just going to resolve this little situation and I'll be with you.'

Brian wasn't happy but the red mist was lifting now, replaced by confusion. He knew Terry was a badass. Why was he letting this freak jerk him around? For a moment the anger welled but the look in Terry's eyes convinced him to leave. He clambered down. Aksel waited until he disappeared from view.

'That boy's got anger management issues, you need to watch him,' said Aksel.

Terry shrugged. 'He's new, just got out a few weeks ago. My boss is big into rehabilitating offenders, second chance and all that.'

Aksel frowned. 'Gonna have his work cut out with that one.' He waited until Brian's footsteps had faded, then turned to Terry. 'So, what's the real reason you're here?'

Terry tried to appear innocent. His acting ability wasn't really up to it.

'Like I said, Kid and Jimmy are important investments for my boss. When they didn't turn up he got concerned. Jimmy is going to be a star and we need to know what he was up to up here in the middle of nowhere. If there is any scandal, we need to be able to shut it down.'

Aksel looked around at the empty expanse.

'You see any scandal?'

Terry followed his gaze. 'No, just rocks and shit.'

Aksel removed the magazine on the Colt and handed it back to Terry.

'That's us done then, you have a safe drive back.' Aksel was ushering Terry from his property but Terry wasn't ready to go.

'So, what do you do up here?'

Aksel fixed him with a hard stare. 'It's where I live.'

'Used to be a gold mine didn't it?' he probed.

'Fifty years ago maybe. It wasn't a mine though. There's a river which comes out of the mountain about a mile below here. They used to pan down there, even did some open cast trenching to gather in the gold, but that thing ran dry years ago.'

'So why was the ranch up here?'

'Because the valley sometimes floods in winter and early spring, it's too open down there. There was nowhere to build a secure place, so they made the ranch and the compound up here.'

Terry looked around. 'Any chance of a tour?'

Aksel slowly shook his head. 'Afraid not, I'm not in the business of showing snoopers around. You just get back in your vehicle and go.'

'Now that ain't very neighbourly,' said Terry.

For the first time Aksel let his anger show. 'I'm not your neighbour,' he hissed.

Terry backed off. 'Ok, I get the message, it's just that my boss, he's kinda persistent and he won't take my word for it unless I do have a good look around.'

Aksel wanted to kill these men, he felt the need to do it but he knew it would just complicate things. He sighed.

'Anybody ever tell you that you're a pain in the ass?'

'Everybody, including my parents.' Terry smiled.

Aksel smiled too. 'Ok, I had a boss like that once. If I give you a quick tour, will you leave me alone?'

Terry held up his hand. 'I promise.'

They climbed down onto the drive and met Tony and Brian who were jogging up the track. Now Aksel was looking at a three-to-one situation, and Brian was still looking for a fight. He lunged towards Aksel. Aksel rocked back and dodged the blow, grabbing Brian's arm and twisting it backwards as the weight of his lunge took him forwards. He turned rapidly and twisted the arm around and upwards. Brian was forced to follow and somersaulted forwards trying to take the rotation out of his arm. He landed on his back with a thud. Aksel flicked the arm across his knee and there was a sickening crack as it broke. Brian screamed.

'You do that again, you won't have an arm,' hissed Aksel.

It all happened so quickly that even Terry hadn't moved. Aksel let go of Brian's arm and, raising his voice above the level of Brian's screaming, called to Terry.

'Come on then if you want a tour.' Tony stepped forward but Aksel held up his hand.

'Not you, just him.' Tony looked to Terry for guidance and Terry gave him a brief nod.

'Ok, let's go take a look.'

Aksel looked down at Brian as he moaned. 'Shut up, it's only a broken arm. Thought you were a tough guy.' He backed away slowly, watching all of his visitors. Once he and Terry were around the bend, he switched his full attention to Terry.

'You're pretty handy with your fists,' said Terry.

'I didn't hit him, I just used his own momentum against him, you got a problem with that?'

Terry shook his head. 'No, he asked for it. Guy's a hot head, the boss should never have hired him.' They walked for a few seconds in silence and then Terry spoke quietly. 'Ex forces?'

Aksel nodded. 'Long time ago,' he pursed his lips. 'You never forget though.'

'I guess not. You know I'm going to have to listen to that motherfucker whine all the way back to Vegas?'

Aksel grinned. 'You want I could kill him for you? Be a much quieter journey?'

'It's tempting.'

As they walked, despite his small talk, Aksel could see that Terry was absorbing every detail of the place, looking for something that didn't fit in with his story.

'You want a look in the ranch first?'

'Please.'

When they reached the ranch, Aksel took him through each room like an estate agent showing a house, only quicker. He then took him across to the barn. The false wall filled with tools and shelves hid the way into the cave and Terry saw nothing that looked suspicious. They walked back out into the yard.

'You satisfied now that I don't have wall-to-wall hookers or a cocaine den?'

'Yep!' It was a concise answer delivered in Terry's Texan drawl. 'Only thing you could die of out here is boredom.'

Aksel smiled. 'Just how I like it. Me and Kid go back a long way. He and Jimmy were just passing and called in to catch up.

They stopped the night, and we had a meal and a few beers, end of story.'

Terry couldn't argue. 'Thanks for your time, Mister?' He tried again to get Aksel's name, but Aksel wasn't playing.

'You're welcome.' Aksel watched Terry walk back down the drive. 'Oh, just one thing.' Terry turned back. 'You bring that hothead here again and I will kill him.'

'If I don't kill him first,' smiled Terry.

Aksel stood and watched Terry walk down the track until he disappeared around the corner. He regretted breaking the idiot's arm. He didn't want to show his skills. Too late now. This wasn't the end of the matter; they would be back, and he was going to have to kill them.

As Terry reached the pick-up Tony came up to meet him.

'Brian's hurting pretty bad.'

'Good,' said Terry angrily. 'Who the hell does he think he is?'

'Chuck Norris.'

A smile cracked the edge of Terry mouth. 'You're a funny guy, Tony.'

He shrugged. 'That's what they say.'

They walked up to the pick-up and Brian was groaning in the back. In between waves of pain, he was cursing and telling Danny what he was going to do with the fucking Viking when he got his hands on him. Danny wasn't listening.

'Whatever you say Brian, but he kicked your ass pretty bad so I wouldn't be shouting too loud, just in case he hears you.'

'Fuck you, Danny!'

From outside the pick-up Tony and Terry exchanged looks.

'Shall we just whack this guy on the way back? He's trouble.'

Tony thought about it for a moment. 'Bound to be some old mine shafts around this area.'

'Is that a yes?' Terry asked.

'In principle, I'm all for whacking him, but he doesn't work for me. He works for Jack and we can't just kill him because he's annoying.'

'You sure?'

'Pretty much, Terry. My girlfriend is in HR and from what she tells me, it would be frowned on.'

Terry laughed. 'Shit Tony, you're on fire today.' He pulled some gum out of his pocket. 'You want some?' Tony shook his head. Terry pulled a piece from the wrapping and popped it in his mouth. 'You know Jack will probably kill him when we get back.'

Tony knew it. Jack didn't like people who couldn't follow instructions. Come to that, neither did Terry. Brian was clearly unhinged and totally unsuited to the pressure situations that he would face working for Jack.

'Did you see the way he put Brian down?'

Terry nodded.

'He's got special skills.'

'And a bag full of secrets,' said Terry.

'You find anything?'

'Nothing, it was all clean as a whistle,' Terry rubbed his chin. 'Something doesn't add up here. Don't know what it is, but it's just wrong.'

Tony looked puzzled. 'So, what do we tell Jack?'

'Nothing. I say we give this place a clean bill of health. We found nothing. Let's just leave it at that. If we go back telling Jack we are suspicious of this place and that the owner is ex special forces he's going to want us back here and tearing the place apart.'

It all made sense to Tony, he nodded. 'Suits me, I don't fancy tangling with him. How do we explain Brian's arm?'

Terry laughed. 'Watch and learn Tony.' Terry went over to the passenger door and opened it. Brian's moaning became louder.

'Shut the fuck up, Brian.' As always, his bedside manner was impeccable.

'But my arm.'

'Your arm is broken. Man the fuck up. It was your own fault. Shouldn't have fallen off that rock.'

Brian stopped moaning. 'I didn't fall off the rock, you saw what happened.'

Terry shrugged. 'We all saw you fall off the rock,' he looked at Danny. 'What did you see Danny?'

'He fell off the fucking rock!'

Brian turned to Danny. 'I didn't, you saw what happened.'

'Yeah, you fell off a rock.'

Before Brian could argue any further Terry leaned over him. 'Now listen closely Brian. You're new here and you don't understand how Jack Lantern works, so I'm going to tell you.' Brian went to interrupt but Terry raised a finger to his lips. 'Jack told us to come up here and scout around. He didn't say come and start a fight. If he wanted that he would have told me so. If he finds out that you went for that guy, he would probably beat you to death with a baseball bat.' Brian went even paler. 'Or, if he was in a good mood, give you a good beating and sack you.'

———◆———

Jack sat back in his office chair. Terry had just called and let him know that there was nothing going on up at the old goldmine near Etna. Jack didn't buy it. Why would the guy go to the trouble of setting up a false view for them to watch? That was clever. He made a mental note to come back to this at a later date. The sudden arrival of untraceable money coincided with Jimmy and Kid's arrival at the goldmine. He smelt a rat, a very wealthy one. Whilst he was pondering the situation, his intercom rang. It was Margo, his secretary.

'Got a visitor for you Jack.'

Jack glanced at his diary. 'I don't have a visitor.'

'Well I got one here.' Margo had been with Jack a long time. She was a tough cookie with the empathy of a brick.

'Tell whoever it is to fuck off.' Normally that would have been enough for Margo, but not today.

'He seems like a lovely old chap Jack.'

Jack looked at the phone. Was he imagining things or was there a note of compassion in Margo's voice? He'd never heard it before, it made him curious.

'What's he look like?'

'Oh, he's lovely.'

Was that a swoon in her voice? 'You been drinking Margo?'

'No Jack, it's morning.'

'Describe him to me.' Normally Margo would just say whatever she thought, not today.

'Well, he's very handsome. He has a brown suit and matching hat. Maybe in his sixties and,' she hesitated then whispered, 'he matches his suit.' She sounded a little embarrassed.

'What do you mean, he matches his suit?' There was a pause at the end of the phone and when she spoke it was clear that Margo was covering the mouthpiece with her hand and had lowered her voice.

'His suit is brown, Jack.'

'I heard that.'

'He matches it.'

'You trying to tell me he's Black?'

'Yes, Jack.'

Jack smiled; he didn't get many Black visitors. Jack wasn't racist. He was happy to exploit anyone regardless of creed or colour.

'Guess you better show him in them Margo. Did he say what he wants?'

'Er no, I didn't ask.'

'Isn't that your job?' he asked, curious now as to what kind of a visitor could possibly win over the flint-faced, stone-hearted receptionist from hell.

'Sorry Jack, he's just such a nice gentleman I never thought to ask.'

'Better send him in then.' Jack really wanted to see this visitor who had found the softer side of Margo. She was like the Presidents at Mount Rushmore; stone masons could have been chipping away at her hard veneer for years without making a mark, but this chap seemed to have charmed her in moments. There was a brief knock on the door and in came Margo. Her face was flushed, and she seemed excited, like a schoolgirl with a crush. Jack found this very amusing.

'This is Mister John R. Deal.'

In walked a gentleman in a brown suit and a matching trilby. It was hard to tell how old he was because his face had a cheeky youthfulness that hid the years, but it was impossible to see past his eyes. Deep blue unblinking pools. Although he didn't know why, Jack found himself standing up as John Deal entered the office.

'How do you do Mister Deal?' He pointed to a chair. 'Can we get you a drink?'

John nodded. 'Tea if you have it... English Breakfast or Ceylon.'

Jack glanced at Margo. Normally she wouldn't make anyone a drink. One of the girls in accounting could do that, but she was making an exception for John.

'No problem, I'll do it myself.' She slipped John one more smile and reversed out of the office. Jack sat down.

'Well, you seemed to have made an impression on my secretary Mister Deal.'

'Margo is a warm-hearted woman.' His voice was like honey.

'How did you know her name?' Margo never shared that kind of information.

'Well, Jack, I can call you Jack?'

Normally Jack would have said no. Only a handful of family and senior employees were allowed to be on first name terms with him. John Deal was very hard to say no to.

'Please do, we like to keep things very informal around here.' That was a lie.

'I understand that you are a shareholder in Small Print Records.'

That took Jack by surprise. It was not the kind of info that was generally known. He had been very careful to hide his interests by purchasing through several holding companies. His intention was to launder cash through the label, so he needed to be invisible.

'As it happens I don't believe I am, John. Can I call you John?' Jack heard himself ask. Why had he done that? He called people what he wanted.

John R. Deal leaned back in his chair and smiled a smile that lit up the room.

'Please do Jack, just don't take me for a fool. I know you are a shareholder. Let's not do this dance.'

John's words took Jack's breath away. He waited for the anger to come. Nobody called Jack a liar to his face without repercussions. To his amazement Jack found himself smiling and, worse still, telling the truth!

'You know how it is John? In business, sometimes you have to operate in the shade. The IRS have eyes everywhere.'

John nodded. 'I can see that, Jack. You're a criminal, and honesty isn't in your nature, but I'm not bothered about anything you get up to unless it affects Jimmy Wayne.' He fixed Jack with those clear blue eyes.

'Do you wear contacts?' asked Jack. 'It's just that I have never seen such blue eyes on—' he trailed off.

'On a Black man?' John laughed. 'These are my eyes and blue is my colour. They are special eyes. They let me see into people's souls.'

Jack laughed. 'Really, what do you see in mine, John?'

John sighed. 'You don't have one, Jack, but you knew that already.'

There was a knock on the door and Margo entered with the drinks, she had also put some biscuits on a plate.

'There you go, Mister Deal.' Margo smiled and gazed deep into John's eyes. John reached forwards and took her hand.

'Thank you, Margo. That is much appreciated.'

Margo blushed; she was flustered. 'Oh, it's no trouble John, I mean Mister Deal.'

'John is fine, Margo. Me and Jack here are on first name terms already.'

Margo looked at Jack. Jack looked back at her and both of them thought, what the fuck is happening? Nobody came into Jack's office and took over. Usually, unless they had been summoned, they never got past Margo. Somehow John Deal had charmed his way in and like the witnesses to a slow-motion car crash they were unable to stop him. Margo backed out of the room smiling and Jack began to laugh.

'You find something amusing, Jack?'

Jack stopped sniggering. 'You know John, I do. If anybody came through that door and called me a liar, they would be dead or seriously injured by now. But here you sit drinking tea and eating my biscuits.' He slowly shook his head. 'What the fuck's going on?'

John sipped his tea and then bit a chocolate cookie in half. He chewed quietly and then took another sip before looking back at Jack.

'These cookies are exceptional.'

'Never mind the cookies, why are you here?'

John looked directly at him and Jack felt like he was being tested. 'You are not a nice man Jack, and your mother,' he paused. 'How can I put this? Is a psychopath.'

Jack was about to protest but he knew that John's words were true.

'Doesn't make her a bad person though.' It wasn't much of a defence of his mothers' reputation but it was all he had.

'I'm afraid it does. But your mother's evil tendencies are not why I am here.'

'Then why are you?'

'Because I want you to do the right thing. Jimmy Wayne is about to succeed, and I need you to not interfere with that process.'

'Why would I do that? If Jimmy does well, I do well.'

John thought about Jack's words for a moment. He seemed to weigh them on an invisible scale. 'That's true Jack. Trouble is you just can't help yourself. You're always looking for an angle. Too much is never enough.'

Jack was about to protest but John silenced him with a look.

'Look, Jack, all you and your mother have to do is leave Jimmy Wayne alone. You will do well when he does well. I won't allow any interference, do you understand?'

Jack didn't understand. 'Are you threatening me?' he was more incredulous than angry.

John spoke quietly. 'You misunderstand me, Jack. This is not a threat. I'm just informing you that you cannot harm Jimmy Wayne in any way.'

'I've been harming people for years; it's what I do. Not being funny, John, but an old Black guy in a beat-up suit won't be telling me how to run my business affairs.'

John shook his head slowly.

'You really need to listen better, Jack. I'm not telling you anything, just informing you that if you do try it won't go well for you. You may think you are powerful but there are bigger things at play in the universe, and you, well, you can't control them.'

Jack just sat there trying to comprehend what was happening. There was a baseball bat under his desk. Why hadn't he used it? Nobody in this town would dare to speak to him in this way and yet there was just something about John R. Deal that was strange, different.

'Are you an angel or something?' The words were out of his mouth before he could stop them. 'What I meant to say was—' Jack was flustered and John's smile just got bigger.

'No, I'm not an angel, Jack.'

'That was a slip of the tongue. I... I meant agent.'

Again, John smiled. 'Not many angels in the agenting world. To be clear, Jack, I'm neither an angel nor an agent. All I am asking is that you don't interfere with Jimmy Wayne's progress.'

'Or what?' Jack was trying to gain control of the conversation. 'I'm a powerful man in this town.'

The two men sat there, eyeing each other. John took another sip of tea and nodded.

'Ok, Jack, if that's how you want to play it that's fine.' He stood up. 'Thanks for the tea and cookies.' He moved towards the door.

'That it?' Jack was incredulous. 'You come in here and threaten me and now you're just gonna get up and walk out.'

John turned around. 'We all have to make our choices in life Jack, I can't force you to make the right one, but you have to realise that if you make the wrong one there will be consequences.'

'That sounds like a threat, John.'

'How could I threaten you, Jack? Like you said, you're a powerful man in this town,' he took a beat. 'But powerful men have secrets.'

'Meaning?'

John turned his back and headed to the door. He pulled it open and as he did so he turned those bright blue eyes back on Jack and smiled. 'I know your secrets, Jack!'

Jack sat there looking at the empty doorway. Margo came bustling through blushing but smiling.

'He seemed nice.'

Jack gave Margo a weak smile. 'Yeah, a real gent.'

CHAPTER 12

ALL ROADS LEAD TO VEGAS

The V6 on David Parker's F Type Jaguar purred as he and Jimmy cruised up Interstate 15 headed for Vegas. LA was a hundred and forty miles behind them, and Jimmy had been dozing in the passenger seat for the last two hours. He stirred and opened his eyes, blinking at the brightness of the afternoon sun. David looked across.

'Sleeping Beauty awakes.'

Jimmy smiled. 'Please tell me that you ain't the sweet Prince.'

David laughed. 'Rest assured Jimmy, you are not on my kissing list.'

'Where are we?'

'About a hundred miles from Vegas.'

'How long have I been asleep?'

'Two hours, give or take.'

Jimmy was surprised. 'Man, tracking those vocals must have taken more out of me than I thought.'

'Well, you can relax now Jimmy. You sounded great and the record's in the can.'

'It ain't film. It's all digital these days.'

David sighed. 'I know but saying it's in the can sounds so much more romantic.'

'You are so English!'

'I know, it's one of my best features.'

Jimmy said nothing, happy to let his friend reside in his own self-image. David had done a lot for Jimmy and he trusted him completely.

'Why are we going to Vegas?'

'I want you to meet Frank Carpenter. He's taking a big risk on you and I thought it would be a good idea for you two to get to know each other before you are actually working together.'

Jimmy could see the sense in that. If Frank could see that Jimmy was ready for the next step, convince him that he was going to bring in the crowds, it would ease his arrival.

'You know that Frank has a partner, don't you?'

Jimmy didn't. 'Should I?'

'I don't want to put you under any extra pressure but not only does Sam Estrin own the Riviera and the Golden Flamingo.'

'He is also a close friend of Frank Carpenter.' Jimmy finished the sentence for him.

'Exactly, so do well here and the next step is already in place.'

Jimmy chuckled. 'Or fuck it up and I'm back at the Riviera!'

'If you're lucky, but let's think positive.' David glanced at the dashboard. 'Looks like we are going to arrive early.'

'I always liked to get to gigs early when I was touring. Get to know the stage managers, the sound guys. Form a relationship. If you can get them liking you, chances are the sound will be better and the spotlight will actually shine on you when you're singing.'

David smiled. 'Yes, you never want to annoy the crew.'

Jimmy started to chuckle.

'What's so funny?'

Jimmy shook his head. 'You just reminded me of a tour I was on back in the late nineties. You ever heard of Meteor Mike Kelly?'

David gave Jimmy a look of disdain. 'Do I look like someone who would have heard him?'

Jimmy sighed. 'Yeah, you're not his kinda fan demographic.'

'Is this a cautionary tale?'

Jimmy grinned. 'Fuck yeah! We were on a tour around the Rust Belt. Meteor Mike was pretty big back then. They called him Meteor because he played so fast. He was like a poor man's Van Halen.'

'I know Van Halen,' said David.

'Yeah, well imagine a second division version of him with a receding hairline and a paunch.' Jimmy paused for a moment remembering the image of Meteor Mike in full flow. 'He didn't look too appetising but boy he could play; he was a pretty good singer too. Trouble with Mike was he had got touched by the star bug. A couple of top thirty hits and an album that had got into the top three on the Billboard Rock charts and that fame turned him into an ego on legs.'

'Sounds wonderful,' sighed David.

'Oh, it wasn't. He turned into a right pain in the ass. He used to scream and shout at every soundman and lighting engineer in every venue we played in. Me, I always got the boys some doughnuts and coffee when we were setting up. Just as a thank you and to keep them onside. Needless to say, my sets, when I was opening for him, usually went perfect. Not Mike. If he had any sort of a problem, he would just scream and shout, but when people don't like you, they just don't try as hard.'

'Treat other people the way you would like to be treated, that's what my father taught me.'

Jimmy nodded. 'Only way to be David, only nobody seemed to have told Mike this. This one night we are playing a gig somewhere in Ohio. It was a nice venue, about twelve hundred capacity, and it was full. Now my set had gone perfectly, and the guys were great, but Mike had been throwing his weight around from the moment we arrived. He had pissed off everybody, including the guy in charge of the lights, and that was a big mistake.'

'This is the cautionary bit, isn't it?'

Jimmy nodded. 'Fuck yeah! So, the lighting guy was also the owner of the venue and Mike had really pissed him off. Now a big part of a Meteor Mike show was the solos. To be fair, that was the show. It was like a big solo with a song attached. When he started shredding, he would move to the front of the stage and the spotlight would hit him, but not this night. Mike moved to the front of the stage and launched into his first solo, and the spotlight hit the drummer. The drummer was as surprised as everyone else. I was at the back of the hall with one of my roadies and he knew what was happening straight away. "Holy Shit," he said. "Maurice told me he was going to stick it to Meteor Mike tonight." "What do you mean?" I asked. "Mike ain't getting no spotlight. He's pissed off the wrong person."

'Stan was right. Halfway through that first solo, Mike edges into the spotlight in front of the drums. He looks pissed, but the crowd go wild. Solo finished and the normal lights come up and Mike comes back to the microphone for the next verse looking mighty pissed. Next song he gets to the solo, and the spotlight hits the bass player. Sure enough a few seconds later a red-faced Meteor Mike barges into the spotlight and goes on with his solo. From where I'm standing at the back of the hall I can hear the laughter coming from the lighting gantry. Maurice the owner is really sticking it to the Meteor tonight!'

'Nasty case of Schadenfreude,' observed David.

Jimmy looked questioningly at David. 'What does that actually mean?'

'Taking pleasure in the misery of others.'

'Well, Maurice was certainly doing that. He was waiting for Mike to get to wherever he had put the spotlight and then, when he got there, moving it somewhere else. By now the crowd was thinking that this was part of the show – a bit of humour injected by Mike – and they were laughing and cheering every time he made it into the spotlight. Now Mike wasn't a fit guy, but he was a showman and he played every solo and never missed a beat. He must have covered about six miles on stage that night. At the end of the show the crowd went wild and Mike had a heart attack! Man, we all laughed.'

David looked shocked. 'That's a bit harsh.'

Jimmy shrugged. 'Mike was a dick… He recovered though. Never did shout at the engineers much after that!'

Jimmy fell asleep again, occasionally chuckling as he did so. Soon David and Jimmy would be in Vegas. Jack and Ma Lantern were already there. Standing at the crossroads opposite Carpenters Casino stood John R. Deal, waiting. Moving down Highway 93, Terry Moist, Tony C and Danny Baker were trying to close their ears to the moaning of Brian McCumber as he cradled his broken arm. And Wendy? She too was there. She had always wanted to return to Vegas and now she had 'Access All Areas'. No club could bar her and no celebrity could refuse her entry to their homes. She could have written the perfect gossip column, if only she was alive.

'Why can't we just kill him?' growled Terry, growing tired of Brian's complaining.

'I think we need to give him a written warning first,' replied Tony, once again falling back on his scant knowledge of HR gleaned from his girlfriend. 'That or thirty days' notice.'

Terry looked across at him. 'We ain't talking about workers' rights here, Tony.'

'Maybe he could strangle himself. He strangled his fiancée,' suggested Danny.

'With one fucking hand? Jeez, am I the only sane person in the vehicle.'

'I'll strangle him if you like. He's starting to irritate me too.'

Brian sat up. 'I am here you know.' He sounded hurt. Terry started to chuckle.

'Congratulations boys, we've managed to hurt the feelings of a guy who strangled his fiancée.' There was a round of sniggers except for Brian, who was indignant.

'You guys don't know me. You don't know what happened or why it happened.' Terry looked at him in the mirror.

'Way I heard it you strangled her at your hotel the night before your wedding. What else do I need to know?' There was silence as they waited to hear Brian's justification. He wiped his nose with his good arm.

'I loved her.'

'Funny way of showing it,' said Danny.

'Any of you guys had a wedding? They're very stressful.'

'Well, it was for her!' Danny again.

'Muriel was a very attractive woman.'

'Muriel!?' they all said it together.

'Were you marrying your maiden aunt?'

Brian rounded on Danny. 'Her parents were from Vermont,' he said, as if that explained it.

'Why did you kill her at your hotel? The place was full with all your family for the next day. Surely you didn't think you would get away with it,' Tony asked sympathetically.

'I didn't think at all. It was a crime of passion. We had just done a run through of the service with the wedding co-ordinator, she glanced at the ring on her finger and then turned to me and said, "Why didn't you get me the ruby?" The co-ordinator didn't know where to look. It was embarrassing. "I thought you wanted the diamond," I said. She just let out a sigh. "Suppose it will have to do then." 'That's when I lost it. I strangled her right there and then in front of the co-ordinator. She tried to get me off her but that look she had given me and the way she sounded; I guess I just realised I couldn't face that for another fifty years.'

Brian fell into silence as he remembered. The boys exchanged glances and shook their heads but remained silent until Tony spoke.

'Let me get this straight. You strangled Muriel—'

Terry and Danny sniggered.

'—in front of the woman who was organising your wedding, in a hotel full of your family and friends.'

Brian nodded, a look of regret falling across his features. 'I've always been impetuous.'

Tony bit his lip. 'Yes, that was a little impetuous Brian.'

'I know,' he agreed. 'I deeply regret it. We were going to honeymoon in Barbados. I could have drowned her snorkelling and made it look like an accident!'

'Did you get your deposit back?' asked Danny.

Brian's answer was drowned out by the laughter of the others.

———◆———

'Wake up, Jimmy, we're here!'

Jimmy opened his eyes and there, laid out like a taster menu of vices, were the delights of Las Vegas. As they cruised up the Strip, they called like sirens tempting him, every base desire your heart could wish for and your mind could imagine. When you fell for Vegas, you fell hard. Last time he was here, he was a drinker. He had indulged. After three months he barely knew who he was anymore. The days and nights just blurred into one another like a kaleidoscopic nightmare. Not this time, he thought. This time Vegas will serve me. He would take what it offered, on his terms. He hadn't been to Vegas for a while. He had driven through with Kid two weeks back but now he was coming back to stay.

'Man, I've missed this place.'

David nodded. 'Yeah, me too. It's brash and it's vulgar but it's,' he reached for the right word, 'alive.'

Jimmy knew what he meant. There were a lot of bad things about Vegas, but it was an exciting place. It built dreams and it shattered them. Made people do the wrong things. Like a modern-day Sodom and Gomorrah, it was where the masses came to get their fix of the forbidden. Everything was available if you had the money and the desire. The perfect place to build an empire based on exploitation and greed. The perfect place for the Lanterns to live.

———————◆———————

Jack Lantern pulled up on his drive. His meeting with John R. Deal had disturbed him. He decided to get out of the office and go home for lunch. As he walked through the doorway, Ma was coming in through the French windows facing the pool.

'Oh, hi Jackie, what you doing home?' She was smiling but looked flushed. Jack eyed her suspiciously.

'What you been up to, Ma?'

He watched the emotions play across her face.

For a moment she thought about lying but then her shoulders sagged a little and she gave him a wicked smile. 'I just been interviewing the new pool boy.'

'Does he know his stuff?'

Ma shrugged. 'Never got that far, he passed his physical though!'

Jack sighed. 'Jeez, Ma, you gotta stop fucking the staff, that stuff ain't in their contract.'

'He's a pool boy!' she said as if that was all the explanation that was required.

Jack headed for the fridge. He had long ago given up trying to understand his mother. She danced to a different drummer, a voodoo one.

'You want a pastrami on rye, I just made one for the...' she hesitated, and Jack finished her sentence.

'The pool boy?'

Ma winked at him. 'The boy's got to keep his strength up. He won't be needing it now. He headed out the back gate when he saw you pull up on the drive. Probably thought you would take a dim view of him making out with your momma.'

Jack sat down at the table. He knew the pool boy would not have had a lot of say in the matter.

'Will he be coming back, or do I have to find a new one?'

'Oh, he'll be back, Jackie. Your Momma showed him some stuff he never even dreamt of.'

'Maybe in his nightmares,' he said quietly under his breath. Ma slammed a plate of pastrami and rye with a selection of pickles down on the table in front of him. There was homemade mayo and some chips, even some olives. 'Man, you look after the pool boy better than me.'

'Yeah, well, I like him better. You, I just love!'

A mother's love is a strange thing and Ma's love for Jack had been unconventional. By the age of eight she was teaching him how to manipulate people, showing him the value of fear. She even introduced him to her torture chamber, to toughen him up. It was all part of her succession planning and Jack had turned out OK. He wasn't as ruthless as a properly raised girl would have been but for a boy he would do. Jack knew that his mother had wanted a girl, but when you get pregnant at fifteen family planning doesn't really come into it.

Jack took a bite of his sandwich and chewed it thoughtfully. His Ma came over with a pot of tea and pored them both a mug.

'You look thoughtful. What's eating you, Jackie?'

'I don't know Ma. I just had the strangest meeting.' This got Ma's attention.

'Someone trying to move in on us?' Anger flashed in her eyes, the bitch defending her brood.

'No, Ma, nothing like that. Just an old black guy.'

'What did he want?' There was an urgency in her questioning. Jack shook his head.

'I'm not sure.'

'What do you mean you're not sure? He must have said something.'

'He just told me not to mess with Jimmy Wayne.'

'Motherfucker! Who the hell does he think he is? I do hope you beat him to a pulp.'

Jack never liked to disappoint his Ma but, on this occasion, he didn't have a choice.

'No, I gave him tea and biscuits.' Momentarily Ma had lost the ability to talk, her mouth opened and closed a couple of times. Jack could see her inner volcano was close to erupting.

'Ma, he didn't really threaten me. He was *different*. He just told me that Jimmy was going to do great and not to get in his way and everything will work out fine.' Jack held back the bit about John knowing his secrets. That kind of talk would have John ending up in Ma's chamber of horrors, and for some inexplicable reason he didn't want that for him. 'Do you believe in God, Ma?'

Ma stared at him. She looked both worried and angry, which is not an easy expression to convey. Ma seemed to have mastered it.

'Do I need to call a doctor, Jackie? I think you're having a stroke or something.'

Jack smiled. 'You don't understand Ma. He's different. You should meet him.'

'I plan to,' she snapped. 'Where's he live?'

Jack shrugged. 'I don't know.'

'What's his phone number?'

'Don't know that either.' Jack heard himself utter the words, but he couldn't quite believe them. How had he and Margo allowed a total stranger to enter his office without an appointment and tell him what to do with a veiled – albeit nicely veiled – threat. He glanced up at Ma. She was looking at him the way an owner would look at a dog that needed putting down.

'You had to be there. He was,' he paused for a moment, 'beguiling. Yeah, that's the word. Beguiling. When he smiled it was like when the sun bursts through the clouds on a sunny day and you feel that warmth wrapping itself around you.'

Ma's fists were clenching and unclenching and the veins in her neck were starting to resemble rope. If she had been a cartoon, steam would have been coming out of her ears. She fought to control her emotions. Jackie was her only child, and to bash him over the head with the frying pan that was oh so temptingly sitting within reach would have been counterproductive to her succession plan. She sat down opposite her son and forced a smile.

'Jackie, I'm worried about you son. Maybe you're working too hard.'

'I'm fine Ma. I know it sounds crazy, but there was something good about him, you know what I mean?'

'No, I don't have a fucking clue what you mean. I tried to raise you proper. It wasn't easy being a single mother in a man's world. I showed you how to intimidate and exploit. Taught you how to cheat and steal, I did everything for you and now this!' She paused as if trying to comprehend the terrible misfortune that seemed to have overcome Jackie at his office. She reached across the table and took his hand in hers. 'Jackie, you've done so well since you took over the business, don't spoil it now by being kind. To swim with the sharks in this town you gotta be the biggest shark. Nice won't cut it. It won't do son; it just won't do!'

Jack sat there for a few moments considering his mother's words. They were genuine and she meant every word. She was right, he had let John R. Deal get to him. He was a mean bastard, just how his mum had raised him. He felt himself coming to his senses.

'You're right Ma. Didn't have breakfast this morning, maybe I was hypoglycaemic.'

'Or a dumb fuck.'

He nodded. 'That too.' He sipped his tea. 'Relax Ma, next time I see him I'm gonna knock his block off.'

'That's my boy, Jackie.' Ma gave Jack a reassuring smile secure in the knowledge that he would never see John R. Deal again, not if she had anything to do with it!

———◆———

David and Jimmy cruised towards Carpenters Hotel and Casino at the northern end of the Strip. It was one of the older establishments. When it was built it was outside the town, but as Vegas had grown the strip had extended to now include it. Too small to compete with the big venues, it had built its reputation on good value for money, a friendly atmosphere and being one of the best music venues in town. Headlining here would definitely put Jimmy Wayne and the Second Chance on the map. David glanced across at Jimmy.

'You excited?'

Jimmy smiled. 'You know I am.'

They cruised up to the crossroads on which Carpenters sat. There wasn't much traffic, but the lights were against them. It was just then that Jimmy noticed an elderly Black gent in a brown suit and matching trilby standing by the entrance to Carpenters, just watching the traffic on the crossroad. John R. Deal! Not in a dream, but standing there plain as day. Jimmy pointed and David gazed in the direction Jimmy was indicating.

'Do you see that old guy?

David looked across to where John stood. 'Looks like an old bluesman, maybe he's been playing with somebody at Carpenters.'

'Maybe,' acknowledged Jimmy. 'But why do you think he's waving at us?'

David looked again; he was waving at them.

'Did you have any male Waynettes?'

Jimmy sighed. 'That's real funny.'

'Then I guess he knows you.' The lights changed and David eased the Jaguar across the junction and into the parking bay at the front of Carpenters. He turned off the engine.

'Welcome to your new home from home.'

As they climbed from the car they heard the soft footfalls behind them and turned to see the old guy in the brown suit walking towards them.

'Jimmy Wayne, so good to see you, son!' John held out his hand and Jimmy politely accepted it.

'Nice to meet you, sir. Do I know you?' He recognised him but only when Jimmy looked into those deep blue eyes did he understand that John R. Deal was not a figment of his imagination. He was real. John nodded at him.

'Is it coming back to you?'

Jimmy nodded.

'Tell me my name.' John asked it in a gentle, unchallenging way.

Feeling a little stupid Jimmy answered. 'I believe it's John R. Deal.'

A look of delight spread across John's features. 'That's right Jimmy, I'm here to help you.'

David had observed this strange encounter and he moved towards John and offered his hand.

'Pleased to meet you sir. My name is...'

'David Parker,' said John. 'I'm very pleased to meet you too.'

David was confused. 'I'm sorry, have we met?'

'Never.'

'Then how do you know my name?'

John still held David's hand, he pulled David gently towards him. 'We share a purpose.'

'We do?'

John nodded. 'We are both here to look after Jimmy. You are like a big brother to him, and I am like the father he never had.'

'I had a father; he wasn't much of a father, but I did have one.'

'What did he teach you, Jimmy?'

Jimmy thought about John's question. 'He taught me not to get caught, not to get married if you want to play around and always write about what you know.'

John slowly shook his head. 'Apart from the last one he doesn't sound like much of a role model.'

'He wasn't. Maybe as a role model for what not to do, but you don't realise that when you're a little kid.'

David was a polite man, but their meeting with Frank Carpenter was in five minutes.

'Look, John, I don't mean to be rude, but we are expected in a meeting in five minutes. Jimmy will be on here in a few weeks and we just have to nail a few items down with the owner.'

John clapped his hands with delight. 'I know, it's marvellous that Frank is giving Jimmy a chance.' Both Jimmy and David were surprised at this revelation. The publicity wasn't going out until next week, how did John know this?

'Why are you here John?' Jimmy paused mid-sentence, finding it hard to say the next part. 'You know I have been dreaming about you.'

John nodded. 'Of course, and now we finally meet.'

'Why are you here, John?'

'To help you write songs.'

'He writes great songs these days,' said David.

'I know he does but I want to help him write them a different way!'

Jimmy wasn't sure he understood what John was trying to say. John spelled it out for him.

'I think the Song Cemetery is full now Jimmy, don't you?'

Jimmy felt dizzy. He knew! This man, who he had only seen in his dreams, knew his secret. He didn't know how to respond.

'Look Mister Deal, it seems like you and Jimmy have a lot to talk about. Could we maybe meet up tonight and discuss it over a meal?'

John considered it for a moment. 'That would be most agreeable Mister Parker.'

'Excellent, where and when shall we meet?'

'I'll be here when you come out.'

David looked concerned. 'We could be in there for hours.'

John shrugged. 'The passing of time is just history in the making.'

Jimmy pulled a fifty-dollar bill from his wallet. 'There's a nice bar at the end of this block, go get yourself a drink and something to eat and we will meet you there.'

'Ain't no need for that, Jimmy, I already have everything that money can't buy.' Regardless of that he took Jimmy's money and with a wink turned and headed for the bar, calling back over his shoulder as he went. 'See you later gents.'

They watched him walk away until he was well out of earshot. David looked at Jimmy. 'Do you want to tell me what on Earth that was about?'

'Damned if I know.'

'But you said you dreamed about him, and you knew his name.' Jimmy looked at David, unsure whether he should explain. He wasn't even sure if he understood it himself.

'I had a dream with John Deal in recently. In my dream he was like a mentor to me. An old bluesman who knew the game, how to play it and how to survive.'

David wasn't buying it. 'You must have met him Jimmy, you've been around a long time. Maybe you worked with him, and your brain has worked him into your subconscious and then into your dreams.'

'No, I never met him. Look at his eyes, have you ever seen a black guy with eyes so blue.'

'You mean African-American.'

Jimmy shrugged. 'African-American Black guy then.' He watched John turn down into the entrance of the bar and disappear from view. He turned back to David. 'I'm telling you, I dreamt of John recently, and today I met him for the first time. He knew my name and I knew his, how do you explain that?'

David couldn't explain. He glanced at his watch.

'Come on Jimmy, we can discuss your Twilight Zone adventures with John R. Deal when we have sorted out the real world with Frank Carpenter.'

———◆———

Back at the studios, Kid was sitting on the patio watching the sun starting to go down over LA. He felt at peace. It had been a long time since he had felt this good. It was a strange feeling. Maybe this could be happiness. He had heard a lot about it and, when he was younger, he'd had an occasional skirmish with it, but nothing that ever lasted. Now here he was playing in a band he loved, arranging the music. They had just recorded a great record on one of the best labels around and they were booked into a run in Las Vegas. Could it get any better? He leaned back in his chair, took a sip of his beer and let the moment wash over him. Happiness and success, a great combination. The sound of his mobile disturbed his meditation. Only a handful of people had his number. He looked at the caller ID. Aksel!

'Hi brother, how you doing?'

'I'm doing ok,' he answered cautiously.

'Something wrong?'

'I had a visit today from four of those guys that work for Jack Lantern.'

Kid let the information sink in for a moment. 'Are they still alive?' He said it in a joking voice but he knew it was possible that they weren't. Like him, Aksel was capable of serious levels of violence when forced.

'Yeah, I was diplomatic! Had to break one arm but the other three were fine.'

Kid was impressed. 'You should be working at the United Nations.'

Aksel laughed. 'Too late for that.'

'What did they want?'

'I'm not sure. My guess is that somehow this Jack Lantern knows that you and Jimmy have come into money since they tracked your visit here. This is an old goldmine and they have put two and two together and come up with...'

'Four!' said Kid.

'Exactly. I showed the boss man round.'

'What did he look like?'

'About five ten and two hundred pounds, dangerous eyes and a Texan accent.'

Kid nodded. 'Congratulations, you just met Terry Moist and survived.'

Aksel sighed. 'He was the one who was lucky to survive. If he hadn't bought the story I was planning on killing them all.'

'I thought we were pacifists now, Aksel.'

Aksel laughed. 'Whenever possible.'

'Do you think they bought it?'

Aksel considered it for a moment. 'I think that Terry decided I was more trouble than he wanted.'

'Sounds like a wise man. So, what you going to do?'

'I got a tracker on his vehicle and put one in his camera, which he will never find. Got a mic in it so I can keep tabs on him if he brings it back.'

Kid smiled. 'You always were the best tech guy the FS had.'

'You know it. I got pressure pad alarms that warn me if anyone comes onto the drive, so they won't be sneaking up on me.'

'Still getting plenty of gold?'

'You wouldn't believe it. It's still going the way it was when you were here with Jimmy. I think there must be a huge seam that has been exposed upstream in the river and it's just coming down in big lumps of Placer gold as its, washed out. I'm going to be able to do a lot of good with this money.'

Kid smiled sadly. His friend was a good man, and he was trying to atone for the sins of his previous life by helping those less fortunate souls. But Kid knew only too well that all the gold, and the good it could do, would never wash away the memories of the things they had done in the service of their country.

'You take care brother, I'll come up and see you before we start in Vegas.'

'I'd like that,' said Aksel. 'Bring Jimmy.'

There was a click and Aksel rang off. Kid sat there looking at his phone. Aksel was his best friend in the world, they had been through a lot together and he owed it to him to help him find his way back to a normal life. He made a promise to himself that he would go to see Aksel as soon as he finished in LA.

CHAPTER 13
CARPENTERS' CASINO

As they entered the reception area of Carpenters, Jimmy looked at the high ceilings and the clean Art Deco lines. This place was a lot smarter than he had imagined. David had told him it was a hidden gem, and it was certainly living up to his description.

'How can I help you gentlemen?' asked the young lady at reception. Her smile and her question seemed genuine; it really was a warm welcome.

'David Parker and Jimmy Wayne to see Sam Estrin.'

Jimmy recognised that name but before he could say anything the receptionist shot him a dazzling smile.

'Oh! So nice to meet you Mister Wayne. I'm looking forward to hearing you play.' Jimmy smiled. 'Thank you, Ma'am.'

'My mother has told me lots about you.' That took the smile off his face and David, standing at his side, tried to suppress a smile. 'All good. She was a Waynette!'

'Was?' asked David, keen to enjoy Jimmy's discomfort.

She blushed a little. 'No, she still is. She actually tried on her old Waynettes cheerleader outfit when she heard you were coming.' She paused. 'Apparently it's shrunk.' She winked at David. 'Momma's put on a couple of pounds.'

'Yes, Jimmy's fan base has remained stable over the years. It's just the overall weight that has increased.'

Jimmy wanted to kick David, but he stood there and pretended to enjoy the joke with the others. The receptionist excused herself and then headed off to get Sam.

'Enjoying yourself?' he asked David.

'Immensely, thank you for asking.'

'Sam Estrin?'

David looked at Jimmy. He winced. 'Little white lie. I know you were disappointed when the Golden Flamingo fell through, and I thought if you knew Sam owned Carpenters you might say no.'

'You think I'm that precious?'

David shrugged. 'You're an artist, of course you are.'

'I'm just grateful to get booked in Vegas, I would have gone on in the car park if that's what it took!'

David nodded. 'Well, if it doesn't go well here it may come to that.'

The door swung open and Sam Estrin burst into the reception area. He was younger than Jimmy expected, maybe in his late fifties. He looked lean and tanned. He smiled and forty thousand dollars of dental work gleamed at them.

'Great to see you, David.' He embraced David in a bear hug and Jimmy could see that David's English reserve was being breached.

'Easy Sam, no tongues,' he joked as he deftly extracted himself. He stepped back. 'Boy, you're looking good Sam. You must have lost forty pounds.' David squeezed his shoulder. 'You got toned too.'

Sam nodded enthusiastically. 'I got married.'

'I thought you were married.'

Sam's gave him a guilty but unrepentant smile.

'This is Vegas, David. Nothing lasts forever.'

'I'm guessing she's younger,' said David, sardonically.

'Twenty-two!' he exclaimed proudly.

'That's good, your kids can babysit her.'

Sam frowned. 'You cheeky bastard.'

David shrugged. 'I'm guessing that with the sex you're having you can rise above it.'

'You guess correctly, my friend. I'm shallow, but it doesn't make me a bad person.' Jimmy could think of several responses to that statement but given the fact he didn't know Sam he opted for saying hello. He held out his hand.

'Jimmy Wayne, pleased to meet you Mister Estrin.'

Sam turned and looked at Jimmy for the first time. 'Pleased to meet you too, Jimmy.' They shook hands and Sam looked him up and down. 'You look well, Jimmy. You ready for the big stage, I need you to bring in the punters.'

'I will Mister Estrin.'

Sam waved his hand.

'Don't call me Mister Estrin, Sam will do just fine, you want a guided tour?'

Both Jimmy and David said yes.

'Then walk this way gents, let's go to the auditorium first.'

They followed Sam down the corridor through two sets of doors. Up two flights of stairs and out onto a large concourse, and then they went through a set of double doors and they were in the back of the middle balcony. It took Jimmy's breath away for a moment. It was beautiful, three-tiered Art Deco perfection. It held six hundred people. Here, finally, was a venue worthy of his talent. He just stood there and took it in. He was like an awestruck kid. Everything up to this point in his life had led to him being here. The murder of his father and the suicide of his mother. There were so many ups and downs in a turbulent life, but it was Wendy who had made it possible.

Sam thought otherwise. 'Magnificent isn't it, Jimmy? Best kept secret in Vegas. You gotta thank David for getting you here.'

Jimmy smiled. 'I know that it was David who convinced you I was worth a go.'

Sam laughed. 'That's true Jimmy, but I was thinking that if David hadn't fucked the Finance Director's wife on the boardroom table at the Golden Flamingo I wouldn't have moved him to the Riviera and you guys would never have met. Funny how fate works, eh?'

'Hilarious,' said David. 'I just wish you wouldn't be so crude when you talk about my lady friend.'

Sam shrugged. 'So how would you describe it?'

'Horizontal manoeuvres has a nicer ring, don't you think?'

Sam looked at Jimmy. 'You believe this guy?'

'Always.'

David slapped him on the back. 'Correct answer Jimmy.'

Sam continued the tour, and everything was pristine. David had a huge smile on his face.

'Why didn't I know about this place, it's an absolute gem!'

'It is,' beamed Sam. 'I bought it two years ago from Frank Carpenter. He didn't want it falling into the hands of one of the big corporations, figured they would just knock it down and use the plot for a skyscraper.'

'That would be a sacrilege.'

'Yeah, it would have been unfortunate, but they didn't see the big picture. This place will appeal to old money and punters with a bit of style. We won't be catering for the cattle class here. It's only got four hundred rooms, but the spec is very high now. It's been a costly restoration, but this place is going to do well.' He turned to Jimmy. 'Concert hall will have classy acts as well, but we are going to open with you.'

Jimmy looked offended. 'I can be classy.'

Sam smiled. 'I'm sure you can, Jimmy, but what we going to do about the Waynettes?'

'Subdued lighting,' suggested David.

The tour had gone well and when, one hour later, they were standing in the reception foyer, Jimmy was happier than he could ever remember being. David could see it and he was happy for his friend.

'Shall we wander down to that bar and meet Mister Deal?'

Before Jimmy could reply, the doors to the lounge burst open and six foot two inches of bald German campness engulfed them.

'Jimmy Vayne?' Jimmy nodded. 'Das iss goot.'

David shot Jimmy an amused but questioning look. It's not every day that you get accosted by a six foot two, bald headed, camp German wearing a monocle. Yes, he was wearing a monocle!

'I am Herr Kessler, zee entertainments director,' he smiled coyly. 'But you, Jimmy Vayne, can call me Flare.'

'Ok,' replied Jimmy cautiously. 'Is that a real name?'

'Vot, Kessler?'

'No. Flare.'

He sighed. 'My mother verked in a munitions factory when she vas a girl.'

'Could have been worse,' said David, sniggering slightly.

'Jah, Mine Kessler for instance.' He smiled. 'Ve are very much looking forward to your stay vith us Jimmy.'

'Me too,' stammered Jimmy. 'It's a great place.'

Herr Kessler grinned. 'It's vonderful, and Sam has turned it back into a palace.' Herr Kessler was very expressive as he spoke, he was one of those people that if you tied their arms behind their back would be rendered speechless.

'What part of Germany are you from Herr Kessler?'

He touched David gently on the shoulder. 'Oh David, I am not German. I vas born in Birmingham, England, but my mother vas German so I got my accent from her.'

'Birmingham, I know it well.'

'Then you will understand vhy I kept my German accent as opposed to zee local dialect.'

'Oh, I quite like the Brummie accent.'

'Brummie! You do know my hometown zen.' He removed his monocle and gave it a quick polish on his jacket.

'How does that work, Flare,' asked Jimmy curiously.

'Ze monocle?' he leaned towards Jimmy conspiratorially. 'Truth be told Jimmy, it's just plain glass but zee eye it iss behind, it iss also glass.'

'Oh, I'm sorry... I didn't realise.'

Her Kessler burst out laughing. 'I make a joke vis you Jimmy; I wear it just for show. I am zee entertainments director, I have to entertain!'

Herr Kessler certainly did that. It was just then that David noticed Sam Estrin standing near the entrance to the Casino, laughing to himself. He wandered across.

'Good, you boys have met Flare.'

'We certainly have,' said David. 'And it's been quite an experience.'

'Oh, Flare is great but he watches a lot of musicals.'

'That explains everything,' said Jimmy. Herr Kessler gave Jimmy a big hug.

'You, Jimmy Vayne, are a very naughty man, ve are going to get on very vell!' He turned on his heel and dashed off in the direction of the elevators. They watched him go in stunned silence. Sam was the first to break it.

'He's quite an experience, ain't he?'

'He's that all right. It's like being run over by a Bavarian Hurricane.' David turned to Jimmy and smiled mischievously. 'He seems to like you though, Jimmy.'

'I got no problem with gay men.'

Sam laughed. 'Don't be fooled by Flare, it's all an act. Think he must have slept with every waitress at the Golden Flamingo.'

'He's not gay?' Even David was surprised.

'No, he pretends he thinks he is but lets the girls convince him that he's actually straight. Reverse psychology, or as he would say. "Sam, every voman likes a challenge!"'

They all laughed. 'He's a great entertainment director though and he has a great managing director.'

'Who's that?' asked David.

'It's you, fool. I want you to run this place and the Riviera.'

David was stunned for a moment and for once in his life didn't know what to say.

'You wanted to get back into Vegas, well here's your chance. I'll even cut you into the action if you hit the targets.'

'I don't know what to say Sam.'

Jimmy slapped him on the back. 'Say yes, David.'

David turned to Jimmy. 'But what about me managing you?'

Jimmy shrugged. 'I'm only going to be playing here for the next few months and then back to the Riviera to rehearse new material for the next album, so it won't be a problem.'

David looked at Sam. 'Would you be ok with that?'

'You're the most capable man I have ever met David. You can do all three as long as it doesn't affect business. And I know it won't.' It was a huge vote of confidence but David still had doubts.

'What about touring?'

'We can get a tour manager to work to your instructions.'

David thought about it for a moment. 'Well, when you put it like that, it does seem plausible.'

Sam offered his hand. 'We got a deal then?'

David reached out and took it. He smiled. 'I think we do.'

'That's great. Come and see me next week and we can sort out the paperwork.' He turned to Jimmy. 'Welcome to Carpenters Jimmy, I think you know your new boss!'

Jimmy walked down the street towards the bar where John R. Deal was waiting. David had told him to go on ahead while he sorted a couple of things out with Sam. Jimmy knew it was about the contract for the band, so he left him to it. It was late afternoon, and the air was warm and still. He was looking forward to meeting John, but he was nervous, he had a feeling that John was going to be important in his life only he didn't know how important.

'Hi Jimmy.'

He turned and there just two steps behind him was Wendy. He checked to see there was nobody near. He didn't want to look like the nutter on the street talking to somebody who wasn't there. The coast was clear.

'Hi Wendy, did you get a look inside Carpenters?'

'Sure did, it's a pretty fancy place. Not sure if it's really Art Deco though. Designed by the same architect that did the Huntridge Theatre back in 1944.'

Jimmy shrugged. 'It looks pretty nice to me.'

'Oh, it's nice all right, but it's gotta be thirties to be real Deco. Hey, talking about real, that Herr Kestler is pretty off the wall.'

'I liked him.'

'Yeah, he's definitely a character. Kinda sexy in a strange way. I don't usually go for gay men.'

'He's not gay, Wendy. It's all part of his act.'

Wendy wrinkled her brow. 'It's a hell of an act. Next your gonna tell me he ain't German.'

'He's not. Born in England.'

Wendy looked confused. 'Ok, I give up. I'll wait until I get to know him better.'

Jimmy felt happy, that meant Wendy intended to hang around for a while.

'You going to meet John now?'

He'd expected Wendy to know about John. Since she'd been dead, she seemed to know something about everything.

'Listen to John, he has your best interests at heart. He's special.'

The way she said it made Jimmy stop walking and turn to her. 'In what way, is he a ghost like you?'

Wendy shook her head. 'Don't think so.'

'You mean you can't tell?'

'He's no ghost, but he ain't a normal person.'

'Well, if he's not dead and he's not alive, what is he?' Jimmy was confused. He felt that there was something very different about John, but he was sure Wendy would suss it out.

'If I was a guessing person I would say he's an angel.'

'But there's nothing religious about you, Wendy. You're all about science. Why would you think he was an angel?'

Wendy shrugged. 'I dunno. Not the bible kinda angel. The guardian kind.'

'Is that a real thing?'

'I guess you're about to find out.'

'You gonna come in and listen?'

She put her arm around his shoulder. 'Course I will, I don't want you forgetting who your real guardian angel is.'

He wrapped his arms around her.

'Thank you Wendy, none of this would be happening without you.'

She gave him a peck on his cheek and then dissolved through his arms.

'When did you learn to do that?'

'Every day is a school day, Jimmy.' He heard her voice, but he couldn't see her.

'Where are you?' he called. She materialised next to him. 'Right here.' She winked at him. 'Got my invisibility cloak working now.'

Jimmy sighed. 'You're a regular Klingon Warship, Wendy.' He knew she would get the comment. Wendy loved Star Trek.

'See you in there, Jimmy.' And with that she just disappeared, leaving Jimmy standing alone on the sidewalk.

———————◆———————

Back at Jack Lantern's office, Margo was still thinking about John's visit. Just talking to him had rekindled feelings she hadn't had for years. Maybe working for Jack and Ma all these years had made her hard. Since looking into those beautiful deep blue eyes and feeling the gentle touch of his hand she had been filled with warm and generous thoughts. This was most unlike her. Even Jack had failed to be his usual violent, rude, bad-tempered self. She wanted to meet John R. Deal again. As she sat there thinking happy thoughts Jack barged into his office like a bull with indigestion.

'Hi Margo.' Before she could answer, Jack continued. 'I don't want any more shit like this morning. You should never have let the old guy in.'

'But you told me to show him in.'

'You shouldn't have asked me; you know the rules. No appointment, no admission.' He looked at her pointedly. 'You got that, Margo?'

She nodded. 'Yeah, I got it, but you liked him too!'

Jack winced. 'I know I liked him, but I shouldn't have been given the opportunity to like him, should I?'

'Sorry Jack, he just seemed so nice.'

'Shut up with this nice already Margo, I just had my ass chewed out by Ma over this. She thinks we've both gone soft.'

He thought for a moment. 'She may have a point! Ma told me to whack him.'

'You can't do that Jack; it wouldn't be nice.'

'For fuck's sake Margo, listen to yourself. We've attacked plenty of folks in the past, what's different with John?'

Jack had a point. She had seen people walk into Jack office on many occasions only to be carried out in a bag later. Something had changed for Margo the moment she met John. Hopefully he was like a case of the flu, and she would get over it.

'Sorry Jack. I'll try to be meaner from now on.'

Jack smiled. 'That's my girl. Take no prisoners.'

'You want a coffee, Jack?'

'Yes please, Margo,' he heard the politeness in his voice. 'And don't take all afternoon about it,' he snapped. Better, he thought. He would start with rudeness and build up to GBH. He went into his office and slammed the door behind him. Slumping in his seat, he thought about John. The man had unsettled him, Jack fed off his greed and his anger, but John seemed to have robbed him of it. He needed to kill the man.

———◆———

Jimmy walked into the bar and there, sitting alone at a table by the window, was John. He saw Jimmy and a huge grin spread across his face.

'Good to see you, Jimmy.' He ushered Jimmy to a seat. 'Get you a drink?' he winked. 'With your money.'

'Beer would be nice,' he sat down.

John didn't raise his hand or try to catch the attention of the waitress, but she drifted across to their table as if drawn by an invisible force.

'What can I get you, John?' First name terms already, thought Jimmy. John Deal doesn't hang around.

'Two beers please, Susan, and a gin and tonic for our friend who will be along shortly.'

She smiled at John. 'My pleasure, John. Be back before you know it.'

'I shall look forward to it.'

Jimmy was impressed. John seemed to go around giving off an aura of warmth and kindness. The lives of everyone he came in contact with seemed to be made better.

'How did you know David drank gin and tonic?'

A sly look crossed his face. 'Well, he is English.' It was an answer but not the right one.

'So who are you, John, and what do you want with me?' He sounded a bit abrupt, but he wanted answers. John seemed unconcerned.

'Those are two big questions; are you sure you want to know the answers?'

Wendy appeared behind John. 'Go on Jimmy, ask him.'

Without turning around John spoke. 'Hello Wendy.'

Jimmy looked at Wendy. she looked more surprised than a ghost had a right to be. He then looked at John, who smiled serenely at him. This meant that he wasn't crazy. If John could see Wendy too, it meant that Jimmy wasn't imagining it. Unfortunately, it could also mean that John was just as crazy, and he had another nutter joining him in his delusion.

'Do you see Wendy?'

He shook his head. 'No, I sensed she was there, and I could hear what she said, not in my ears. Like a voice in my head.'

'That doesn't really make things clearer, it just increases the chance that I'm going crazy.'

John shrugged. 'Maybe, but I don't think so. What do you think Wendy?' He asked the question without turning to look at her. Wendy hesitated.

'Well… Jimmy has always been a bit crazy, but I don't think he's round the bend.'

John nodded. 'I would agree.' He leaned towards Jimmy. 'What would you like to know son?' He looked Jimmy straight in the eye with those deep blue pools of his. Jimmy felt like John could see right into his soul.

'Who are you? I don't mean your name, I mean where do you come from?'

'Maybe when did I come from would be a better question.' He let that hang there between them for a moment.

Jimmy could feel himself starting to freak out. 'Let's concentrate on the where, we can tackle the when later.'

'Good answer Jimmy, you ever thought of going into politics?'

'No, I've only got one face.'

John and Wendy laughed.

'I'm from a little town called Greenville. It's a city now but when I was a boy it was just a small town.'

'Where's Greenville?'

'Mississippi, not too far from Memphis, you heard of it?'

Jimmy nodded. 'Think I played there twenty years ago at an old place that used to be on the Chitlin Circuit, Southern something.'

John beamed. 'The Southern Whispers Restaurant!'

'That's it, you know it?'

'Know it? I've played there.'

'Ok, so you play then, what do you play? I never heard of you, John.'

'Don't be so rude, Jimmy.'

John looked up, he couldn't see Wendy but he knew she was scowling at Jimmy. John didn't seem bothered.

'It's a fair question. I been a bluesman all my life, plus a bit of soul. I never left the Chitlin Circuit because my life went another way. I decided to help people. People like you, Jimmy. You want to write great songs without killing people?'

It was a simple question. There was no preamble, he just came right out and said it. Wendy's mouth fell open, but she recovered before Jimmy.

'You know about that?'

'I know about everything, Wendy; it's what I do.'

Jimmy sat there just looking from John to Wendy and back again.

When Jimmy finally spoke, it was in a whisper. 'Could you do that?'

'Course I could, you're halfway there already. Look at that song we wrote together the other night, and what about that duet you wrote for you and Wendy? That was lovely and you didn't kill anyone for that!'

'How do you know that? We only ever did that at the Song Cemetery, no way you could have heard us do it.'

John clapped his hands and looked upwards before returning his gaze to Jimmy.

'Don't go expecting normality when I'm around because things change. Normal is not what I bring.'

'Say that again.'

'How you gonna help Jimmy write songs without the, you know?' Wendy suddenly became coy about the killings.

'The "you know" is all I got. Without it I'm just another bum with a guitar.'

John shook his head. 'No Jimmy, you are much more than that. Let me show you how, let me teach you.'

Wendy was nodding at Jimmy. She wanted him to take John's offer. He wanted to take it too but there was something he needed to clarify first.

'Ok, if I believe that you can help me I need to know more about you. I know where you're from and I know some of the stuff you do. What does "When I'm from" mean?'

For nearly thirty seconds John was silent. Thirty seconds isn't a long time when measured in the span of a normal day. When it's a pause in a conversation it feels like a lifetime. Then, without any preamble, John began to tell his story.

'I was sixteen when the siege of Vicksburg began. The year was 1863. I had decided to try and cross the Mississippi the next night and try and join up with the Union forces. I was picking cotton on Mister John Landry's plantation; he wasn't a kind man. I never did figure out how a man like that could love God so much but treat Black folk like beasts of burden.' John sighed. 'I guess we were just not white enough for his God. I had planned my getaway and had a little raft hidden beneath some trees; I just had to pick cotton for one more day. It was a normal day but everything changed forever around midday. General John Pemberton, who was in charge upriver in Vicksburg, had positioned cannons at Greenville to try and pick off the supply boats and troops from getting through. Some of those good old boys decided to let a passing gunboat have it. That was a big mistake. The Gunboat took out the cannons and then covered a troopship that came ashore. When the gunfire had started, me and my brother had run down to the ridge to see what was happening.'

John ran his hands through his hair and rubbed his neck, he looked troubled by the memories.

'I had seen a lot of cruelty in my life, but I had never seen war. The Union was our ticket to freedom, but they came ashore like avenging devils. They killed any man that got in their way and burnt the town to the ground. Mister Landry and his sons thought they were going to push inland from the river, and they packed up and ran. It was strange seeing fear in the eyes of the people who had ruled us by fear for so long. I couldn't take pleasure in it. Fear is not a pretty thing to see. I decided that my days' work was done, and my brother and I ran down to the river and sheltered underneath the trees where my raft was hidden to wait for the river to clear and be safe to cross.'

Jimmy and Wendy were hanging on John's every word. 'What about the rest of your family, John?'

'My brother was my only family. My dad had tried to get north two years previously. Mister Landry's men caught him and bought him back to the farm. It was the second time he had run. First time they gave him a whipping, but not this time. They hanged him from a tree down by the pond that evening, made us all watch just to teach us a lesson. After that they sold my mother and sister to another owner near Shreveport and me and Joseph were alone.'

Jimmy was angry. 'Man, I hope you got to kill Mister Landry.'

John smiled at Jimmy and his eyes were full of warmth. 'No, I never did, and you know what, I never wanted to. Something clicked in my head that day and I knew that piling violence on top of violence was like throwing wood on a fire. I hated what they had done to my family, but if I did it back to them, I was no better.

'We crossed the river that evening and then spent the next week floating up the north side headed towards Vicksburg. When we got close enough to hear the artillery we went ashore and made our way on foot. We were found by a Union patrol. When they heard our story, they took us back to their camp and we worked in exchange for food and shelter. I guess, being as I was sixteen I could have got a gun and fought, but Joseph was only thirteen and he needed me so I washed dishes and waited. I didn't have to wait long though.

'On the 47th day General John Pemberton surrendered, and General Grant took the town of Vicksburg. The very next day, Robert E. Lee was defeated at Gettysburg. The Union now had control of that part of the Mississippi and the Confederacy was split in half. I guess it was a turning point, but the war had one more nasty surprise left for me.'

John hesitated; he was struggling with the emotions that the memories brought.

'Me and Joseph decided to borrow a boat and go upriver and take a look at what was left of Vicksburg. We were about a mile upriver. We should have known better; *I* should have known better. There were still a few confederate renegades around and they decided that two young Black boys, who were obviously escaped slaves, would be good sport. They had a small mortar and they opened fire on us. The first one missed, the second did not.'

John stopped talking and a singled tear rolled down his cheek.

Jimmy had barely taken a breath as he listened to John's story. 'What happened to Joseph?'

John slowly shook his head. 'I never saw him again. I woke up on the river shore two days later. I don't know how I got there, but I knew I was different. I felt a fire inside me. It wasn't an angry flame but a warm glow of strength and purpose. I should have died, maybe I did. For some reason I was spared and I had a purpose.' He looked at Jimmy and his cool blue eyes glowed with that purpose. 'I knew I was here to make things better, find the underdog and lift them up. I needed to travel, and I needed to heal. That day was the start of my journey. It was 1863 and I was sixteen years old!'

Jimmy and Wendy said nothing. They were transfixed by John's story. Jimmy broke the silence.

'John, that would make you over a hundred and eighty years old!'

He smiled. 'I look good on it, don't I?'

'But that's just not possible.'

John shrugged. 'It may not be possible, but it is true.'

Wendy had been unusually quiet.

'Einstein's *Theory of Relativity* could give us a clue.'

John looked questioningly at Jimmy.

'She does this all the time John, she's a bit of a science geek.'

Wendy pulled a face. 'You want to hear my theory or not?'

'Not!' said Jimmy firmly, but John was interested.

'You can run it by me Wendy, I'm interested. Einstein was that dude with the crazy hair, wasn't he?'

'Crazy hair but a brilliant mind.' Wendy sat down between them so anyone else in the bar would think they were chatting to each other instead of listening to the words of an invisible dead woman. 'Einstein proved that time was not a constant, John. Depending where you view it from in the galaxy, it can appear to go at different speeds.'

'Always seems to go real slow for me. Guess it's because I been around so long.'

Wendy pushed on. 'Einstein worked out that massive objects can cause a distortion in the space-time continuum.'

'He was talking about planets or black holes though.'

Wendy was impressed. 'Jimmy, you been watching documentaries?'

'Nah, think it was in a magazine in the doctor's waiting room.'

'Anyway, let's say that the mortar shell that hit you and your brother caused a distortion in time. You say you woke up two days later but with no memory of how you got to the shore?'

John nodded. 'Yeah, that's all I remember.' Wendy was in full flow now.

'So, before that John, did you age normally?'

John thought about it for a moment. 'I guess I did. I was three when my brother was born and we just kept on growing at the same pace until,' he paused for a moment looking for the right words, 'until the day we were attacked.' This seemed to please Wendy, she leaned forwards enthusiastically.

'That backs up my theory.'

'You got a theory?' said Jimmy with more than a touch of sarcasm in his voice.

'Yes, I do, Jimmy.' She looked back at John and even though John could not see her he knew exactly where she was and could hear and understand every word she was saying. 'A mortar shell isn't a planet, but what if it caused a very local distortion in the space-time continuum affecting only you, did your aging slow down after the attack?' John rubbed his chin as he considered Wendy's theory.

'You know Wendy, I think it did. I seemed to age at about a third the rate of other people. That's why I have always kept moving. Hang around and folks start to notice that they are getting old a lot quicker than me.'

'Boom!' cried Wendy triumphantly. 'My theory works.'

Jimmy shrugged. 'Sure, it does, but that don't make it the truth.'

'Got any better ideas?' Jimmy, of course, hadn't.

'I like it,' said John. 'Up till now all I've know'd about time is that there is a lot of it, and it goes real slow!'

'So, what would that make John then?'

Wendy ignored Jimmy's sarcastic tone. 'He's going to be in his mid-sixties.' He certainly looked like he was, but when you watched him move he had a casual grace like a panther moving through the forest floor. The muscular definition in his arms, shoulders and legs pushed against the outline of his suit.

'You look a lot fitter and stronger than an old man,' observed Jimmy.

John laughed. 'Well, I'd whip your ass and no mistake.' Jimmy looked at John's physique and knew that he probably would.

John turned to Wendy. 'There is another explanation.'

'Go on.'

'Well science is all very well, Wendy, and in most cases it's the answer, but not in this one.' Jimmy and Wendy hung on John's words. 'Sometimes fate just takes a hand. I was spared for a purpose. I don't know what that purpose was, but I know that if I just keep moving, I'm going to find people who need my help. Wrongs that I can right. There is a light within me and it's burning bright and I intend to keep walking until that light goes out!'

Jimmy and Wendy looked at each other. It wasn't much of an explanation; it wasn't really an explanation at all, but it kinda made sense. When they looked back at John, they were just in time to see him walking out the door. He had slipped away like a ghost in the night. He paused and held the door open for David.

'Good evening, Mister Parker.' He raised his hat and just slipped into the night like a dream of a time gone by.

'Where's Mister Deal going?' asked David.

'He had to go. Sends his regards though.'

David nodded doubtfully. 'Surprising, he seemed pretty keen to talk to you.'

'He did,' Jimmy glanced at his watch. 'You been gone nearly an hour David.'

'Yes, sorry about that but Sam and I had some details to finalise about your contract.' Jimmy gave him a concerned look.

'Don't worry Jimmy, it's all good.' Jimmy was reassured and returned to the subject of John R. Deal.

'John's a great songwriter, he's going to help me with my writing. Reckons he can see a funkier, bluesier side to me.'

David didn't look convinced. 'You think you need help in that department?'

Jimmy nodded. 'Yeah, writing songs is hard work. This record has taken its toll. If it does well, Michael's going to want another one in the can as soon as possible. You know, that difficult second album syndrome?'

David had heard of it. 'Suppose that's the problem for any artist who has a big success with their first album or film or book. There's going to be a lot of expectation on the follow up. Puts the pressure on.'

'It does, having John do some writing with me will spread the load. We can do some demos, and if we don't like them we won't use them. If he comes up with two or three that work, then that's a big win.' Jimmy turned and smiled at David. 'I think we both know that this record is going to work. The band is on fire and a run at Carpenters and all the PR that's going to come from that will really up our profile. I need to start working on the next set of songs now.'

David could see exactly what Jimmy was saying. 'Great expectations, they can make you or break you.'

'Thanks, that helps a lot.'

'Listen Jimmy, why don't you take a moment and just enjoy the success that's coming your way. You can start writing songs in a couple of months.'

David had a point, maybe he should just kick back and enjoy the moment.

'"Great Expectations" would make a great song title.'

'I'm sure Dickens would be delighted.'

Jimmy didn't have a clue who Dickens was, but he decided to jot the title down on a pad when he got back to his hotel room. He was going to start writing again and take his time. Not killing anyone would be a bonus.

CHAPTER 14
A STAR IS RE-BORN

Two days later Jimmy and David were back at the studio in Laurel Canyon. Michael had mixed and mastered the record and they were all sitting around waiting to hear the finished master for the first time.

'Everyone sitting comfortably?' asked Michael.

Nobody spoke, they were all keen to hear the finished product that they had been developing for months.

'Then let's begin!' Michael hit the play button on the console and the first bars of *Vacant Stare* come wafting out of the speakers.

It took forty-four minutes to play the whole album, and nobody spoke. They nodded and smiled but they just listened intently. When it finished, everyone was nodding and smiling with satisfaction and a deep sense that this record was special. Kid was the first to break the silence.

'Is it me or was that awesome?'

'It was awesome,' agreed David.

Michael smiled. 'Gentlemen, I think we have a hit on our hands.'

'Drums sound great.' They all turned round to look at No Relation.

'Is that all you got to say?'

Joe shrugged. 'But they do.'

'Took a bit of editing to get them in time.'

Joe gave Michael a hurt look. 'Cheeky bastard.'

'Take no notice Joe, wherever you go we will follow, we don't have much choice!'

Jimmy sniggered. 'That's a little harsh, Kid. I think it all sounds great.' Jimmy turned to Michael. 'Thanks Michael, I can't tell you how much this means to all of us.' Jimmy turned to face the rest of the band. 'Whatever else we do with our lives we will always have this record. It proves that we had something, and for once in my life I didn't fuck it up. I'm proud of it and I'm proud of you!'

Kid nodded. 'I gotta agree with Jimmy, this record is the nuts. We're headed for the big-time boys, what could possibly go wrong?'

Sadly, for Kid and Jimmy there was plenty that could go wrong. Eight hundred miles away in Jackpot, Nevada, the past was about to catch up with Jimmy Wayne.

———◆———

There was a knock-on Sheriff Pence's door, he looked up and saw his secretary, Dolly.

'What is it, Dolly?' She walked into the room clutching a notepad in her hand.

'You remember that body we found in the back of the burnt-out pick-up near Twin Springs.' Pence set down his coffee.

'I do.'

'I think we may have a name.' She glanced at the notepad she was holding. 'Seems there was just enough left to get a DNA sample, and the forensic guys have come up with a match.' Pence felt a tingle of excitement.

'That's great news.'

Dolly frowned. 'I'm not so sure.'

She held out the notepad. Sheriff Pence leaned forwards and took it from her. He recognised the name at once, but it didn't compute.

'Are you sure about this, Dolly?'

She nodded. 'Afraid so. I already went back to them and checked. The father of the deceased is on the way here now, from London, England!'

'Oh, fuck!' Pence leaned back in his chair.

The name on the paper was Davy Digbeth. If you were in law-enforcement in Las Vegas, you knew who the Digbeths were. The first family of crime back in the good old United Kingdom had been moving in on the Vegas scene for the last four years, having already established a foothold in Miami. This was bad, very bad. Moving into Vegas made you an enemy of Jack Lantern. Davy Digbeth had turned up dead with two of Jack Lantern's boys, which surely wasn't a coincidence. Sheriff Pence worked for Jack Lantern; things were about to get very complicated.

'What time is Big George landing?'

'He's landed already. FBI informed him yesterday.'

'Fuck! How long I got?'

Dolly shrugged. 'He left LAX about three hours ago.'

'Ok, that gives us a bit of time.'

'By helicopter!'

He waved Dolly away.

'Let me know when he arrives at the casino helipad. I got some calls to make.'

'Sure thing, boss.' Dolly backed out the door and closed it behind her. She decided to cancel her lunch reservation. Things were about to get interesting.

Pence looked at the phone, knowing he had to make the call. Jack Lantern was bad, but the reputation of the Digbeth family was darker. They had moved into the Miami nightclub scene like a cancer wearing a glitterball, swiftly inserting themselves in drugs and prostitution, whilst maintaining the thinnest veneer of respectability with a chain of English Pub-styled restaurants which had proved to be surprisingly popular. Good taste in Miami was apparently in short supply.

'Hi Jack, it's Marty Pence.'

Jack smiled to himself, clearly Sheriff Pence did not understand caller ID.

'What can I do for you Sheriff?'

Pence swallowed hard. 'I got some news.'

'Better be good,' said Jack.

Despite the fact it wasn't a video call, Pence shook his head. 'Nah, imagine the worst news and then double it.'

Jack was getting irritated. 'Spit it the fuck out, Sheriff. I'm not in the mood for guessing games.'

'We've got an identity for the body in the back of the burnt-out pick-up.'

Jack felt the hairs on the back of his neck lift. 'Ted Baker's pick-up?'

'Yep.'

'And?'

Pence could hear the irritation rising in Jack's voice. 'It's Davy Digbeth.' He paused for a moment, but Jack didn't say anything. 'You know who he is, Jack?'

'Course I fucking do. Are we sure about this?'

'Afraid so. FBI lab are 99.9% certain.'

Jack put the phone on loudspeaker and slumped back in his chair. He looked around his office for a dog to kick, but the dogs were back home in the garden with Ma and the pool boy. This was bad. If George Digbeth was on the way to see Pence, the shit was well and truly about to hit the fan. Jack had known this day was coming ever since Davy had showed up in Vegas and started throwing his dad's money about. A little digging had revealed that the Digbeths were the first family of crime in the good old UK and were now well-established in Miami. It didn't take a genius to work out that the Digbeths buying a few old bars and restaurants up in Vegas and rebranding them as The Old England Pie House was a Trojan Horse for far bigger and darker enterprises.

'Here's how you gotta play this, Marty.'

Pence smiled. Jack only ever called him Marty when he wanted something. 'When Digbeth gets in your office he is going to want all the details. You are going to have to make it sound like his son and Ted Baker were working together and got murdered by an accomplice of that other dealer scumbag that died with them. What was his name again?'

'Jackson Pollack.'

'Yeah. You gotta make it look like that drug-crazed piece of shit got into a fight with them, they killed him, but Jackson had an accomplice that took them out. We could blame it on some of the Delta Biker gang.'

'But they're all dead.'

'I know, it's perfect. Dead men tell no tales. We could say that one of them was a psycho and knocked Davy out, locked him in the trunk of the pick-up and roasted him alive.'

Although he really did not like Jack Lantern, Sheriff Pence had to grudgingly admit that he had a real talent for distorting the truth. In just a couple of seconds Jack had come up with a story that fit all the known facts and pointed the finger of blame at a dead third party and in the opposite direction to Lantern and his boys.

'I could sell that Jack.'

Jack gave a terse laugh. 'You're going to have to sell it. George Digbeth is going to be angry. He's gonna have a mouthful of hate that he just can't swallow. I know I would if it was my son that got barbecued!'

'What if he asks me about Ted? He could soon find out that he worked for you.'

Sheriff Pence had a point. Digbeth could easily find out that Ted was working for him. He had to make it seem like they were working together and were both the innocent victims of a third party... namely the late and unlamented Deltas.

'Why don't you suggest that they had been seen drinking together in a local bar. You don't have to say any more than that, but it would give the impression that they were working together. That will send him to me eventually and by the time he gets here I will have a bullet proof story to give him.' Jack waited for a moment. 'You reckon you could do that, Marty?'

There it was again; the 'Jack-needs-a-favour' voice, but when you're a bought man you really don't have a say in it.

'Ok Jack, leave it to me.'

'Call me when he leaves, Marty.'

The line went dead. Pence sat there with the phone in his hand knowing that within an hour he would once again be telling lies to cover the tracks of Jack Lantern. It didn't feel good, for the thousandth time he asked himself why he had sold his soul for dirty money. The answer was easier than the question. Dirty money went a long way, mainly because it tended to be tax free!

Jack leaned back in his chair and stared at the wall, his brain racing to try and form a plausible story to tell Big George Digbeth. The body in Ted Baker's burnt-out pick-up turning out to be Davy Digbeth was a complication he could have done without. The Digbeth family was a powerful one and they were just as ruthless as he was. He had two problems.

Firstly, he had to try and avoid a stand-off with George Digbeth. That day would surely come, but now wasn't the moment. His second and biggest problem was to keep Ma on the leash. If she got wind of what was going on, she would be loading the flame throwers and sharpening her knives. She was a strong believer in getting her retaliation in first. Whilst this attitude was excellent at spreading fear into lesser mortals, it wasn't going to work with the Digbeth family. They could fight fire with fire, literally, and then everybody loses. No, he had to find a way to resolve this problem without conflict, for now. George Digbeth and his family needed a longer more elegant solution and that required time and planning. Jack was good at that.

Sheriff Pence heard the helicopter before Dolly had a chance to inform him of Big George Digbeth's arrival. The door of his office swung open and there was officer Feemster. The brightest and the best of his deputies, unfortunately he had two things going against him – integrity and intelligence. These were not attributes that Pence wanted from his deputies, but Feemster was the only bad apple in the Blackjack force. All his fellow officers were scrupulous in maintaining the high levels of dishonesty that Sheriff Pence required to ensure that the Jack Lantern slush fund flowed like a steady river of dollars into various accounts that would supplement their Blackjack police department salaries.

'You won't believe who has just arrived at the Riviera, boss.'

Pence knew but he was savouring the shocked look on Feemster's honest countenance.

'Jimmy Hoffa?'

Feemster frowned. 'Big George Digbeth.' Feemster seemed genuinely shocked by his arrival. Sheriff Pence was more shocked by the fact that Feemster even knew who he was.

'How can you be sure it's Digbeth?'

Feemster shrugged. 'I've been reading up on the Digbeth family. They've been moving in on Vegas for a few years now. Only a matter of time before they start showing up at the smaller Casinos like the Riviera. Easier targets than the big boys in Vegas.' Pence nodded. Feemster had already got it all figured out. Too clever for his own good, that kid.

'You may be right, Feemster, but not today. Big George is here about the death of his son. You remember the unidentified dead body in the trunk of the burnt-out pick-up last year.'

Feemster nodded. 'The one up at Twin Springs!'

'Yep, the very same.' Pence paused for a moment and then looked Feemster straight in the eye. 'Turns out our barbecued boy was his son, Davy Digbeth.'

Feemster winced. 'Shit!'

'Shit indeed, Deputy. Looks like Big George Digbeth is going to be poking around Blackjack for a while.'

'That's not going to sit well with Jack Lantern, boss. Especially as Davy was in the back of Ted Baker's pick-up. Won't take him long to find out that Baker worked for Lantern.'

Pence nodded in agreement. Man, this kid was quick, he made a mental note to get Feemster promoted and moved on as soon as possible. He was far too clever to be in the Blackjack force.

'I suggest you make yourself scarce. Big George is going to be barging through that door any minute now and he's not going to be in the mood for making small talk.'

Feemster nodded. 'Ok boss, I'll head over to the helipad and see if there is anything I can get out of his pilot. Might even have brought a couple of goons with him.'

'You do that Feemster.' He watched him go. That boy is just too switched on for his own good. Maybe he would have to have an accident in the line of duty.

Pence heard voices from the reception area. He couldn't make out what was being said, but he could just about hear the flat tones of an accent he was unfamiliar with, that had to be Big George. His phone rang.

'Mister Digbeth is here Sheriff.'

'Thanks Dolly, please show him in.'

He put down the phone and took a deep breath, this was going to be interesting. If Digbeth was ever going to go head-to-head with Jack Lantern, he knew he needed to position himself somewhere in the middle. The only loyalty Sheriff Pence owed was to the winner!

There was a tap on the door and Dolly ushered in Big George Digbeth. For a moment Sheriff Pence did not know what to say. Big George Digbeth was decidedly not big. Five feet six in his hand-made brogues, but built like a bull. He offered his hand, which was like a bunch of bananas, and flashed Pence a brief smile which highlighted the cold blue steel of his eyes.

'George Digbeth.' His voice had a quiet power and a heavy regional English accent which Pence could not place. Pence waived to a seat.

'Please take a seat, Mister Digbeth.'

Digbeth seated himself like a gorilla flopping onto a tree stump. The latent power of his movement belied his sixty-four years. This was a man who had kept himself in shape.

'I'm so sorry about the news regarding your son. I can assure you that my department will not rest until we have found the culprit for this crime.'

Digbeth nodded solemnly. 'Thank you, Sheriff. I'm going to make sure we find out what happened.'

Pence didn't like the sound of that. 'Don't worry, Mister Digbeth, my boys are all over this.'

George looked around the office. 'I don't see anyone being questioned; you even got a suspect?' The interview was getting ugly real fast.

'It's early days, Mister Digbeth. We only just found out it was your son in there.'

Digbeth looked away impatiently. Pence could see the muscles at the edge of his temples flexing as he fought to contain his anger.

'My boy has been dead for months and you only just found out who he was. You're not filling me with confidence, Sheriff.'

This was not the conversation Pence had been hoping to have. He opened his notepad and picked up a pen.

'Could you give me any idea of your son's reasons for being in Blackjack.'

Digbeth stared at Pence with contempt. 'He wasn't supposed to be here. He had business in Vegas. Why would he end up here, nearly eight hundred miles away?'

'Yes, that's a bit of a mystery.'

'Bit of a fucking mystery!' Digbeth hissed. 'He was fucking kidnapped.'

'We don't actually have any proof for that.' Pence was desperately trying to calm the conversation, but his words fell like petrol onto flames.

'You think he locked himself in the back of a pick-up and then set it on fire?'

Pence shrugged. 'That seems unlikely.'

Digbeth jumped up out of his chair and towered over Sheriff Pence's desk. It's hard to tower when you are only five foot six, but Big George had an aura of barely suppressed violence that made him seem bigger. He seethed with anger and was struggling to keep himself in check. He leaned over towards Pence, standing on tip toe to counteract his vertical limitations.

'There's something wrong here, Sheriff. It just doesn't fit. I'm getting a bad feeling and when I get a bad feeling people tend to get hurt.' He sat back down without taking his eyes from Pence. 'Now I suggest you tell me everything you know, Sheriff, or I may just have to assume that you have something to hide.'

Pence nodded slowly. He realised this was the moment for him to turn the conversation in the direction that both he and Jack Lantern wanted.

'Ok Mister Digbeth, there are several facts about your son's death that you won't be aware of. We kept a lid on the reporting of the incident because we needed to work out what was going on before the press put two and two together and came up with five.'

'So, what happened, Sheriff? What is it I don't know?'

Pence reached across his desk and took the case file he had pulled out just a few minutes before. He knew exactly what it said but he made a show of reading the first few lines.

'Seems to me that your son got caught up in some kind of local conflict.'

George Digbeth did not seem impressed. 'What the fuck does that mean?'

Sheriff Pence kept his voice calm and slow. 'Your son wasn't the only person to die that day. The pick-up he was locked in belonged to a guy called Ted Baker who worked for a Las Vegas club owner called Jack Lantern.'

Digbeth let out a terse laugh. 'Ha, should have known that slimy bastard had something to do with it.'

Pence held up his hand. 'Not so fast George,' he looked up. 'Can I call you George?'

George smiled. 'Sure, call me what you like Sheriff, just help me find the killer of my boy.'

'We believe that Jack Lantern's man was as much a victim as your son. Ted Baker has disappeared. We think the killer is responsible for the disappearance of not just Ted Baker, but a local drug-dealer called Jackson Pollack.'

'So where is this Jackson Pollack and who was he working for?' demanded Digbeth.

'That we don't know. He was only a dealer; we don't know who his supplier was.' Despite the fact that he knew exactly who Pollack's supplier was, Pence leaned forwards conspiratorially. 'We have reason to believe that there was a fourth person on the scene.'

'Then why isn't he in custody?'

Pence's face creased into a pained expression. 'For several months we have only had the two burnt-out trucks belonging to Baker and Pollack to go on.' He paused for a moment trying to find the right words to describe the charred remains of Davy Digbeth. 'And the remains of your son. I'm afraid the fire was quite intense and that's why it's taken so long for the forensic boys to identify the body.'

George Digbeth nodded slowly. 'Ok, Sheriff, let's see if I have this straight. You guys eventually discover two burnt-out trucks at this Twin Springs place. The trucks belong to a local dealer and one of Jack Lantern's men. Both these men have gone missing, and my son's body was found locked in the back of one of the burnt-out trucks.'

Sheriff Pence sighed. 'Yeah, that's it in a nutshell George. There was a lot of blood at the scene and the blood types match the missing men, but as yet we have been unable to find their bodies. There has to be a fourth person.'

He could see that Digbeth was trying to absorb this new information. Before he jumped to any conclusions, especially ones unfavourable to Jack Lantern, Pence took his chance.

'We believe that Pollack had attacked Baker and killed him. We also believe that Baker and your son were working together.

They had been seen drinking together the day before. We think that Pollack was trying to kidnap Davy.'

'Why would he do that?' interrupted Digbeth.

'Because your son had gathered himself a reputation in Vegas since he moved up from Miami. He had a profile and Pollack obviously saw him as a threat, or more likely Pollack's supplier saw him as a threat.'

George Digbeth raised his hand to stop Pence. 'Sheriff, are you suggesting that my son was involved in criminality? That's quite an accusation.'

Pence considered his words carefully. 'Can I be candid with you George?'

'I wish you would be, Sheriff.' There was a terse edge to his voice. Pence knew that now was the moment to drop his bomb.

'We all know why you and your family are here. You have business interests, some that pay tax and others that are more cash-oriented.'

A slow smile crossed Digbeth's face. 'Go on, Sheriff, I'm listening.'

'Jack Lantern has business interests that also have flexible taxation options. You both have legitimate interests and there is no benefit in descending into murderous criminality. It's bad for business. I think that this is a crime against both of you and you have a common interest in getting to the bottom of it.'

This took George Digbeth by surprise. 'Let me get this straight, Sheriff. You, an officer of the law, are suggesting that Jack Lantern and I join forces to try and catch this killer. Sounds to me like you are making us deputies to send us out as vigilantes.'

Pence nodded. 'It does sound a little like that, but I have to tell you, George, I've been a lawman for over thirty years and sometimes you have to bend the rules to make them stick. All I'm suggesting is that you and Lantern work together to help me find the killer. Three heads are better than one.'

Digbeth sat and considered Pence's suggestion. He had a goatee beard and he began to stroke it deep in thought.

'Let me give you a hypothetical, Sheriff. Suppose we do that, and just suppose we find out who the culprit was.' He paused for a moment. 'What would be your position if we whacked him?'

'Or her,' interrupted Pence.

'Her!' Digbeth seemed surprised. Pence just smiled knowingly.

'This is Nevada. There are some pretty tough women.'

'Really? You're kidding, right?'

Pence smiled. 'Clearly you have not met Jack Lantern's mother, Ma Lantern. She is tougher than Jack and the only person I have ever met that I would consider to be truly evil.'

George nodded. 'I shall look forward to meeting the lady, but if she's Jack's Mum, she must be sitting in God's waiting room. How old is she?'

Pence thought for a moment. 'Hard to tell, George. She looks about fifty if you cut through the heavy make-up, but she has to be early seventies.'

George Digbeth snorted with derision. 'So, you're telling me the most terrifying person in these parts is an overly made-up old lady in her seventies?' George appeared genuinely amused by this but Sheriff Pence wasn't fazed.

'Can I tell you a story about Ma Lantern?'

Digbeth shrugged. 'If you must.'

'I think I should. You seem like a decent person,' Pence lied. 'I wouldn't want you to come to harm because I hadn't warned you.'

Digbeth smiled but said nothing. It was clear to Pence that he did not even consider the possibility of a septuagenarian female being a threat.

'About five years ago we had two young men come down here to spend a few days gambling and drinking at the Riviera. They were from Chicago. Blue collar background, but clearly they had made a few dollars. They were drunken and loud, but in the main harmless. Now one day after spending all of the morning and part of the afternoon drinking and gambling, they came out of the Riviera and stumbled onto the sidewalk, and who did they bump into walking her dog but Ma Lantern? They were unlucky because Ma Lantern doesn't spend much time in Blackjack, but her son has business here and there was a singer on at the Riviera who she wanted to see. Now, Ma's dog was a friendly little thing and he wagged his tail and jumped up at the fellas looking for a bit of fuss. These boys were drunk and slapped the dog down and then gave it a good kick to send it on its way.'

Digbeth sighed. 'Is there a point to this story Sheriff?'

'I'm getting to it George.'

'Any chance you could get there a bit quicker? I've got people to maim!'

Pence ignored the threat that Digbeth had just made to parties unknown and continued. 'Ma didn't even raise her voice to those boys. She just followed them to their hotel and found out where they were stopping. Later that day someone broke into their rooms and kidnapped them both. We looked for them boys for four days before we found them, or should I say what was left of them!' Pence's face creased in a pained smile. 'There is an old farmstead up a gravel road headed up onto the hills behind Shoshone Creek. Been abandoned for twenty years or more. Nobody gets up there much, but a couple of backpackers were walking nearby, and they got the scent of something that one of them recognised. Turned out he was an undertaker, and he knew the smell of a decomposing body when he smelled it. When they investigated, they found a pit about twenty feet square and six foot deep. The two boys were in there, been stripped naked and staked out on their backs to the floor of the pit, spreadeagled!'

Pence waited for a moment for Digbeth to say something. Digbeth said nothing. For once in his life, he was listening.

'Now somebody had put doggy meat on their balls and smeared their arms and legs with the stuff. We only found out about the dog food when the forensic reports came back. Those boys were tore up so bad they had to be identified by their dental records. When I spoke to Bill Philips, the local pathologist, he reckoned the wounds had been inflicted by six or more pit bulls. Judging by the blood loss on the ground they had had their balls torn off first. Bill reckoned that their screams had sent the dogs into an attack frenzy which probably meant that they had their throats torn out next. Them dogs must have been starving because they ate a good chunk of those boys.'

'Were the dogs ok? Some kids these days are just fat balls on legs. Don't want them getting indigestion.'

'We don't know about the dogs, George. We never found them. The only thing we did find was the imprint of a folding chair at the side of the pit. Somebody had sat down and watched the whole thing.' Pence shook his head. 'Can you believe that? Just sat down and watched two young fellas get torn apart by a hungry pack of dogs.'

George smiled. 'I can imagine that, Sheriff. You're never so alive as when you watch someone die. Kinda brings home the fragile nature of existence.'

'Well, you sure are a cold-hearted bastard, George.'

'Goes with the territory, Sheriff.' Digbeth stroked his beard again. 'Is there actually a point to this story?'

Pence chuckled. 'Oh yeah, guess I got a bit side-tracked. You can imagine that a double murder like that got some pretty serious attention from the press and some cops from Chicago came down.'

'Can you charge dogs with murder?'

'Only if we could prove that they dug the hole and staked the boys out in the first place. Failing that we have to assume they had some human accomplices.'

'Is this where Ma Lantern comes in?'

'Pretty much. The press speculated about it being a gambling debt related double murder. The detectives from Chicago tried to link it to the boys having seen or heard something they shouldn't, but nobody could find a thing. But I knew. You see I saw those boys kick Ma's dog, and I saw the look on her face when she followed them across the street. I had no doubt she had them kidnapped, stripped, tied down and then sat back and watched them being fed to those pit bulls.'

'So why didn't you arrest her, Sheriff?'

'And charge her with what? Giving them a nasty look!' Pence leaned back in his chair. 'I went up to see her in her house in

Vegas. Big place. Crime obviously pays. She made me a coffee and we sat in her kitchen and I just came out with it. "I know you killed those boys, Ma." She just looked at me cool as you like, took a slow sip of her coffee. "You want a biscuit, Sheriff?" she said. As it happened, I did want a biscuit. I took one from the plate, but I hesitated as I went to bite it and Ma laughed. "It's not poisoned Sheriff, if I was going to kill you it wouldn't be in here.'"

'That must have been reassuring,' smirked Digbeth.

'Not really, but I pressed on. "You know I saw those guys kick your dog in Blackjack. I saw you follow them to their hotel, the same one they were kidnapped from just a few hours later. I would say that's more than a coincidence, wouldn't you?" She just smiled at me.

'"You can say what you want, Sheriff, but that won't make it true. So far I haven't heard a single thread of evidence to support these terrible accusations."

'She was playing with me, George; we both knew it but I was just too stubborn to back off. "Why did you have to kill them, Ma, and why like that?" She poured herself another coffee and sat down opposite me. She has a really big island in her kitchen. "Sheriff," she says. "You know that I'm a dog lover." "But feeding those boys to a pack of wild dogs, you went too far Ma." "Obviously I didn't, Sheriff, or you would be arresting me, not drinking my coffee." Ma took a long sip and then gave me this look; it was quite disarming. "Look, Sheriff, I hear them boys had stuff on their wangs. Now that would have made a real nice doggy treat, don't you think? And you're right to be looking for a dog lover, but I'm not the one." "Do you have an alibi?" I asked her. "Of course," she says. "What time did it happen?"

'"How do you know you have an alibi when you don't even know when it happened?" She shrugged. "Tell me when it happened and I will find you an alibi."'

George Digbeth was smiling. 'I'm liking the sound of Ma Lantern, Sheriff.'

Sheriff Pence sighed. 'I would reserve judgement until you actually meet her. She's terrifying.'

Big George rose quickly from his chair. Being five foot six it didn't take long.

'Sounds to me, Sheriff, that you are out of ideas and I need to go and have a chat with the Lanterns.'

Sheriff Pence inwardly gave a whoop of joy. The conversation had played out just how he had wanted it. Big George Digbeth was now headed for Jack Lantern and Jack was going to make him an ally in a joint quest for revenge. Sheriff Pence really didn't need to say another word, but a sweet little idea had been running in the back of his mind all the time he had been talking to Big George. Jack wouldn't like it if he ever found out, but Sheriff Pence just couldn't resist this chance to make Jimmy Wayne's new life as awkward as possible. That bastard was due some and he was going to make sure he got it.

'Before you go George, you might want to check out a guy called Jimmy Wayne.'

This made Wendy, who had been leaning by the window throughout the whole meeting, jump to attention.

'Jimmy Wayne? Who the fuck is he?'

'Just a blues singer who's been down but by some miracle is on the way back up.' Sheriff Pence pretended to consider his words although he knew exactly what he was going to say. 'Now

I'm not saying he killed Davy. I have nothing to link him to the events of that day. Truth is we have had a lot of bad shit go down around here over the last year and Jimmy Wayne was around for most of it. He's in LA and Vegas now but since he's been gone it's stopped.' He paused again for dramatic effect and a cunning grin momentarily washed across his vulpine features. 'Might just be worth checking him out.'

'Oh shit!' said Wendy as she floated through the wall and headed back to LA to warn Jimmy.

CHAPTER 15
SIGN OF GOOD FAITH

After the album listen-through, the band had had a small celebration. As half of them were recovering alcoholics, it had been a
fairly understated affair but the mood within the camp was buoy-
ant. David and Michael had headed off to some meetings about
distribution for the record. No Relation and Doug had headed
down into LA to have a real end of recording celebration, and Kid
had headed to bed to try and sleep off the seven plates of food he
had harvested from the buffet that Michael had laid on. Jimmy
was the last man standing. Despite the initial feeling of elation
Jimmy couldn't help wondering if he would ever be able to record
anything this good again, without killing somebody. His writing
was definitely getting better, but he could still tell the difference
between an innocent song and one that was a bit murdery.

Looking down the sweeping lawns that ran down the hill
towards LA far below he thought he saw something move in
the trees in the woodland at the end of the lawn. He watched
closely. There it was again, a tiny flash of brown moving steadily
along the woods about two yards in from the edge. Curious,
he headed down to investigate and the memory of walking
down to the woods where his mother's body had lain came

flooding back to him. Coming home that day and finding his father's dead body seated at the kitchen table. A glass of whiskey clenched, undrunk, in his cold dead fingers. The spatter of his brains across the back of his chair and down onto the floor like an undercooked pasta.

It had taken the police two days to find his mother's body. She had been sitting in the small woods at the bottom of the field, on the old bench her father had made. It was here, as a girl, she had sat with her dad and talked as they looked out through the opening in the trees towards the Poconos Mountains. That final day, she had sat looking out at the view for one last time, the shotgun jammed beneath her chin, waiting for the moment when she would find the courage to pull the trigger. Wayne Corvella had humiliated her for the last time, but in killing him she had closed the door on any future. There was no escape in life. Every decision she had made had brought her to this place. Jimmy would be fine; her mum and dad would see to that. The realisation that her son would probably be better off without her brought tears to her eyes. Why had she failed so completely? Her finger tightened on the trigger. She had fallen for a good-looking man who was beautiful on the outside but emotionally bankrupt on the inside. If only she had listened to her father's warnings. As she sat there, the hills disappeared in the fog of tears, she heard the call of a faraway chickadee.

'Feebee, hey sweetie... feebee, hey sweetie!'

As the shot rang out the chickadee took to flight and the woods fell silent.

A movement near a clump of birch trees brought him back to the present. Against the silvery white trunks, he could clearly see that the flashes of brown were not a mule deer but an old man in a brown suit. He didn't move like an old man. His movement was smooth and his progress steady. He stepped out of the woods and onto the lawn.

'Jimmy Wayne, fancy seeing you here.' John R. Deal beamed a smile that radiated warmth. His eyes sparkled and were edged with humour.

'How the hell did you know I would be here, John?'

He dismissed his question with a wave of his hand. 'Jimmy, you need to stop asking dumb questions and just accept the fact that I know stuff. Lots of stuff. Living nearly two hundred years means you get a lot of experience, some good...' He let the sentence trail off and looked at Jimmy. 'You going to offer me a drink or what?'

'Sorry, John, would you like a drink?'

John snorted. 'I'm a musician, ain't I?' He took Jimmy by the arm and walked him back up the lawn towards the studio. 'Why don't we take our drinks into the studio and have a listen to what you've done? I've a feeling it's gonna be good.'

Jimmy nodded. 'It's good, John, it's very good.'

'I'm sure it is, son. I just want to hear how good you are when there is blood on the tracks!'

Jimmy stopped walking, it still shocked him that John seemed to know all his secrets.

'What exactly do you mean, John?'

John slowly shook his head. 'How many times I got to tell you Jimmy? I know stuff. There's nothing you can hide from me, but don't be afraid of that. I'm your friend, here to help. Besides, all them fellows are better for being dead.'

John gently pushed at Jimmy's arm and got him moving again.

'So, if you think you know what I did, why do you want to help me?'

John smiled. 'I don't think Jimmy my boy, I know! It's like I said, killing folks don't make you a bad person if the folks you are killing need killing.'

Jimmy thought about this for a moment. 'So, you're ok with it?'

John laughed. 'Looking at some of the folks you killed I would say you were doing a public service, apart from Wendy and Sammy, but they were accidents. We all have accidents.'

Jimmy's mind was reeling. He had only met John R. Deal twice, and yet he seemed to know everything about him, even his darkest secret. As they reached the studio he decided that whatever John suggested, he would go along with it. He knew too much with no way of knowing it, but more than anything else he had a feeling that John was here to help him.

'Are you my angel, John?'

'I'm no angel, Jimmy. I'm just a traveling bluesman who is trying to help you become a better songwriter.'

'Without the killing.'

John thought for a moment. 'Let's not rule out a bit of killing. Lot of assholes out there, Jimmy. Sometimes they just need thinning out. It's the way of the world. All I'm saying is you need to develop your talent so you don't need to be killing for every song. Makes your music depressing.' He nodded towards the desk in the studio with its rows of faders casting shadows in the low sunlight. 'I'm guessing that this album is going to be dark and introspective, kinda like a bi-polar Leonard Cohen on a really down day.

Jimmy nodded. 'Kinda.'

'Figured as much. Hard to be upbeat when you're swimming in blood.'

'Well, this ain't disco, John.'

'Ain't that the truth.' He squeezed Jimmy's arm. 'I'm sure this is gonna be fine. Depressed people need music too.' Jimmy had the distinct impression that John was making fun of him. He pointed John towards a seat.

'Sit down and we can have a listen. Make sure to remove any sharp objects from your pockets, just in case!'

'No worries, Jimmy, I don't much go for that happy clappy shit. Give me a song with meaning that makes me think any day. I want to be moved.'

Jimmy nodded. 'Oh, you're going to be moved, just don't know how much you are going to like it when you know about the inspiration for every song.' Jimmy opened the file and the first track started to play.

You look at me with your vacant stare
I see you but there's no-one there.

The song drifted on the breeze down the lawn from the studio and all seemed calm in the world. But nothing is ever truly calm. Events were gathering pace. On the road, moving towards Aksel Lund's gold mine, was a blacked-out Escalade. Inside, with a recently broken arm, was Brian McCumber and three Las Vegas thugs he had rented for the day. He had promised them gold, and they had bought into his promise. Brian would take gold but more than anything he wanted revenge. Aksel had made him look stupid. His fiancée had once made him look stupid, and for that he had strangled her. He looked down at his injured arm still in its cast. Strangling Aksel would be out of the question but at least he could hold a gun and shoot him.

Brian was too full of revenge fuelled anger to realise he was already a dead man. If Aksel didn't kill him, Jack Lantern surely would. Jack didn't take kindly to employees moving in on scams that he viewed as his own, but when you strangle your fiancée in the honeymoon suite of a hotel that is full of all your family and friends on the eve of the wedding, careful planning is not your strong point!

CHAPTER 16
STREETS PAVED WITH GOLD

The crew of thugs and killers that Brian McCumber had assembled were not drawn from any of Jack Lantern's private army. He had made the fatal mistake of trying to recruit Danny Baker. When Danny had said no, he should have killed him, but Brian had failed to realise that his refusal also meant that Danny would be telling Terry Moist what he was planning. Terry, in turn, would be informing Jack that Brian was on a solo mission to steal his gold. That's how Jack would view it, his gold! Dead man walking. Brian hadn't worked this out yet.

'So, what's the plan boss?'

Brian turned to Gino; it wasn't a pleasant view. A face that bore all the marks of a lifetime spent in violent endeavours. The broken nose and scarring above the eyes of many cuts that had been stitched by veterinarians and other less qualified medical professionals. Clearly he had been enthusiastic, but less than successful.

'The plan is to kill this Viking asshole and take his gold.'

Gino nodded but still looked confused. 'Shouldn't we take his gold then kill him, boss?'

Brian shot him a withering look and he hesitated before continuing.

'Like you said boss, you never saw the gold, you just think it's there.'

Brian let the moment of anger pass. Clearly, despite being hit on the head on many occasions, Gino still had moments of clarity.

'Fair point. We take him, and then beat the info out of him.'

'Then can we kill him?'

Brian smiled at Walter. ''Course we can. You want to do the honours, Walter?'

Walter licked his lips and let a grin pass across his vulpine features. 'I would like that very much. I ain't killed nobody in months.'

Gino sighed like an annoyed teenager; Brian put a reassuring hand on his shoulder.

'Cheer up Gino, you can beat the shit out of him first. You know Walter likes to finish them off.'

This seemed to reassure Gino.

'Ok, but I want to kill the next one.'

Brian shrugged. 'Maybe he has a dog you could shoot.'

The Escalade was being driven by Kenny Wogstad. Kenny never said much. He just drove. Hell of a wheelman but totally devoid of empathy. He had witnessed many severe beatings from behind the wheel of a car, even some murders. His only response? 'Where to?'

Kenny pulled off the mountain road and onto the track that led to Aksel's cabin.

'Mesa Ridge, Etna. We're here.' He turned off the engine and set the Satnav for retrace route before leaning back and folding his arms.

'You not joining us for the fun, Kenny?' asked Brian.

'Nope.'

'What about the gold?'

'You find it and I'll help you load it. Apart from that I just drive.'

The other three looked at each other and Walter said what they were all thinking.

'Why should we share the gold with you if you don't help us get it?'

Kenny shrugged. 'If we get chased, you're going to need my driving to help you keep the gold.' Kenny didn't do violence of any kind unless you counted running other vehicles off the road, into trees or over cliffs. Collateral damage inflicted from his driving was just that.

'You want me to turn round for a quick getaway?'

Walter sniggered. 'We ain't going to need a fast getaway. Once we have got that Viking asshole to give up the gold, I'm going to kill him and then we can just take our time.'

'Whatever, Walter,' Kenny sounded bored. 'But he did sorta break Brian's arm last time and sent Terry, Danny and Tony home with their tails between their legs. Sounds like a tough guy to me.'

'Just a lucky cheap shot,' snapped Brian. 'He's all out of luck today.'

While the three thugs were debating just how unlucky Aksel was going to be, Aksel was busy watching them on his security cameras. He had already hidden several weapons about the property so he could gather weapons as he moved. He banged another magazine into his HK G90 sniper rifle. He had a 20-shot magazine fitted and three more magazines in his belt.

With a twelve-magnification scope and a suppressor fitted, his unwanted guests would be dead before they even knew they were being fired upon. Aksel liked to plan ahead and had taken the trouble to place three more HK MP7 lightweight machine guns around the property. These were his favourite weapon for fighting on the move, super light with a twenty-shot magazine fitted and a practical range of 200 metres. They were also suppressed. Today he planned to deal in Whispering Death. He had made the decision several days back, whoever came to call was not going back. He took one last look at the Escalade on his screens. Three men had climbed out. He recognised the one with his arm in a cast; he had put him in it. He couldn't help smiling.

'You come to take my gold and you only have one arm,' he thought. Clearly these men were not only missing a useful arm but also the power of rational thinking. Shame that he had to kill them, but people this stupid should clearly not be allowed to breed. The world's gene pool already had enough stupid in it.

Aksel zoomed in and could see they appeared to be armed with Glock 19s 9mm handguns. They were a good handgun but that was like turning up to a knife fight with a cocktail stick. He was just about to move out when he noticed a fourth man. Sitting behind the wheel with his head leaned back on the headrest, this guy wasn't going anywhere. This made things tricky. If he was just here to drive, chances are he would be on the gas and gone at the first sign of trouble. Somehow Aksel had to kill the other three without letting the driver see. He picked up his weapon and crept out of his office by the back door and headed for the ridge behind the workshop.

There was a narrow pathway through a crack that ran up the rock to the ridge. Aksel moved swiftly, staying low and watching the drive that led to his cabin. Any moment now his three attackers would be appearing round the curve in the drive and would no longer be shielded by the rocks that lined the drive. He took up position, breathed deeply and aimed his rifle at the middle of the drive, waiting for them to appear in his sights. But they didn't. He cast his eyes anxiously around, scanning the approach and there, moving rapidly to the left across the rock field, was the small man with a fox-like face. He scanned back to the other side. For a moment he could see nothing, then he saw the top of a head bobbing as he ran. There was a corridor between the rocks and it would shield him from Aksel's fire but Aksel knew that that corridor was a dead end. When he reached it, he would have to climb into view to keep moving towards his cabin. He glanced back towards the small guy and saw him drop down behind some rocks near to the edge of the rocky ridge on which he was positioned. To make the shot he would have to stand up and lean over the edge. The situation was getting tricky. He scanned back and forth between the two men, waiting for a shot to open up, and as he did so the man with the cast on the arm he had broken came into view. He was hugging the rocks as he came around the corner, thinking that he could not be seen from the cabin, and he was right. But Aksel wasn't in the cabin, and from where he lay Brian McCumber was an unmissable target. He really wanted to interrogate this annoying thug, but circumstances dictated that he needed to reduce the odds in this encounter. He lowered the G90 and took aim on Brian McCumber's forehead. Gently he squeezed the trigger and with a silent 'Whoosh' the shot was gone. The man flew backwards and upwards as his head exploded. Aksel watched him fall to the ground, twitch a couple of times, and then was still. For a man who had such a stupid attack strategy he appeared to have a large amount of brains. Now they would remain in death as they had in life – unused!

Aksel swiftly refocused and saw the big man climbing up the side of the cliff trying to reach the ridge that he was on. He was a powerful man but way too big to be a climber and was struggling like a pig on ice skates. He could leave him for a moment. He scanned back the other way. Nothing. The small man had disappeared. The only place he could have gone was beneath Aksel's position along the foot of the cliff. Aksel risked a look over the edge and was greeted with a bullet. It hit the rockface about a foot beneath him. He ducked back down. This was bad. The little guy had worked out where he was. He had to get back down the ridge before he became a sitting duck. Swiftly he made his way down towards the cabin. He glanced over to the rockface on the other side of his cabin and the big man was nearing the top of the cliff. Another twelve feet and he would be there. He needed to take him out but before he could take aim another bullet smashed into the rocks just in front of him. He dived to the ground, thankful that these guys had only bought handguns. Clearly the small man was cleverer than his colleagues.

Back in the car, Kenny Wogstad had heard the two shots from Walter's Glock. He jumped out of the car and ran down the drive, keeping close to the rocks. As he rounded the curve he was greeted by the sight of Brian's body. The top of his head was missing but his face was unmarked. It bore a look of surprise. The arm in the cast pointed to the heavens.

'You won't be going there,' thought Kenny. Another shot rang out from the cliff face to the right. He pushed himself back into a gap in the rocks at the side of the driveway. From where he stood, he was hidden from the cabin and could only see the rocks and the cliff to the left of the cabin. Hanging precariously, like a drunken spider, was Gino. Just a couple of feet from the top but unable to make the final moves to get over the slight overhang. Kenny wasn't a gambler, but he knew bad odds when he saw them. He took a deep breath and burst from the shelter of the rocks and ran back down the drive to the car. These fools were on their own.

On the top of the ridge Aksel heard the roar of the Escalade's motor as Kenny Wogstad performed a rapid U-turn and floored the throttle. Aksel cursed under his breath. Now there was a witness.

Walter wasn't too happy either and made a mental note to kill Kenny when he caught up with him. Gino on the other hand didn't even notice. He was stuck. He couldn't go forwards, and he couldn't retreat down the rockface. He was only a couple of feet short of the ridge but there was a slight overhang, and if he went for the one hold that was just outside his reach, he would lose his foothold. He glanced down at the 60 foot drop. There was nothing to break his fall.

Aksel was approaching the part of the ridge where there was a small crack in the rocks that descended to his cabin. Once he started down, he would be a sitting duck if the small man had reached the cabin. He crouched down behind a rock just a few feet short of the crack. Reaching into a fold in the rock, he pulled out his MP7. It felt reassuringly deadly. He was going to have to take a calculated risk. Chances were that the small man was scanning the rocks and waiting for him to appear. The second he started down the path in the crack he would be spotted. The chances of his attacker hitting him with a hand-gun from that distance were slim and the second he fired Aksel would know his position and he would unleash a magazine of rapid fire that would send him diving for cover. He took a deep breath, removed the suppressor – no need for that now – and sprang from cover. As he reached the top of the pathway a bullet slammed into the rock behind him. The flash from the Glock had come from the rocks on the other side of his cabin. He pulled the trigger and the world exploded. Splinters of rock erupted, and Walter dived for cover. He scrambled back along the foot of the cliff edge. He was outgunned. This guy had clearly been expecting them.

When Aksel's machine gun had fired, Gino had nearly fallen and as he clung to the rockface he could hear the tinkling of shards of rock as they fell to ground. He was a sitting duck. If that gun could shatter rock, what would it do to him?

Aksel glanced down the track as he snapped a fresh magazine into the MP7. The little man was retreating across the rocks at the foot of the cliff. He was heading for the cutting in the rocks that the big man had used to reach the cliff face. If he reached there, he would be able to make a break for the driveway under cover. Aksel couldn't allow that to happen. He glanced up and there was the big man, like a spider in a bath. He wasn't going anywhere. Aksel bounded down the pathway and sprinted across the driveway in front of the cabin. The small man was scrambling across the rocks towards the cutting, but leather-soled shoes and short little legs do not really work when an athletic trained killer in rubber soled climbing boots is chasing you. Aksel sprang up the rocks, clicking the MP7 onto single shot as he did so. He put a shot to the left of the small man and then one to the right.

'Stop right there, or the next one's going in your back!'

Walter looked at the distance to the cutting, another ten meters. He would never make it.

'Drop your gun.' Reluctantly Walter did so. 'Turn around.' Slowly he turned to face Aksel. The guy really did look like a Viking. Tall and blonde and powerfully built. Aksel moved towards him.

'Who sent you?'

Walter shrugged. 'Nobody sent us, we work for ourselves.'

'Who is we?'

Walter thought for a moment. No point lying to this guy, but maybe if he thought he worked for Jack Lantern he might think twice about killing him.

'Jack Lantern. You know him?'

'I know of him.'

'Well, you know that you don't want to be messing around with his boys, do ya?'

Walter gave Aksel a cocky grin which Aksel wanted to wipe from his weasel face with a bullet. He couldn't afford to do that, he needed to know who had sent these guys. He never got the chance. Before he could ask another question there was a stifled scream from above. Walter got a split second to glance up before two hundred and forty pounds of Gino Del Monte landed on him, compressing his already vertically-challenged body into something more compact. With a dull thud accompanied by a cracking of compressing vertebra, Walter splattered across the rocks. Gino had found something to break his fall, but not enough to save him. Aksel just stood there for a moment unsure whether to laugh or cry.

———◆———

As the last track faded out John R. Deal nodded slowly.

'You nailed it Jimmy, this will make you a star.'

'You think, John?'

'I'm positive,' he paused for a moment. 'Good as this is, Jimmy, it's only a steppingstone. This will put you back up there, but you have a problem.'

'I do?'

'Same problem every band has with a breakthrough album.'

Jimmy was confused.

'That difficult second album?' said Kid. He had slipped into the studio whilst they were talking.

'But we've only just finished the first album,' protested Jimmy.

'Kid's right,' said John. 'Fame is like an incinerator; it just burns up material. You need to have something ready to go within six months or you are going to lose momentum. Nobody's heard from you in twenty years and suddenly you are coming out with a really good album. Fans are going to be expecting lots of songs that you have written over those twenty years. You have to pretend that you have been writing great songs all this time but never got the chance to release them. They won't wait another twenty years for the next one!'

'John's right, Jimmy, if we want to ride this wave, we can't afford to leave a big gap before the next album.'

Jimmy shook his head. 'That's easy for you guys to say, you don't have to kill anyone.' John walked over to Jimmy and put an arm around his shoulder.

'Cheer up Jimmy, I think we could write a few songs without you killing anybody.'

Jimmy looked up at John hopefully. 'You really think so, John?'

'Yeah, maybe need two or three. Strong singles are important.'

Kid wasn't so sure. 'You ever listened to any of Jimmy's stuff when he hasn't killed someone?' The look of pain on John's face convinced Kid that he had. A big smile spread across Kid's face.

'Hey, let's do some covers!'

'That's a great idea,' said John. 'You can make them your own by using that new style you're developing.'

Jimmy thought that this was a great idea. 'What about *Low Spark of High Heeled Boys*?'

'I love "Traffic",' exclaimed Kid. 'We could do an amazing take on that; you sound a bit like Stevie Winwood.'

Jimmy was genuinely excited now. Every cover was a song he didn't have to write or a person he didn't have to kill. He turned to John. 'You got any suggestions?'

John nodded. 'You ever heard of a dude called Mike Zito?'

They both shook their heads.

'Well I met him in Texas once and he wrote some pretty cool stuff. He got this one song called, "Judgement Day". Could have been written about you, Jimmy. I think you should try that one.'

Jimmy nodded. 'I'll give it a listen.'

'Me too,' said Kid. 'And look on the bright side, we are going to be based in Vegas for weeks, and if you can't find anyone that needs killing there, well, you just ain't trying hard enough!'

'How many songs you got, Jimmy?'

Jimmy shook his head and looked sadly at John. 'Five.'

John asked the question that both he and Kid were thinking.

'And how many were related to death?'

'Two,' he sounded dejected but then brightened. 'The two I wrote are pretty good though!'

'I think you should let me and Kid decide that.'

Before Kid could answer, his phone vibrated in his pocket. It was a text from Aksel. Jimmy sensed that it was important.

'Who is it?'

'It's Aksel.'

'What's he want, everything OK?' Kid scanned the text.

'Good news and bad news.' Jimmy didn't like the sound of this. 'A bunch of thugs just attacked him, sounds like Jack Lantern's men.'

'Shit!' This was something that Jimmy had been hoping to avoid. 'So, what's the good news.'

Kid smiled ruefully. 'I reckon you got three new songs coming.' John clapped Jimmy on the back.

'That's the singles taken care of. Now you and me are going to have to work on some songs without anyone dying. Want to give it a try?'

Jimmy nodded. Like Lady Macbeth he was sick of having blood on his hands. He needed to get it off.

———◆———

Over the next couple of days things began to gather pace. Michael and David were off doing lots of meetings, setting up distribution deals and personal appearances for Jimmy. They were running a big campaign for Jimmy's residence at Carpenters and were away from the studio. If Jimmy thought that this would give him some downtime he needed to think again. Sonny Castiglia had plans for him.

The roar of Sonny's Hummer announced his arrival. The gates of the property swung open and it trundled into the court-yard like a tank. The door clicked open and Sonny Castiglia free-falled to the ground. Whilst Jimmy was sniggering Sonny jumped self-consciously to his feet and brushed off his jeans. He glanced down to the patio where Jimmy and Kid were sitting.

'He really does need to get a ladder,' observed Kid.

'Or a smaller truck.'

'Clearly he's compensating.'

'Or maybe he's just a crazy survivalist.'

'That he may be Jimmy, but if he takes too many falls like that, he ain't going to survive getting out of his vehicle. Armageddon will have to take place without him.'

Sonny walked jauntily towards them oblivious of the fact that he had been entertaining his client. 'Morning boys, you ready to go do some interviews?'

Jimmy groaned. 'Do we have to?'

Sonny laughed. ''Course we do. It's my job to make you famous. Gotta sell those albums and fill those seats at Carpenters. I even got you a rematch with Ron Blazer.'

Jimmy shook his head. 'No way, Sonny. That guy is a stitch-up artist.'

'Sure, he is, but he got you over five million views. That's some major PR.'

'Guy's an asshole.'

Sonny couldn't disagree. 'Yeah, but you're smarter than him. You ran rings around him, and it turned out real good for you.'

Kid leaned towards Jimmy. 'It was great TV, Jimmy, and I haven't laughed as much in years. Look at the hits you got on Facebook and Instagram afterwards. I really think Sonny is right.'

In his heart Jimmy knew it too. 'Do you think he wants me back after I made a fool of him?'

'This is LA Jimmy; you could take a dump on Ron's head if it gave him good ratings. Since the show his advertising revenue has doubled.'

'Why would companies want to be associated with Ron Blazer?'

'It's called ironic advertising. The kids are laughing at him not with him, that's why Head Blast Vodka have put in a new advert. Do you know what it says?'

Jimmy shook his head.

'Watching Ron Blazer? Then you need alcohol. Head Blast Vodka to soften the blow!'

Jimmy couldn't believe it. 'And Ron doesn't mind?'

'Ron's getting five thousand dollars every time it's broadcast, which is three times on every show. The guy may be stupid but he's no fool.'

Jimmy thought about it for a moment then looked to Kid for an explanation.

Kid just shrugged. 'Welcome to Hollywood.'

'Are we getting paid for this interview Sonny?'

'The exposure is priceless. You can't buy PR like this!'

Kid gave Sonny a sidelong glance.

'From the look on your face I'm guessing Ron isn't buying either?' Sonny shifted uncomfortably.

'We are getting paid?' asked Jimmy.

Sonny tried to move the conversation on. 'I really don't think we need to focus on money for this Jimmy. The exposure is reward enough.'

Jimmy knew bullshit when he heard it. 'How much, Sonny?'

Sonny knew when he was beaten. 'Four grand.'

'Is that before or after your fifteen percent?'

'Before.'

'So you get six hundred dollars.'

'I know, doesn't seem enough, does it?'

'I think it's plenty, but I don't begrudge it. You're doing a good job, Sonny, just don't start taking liberties. Speak to David. I got him to set up a trust fund for my son and I want to pay all the cash from interviews and public appearances into the fund.'

'You trying to give young Wayne enough money so he can afford to change his name, maybe to John?'

Jimmy smiled. 'No, I'm just trying to help the kid, with Elaine as his mother he must have had it pretty tough. I want to give him a chance at some independence, something she can't get her hands on.'

'Any plans to meet him? Make a great human-interest story.'

Jimmy shook his head. 'No chance. When I meet up with my son it's going to be a private matter.'

'I could get you ten thousand dollars for his trust fund.'

'Less fifteen hundred for your fees Sonny.'

Sonny shot Jimmy a big grin. 'Man's gotta eat.' Sonny just never let go and, despite his avaricious tendencies, Jimmy couldn't help but like him. The guy never stopped, and it was great having him in his corner.

'So, when do you want to go back to Ron Blazer?'

Sonny glanced at his watch. 'In about sixty minutes.'

'It's already booked in?'

'Yep!'

Jimmy looked over at Kid. 'Do you believe this guy?'

'Only about sixty percent of the time,' Kid smiled. 'But I believe he is in your corner one hundred percent of the time.'

'You need to listen to Kid, Jimmy. He seems to understand this town. You gotta get out there and shake your booty. Right now you're just another dancer in a huge chorus line. If you don't shake your ass, nobody's ever going to see you. Get out there and give the people what they want.'

'And what do you think that is?'

Sonny pointed at him. 'It's you Jimmy. You gotta give yourself. You gotta meet and greet. Hug the Waynettes, talk to the press and go to the opening of every show you get invited to. You need to be seen and heard. This town is all about who makes the most noise. I have you down for three parties tomorrow, one A List and a couple of B listers.'

'I ain't hanging with no B Listers,' said Jimmy, with an outrage he didn't really feel. Both Kid and Sonny laughed.

'Hell Jimmy, you are barely a D Lister right now,' said Sonny.

'I'd have said borderline C myself,' observed Kid.

'Go fuck yourselves,' smiled Jimmy. 'Looks like my dance card is full for the foreseeable.'

Sonny nodded. 'Yep, for the next three days your ass belongs to me and I'm going to make you work it like a bitch!'

Fifty minutes later Jimmy found himself parked outside of Blazer TV with Sonny.

'So, what's on the agenda today? We did crazy ex-girlfriend and son I never knew I had last week.'

'Not forgetting an ex-manager who wasn't,' added Sonny, clearly proud of his handiwork.

'Yeah, let's not forget that little doozy.' Sonny gave Jimmy his best reassuring agent smile. Every one of his teeth was on show and he gave the distinct impression of a crocodile auditioning for a toothpaste advert.

'Just you and David today.'

'I thought David was in Vegas.'

'He was but the contract details are signed. I arranged with Ron for you and David to do a follow up interview, talk about how you guys met at the Riviera and how David re-discovered you and got you a deal with David's buddy at Small Print records… Nice human-interest piece.'

Sonny painted a lovely picture but Jimmy had a feeling that nothing was straightforward where Sonny and Ron Blazer were concerned.

'That won't get five million viewers.'

Sonny gave Jimmy a look that told him that he knew something Jimmy didn't know. The question, thought Jimmy, was does David know? He would find out in the next few minutes.

'You got something up your sleeve, Sonny?'

'Maybe, but it's going to get you ratings buddy. Five million watched that last shit show and now that you are a C Lister, with a bit of a profile, even more will tune in. As long as we grab them in the first couple of minutes, we could hit six or seven.'

Those numbers were impressive, and Jimmy should have been jumping up and down with happiness, but he knew that those ratings needed feeding – with some raw meat. He felt that knot in his stomach start to tighten once again.

Before he could change his mind Sonny opened his side-door and virtually pushed him out. He grabbed for the door handle and swayed out as the door opened, scrabbling to get his feet beneath him on the step. As he hung horizontally Ron Blazer's moustachioed features appeared next to his face. This close up, Ron looked like a walrus in a sports jacket.

'Jimmy my boy, so good to have you back.' He grabbed Jimmy by the shoulders and eased him back into a vertical plane. Jimmy managed to get his feet beneath him as he dropped to the floor.

'Thanks, Ron. I think Sonny was a bit too enthusiastic.'

Ron just laughed. 'No shit. He just pushed you out, because he knows the second your ass hits my carpark I have to pay your fee!'

Jimmy glared up at Sonny. 'That true?'

There was a glint in Sonny's eye. 'In principle, but let's not forget you get 85% of it.'

'Well, that should cover my medical bills.'

'Not in this town!'

Before Jimmy could get into it any further, Ron took him firmly by the arm and guided him towards the entrance to Blazer TV.

'Very exciting show today, Jimmy. Got a full house in, even put in another twenty seats.' Ron steered Jimmy through the doors straight into the studio. As soon as the crowd saw him, they started cheering. Unlike last time, Jimmy knew his entrance would be straight onto the stage and he waved cheerfully as he moved towards the side of the stage and the entrance to the green room. The door was opened by the floor manager who scowled at Jimmy.

'Welcome back, smartass.'

'Nice to be back.' Jimmy grinned at him. 'I thought you would be pleased to see the man who upped your ratings.'

The floor manager shrugged. 'I am. Don't mean I have to like you though, does it?'

'Guess not.' Jimmy did his best to stand on his foot as he went through the door but the floor manager backed away as if he expected some form of physical assault. As Jimmy entered the green room, David stood up to greet him.

'Hello Jimmy, how are you this fine morning?'

'Well as can be expected for an ambush victim.'

David smiled. 'I'm sure it won't be that bad.'

'Did you see the last show?'

David couldn't supress a smile. 'Yes, it was a little combative.'

'It was a shit show,' exclaimed Jimmy.

'True, it wasn't very good, but I thought you came out of it rather well.'

Jimmy looked at his friend. Not a hair out of place, brown brogues polished until they gleamed, and a pair of cream chinos topped off with a crisp white shirt and a brown and blue tweed jacket. In the breast pocket was a folded silk handkerchief which was speckled with blue and brown to complement his jacket. Jimmy glanced down at his grubby trainers and scruffy jeans.

'You're making me look underdressed.'

David looked him up and down. 'You're barely dressed at all. Have you slept in those clothes?'

'Rockstar chic?'

David smiled. 'Lazy bastard more like.' David ushered Jimmy to a seat and sat down next to him. 'You know what this interview is about?'

Jimmy shook his head. 'Nah, I guess old Ron is going to try and stitch us up. Seems like his style.'

David nodded his agreement. 'Yes, that would be my opinion. He is going to ask us about how we got to know each other. Let me take the lead and you follow; I don't want him going on about your drinking years.'

'That would be all of them at the Riviera, until last year.'

'Exactly! We don't want to dwell on the negative stuff. Let me brush over it and we can get onto the good stuff.'

Jimmy looked at David with affection. 'You really don't know Ron Blazer very well do you, David? He doesn't do interviews. He does ambushes! Be on your guard and expect questions about anything. With this guy, nothing is off limits.'

David looked unperturbed. 'I'm sure I can handle anything that this chump has to offer.'

'You probably can. All I'm saying is, be on the lookout for the grenade. He's going to chuck it in at the first opportunity.'

———◆———

Two hundred and seventy miles away Jack Lantern sat in his office. There was a knock on his door and in came his secretary, Margo. She smiled with a face that carried all the warmth of a block of granite.

'Ronnie Reich is here, Jack.'

Jack nodded. 'Show him in Margo, oh and get us a couple of coffees.'

Margo nodded. As usual with Jack, there were no pleases or thankyous. She had never noticed before but since she had met Mr John R. Deal, she had felt this warm glow inside her and emotions she had never felt were now bubbling away beneath the surface. Like a long dormant volcano, stirring after a long period of inactivity, small tremors were beginning to register. She walked into her office and hooked her thumb over her shoulder in the direction of Jack's office.

'You can go in, Ronnie. Still take your coffee white?'

Ronnie nodded. 'Yes please, Margo.'

Margo smiled at him. Ronnie was a nice man. Such a shame that his dad had been a Nazi. Ronnie tapped the door of Jack's office before entering. Jack looked up.

'Morning, Third.'

Ronnie winced as he sat down. 'Do you mind not calling me that, Jack. It's not a nickname I appreciate.'

Jack leaned back in his chair. 'But your name is Reich, and your dad was a Nazi. It's perfect.'

Ronnie shook his head. 'It's distasteful Jack. You know me and my father weren't close.'

Jack nodded. 'Ok, ok, but I still think it's funny.'

Ronnie wanted to move the conversation on, the best way to distract Jack was to talk about money.

'I've been doing some digging into this Aksel character and his accumulated wealth.' Now he had Jack's attention.

'What you found?'

Ronnie opened the folder he was carrying and spread out several pages of handwritten notes on the desk. 'This Aksel chap is hiding something, and he is very good at it. That said there is a picture emerging from all the data I have gathered. The money that appeared in Jimmy and Kid Oscarson's accounts had come from a Swiss bank, and Aksel Lund has an account with this particular bank.'

'How did you find that out?'

'Like you said, Jack, I'm from an old German family and I still have contacts, especially in places like Switzerland. They may have been neutral in the Second World War but the Swiss were happy to invest money from anyone.'

Jack nodded his understanding. 'Sons of the fathers?'

'Let's just say they didn't all come to America!'

'So, what have you got?' Jack was eager to have his suspicions about Aksel Lund confirmed. Ronnie looked down at his paperwork.

'Well, we know that it was probable that Aksel Lund put the four million dollars into the boys' accounts. I also know, through my contact at the bank, that Aksel has paid tens of millions anonymously to several charities in the last year or two.'

Jack whistled under his breath. 'Go on Ronnie.'

'Checking back through his banking history, Aksel Lund had no money to speak of until two years ago. He had a few hundred thousand from a compensation pay off from the Norwegian armed forces, but I couldn't trace what branch of the forces.'

'Special Forces. Terry told me the guy really knew how to handle himself,' said Jack. 'Broke that Brian McCumbers's arm.'

'What, the crazy guy who strangled his fiancée?'

'Yeah, that's the one. He's a bit highly strung, but he shows promise.'

Ronnie sighed. Only Jack would think strangling your future wife would be a positive character statement.

'Takes all sorts, I suppose.' Ronnie pulled a sheet from the papers he had laid out on Jack's desk and handed it to him. 'Based on every payment he has made to the charities I have found and assuming, which I think is a safe assumption, that the four million paid over to Wayne and Oscarson came from him...'

Jack was reading the paper and beat Ronnie to the punchline. 'You reckon he is worth forty million dollars!' Jack looked aroused.

Ronnie found it disturbing and looked down at his other papers. 'No, he's had far more than that. This figure has come from payments he made that I can trace. I haven't managed to find any other accounts yet, but there will be others. Conservatively I would estimate that our Mister Lund has probably generated close to a hundred million in the last two years.'

Jack leaned back in his chair his aroused face now thankfully turning into a broad grin. 'Seems to me, Ronnie, that we are going to have to pay Mister Lund a visit.'

'Or set yourself up as a registered charity, because he seems to be giving it away at a rapid rate.'

The grin on Jack's face subsided. 'Maybe we could get him sectioned. Giving all that lovely cash to the poor and the needy. What's wrong with the guy?' Jack seemed genuinely incredulous. The idea of giving without receiving was totally at odds with the upbringing that Ma had given him. Jack had done a lot of receiving in his life, mostly stolen goods, but that felt natural. Giving away money to the poor and needy – that just wasn't natural.

'He's clearly an altruist. Maybe, if he was Special Forces at one time, he's trying to make amends for the things he did by helping those less fortunate. Atonement, I believe is what they call it.'

Jack didn't look convinced. 'Like you giving back the artworks your Nazi father stole from wealthy Jews back in 1942?'

'Those pictures have been in the family for years,' protested Ronnie.

'Yeah, but not your family. Don't forget Ronnie, I've been to your house. Don't get me wrong, you're a very talented accountant. You make a lot of money working for me and I know you do a bit of moonlighting, but that don't buy what you got. Monets and Sisley's, seem to recall a couple of Turners. I looked them up, you know, and they were all down as missing in the Second World War. The value was estimated at over one hundred and forty million. Now I don't know how much a Brigadier General in the Waffen SS made but I'm guessing it didn't run to buying that little collection.'

For a moment Ronnie didn't know what to say. How did Jack know what rank his father had been and how the hell did he know he was SS?

'Listen Jack, you know I did not approve of my father's life choices.'

'He was a murdering SS Nazi bastard, Ronnie!'

'Well, you're not exactly Snow White!' snapped Ronnie.

Jack smiled. 'Don't take this personal, Ronnie. I'm not saying I don't approve of accumulating wealth by dubious means. Your dad was never going to be humanitarian of the year, but we all know he left you sitting very pretty, so don't go denying it!'

Ronnie couldn't deny it. His father had left him very comfortable when he died. His dislike of his father didn't go as far as trying to return his ill-gotten gains to the families they had been stolen from.

'You know I could never sell them on the open market, Jack. They are all listed as missing.'

'I know that, Ronnie. Wouldn't take them long to find out who your father was and what he did in the war now, would it?'

Ronnie shuddered. He had built himself a very nice life in Vegas. He went to all the best parties and was respected. Being outed as the son of a Nazi war criminal would have a disastrous effect on his standing in the community.

'Your valuation is wrong. To me they are worthless because I can't sell them.'

Jack sneered. 'On the open market no, but I could pick the phone up right now and find you a private collector for most of those, no questions asked. So, let's not play the poor card, Ronnie. I'll get you half the market value less my commission.'

'Thanks Jack, but I'm not selling. How about we concentrate on Mister Lund's assets?'

Jack nodded. 'Yeah lets,' he leaned forwards. 'So how much do you think we could shake him down for?'

'Hard to say, Jack. It's clear he is generating a lot of money, but he seems to be spending it as fast as he makes it. My guess is he has struck a rich seam of gold and he is disposing of it through multiple outlets under a series of untraceable shelf companies.'

Jack thought about this for a moment. 'So do we stake out every bullion bank in Nevada and California?'

'Pointless, Jack. He could be using several different independent agents in different states who are all unaware of each other. That way he has been spreading it...'

'To try and stay under the radar,' Jack interrupted.

'Yeah, he's a cute one.'

'He may be cute, but that's a lot of gold. These banks are going to start wondering where he is getting it from.'

Ronnie shook his head. 'I reckon I could find over forty bullion banks operating legitimately in the world right now. Then there will be smaller traders. My guess is that our Mr Lund is smelting them into ingots so he can have them stored with a bullion bank and then trade them where and when he wants. That's going to be more or less untraceable.'

Jack sat back and thought. 'This is panned gold then?' asked Jack.

Ronnie shook his head. 'We call that Placer gold, but he couldn't possibly generate that much gold by traditional panning.'

'Well how the hell is he doing it? He's all alone up there.'

'I have a theory.'

'Let's hear it,' said Jack. He was becoming irritable as he began to realise that proving Aksel had gold and then finding a way of getting hold of it was going to be more difficult than he had anticipated.

'We know there is a river that runs through the mountain coming from the Etna Station side within the Mesa Ridge. The panning used to take place below the ridge where the river comes out into the Valley. What if there is a rich seam of gold within the ridge which is being washed from the rock by erosion of the river. Aksel could be getting big chunks of gold breaking away which is going to be just like mined gold, big nuggets!'

Jack nodded his approval. 'That makes sense, Ronnie, but it's a bit far-fetched!' Jack didn't realise it, but Ronnie had just revealed Aksel's big secret.

———————◆———————

Sonny Castiglia perched on a stool in the green room at Blazer TV. 'Back in Black' came roaring through the PA. He was looking forward to this. Ron Blazer was sure to ask Jimmy and David some tough questions. He knew that because he had given them to Ron. A big shit show gets far more attention than a nice, safe interview.

Ron let the applause die down.

'Welcome to *Back from Oblivion*, today's guest is an old friend of the show, Jimmy Wayne, and his friend and manager, David Parker.' There was a huge roar from the capacity crowd. Only sixty people but in a small studio it sounded huge. Jimmy waved to acknowledge the crowd. David, on the other hand, maintained a cool debonair appearance and simply nodded his gratitude. Ron looked at Jimmy.

'Does it feel good to be back so soon, Jimmy?'

Jimmy grinned. 'Yeah, it's like going to the dentist. You don't want to, but you know you should!' This brought a healthy round of applause. Ron laughed.

'Well I am sure we can find some cavities in your history, but more of that later.'

Jimmy didn't like the sound of that much. Ron had been doing his research. Ron turned to David.

'So, David, England is a long way to come to be working at the Riviera, especially after you had been managing one of the biggest casinos in Vegas.'

David showed no outward sign of surprise but now realised that the grenade that Jimmy had warned him about had just been thrown.

'Have you been to the Riviera, Ron? It's a lovely place.'

'But it ain't Vegas, is it?' Ron was smiling as he spoke but there was an edge to his voice. David calmly gestured around the studio.

'To be fair Ron, this isn't exactly primetime, but it's still a nice little venue.' David put special emphasis on the little. There was a snigger from some of the audience. Ron wasn't fazed.

'Good point, David. I got canned from primetime by the woke mob. What did you do?'

'Well I'm not sure I even understand what woke is Ron.' Again, the audience laughed but Ron would not be deflected.

'I heard it was a public relations issue?'

David gave Ron a look of mock surprise. 'Really? Tell me more.'

'The story goes that you were having... public relations... with a fellow director's wife... on the boardroom table!'

There was a collective sharp intake of breath from the crowd but David was unflappable. 'On a vintage walnut desk? That would be sacrilege.'

'Does it matter what type of boardroom table it was; we just want to know if you had sex on it.'

David thought for a moment. 'Well Ron, to be candid, I have been bored stiff in many a meeting but never stiff on a boardroom desk.' Jimmy watched in wonder as David calmly played with Ron. Ron, though, looked happy; this was great television.

'So, you are denying it then?'

'Regrettably I can neither confirm nor deny it, Ron. When I left Las Vegas I went to the Riviera, another casino hotel within the group. True, it needed a bit of an upgrade, but I was given shares. Now that's hardly likely to have happened if I had been carrying on as you suggest!'

'So, you are refusing to comment then, David?'

'There is nothing to comment upon, Ron. When I left to go to the Riviera the whole transfer package was covered by a Non-Disclosure Agreement, something I am sure, given your background, that you are familiar with.'

This time Jimmy couldn't help but join in with the laughter from the audience, even Ron joined in.

'Touché, David. Let's just say that it was a fortuitous move, because the Riviera is where you met Jimmy. What were your first impressions?'

A pained expression crossed David's face. He turned to Jimmy. 'Well, no offence to Jimmy, but you weren't at your best.' Jimmy pretended to look hurt. 'In fact, he weren't even average.'

'But you saw potential?'

'No Ron, I just saw a problem. A likeable one, but a potential problem nonetheless. His heart wasn't in it, and he wasn't looking after himself.'

'So how did you turn him around?'

David thought for a moment. 'I don't think I did turn Jimmy around. He turned himself around. All I did was create an environment where he could flourish. It took a while.'

'How long?' asked Ron.

'About six years.'

'You obviously have a lot of patience, David.'

'I do,' he agreed. 'But Jimmy was very cheap, and he is quite likeable. Let's face it, most people are there to gamble – why not me?'

'I can hear you, you know!' Jimmy sounded hurt but he was smiling.

'I know, Jimmy, but you need to let me finish.' David turned to the audience. 'One day Jimmy just started writing really good songs and the audiences began to listen. None of us saw it coming.'

'Neither did I!'

'So how did you do it, Jimmy?' asked Ron.

'You won't believe me, but the songs just came to me while I was sleeping. I kinda dreamed up an album's worth.' Jimmy was being economical with the facts but there was a grain of truth. He just didn't mention the murders.

Ron turned to the camera. 'Can you imagine what Jimmy could do if he were in a coma.' There was a big round of laughter from the audience.

In the green room Sonny Castiglia permitted himself a good chuckle. It hadn't been the shit show he was hoping for, but this interview was coming over really well. Sometimes, even in LA, you can still be surprised by an outbreak of niceness.

CHAPTER 17

VEGAS BABY!

Jimmy walked out onto the stage at Carpenters. Finally, he was in Vegas. He stood there looking out into the theatre, soaking up the atmosphere and the ghosts of the performers that had played this stage before him.

'Try not to fuck it up this time.' He turned and there behind him, leaning on the speaker stack at the side of the stage, was Wendy.

'I'll do my best.'

'Hope that's gonna be good enough, Jimmy.'

'You know it will.' Jimmy turned back to look into the theatre once more. 'It's a great place, ain't it?'

Wendy sighed. 'Sure is, you think this is where your dream comes true?'

Jimmy thought about it for a moment. 'Nah. The real dream would be to have you here too.'

Wendy shrugged. 'I am here.'

Jimmy turned back to her. 'You know what I mean. It just seems a bit hollow, none of this would have happened if you hadn't died.'

Wendy floated across to him and put an arm around him.

'We all gotta die sometime, Jimmy. At least I get to travel in this life. Could be worse.'

Jimmy looked doubtful. 'How could it be worse?'

Wendy thought for a moment. 'I could have died in a public toilet and ended up having to haunt that for the rest of my days.'

'Inconvenienced, in perpetuity,' said Jimmy, a wicked smile playing on his face. For a moment Wendy was genuinely surprised. Sometimes, very occasionally, Jimmy would say something that made her believe that there had been an odd day or two in his school life where he had actually paid attention.

'That was pretty witty, Jimmy. You read that in a cracker?'

'Maybe.' Jimmy pointed to his head. 'Don't be fooled by these pretty looks. Inside this sexy head lurks the brain of a genius.'

'Let's just hope he don't want it back!'

Jimmy laughed. 'You going to be staying around?'

'For a while. I want to see you debut to a full house and, once I know you're ok, I'm heading off to the Grand Canyon for a while. You know I always wanted to go there. Now I'm dead, it seems that I can go anywhere I please.'

'Hell of a price to pay for free air miles!'

'Always gonna be a trade-off, Jimmy.' Wendy curled herself around him and gave him a long tender kiss. 'Enjoy the moment, you earned it.'

Before he could reply, Wendy dissolved from his arms and he felt the slightest breeze as she brushed past him on the way to who knew where. Even after all this time Jimmy still didn't know if Wendy was real or just a figment of his imagination. Before Jimmy had time to miss Wendy she suddenly reappeared through the wall.

'Couldn't stay away?'

Wendy looked sheepish. 'More a case of forgetting to tell you something.'

Jimmy could tell by the look on her face that this wasn't going to be good news.

'Spit it out, Wendy.'

'You know the body in the pick-up, the one that turned out to be the gangster from the UK?' Jimmy felt that familiar tightening in his gut.

'Yeah.'

'Well, his dad has been to see Sheriff Pence.'

'And?'

'Pence kinda suggested that you had something to do with it!' Wendy gave him a sickly smile. 'Don't think the Sheriff likes you, Jimmy.'

'No shit.' Jimmy tried to think. 'Anything else you forgot to tell me?'

'Apart from the fact he is coming to Vegas to question Jack Lantern? No, don't think so!'

Jimmy stared blankly at Wendy, trying to absorb this new information. This was bad, but how bad?

'Look on the bright side. It's in Jack's interest to protect you. Ted Baker was working for him, and Jackson Pollack was dealing Jack's drugs.' That made sense.

'So just deny everything?'

Wendy nodded. 'There are no witnesses apart from me, and I'm dead. Jack has money invested in you via the label. It's not in his interest to drop you in it.' This made sense to Jimmy. The knot in his gut started to relax.

'What's he like?'

'Big George Digbeth?'

'Who else?'

'Well, he ain't big. Five foot six tops, but he's built like a gorilla and he's got that cold look in his eye. Sheriff Pence knew that Jack wouldn't be happy with him dropping you in it, but he did it anyway.' Jimmy knew that Pence didn't like him and now he realised just how deep that went.

'One day, Wendy, I'm going to go back to Blackjack and write a song about Sheriff Pence.'

For the next few days, the band were going to be rehearsing hard. Learning how to fill the stage and discovering the amp settings that would give them the best sound. Phil Butters, the sound engineer at Carpenters, was brilliant. He understood the space and, by the end of day one, had all the levels set to perfection. All they had to do was get their set perfect.

Everything was lined up and now for the first time in his career Jimmy had no excuses. That was a daunting place to be. Everything was looking rosy but there was a black cloud in the vertically challenged shape of Big George Digbeth coming his way. The seed that Sheriff Pence had planted had now grown into a forest and George Digbeth was now convinced that Jimmy Wayne knew something about the death of his son.

———◆———

Less than four miles away Jack Lantern was looking for something to throw. Terry Moist had just given him the news about Brian McCumbers unauthorised visit to Aksel Lund's gold mine.

'What the fuck was he thinking?'

Terry shrugged. He had seen Jack go ballistic on so many occasions it was no longer the thing of awe that it had once been. 'This is the guy who strangled his fiancée at their hotel the night before the wedding. Not too sure that thinking was part of his DNA.'

Jack knew that Terry was right. He also knew he had warned him about Brian. Terry was far too clever to remind him, but the look on his face made it clear what he was thinking.

'Ok Terry, you were right. He's a loose cannon.'

Terry didn't say anything, just raised his eyebrows in a way that implied that he knew this would happen. Jack tried to justify himself.

'He just seemed so menacing. I like that in an employee, strangling his fiancée in a hotel full of her family showed commitment. Surely a man that could do that would be up for anything I told him to do.'

Terry leaned his head to one side. 'Trouble is boss, a man that would do that would also do other stuff without considering the consequences. When we need to whack someone, we pick our moment, think it through. That way we don't get any problems come knocking on our door.' Terry was right and Jack knew it.

'Ok Terry, round him and his boys up and get them over here,' Jack paused for a moment. 'Let's send Brian over to visit Ma, I think he has earned it don't you?' For once Terry agreed, Brian and Ma were as crazy as each other.

'I'm not sure that's going to be possible.'

Jack looked hard at Terry. 'That's an order Terry. It ain't negotiable!'

'I'm not questioning your order, boss. I just don't think he's alive. Brian took Gino and Walter with him.'

Jack shook his head. 'Del Monte and Karp!'

'Yep,' said Terry.

'Well, that ain't no fucking A-team, is it?' Jack was angry. 'Maybe I should send them all to Ma. Might stop her buying handbags for a while!'

'I think they're all dead, boss.'

Jack stared at Terry. 'Why would you think that?'

'All their phones are off and the trackers have stopped.' He let that sink in for a moment. Jack knew that if the phones were all off and the trackers were dead the phones had been destroyed.

'What about the truck?'

Terry shook his head. 'Kenny Wogstad was driving.'

First good news of the day, thought Jack.

'Kenny's a good guy, have you tried calling him?'

Terry shook his head. 'Phone's dead like the others and the tracker on the car has stopped,' Terry paused. 'That Aksel is dangerous and clever. If he destroyed all the phones and kicked out the tracker on the truck, we have to assume that he has whacked them all.'

Jack nodded as the full realisation began to dawn. Aksel Lund definitely had something to hide, apart from four bodies, and he was going to find out just what it was!

———◆———

Aksel slid back the secret access wall into the Goldmine. He had spent the last two days tidying up all evidence of the gunfight with Brian McCumber and his gang of thugs. Bullet casings, bloodstains, tyre marks. He had even used a power grinder to disguise any obvious bullet strikes that could be seen. If any police came calling, he didn't want evidence on display.

It was cool in the mine. Deep within the Mesa Ridge with the river running through it would have made a great wine cooler. The only vintages being kept cool today were of the barely human variety. Brian McCumber, Gino Del Monte and Walter Carp. When Aksel hit the lights, their faces seemed to glow in the golden reflection of the precious ore sparkling in the terraced bays of the subterranean river. Aksel sighed, he didn't like killing, but they had left him no choice. Now the three of them would be buried in waters full of gold. Buried wasn't the proper description. Dumped, that was the word. Aksel had put several bodies into the river before. He knew from the camera that he had lowered down the river on a reel that within the mountain was a huge waterfall. Heavy ores such as gold would fall to the bottom and eventually emerge in the river as it exited the mountain in the valley several miles below. The bodies from last year had failed to reappear. Aksel thought that there must be some subterranean caverns along the river, which had captured the bodies. He bent down and grasped the small man with vulpine features by the collar of his jacket and pulled him upright. He was light and still a little stiff with rigor mortis. This made him easy to move. Aksel hoisted him to the edge of the river beyond the last of the terraced bays. There the gold he had lost his life trying to steal glittered, mocking him in death as it had in life. He took one last look into the mean little face and pushed him into the current. As he bobbed down the shallow river, he looked small. Death always seemed to diminish everyone, he thought. Aksel turned to the 240 pounds of Gino Del Monte. Well, maybe not everyone!

Once the three bodies had floated downstream to their appointment with oblivion Aksel moved back up the river to the terraced bays. Yesterday's harvest had been good and the river-bed was illuminated with gold. Time to start filling the wheel-barrows, he thought.

———◆———

Big George Digbeth was headed for Jack Lantern's office in Vegas. He knew Jack worked by appointment only, but George had never been refused a meeting. He was sure Jack knew more than he was letting on. Patsy Broadhurst, his most trusted employee, had done some research into Jimmy Wayne. Seemed he was on the way back to something big, and Jack had shares in the label that Jimmy was on. There was never smoke without fire in George's world, and nine times out of ten he would be the one that applied the flame. If Jimmy Wayne was involved in the death of his son, he was going to find out. And if he did find out? Well, being one of Jack's investments would not save him.

As his driver cruised down the main strip in Vegas, George wondered what Davy had done to get himself killed. The nature of their business was high risk, and this town was a dangerous place to try and break into. Davy had done well in Miami. Muscled in on those that could be outmuscled and done deals with those he couldn't intimidate. In a matter of a few short years, he had built a very strong business based on drugs, gambling and business class prostitution. His girls were for hire, but the rent was high and the kerb appeal was off the scale... Not that Davy's girls ever saw a kerb. Everything was self-contained within the rooms in his pub chain hotels. A nice clean environment for something that was very tacky.

Davy had called it, 'Sleaze with Ease.' George could understand that, but he wasn't comfortable with it. To him prostitution sent the wrong message about the Fewhurst Empire. Call him old-fashioned, maybe even a traditionalist, but George preferred armed robbery, extortion via protection money and corrupt gambling. Prostitution, however nicely you dressed it up, felt wrong to him. His mother had been a strong woman and would never have let him do it when she was alive. He had tried to stop Davy from doing it but once he got to Miami, he forged his own path. To be fair he made big profits. He also made enemies, one of whom had killed him. He was hoping Jack Lantern would be able to shed some light on it. Davy was killed with one of Lanterns best men... There had to be a tie in.

Five minutes later, George's driver turned off the strip and onto Cleveland Avenue. It was a non-descript road. Lots of scrubby empty lots and two storey industrial units from the late sixties that looked well past their best. Two hundred yards down was a single storey building. It looked like a private home, but the lot next door had been purchased and was now a carpark with a unit which appeared to act as an office for the security guards who watched their approach from behind high security fences. All this was filmed by several security cameras that sprouted like antenna from the roof of the unit. It wasn't much to look at, but nobody would surprise Jack Lantern. They pulled up at the gate and were greeted by a voice from the intercom.

'Who are you and what's your business?' Greeted was not the right word. George's driver leaned towards the speaker.

'Mister George Digbeth to see Jack Lantern.' From where he sat George could see the guard looking down a list on his desk.

'You ain't on the list!'

George's driver looked questioningly at him in the mirror. George just nodded at him. He leaned back towards the intercom. 'Jack Lantern will want to see Mister Digbeth.'

'But you ain't on the list... Turn your vehicle around and clear the entrance.'

The door to the security unit opened and George saw a powerfully built man move down the steps towards his car. Beneath his jacket he could see the outline of his gun. George opened his door and climbed out. He moved to the closed gate and waited for the guard to reach him. When he was within 20 feet the guard started to speak.

'You're going to have to clear the drive, sir... You do not have an appointment.' It was a clear instruction reinforced by the guard's hand resting on the bulge in his jacket. George smiled and then spoke.

'My name is George Digbeth. I have come to see Mister Lantern about my son who died with Ted Baker... You knew Ted?' The guard hesitated. George had clearly touched a nerve.

'Yeah, I knew Ted.'

'Well then, you know that he was murdered with another man. That man was my son!' George waited for a response. He could see the guard considering the implications of his words. The other guard appeared at the door of the security unit.

'We got a problem Stan?'

Stan shook his head. 'Mister Digbeth here says his son was a killed with Ted last year.' The second guard looked over at George.

'We don't know anything about it... Police have closed the case on it.'

'I haven't,' said George. He was very calm. 'I don't think Jack would be very happy if he found out that someone who may be able to help him solve the murder of one of his best men had been turned away... Do you?'

Stan paused for a moment, caught between the desire to tell this cocky Englishman to bugger off and the fear of incurring his boss's anger if he really did want to see this guy. He decided to play it safe.

'Stay there, and I will call Mister Lantern's office.'

George looked across the yard to the single storey building. 'Why don't you just knock on the door, it will be quicker!' George tried to hide a smile but he couldn't. He could see this guy really didn't like him, but he was caught in a dilemma.

'Stay in the vehicle, sir,' he said tersely as he headed back inside the security cabin. He picked up the internal phone and punched in Margo's extension.

'Hi Stan.'

'Hi Margo, I got a fellow called George Digbeth here, says he wants to see Jack.'

Margo glanced down at Jack's diary. 'He ain't in the diary.'

'Says his son was killed with Ted Baker last year.'

Margo felt a flutter of regret at Ted's name. She had liked Ted. Twenty years back, when they were young, they had been some of Jack's first employees. They even went out. Before she could delve further into her memories, Stan spoke.

'This guy seems serious Margo, you better ask Jack.'

'Yeah, sure thing Stan, hold the line.' Margo clicked onto Jack's phone and Jack picked it up after the first ring.

'Yeah?' Jack was his usual perfunctory self.

'Stan's got an English guy called George Digbeth out front, says he—'

'Let him in,' Jack interrupted her. 'I've been expecting him!'

———◆———

Behind Carpenters was a decent sized car park. Sam Estrin had even installed a garden area. Sitting on a bench surrounded by a row of Cactus plants sat Jimmy and Kid. They were having a quiet smoke and enjoying the sunshine.

'So how do you think it's going, Jimmy?'

Jimmy looked at Kid as if he were crazy. 'You been in rehearsal, it's going great!'

Kid took a deep draw on his joint. 'Oh, the music's fine, I was just thinking about all the other stuff.'

'Such as?'

'Well maybe we should be a little concerned that Aksel had some more visitors from Jack Lantern that he had to dispose of.'

Jimmy stubbed his joint out. Aksel had called Kid to let them know what had happened. Three dead, but more importantly the driver had escaped.

'Yeah, those guys could be a problem but it's nothing to do with us. We got an alibi.'

Kid nodded. 'That's true but the driver got away, and if he's still alive...'

'He's alive,' interrupted Jimmy. 'I only got three songs turn up.'

'They any good?'

Jimmy smiled. 'They're always good, I didn't even have to know about it to get them.'

'Third party homicide... It's the future.' Kid squinted into the sun. 'It's a pretty tenuous link. They only died because we went to see Aksel and Jack had us followed.'

'Who cares? We get the songs, and it saves a lot of digging.'

Jimmy and Kid had long ago worked out the strange rules of Jimmy's gift for writing songs. Any death that happened as a result of Jimmy's actions resulted in a song appearing on his bedside cabinet the next morning.

'Got a preference for songs from killing you did yourself and third-party killings?' asked Kid. Jimmy thought for a moment.

'Yeah, I think the first-degree ones are more personal... but hey, some of those third-party ones are pretty good.'

'Makes you wonder, don't it?' Kid left the question hanging in the still morning air. Jimmy turned to look at him.

'Wonder what?'

'How many people did Burt Bacharach have to kill?' Jimmy looked at Kid as if he were crazy.

'Burt Bacharach didn't kill anyone.'

Kid shrugged. 'You don't know that, Jimmy. Look how miserable Bob Dylan has been the last few years. Maybe the weight of all those great songs is weighing on his mind.'

Jimmy studied Kid's face for a tell-tale smile, there was none.

'You serious?' Kid nodded. 'Burt must be in his nineties, no way he could kill anyone.'

'He don't need to with – excuse the pun – the body of work he already has. Besides,' Kid leaned forwards conspiratorially. 'When did he last write a new song?'

Jimmy thought about this, it made absolutely no sense but… and it was a big but, what if Jimmy wasn't the exception to the rule. Maybe the reason that so few singers became famous was that only the ones that learned the killing trick could write the best songs.

'You know what you're saying, don't you? It's crazy!'

Kid held up his hands. 'All I'm saying Jimmy is that you couldn't write a decent song to save your life until you hung Wendy and then… Boom!'

Jimmy wasn't convinced. 'Could you see Joni Mitchell killing a load of people and burying them?'

'Plenty of places to bury bodies up in Laurel Canyon in the late sixties and early seventies. I'm sure Graham Nash would have been more than happy to help her.'

'You can't go suggesting that all great songwriters are serial killers, Kid.'

'So, what separates the thousands that don't make it from the hundred or so that do?' He paused for emphasis. 'The ability to write a great song! People say it's a God-given talent. What if it's from the Devil, the dark side? A trade-off you have to make with the Devil for fame.'

The idea made Jimmy shudder. Sometimes, in the stillness of the night, he had lain awake wondering what the price would be for the songs. There had to be a reckoning. Killing was wrong, even scumbags.

'If that was true, they would have been caught. I've only written a dozen and that's hard enough to cover up. Carole King would need a farm!'

'Carole King could afford a farm.' Kid leaned back. 'Now I'm not saying that Carole has a farm full of dead bodies but aren't you at all curious as to why this gift has been laid at your door?'

Jimmy was curious. The thought that he wasn't the only singer to have inherited this strange song-writing gift seemed incomprehensible, and yet it made no sense at all. When he really thought about it there seemed to be a strange logic to it. Leonard Cohen wrote great songs, and he was really depressing!

Kid held up his joint. 'This is good shit Jimmy... makes you think.'

Jimmy nodded. 'Maybe too much. I'm pretty sure that Bruce Springsteen and Neil Young live on farms.'

Kid laughed. 'Don't stress on it, Jimmy. I was just thinking aloud.'

'Do you think the Osmonds killed anyone?'

Kid held up his hand in protest. 'Hold on there, Jimmy, I said great songs.'

Before Jimmy could respond they were interrupted by the velvet tones of John R. Deal. He appeared at Jimmy's side and took the joint from his fingers.

'Why you boys smoking this shit? You should be rehearsing.' Like naughty schoolboys caught smoking behind the bike sheds Jimmy and Kid sat to attention.

'Where did you come from, John?'

John smiled. 'Everywhere and nowhere, son.'

'That narrows it down,' said Kid. 'How long you been here, John?'

'Long enough to hear you talking all that shit. Not every-one's like you, Jimmy. In fact, I don't believe anyone else is like you. Killing is your USP.'

Jimmy couldn't stop himself from smiling. 'You been to business school, John?'

'School of life, Jimmy, and from where I am standing you ain't passing any exams so far. Time to focus, son.' He looked at the joint held in his hands. He dropped it to the floor and ground it to ash beneath his shoe. 'No more of this shit. I put my trust in you, Jimmy.' John turned to Kid. 'You too, son. You boys are so close to catching the dream. Don't let it slip through your fingers. Life is too short to waste time on regret. Make sure you don't have to.'

There was a gentle intensity in John's words and its effect on Jimmy and Kid was instant.

'We have all the songs nailed, John. The levels are all set and we are ready.'

John nodded his approval. 'That's good, son, because trouble is coming and you have a storm moving in your direction.' Jimmy shot Kid an anxious look which John saw. 'Don't concern yourselves. I'm going to take care of it, but Sheriff Pence has sent Big George Digbeth after you.'

Jimmy looked questioningly at John. 'You know Big George Digbeth is coming?'

'Sounds like a porn star,' said Kid.

'Well, he could fuck you guys up, so you better take him serious.' John said it quietly but there was no doubting the warning tone in his voice. 'You're between a rock and a hard place. Jack Lantern on one side and Big George on the other. I'm going to get in the middle and stop you from getting squeezed. All you need to do is stay outta trouble and concentrate on the show. Can you do that for me?'

They both nodded. John had a way of making you listen and when he spoke every word carried weight.

'Why is this Big George coming after Jimmy?' asked Kid. John sat down on the bench.

'You remember the mystery body in the trunk of the pick-up?'

'The one when I killed Ted Baker.'

'The very same.' John let out a long breath. 'Well, now we know who that body is,' he paused and looked from Jimmy to Kid and back again. 'It was Big George Digbeth's son, Davy.'

'Shit!' The curse slipped from Kid's lips as if he were a deflating balloon.

'Yeah, Sheriff Pence has tried to drop Jimmy in it, and for that there will be a reckoning, but for now we have to sing a song that Big George can believe. Jack too, for that matter. You boys get back to rehearsal and let me smooth the ripples.'

'When is he getting here?' asked Jimmy. He couldn't hide the tension in his voice.

'Already here, I believe. Just arrived at Jack's office.' John stood up. 'Better get over there and smooth this shit out.'

Jimmy shook his head. 'You'll never make it in time.' But before he could finish his sentence, John R. Deal had vanished. One moment he was walking away, the next he was gone.

Kid shook his head. 'How does he do that?'

'Fucked if I know. I'm just glad he can.' Jimmy looked over towards the entrance to the rear of Carpenters but John was long gone. 'Let's just hope he can put out the fire that Sheriff Pence started.' Kid rose to his full height and stretched like a bear coming outta hibernation.

'Pretty sure he will Jimmy… Why don't we just do like John said and do some more practice.'

'Good idea,' agreed Jimmy. There was nothing else to do. Their fate was now in the hands of two hardened gangsters and a two-hundred-year-old bluesman… Nothing to worry about there then!

———◆———

Over at Jack Lantern's office Big George Digbeth was being shown into the inner sanctum of Lantern Incorporated Holdings. As Margo showed him into Jack's office Jack couldn't help but notice that Big George Digbeth wasn't. He hoped that everything else about his reputation was similarly exaggerated.

'Take a seat, Mister Digbeth,' smiled Jack, oozing all the charm of a crocodile at feeding time. 'Can we get you a coffee?'

George shook his head. 'No thanks, do you have tea?'

Jack nodded. 'Of course, you're British, should have guessed.'

George looked offended. 'I'm English actually. Not to be confused with our Celtic brothers.'

Jack glanced up at Margo. 'Do we have any tea?'

Margo nodded. 'We have some Earl Grey.'

George pulled a pained expression. 'That's not tea, that's scented Castrol in a cup. What about English breakfast?'

Just then Margo remembered a tea box selection her friend in Boston had sent her for Christmas, admittedly it was some years back, but they had been kept in a tin in the cupboard here in the kitchen at Jack's office.

'I have some Ceylon.'

George nodded. 'That'll do. Nice and strong with just a bit of milk.'

Margo smiled. 'Almond, oat or...'

'Out of a cow,' said George, before she could finish her menu.

'Udders it is then,' said Margo as she left Jack's office with the distinct impression that Big George Digbeth was neither big nor an English gentleman. He and Jack should get on fine!

'So, George, how can I help you?' Jack knew what George wanted but there was no way he was going to admit it.

Big George had decided not to play games. 'I'm sure Sheriff Pence has given you the heads up about me, Jack. Unless I'm very much mistaken you own him.'

'Own is a strong word, but we do have an understanding.'

'I bet you do,' smiled George. 'So, what do you think?'

Jack feigned ignorance. 'Think of what, George?'

George Digbeth wasn't buying it. 'Come on Jack, be straight with me or I am going to start thinking you have something to hide.' Jack could see that denial was pointless.

'What I know is that someone killed one of my best men and also a dealer who worked for us. I only found out about your son two days ago. Seems to me whoever killed Ted killed your son too.'

George nodded his head in agreement. 'I think we can both agree with that, but who do you think did it?'

For this answer Jack really didn't need to lie. He simply had no idea who would dare to kill one of his top men.

'I don't know, I've had men on it for months but nothing seems to make sense.' He gave George a slow confident smile. 'People that know me don't usually go up against me, tends to be life limiting!'

Big George could appreciate the fact. 'Same here, Jack. I may not be as well-known as you in these parts but in the UK and Miami nobody would go up against my family. This guy is either crazy or he didn't know who he was messing with.'

Jack nodded his agreement. 'Maybe both.'

'Possible, but your Sheriff Pence seemed to think that a character named Jimmy Wayne had something to do with it.'

Jack laughed whilst he was making a mental note to have Pence beaten.

'Sheriff Pence has a history of run-ins with Jimmy, especially since he started to become successful. He would do virtually anything to cause him trouble, so I'm guessing when you called on him, he stuck Jimmy in the frame to make his life awkward.' The way Jack explained it made sense but George knew that Jack had a financial interest in Jimmy. Was that investment enough to make him lie?

'You can't tie this Jimmy Wayne into the killing?'

'No, we dug deep and there is no link or motive. Jimmy is too busy resurrecting his career to have time to be going around killing folks.'

'You got a vested interest in his career though don't you, Jack.'

Jack hadn't seen that one coming but being the accomplished liar that he was he continued without hesitation. 'Yes, I do, but that doesn't extend to letting him kill one of my best men and a valuable dealer,' Jack smiled and leaned back in his chair. 'You need to meet Jimmy. Once you do, you'll realise that he ain't that kinda guy. He's a muso for god's sake, they can barely get out of bed in the morning!'

That much made sense. George had known a few musicians over the years and off stage hardly any of them would have the energy to kill anyone, let alone a professional killer. Before they could get into it any further the door of Jack's office swung open and in swooned Margo with a tray of tea and biscuits. She appeared to float into view on a wave of joy. The reason for her happiness followed her into the office.

'Look who I've found, Jack.' Margo turned and looked behind her. She held out an outstretched arm to usher John into the room. John didn't wait for any further introduction. He just strode into Jack's office and stood between Jack and George. He nodded to Jack and then turned to George.

'Hello, Mister Digbeth. You're a long way from home.'

George looked at John questioningly. 'Do I know you?'

John shrugged. 'That's not important, I can tell that we are going to get on.'

'And why would you think that?' George was smiling but there was a hard edge to his voice.

'People tend to like me, Mister Digbeth.'

'I like you,' swooned Margo. She had draped herself against the doorframe, her ample bosom gently heaving as she gazed at John like a vampire who hadn't had a meal in weeks. John turned and smiled at Margo.

'I like you too, Margo. Do you think you could get me some water, please?'

Margo tilted her head and nodded. 'You only had to whistle, John.'

John looked confused. 'But if I whistled, how would you know what I want?'

It was Margo's turn to look confused. 'Like a sheep dog,' was all she could say.

'Jesus!' said Jack under his breath, and Margo slid embarrassed out of the doorway, the spell that John cast over her momentarily broken. 'You seem to have quite an effect on my secretary John.'

'I do, don't I? Is she married?' One look from Jack told John that this was not a relationship he should pursue. George Digbeth could not believe what he was seeing.

'Is it me or are you lot crazy?'

John turned to George. 'These are strange times Mister Digbeth, stranger than you think.' John stood there and let his words hang in the silence. He wanted a response before he continued. Jack was the first to speak.

'What do you mean by that, John?'

Here was the opening John had been waiting for, the moment when he could plant his story into the minds of Jack Lantern and Big George Digbeth.

'I know why you are here Mister Digbeth, and you have my condolences. The loss of a child, even a psychopath like young Davy, is a tragedy.' George stiffened; he should have been offended by John's words, but he knew them to be true. Davy had been wild. That's why he had sent him to Miami, expecting him to fail, but his crazy, violent nature combined with a certain animal cunning made him the perfect specimen to thrive in the criminal underworld of Miami. Money and power were his gods, and in America he had found the perfect temple to worship at the altar of greed.

'You knew Davy?' George asked.

'I knew of him. He established quite a reputation in a very short time.'

Jack nodded his approval. 'Yeah, illegal gambling, protection money, hookers, you must have been so proud!'

George nodded. 'Yes, Davy had done an excellent job with our new pub chain.'

'Nothing like the pubs back home though,' laughed Jack.

'Over here they have added value.'

John waited for the gangster exchange to subside, when it did, he continued.

'There is a case to be made that you and Jack are enemies, George.' Both men moved to deny it but John silenced them with an upheld hand. 'Hear me out gents.' He paused for a moment until he was sure there would be no interruptions. 'George, your Davy had grown strong in Miami and last year he bought two old bars in Vegas and started to renovate and put in... added value.' John looked at George and then back to Jack. 'Now moving into Vegas is going to put the Fewhurst Empire in direct competition with the Lantern Empire. I'm guessing that Davy hadn't tried to reach an accommodation?'

Jack shook his head. 'No, I had asked Ted Baker to make contact and try and set up a meeting.' He hadn't. What Jack had told Ted Baker to do was to find Davy and trick him into thinking he was interested in changing sides and that he would take him on a collection run to show him how Jack's distribution operation worked out in the sticks. Once he got him out there his orders were to kill him and lose the body. John knew this but he didn't want Big George to know, a war was the last thing anyone needed.

'That's true, Jack. I saw Davy having lunch with Ted in a diner outside of Blackjack last year. They looked to be getting on well.'

'That true, John?' asked George.

John gave him his most sincere look. 'It is George.' It wasn't, they had been arguing because hothead Davy wanted Ted to get him into Jack's office so he could kill him. Playing the long game just wasn't on his agenda. 'Now my guess is that there is a third gang trying to move in on Jack, but they saw Davy and the Fewhurst Empire as a threat to their take-over. That's why both Ted and Davy died.'

It all made sense to George, apart from one thing. 'So why was Davy locked in the trunk of the truck?'

John rubbed his chin thoughtfully. 'That is a tough one, I think Ted was killed first and Davy got captured. They locked him in there because they wanted to use him as a bargaining chip. Something went wrong and they decided to torch the vehicles. Sadly, Davy was still in there. Maybe they were disturbed and had to clean house and get. Whatever the reason, this attack was on both of you and I think you guys need to reach an accommodation business-wise, and then unite to fight this gang who are looking to muscle in.'

The way John had described the events made perfect sense to Jack and George. Jack reached across his desk and offered George his hand.

'Let's work together to catch whoever killed our boys, then we can reach an accommodation about Vegas.'

This seemed to appeal to George Digbeth. 'That works for me, Jack. With Davy gone I just want to secure the business in Miami and consolidate the two premises we hold in Vegas; major expansion isn't in my plans. My holdings in England take most of my time.'

That much was true. Big George had no desire to expand his business in America. That had been Davy's dream. He had a large and very successful empire in the UK. He would rather do a deal with Jack and sell off everything Davy had built out here so he could concentrate on his core business. America felt too alien. It wasn't a place he could live. George's words were music to Jack's ears.

'So, let's do some digging and try to find out who is trying to undermine us.' Jack smiled. 'I can tell you it ain't Jimmy Wayne.'

'I can confirm that too, George,' said John.

George Digbeth looked hard at him. 'You seem an honest man, John, but how can you be so sure.' John leaned on the edge of Jack's desk and folded his arms.

'Because on the day it happened, he was rehearsing at the Riviera. I saw him with my own eyes.' It was a blatant lie, but John sold it well.

'Boy, for an old man you sure get around.'

John shrugged. 'I'm a traveling bluesman. What can I say!'

Just then, Margo reappeared with John's water. While she had been gone, she had clearly freshened her makeup and combed her hair out. It made her look ten years younger. There also appeared to be a couple of extra buttons undone on her blouse. Now there was no mistaking that, like two continents colliding, her breasts were heaving, driven by the rising temperatures her passion for John had created. John looked at Jack.

'You sure she's not married?'

———◆———

Back at Carpenters Jimmy and the band were running through their set one last time, unaware that John had managed to cool

Big George Digbeth's interest in Jimmy. David and Michael stood watching the band from the back of the auditorium.

'These boys are on fire,' said David.

Michael nodded his agreement. 'Yeah, they're sounding great!' He turned to his old friend. 'Thanks for bringing them to me, I think we are all going to do very well.'

David smiled. 'You know, I do believe your right.'

They both laughed.

They weren't the only ones listening. Sam Estrin, the owner of Carpenters, was standing on the west side of the auditorium with Herr Kessler, his general manager.

'What do you think, Flare?'

Herr Kessler clasped his hands to his face. 'I zink they are amazing. Ve vill do so very well wid them. Zey can zing and play, and dat Jimmy, vat I could do for him.'

Sam smiled at his camp manager. 'If only you were gay, Flare.'

Flare sighed with mock regret. 'Yes, if only. It is such a curse to be in the theatre and be straight, ze opportunities I am missing!'

'But you can still enjoy the shows without being gay.'

'I can, but it vould be so much more fun if I vas!'

Sam loved Flare. He was the best theatre manager he had ever had, but man, he made him laugh.

'You're not even German, are you?'

'Nein,' agreed Flare. 'I am from Birmingham, England.'

'Then why don't you speak with an English accent?'

Flare looked horrified. 'Have you heard a Birmingham accent?' Sam shook his head. 'Vell I did, and zat vas when I decided to take up ze German side of my family.'

'Yes, such a lyrical language, German.'

Flare nodded. 'The language of Blitzkrieg, and coming from Birmingham it felt like it!'

They both laughed and turned back to listen to the band.

CHAPTER 18

ALL THE WORLD'S A STAGE

Time is supposed to be a constant, but sometimes it just doesn't feel like it. It had taken Jimmy 20 years to finally climb back to where he had been. Years when time seemed to stand still, everything he had tried turned to dust. A second chance, it's what so many want, but how can you be sure that if it comes along, you won't just fall into the same trap. 'Wanting isn't getting.' That was one of his grandfather's favourite sayings and now Jimmy actually understood what he had meant. He had wanted another shot at fame so bad, but he never had a plan as to what he would do if it came along. Now he had a plan. Great new record, great band and a superb venue to play in. He also had the benefit of David Parker, a great friend and even better manager and the final piece in the jigsaw, Michael Owen. With this array of talent and support, how could he fail? It was the night before the first gig at Carpenters and the place was sold-out, but Jimmy couldn't sleep. It wasn't nerves about the gig. He could do that standing on his head. No, Jimmy knew that there was a whole cast list of characters revolving around him, any one of which could bring him down. Like a sun at the centre of his own solar system he was pulling all these different elements towards him.

Jack Lantern and Ma. They had shares in his label so they also had a financial interest in him. Big George Digbeth, if he ever found out that Jimmy had set fire to Ted's pick-up with Davy inside, it didn't bear thinking about. Sheriff Pence back in Blackjack, still trying to convict Jimmy of something, anything. All the bodies buried at the Song Graveyard, if ever they were discovered, there would be a trail straight back to his door. Aksel and the gold mine. Jack was after that, and it was only a matter of time before he discovered the truth. John R. Deal, he was a good guy but what was he and why was he helping him? So many strands floating in space and if the wrong person caught a hold of one, the whole edifice he was building would come tumbling down. Elaine, his old girlfriend who had had his son. Wayne seemed a fine young man and he was looking forward to getting to know him, but he was also scared that if he got close to his son, Elaine would be back in his life too. Jimmy was on a tightrope and the wind was getting up. Staying on was going to be tricky. Last, but by no means least, was Wendy. Dear sweet very dead Wendy. The love of his life who he had accidentally hanged. That alone would probably send him to the chair in this state. How had his world become so complicated?

It seemed so much easier when he was young. Life was an apparently endless adventure and every step he took was towards something better. The confidence of youth or the ignorance of life. He knew now. Experience had taught him some very hard lessons. Nothing was ever for free, there was always a bill to be paid and now he stood on the edge of fame. The dream he had chased for so long was within his grasp and he wasn't sure that the price he had to pay to get there was going to be worth it.

None of this would have happened if he hadn't killed Wendy. Everything that was now good was built on the death of the only woman he had truly loved. Had her death been the catalyst for his change in fortune, or was it the first step on a road to hell? The bodies buried in the Song Cemetery were a testament to his desire for fame regardless of the cost. Their deaths were a means to an end. He told himself that these men all deserved killing – they were rotten to the core – but who was he to sit in judgement, to act as judge and jury. In the daylight, he could close his mind to his actions but in the quiet lonely hours of the night his ghosts came calling. Their voices drifting on the desert breeze, begging for mercy, cursing him to hell. Knowing that they would all have killed him without hesitation didn't make it any better. He had become death, and death was his guide. His whole success was built on a foundation of bodies. Tonight, like so many other nights, this knowledge overwhelmed him.

Eventually he fell into a fitful sleep and drifted into a dream. He found himself walking along a dusty road in the middle of the desert. It was hot and the sun beat down like a furnace. He remembered the sunglasses perched on his head and pulled them down to cover his eyes. Now he wasn't squinting he could see that the road he was on led to a crossroads a couple of hundred yards away. There was a give way sign which made him smile. There probably wasn't another car within forty miles. This place was remote. Where was he? Arizona? Nevada? He couldn't tell. Just then he caught a movement up ahead. He stared into the bright midday sun and was able to make out a man standing at the crossroads. The man was beckoning him. Who the hell was he? Jimmy tried to focus and gradually as he got nearer, he made out the familiar features of John R. Deal. He waved back and increased his pace. John shimmered in the heat haze. Was he a mirage? Had he imagined him?

'Jimmy Wayne, good to see you, son.' Jimmy was nearly at the crossroads now and he could see John clearly. This was no mirage.

'Hi John, what you doing here in the middle of nowhere?'

John shrugged. 'Waiting for you, I guess.'

'How did you know I would be here?'

'I didn't… Sometimes fate makes the decisions for us. All the world's a stage, and all the men and women are merely players.'

'That's nice.'

'That's Shakespeare, Jimmy. He understood the human condition.'

'Would he understand mine?' asked Jimmy wearily.

John nodded. 'I think so. You're an artist, Jimmy. You stand upon the stage. You have your exits and entrances, and you will play many parts. This is just one of the seven ages.'

'This still Shakespeare? Because I don't understand a damn word you're saying.'

'Sit down, Jimmy. We need to talk.' John indicated a leather armchair that hadn't been there a moment before.

'Where the hell did that come from?'

'Same place as this one.' John sat down in a second chair. Jimmy spun around looking for the source of this mysterious furniture.

'You want a coffee, Jimmy?' Jimmy turned back to see John was now pouring a coffee into a mug on a small table between the chairs. Jimmy took off his sunglasses and rubbed his eyes. He heard John chuckle.

'Relax Jimmy, this is just a dream. Everything is possible.' Jimmy slumped into the empty chair.

'Milk or cream?' asked John.

'You got almond milk.'

'You know it. It's a dream, Jimmy.' Jimmy slowly shook his head. Could his life be any more fucked up? That said, the coffee did taste good. He looked around, there was nothing on the horizon but distant mountains and sand. The leather armchairs and small coffee table seemed a little incongruous set down at the side of the dusty crossroads.

'This your office, John?'

'I don't know, you tell me – it's your dream.' Now Jimmy was even more confused. He sipped his coffee. It had almond milk!

'So, why do you think we are here, John? And don't just tell me it's my dream. You're here for a reason.'

John smiled. 'That obvious, is it?'

'You bought me to a goddamn crossroads in the middle of nowhere. How Robert Johnson is that!'

John leaned back in his chair and grinned. 'Ah dear Robert, I knew him you know.'

'I thought you would,' said Jimmy sarcastically. 'And was he like they say?'

'Oh yes, he was a lazy good for nothing womanizer who couldn't play a lick and then one day... Boom! He was the real deal.'

'And the message is?' asked Jimmy.

John turned to him, he sighed and looked earnestly at him. 'You ain't Robert Johnson, Jimmy, and you can't go thinking you are. All this guilt is no good for you. It's going to get in the way of your talent. It's going to rot you from the inside out. Guilt is corrosive and the only cure is to let it go.'

'Easy for you to say, John. You didn't kill all them people. I'm just like Robert Johnson. I sold my soul to the Devil just to get some crappy songs.'

John shook his head. 'You didn't sell your soul to anyone, Jimmy. You were just a victim of circumstance.'

'Maybe for Wendy, Vinny and Carmine even. That was self-defence, but after that...' he trailed off.

John reached across the table and laid a hand on his shoulder. 'After that, Jimmy, you just did what you had to do. This is fate you don't get to decide. Everything is written, you may think you are changing the future but you ain't. Our wills and fates do so contrary run.'

'That Shakespeare again?'

John nodded. 'Player king, Hamlet Act 3, Scene 2.'

Jimmy nodded. 'Good to know, but what the fuck does it mean?'

'I'd have thought that was pretty self-explanatory.'

'Not to me, I'm from Pennsylvania!'

'They have Shakespeare in Pennsylvania surely?'

'Robert Frost on a good day maybe.'

A broad smile spread across John's face. 'Ah dear Robert, I knew him you know.' Jimmy sighed. 'Strange that you should mention dear Robert, he wrote most eloquently about your situation.'

Jimmy looked dubious. 'Never saw a poem about a serial killing singer in the anthology I read!'

'Don't be so literal, Jimmy. Open your mind. Maybe I can refresh it.' John leaned back and closed his eyes and then began to recite.

I shall be telling this with a sigh
Somewhere ages and ages hence
Two roads diverged in a wood, and I
I took the one less travelled by
And that has made all the difference.

John opened his eyes and smiled at Jimmy. 'Beautiful isn't it? Do you understand what it means?'

'I guess,' said Jimmy uncertainly.

'Tell me.'

'I came to a fork in the road. I had a choice to make. I could choose the road less travelled.'

'Which is?'

'Killing people, and that's what I did. I took the road less travelled and that has made all the difference. Now I have a recording contract, a hit record, a residency at one of the best venues in Vegas. Fame is finally knocking on my door. All I had to do was start killing.'

'Don't be too hard on yourself, Jimmy. Those guys needed killing. It was a public service what you did. As Shakespeare once wrote, "Nothing in his life became him like the leaving of it," although I don't think any of your villains repented like Cawdor.'

Jimmy stared at John, his face a mask of amusement. 'My dreams are very literate, John. Shakespeare, Robert Frost. How can I remember things I have never read? Spiderman comics and music mags – that was all I read.'

'Oh, you would have read or heard these quotes and poems at some time and your brain filed them away and buried them deep. When you sleep you can delve into that hidden memory and find gems you never knew you had.'

'Good to know, but how does that help me?'

'It can only help you if you let it.'

'You want to explain that?'

John gave Jimmy the same gentle smile that he would to a dumb animal. He had dealt with many musicians in his long life, and he understood that behind the glamorous high-rise image was often a single storey person. Nothing upstairs. How best to make Jimmy understand without hurting his feelings?

'Jimmy, don't take this too personal, but you ain't the sharpest tool in the box. You ain't broken you just need sharpening.'

Jimmy sighed. 'This your idea of pepping me up, John?'

'No son, this is just me telling it like it is. You ain't stupid, Jimmy, but for a while you gave up on thinking. Now we got to teach you how to think again. Drink and self-pity do not make for a positive outlook on life.'

'That more Shakespeare?'

'No,' said John, a pained expression creasing his face. 'You really need to read more Jimmy.'

'I will, just been a bit busy killing people of late.'

'I understand. Now you are in a better place. You got the album and the record deal. You got the PR and the Vegas launch pad and you got some new songs and you haven't killed anyone.' John looked thoughtful. 'We may have to kill a couple for the singles, they need to be strong but let's see how we go with our zero expiration songs first.'

Jimmy leaned back in his armchair and gazed out into the desert. A pot plant and a patio umbrella had now appeared, and John was sitting in the shade.

'Can I get one of them?'

'Your dream, Jimmy.' As he finished the sentence Jimmy felt the heat of the sun reduce. He glanced over his shoulder, and sure enough there was the umbrella. He looked down the dusty road that led towards Vegas. He only knew that because the sign at the crossroad bore the legend 'Vegas 24 miles.' He couldn't help noticing that the other three directions had no destination written on them.

'Are you sure this is still a dream, John?'

John nodded. 'Absolutely Jimmy, why do you ask?'

Jimmy pointed in the direction of Vegas. 'You see that low flying aircraft coming our way.'

John squinted into the bright sunshine. 'Yeah, I can see something.'

'That's Wendy.'

John looked again. 'You sure?'

'Positive, she's been creeping up on me for over a year now, I'm starting to get a sixth sense about it.'

'Excellent news,' beamed John. 'I got a soft spot for Wendy.'

A sudden gust of breeze blew sand in their eyes and before they could wipe them Wendy was there.

'Hi boys, this Jimmy's dream?'

'Apparently,' said Jimmy. 'Ask John. He seems to know more than me.'

John nodded. 'Oh, it's Jimmy's dream, alright.'

Wendy surveyed the leather armchairs, the pot plant and the sunshades and nodded her approval. 'This is a lot nicer than some of Jimmy's dreams, if you know what I mean.' Wendy pulled a face. 'Some of them are just... yuk!'

John laughed. 'He's a man, Wendy. Just a victim of his urges.'

'Oh, he's got plenty of urges!'

Jimmy held up his hands. 'Jesus, you two, if you're going to crash my dream, show a bit of respect. This ain't an intervention!'

John and Wendy looked at each other and silently agreed to change the narrative that the dream was taking. John gestured for Wendy to start.

'Ok Jimmy, you're on the launchpad now, you can't blow it.'

'So, what would you suggest, Wendy? I got so much shit coming at me I feel like a sewage farm.'

Wendy winced. 'Nice analogy, Jimmy.'

'Yeah, very explicit,' agreed John, putting down the sandwich that had just appeared on his table.

'Let's take it from the top. What's the biggest problem?'

Jimmy thought for a moment, there were so many it was hard to put them in order of threat level. He tried anyway.

'Well, Ma Lantern wants to kill me, Jack probably wants to kill me if I don't make him money. Sheriff Pence wants to lock me up, once he can trump up a charge to get me on. Big George Digbeth will kill me if he ever finds out that I fired the truck his son was locked in. And then there is the small matter of the eight bodies buried at the Song Cemetery, if someone finds them it won't take the forensic guys long to come knocking on my door.'

'Don't forget about Lena Lantern.'

Jimmy put his head in his hands. Amongst all his other problems he had forgotten that he had accidently had an affair with Jack's wife.

'Jesus, what else can go wrong? Life is so unfair; I didn't know she was Jack's wife.'

Wendy didn't look sympathetic. 'You knew she was somebody's wife, just turned out to be the wrong somebody.'

'I think you gotta give Jimmy a pass on that one, Wendy. Jimmy's a musician, it's lonely on the road, you gotta grab some comfort where you can.'

Wendy let out a high whistling sound like a boiling kettle. 'Geez! You arty types have the morals of a polecat.'

Jimmy threw down the bottle of beer that had appeared in his hand. 'Fuck, fuck! I might as well kill myself now!'

John looked at Wendy. 'For a man on the edge of stardom, he's pretty negative, don't know how you put up with him.'

Wendy shrugged. 'I learned not to listen, John; he does love to whine.'

Jimmy let out a long breath. 'Are you guys listening? Four people, powerful dangerous people, either want me locked up or dead if I don't get this exactly right. I'm tip toeing through a minefield.'

Wendy looked disgusted. 'Jesus Jimmy, you think you got problems? I'm dead!' She had a point. John tried to smooth the troubled waters.

'Listen guys, this is just a little preshow tension. It's all gonna work out fine. You're new to this fame business, Jimmy, and it scares you but it's going to be all right.' John turned to Wendy. 'And you Wendy, you're dead. That takes a bit of time getting your head around. So far you are doing a great job, but sooner or later the fact that this is forever is going to hit you.'

'Forever!' Wendy repeated the word as if realising it for the first time.

John nodded. 'That's a long time, Wendy. You got to make peace with it. There is a whole new world out there for you and it's a wonderful place full of opportunities to enrich your mind and soul.' John paused for a moment, he looked sad. 'But it's still dead.'

Jimmy just sat there. What could he say? He was the cause of Wendy's deadness, not exactly the moral high ground from which to offer advice.

'So, what do you suggest, John?' asked Wendy cautiously.

'Maybe stop mixing so much with the living. You got yourself caught between the two worlds and it's confusing you.'

Wendy weighed John's words before replying. 'But if I leave the land of the living I won't be able to come back, will I?'

John smiled. 'This isn't a movie, Wendy, you won't have to move towards a white light and never return. It's not a Heaven or Hell situation, its simpler than that. There is the world of the living and the world of the dead. Clearly you are in the latter.'

'Thanks,' said Wendy sulkily. 'Tell me something I didn't already know.'

'Wendy, you need to relax. Sit down on the massage chair.' John pointed to an electric massage chair that had materialised behind her. Wendy looked at the chair and then at Jimmy.

'Did you eat cheese last night?'

'Why do ask?'

'Your dreams are weird.' That didn't stop her slumping down on the reclining chair and switching on the massage function to max power.

'So, w-w-w-whattter y-you s-s-saying J-J-J-John?'

John and Jimmy exchanged amused glances.

'Maybe don't talk while the chair is on, Wendy.'

Wendy shrugged. 'W-W-Whattteverr!'

'I guess I'm saying spend more time in the spirit world, it's a great place and it will give you more perspective. Your problem is that you know you're dead, but you still act like you are part of the living world. Move on for a while and then you can pop back and see Jimmy when he needs you or you need to see him.'

'I never want you to just go, Wendy,' added Jimmy. 'I still love you.'

Wendy smiled at him. 'I-I-I s-still l-l-love you t-t-too.' It didn't have the romantic impact she had hoped for but they both understood. As she vibrated at the maximum relaxation level Wendy slowly sank into the brown leather of the chair and disappeared. John and Jimmy sat there looking at the empty recliner. The breeze blew gently, and the muted hum of the electric massage heads drifted on that breeze.

I gotta stop eating cheese, thought Jimmy.

◆

At 11 a.m. the next morning, Jimmy was still fast asleep. Lost in a deep coma filled with strange dreams and fuelled by cheese. Around him Vegas was already humming with activity. Just off the strip Jack Lantern's staff were getting ready for this evening's pre-concert party. Michael Owen and David had raided their address books to gather together a cast of Vegas Glitterati filled out with B and C list wannabees. They also had several powerful Vegas moguls who were curious to find out more of the Jimmy Wayne story. The advertising campaigns, PR interviews and the first single and video had all combined to create quite a stir. Jack had been stirring the pot nicely too, and Jimmy Wayne's debut was quite the talk of the town in Vegas circles. It wasn't Donny and Marie, but he was a lot cheaper with plenty of growth potential to move to a bigger venue. Jack was excited; Ma wasn't so sure.

'You seem pretty keen on Jimmy Wayne, especially considering you were having him killed last year.'

Jack shrugged. 'A year is a long time in show business. Besides he's gonna make us a lot of money.' Ma knew this but still didn't seem impressed.

'He was fucking your wife Jack, you should at the very least castrate him!'

Jack shook his head. 'Too risky, might make his voice too high.'

An evil look crossed Ma's face. 'I could castrate him for you. I'd be really careful to make sure his voice didn't go up.'

'How you going to that with a machete Ma!?' Jack forced a smile. 'Look Ma, Jimmy is good for business, and we are about making money. He won't go near Lena ever again. He never knew that she was my wife because she used a false name.'

'So, what does that tell you, Jack?' Ma was angry.

'It tells me that she was doing what I told her to do. Never let on you're a Lantern unless we are doing something official. That way we get to hear stuff. Outside of Vegas nobody knows who Lena is and that's the way we want to keep it.'

'Your father wouldn't have stood for it,' she spat out.

'We don't even know who my father is now, do we Ma?'

Ma looked sheepish. 'Technically no, but I could narrow it down to three, maybe four guys.'

Jack snorted. 'Cosy. Maybe we could round them up one day and do a DNA so I know which one to ask to take me bowling.'

Ma frowned. 'That's going to be tricky Jack, I killed two of them!'

Jack cried out in mock anguish. 'You killed my daddies. Now I only got two left.' Again, Ma looked a bit sheepish.

'One actually, I kinda had one killed by a third party.'

Jack gave his mother a cool stare. 'You really do hold a grudge, don't you?'

Ma curled her lip. 'I just don't like loose ends or alimony.'

'Alimony?'

'I'm a rich woman, Jack. Those cocksuckers had nothing. If I hadn't sorted them, they would have been coming after you for a paternity test, and then me for cash. So, it wasn't murder; it was just good housekeeping.'

Jack smiled. Good old Ma had always looked after the money and in her own strange and twisted way she had looked after him. Made him strong, made him rich.

'Ok Ma, it really doesn't matter about my father because there is a 75% chance that he is already dead.'

'Hundred percent, Jackie. The other one drank himself to death three years back.'

'Well, that's going to save on Father's Day cards!' Jack smiled and held his arms out to his mother. 'What do I need a father for when I have you for a mother?'

She moved into his embrace and he gave her a big warm hug. As he held her close, he whispered in her ear.

'No killing Jimmy Wayne, Ma.' He felt her tense in his arms. He pulled back slightly so that he could look into her eyes. 'Promise Ma!' Ma pursed her lips. 'Promise!' Insisted Jimmy. He felt her relax.

'Ok, can I beat him up a bit?'

'No, Ma. Jimmy is an asset; we don't damage assets.'

Ma knew Jack was right, but she still wanted to hurt that little singing weasel; she could wait till the time was right. Nobody stayed on Jack's good side for too long.

———◆———

Just a few miles away, on the appropriately named Stardust Drive, Big George Digbeth floated in the pool of his rented mansion. It was already hot, and the cool water helped him think as he floated round the pool on the gentle current. George couldn't swim but the inflatable arm bands that were stuck on his forearms – his biceps were too big to pull them over – kept him safe from drowning. He felt ridiculous but nobody could see him, so he just relaxed and enjoyed allowing his mind to wander. He didn't trust Jack Lantern, or Sheriff Pence for that matter. They knew something about Davy's death, and he was going to find out what it was. He gazed out into the desert and the distant hills beyond. They shimmered in the morning heat and, for the first time since Davy had died, Big George cried. Just a tear at first and then the heavy rain of grief that he had stored as rage. He didn't understand his emotion, and he could not control it. He sobbed like he had never sobbed before, deep and visceral contractions that, but for his arm bands, would have seen him disappear beneath the blue clear water. It took several minutes for his grief to subside and when it did, he was spent. He floated round the pool, his short little legs unable to reach the bottom, like a polar bear trapped on a broken ice flow.

Davy had been his only son and for a long time they had been close. As he grew into manhood, Big George slowly exposed him to the family business to see if he had what it took. A crime Empire like Fewhurst Ltd was built on corruption, violence and doing whatever you had to do to maintain it. There was no place for a nice boy in this world. Davy turned from being a nice boy very quickly. He seemed to thrive on the adrenaline of crime, and feed on the violence which often reared its ugly head. To his horror, Big George had watched his kind, funny and loving son turn into a monster in the space of a few months. He had opened Pandora's Box and Davy had stepped in and taken everything. For this, Big George blamed himself. His tears were not shed for the death of Davy in the back of a burning truck. The Davy he had loved had died the day he took him into the business. The tears were of regret. He should have kept Davy away from the business, kept him on the straight and narrow. He had been selfish, he had punched and clawed his way from the back streets of Birmingham and built an Empire. He wasn't going to let that pass from his family, Davy would be his heir. Sometimes the crown can sit heavy, and power can corrupt. And with Davy, it corrupted absolutely. In the end he was forced to let Davy come to Miami and try to establish the Fewhurst brand. He had done too much damage in the UK to be allowed to continue. This was his last chance and, if he was honest, Big George fully expected Davy to get killed long before he did. Remarkably, Davy's intelligence, fox-like cunning and sheer cold brutality enabled him to muscle into the Miami scene and establish a string of mock English pub venues that hid a multitude of sins behind their semi-respectable facades.

Finally, the current floated Big George to the edge of the pool and he reached out and pulled himself up to the edge of the infinity wall. Stardust Road ran along the edge of a cliff, and he looked out across the desert at the shimmering beauty of nature's creation. Behind him the man-made abomination was already humming with life. Readying itself for another day worshipping at the altar of Mammon. He wanted to turn and look at what greed and thirst for power had built on this once pristine desert, but he couldn't. The vista laid out before him touched his soul. Like his son had once been, it was still beautiful, unsullied by man's avaricious hand. One day, it too would be gone, lost forever buried beneath man's need to dominate everything, even the planet that sustained him. He felt the tears coming again and this time he didn't fight them.

———◆———

'Jimmy! Wake up, Jimmy.' He heard the voice like an echo in a distant canyon. 'Jimmy, Jimmy.' Was he dreaming? 'For fuck's sake Jimmy.'

He wasn't dreaming.

'Wendy, you don't have to shout, I was just resting my eyes.'

'Resting your eyes? Seemed more like a coma to me.'

Slowly Jimmy opened one eye to see what would happen. His worst fears were confirmed when daylight appeared, and with it the irritated form of Wendy.

'I dreamt about you last night,' he said.

Wendy lifted the sheets and glanced at his groin. 'Not that kind of dream then?'

They both laughed.

'No, it was really deep. John was telling you that you… ' He trailed off, not wanting to repeat the words that John had said.

Wendy sighed. 'To go and spend more time with the dead.'

Jimmy sat up. 'You were actually there?'

'Kinda. Me and John floated into your subconscious while you were sleeping. Best time to get a word in edgeways.'

Jimmy sat up. 'But what about the massage chair?'

Wendy smiled. 'Only existed in your mind.' Wendy pointed to the cup in her right hand. 'Made you a coffee.'

Jimmy sat up. 'Is it real?'

'Do bears shit in the woods?'

He reached out and took it. 'Thanks Wendy, I need this.'

Wendy pointed to the clock. 'You sure do, big day today, Jimmy. Headlining the main stage at Carpenters to a sold-out house.' She chucked him a sheet of paper. 'Printed off the Billboard charts for you. *Vacant Stare* is No 1 on the Blues and Americana charts.'

Jimmy took it from her. Through bleary eyes he saw his name swim into focus with the No 1 next to it. He looked up at Wendy.

'Jeez, Wendy, this real?'

Wendy smiled. She looked down at Jimmy and felt the love she had held for him well up inside her. She sat down on the bed beside him and reached out and held his hand.

'Promise me something, Jimmy.'

'Anything.'

'Don't fuck it up this time. You got the talent, don't get in the way of it.'

Jimmy squeezed her hand and smiled back at her. 'I won't, Wendy. I got this. Stick around and you'll see.'

Wendy turned away for a moment and Jimmy sensed an air of finality. 'I'm leaving tonight.'

Jimmy went to say no but Wendy held up her hand to silence him.

'I'm leaving tonight. I want to watch you but I'm leaving after the second number. Dedicate that one to me.'

Fear crept up Jimmy's spine. An overwhelming sense of loss filled him.

'I can't do this without you.'

'Course you can. I've been dead since before you wrote your first song. I got to go and see this world from my side.' She squeezed his hand far harder than any dead person had a right to. 'I'll be back one day, don't know where, don't know when, but when I am you'll know.'

Jimmy wanted to argue but he knew it was pointless, her mind was made up.

'I'm going to miss you, Wendy Walmart.'

She leaned forwards and kissed him gently on the cheek. 'I'm gonna miss you too, Jimmy Wayne.' Something John had said to him came back to him.

'All the world's a stage Wendy, you play yours and I'll play mine!'

CHAPTER 19
NO GOING BACK

The great and the good were mingling at Lantern Rouge, just off the strip. It was Jack's flagship night club and restaurant, and almost legitimate as far as his business dealings would allow. Ma was standing like a hawk near the buffet making sure the freeloaders weren't having too many visits. The ultimate dinner lady. David Parker wandered over to him.

'Great location, Jack.'

That meant a lot coming from David Parker. 'Thanks, David. We thought it was worth it to give Jimmy's first gig a big launch.'

David looked at the champagne bottle Jack was holding in his hand. Pol Roger.

'This must be costing you a pretty penny, Jack.'

Jack grinned. 'Not really, it's all going on Jimmy's album costs. He's just going to have to sell more records to cover it.'

David sighed. He should have known that Jack would find a way to stick the costs to Jimmy. Still, it didn't really matter, there were plenty of press and important bloggers here. It was worth every penny to get Jimmy the launch he needed. David held up his glass.

'And is this really Pol Roger, Jack?'

Jack winked at him. 'Some of it.' He offered David a refill. 'This one here definitely is.' David let him fill his glass and took a sip. It was delicious.

'I can confirm that, Jack. So why not every bottle?'

Jack nodded towards the milling crowd. 'Most of that lot couldn't tell the difference between champagne and a glass of lemonade.'

David looked at the throng and had to agree. 'Still a nice do though, Jack. You're obviously confident that Jimmy is going to succeed.'

'You see the charts, David? No 1 on the Blues and Americana. In the top 20 on the Country Charts and Billboard top 20 on the main chart. Pre-orders are looking great too.'

David already knew all this. 'Exciting isn't it, Jack, especially when you think all four weeks at Carpenters are fully sold out.'

This was news to Jack, he refilled his glass and clinked it with David's.

'Here's to Jimmy Wayne and all who sail in him!' A beatific smile spread across Jack's potato like features and David knew he was hearing the ringing of cash registers.

Before David could comment he was bustled out of the way by the sharp elbows of Ma Lantern.

'Excuse me, Mr Parker, but I need to talk to Jack urgently.'

Like the gentleman he was David smiled courteously and stood back. He was happy to retreat. Ma Lantern gave him the creeps. That said, she was looking very attractive today. He tried to dismiss the thought from his mind and went in search of food to distract himself.

'Jackie, who is that over there?' Ma nodded towards the mass of people circulating in the room.

'Could you be more specific?'

'The one that looks like a ripped Napoleon, but with better hair.'

Jack didn't need to look to know who Ma meant. 'That's Big George Digbeth, Ma, he's big news in the UK and Miami.'

Ma quivered. 'He could be big news in my bedroom. He's gorgeous.' Ma had always had a penchant for small muscular men. Jack suddenly saw a way to ease the tension between him and Big George.

'He's a widower, Ma. Just lost his son too. Maybe you could cheer him up.'

Ma nodded and stared at Big George like he was a starter on a meat menu.

'Oh, I can bring back his smile, Jackie, you just leave it to me.'

He watched his mother cross the room, honing in on Big George like a killer whale approaching a baby seal.

George looked up and saw Ma approaching. His heart skipped a beat. She was sex on a stick, and he wanted to lick it. The way she moved; the way she had her gaze locked on him. Jack watched the pair of them in fascination, it was like watching a wildlife documentary. The two wild creatures had singled each other out and now the mating ritual began. He may not have a father but maybe he was about to acquire a stepdad. He turned away as they met taking one last glance at his mother. She looked good. Losing the heavy make-up had taken years off her and her figure, despite some cosmetic assistance, was still amazing. She could easily pass for fifty. Big George didn't stand a chance.

Lena sidled up to Jack. 'Looks like it's feeding time for your mother.'

Jack smiled. 'Yeah, looks pretty hungry, don't she?'

'Who's the victim?'

Jack looked at Lena reprovingly. 'Give Ma a break. She may not know it, but she is working for the company.'

'How so?'

'That's Big George Digbeth.'

Lena sneered. 'He don't look very big.'

'Maybe not vertically, but he runs the biggest crime family in the UK, Fewhurst Ltd. You heard of them, I take it?'

Lena nodded. 'Yeah, owns a load of venues in Miami. Are he and Ma an item?'

'Looking at the way they are looking at each other my guess is they will be before the night is over.' Jack looked very pleased.

'Two Empires united, happy families all round.'

Jack turned to look at Lena, she looked beautiful and for once he told her so.

'You know darling, sometimes I forget how beautiful you are.'

Lena smiled. 'I know Jack, but I forgive you.'

He took her in his arms and hugged her.

Terry Moist watched from the doorway. He turned to Tony C. 'Looks like all the Lanterns are loved up tonight.'

'Yeah,' agreed Tony. 'I think Mister Deal is opening peoples' hearts.'

Terry gave Tony a pained stare. 'And I think you're going soft.'

Tony pointed to the crowded room. 'Everyone's going soft. You ever seen so much happiness in Vegas? It's all down to John. He's an angel.'

'Well, it sure as hell ain't down to Jimmy Wayne's music. It's depressing as hell.' Tony nodded. 'Yeah, it's kinda sad but beautiful too.'

Terry shrugged. 'It's dark and brooding.'

'Maybe, but do you like it?' pressed Tony.

Terry didn't reply for a moment.

'Yeah, I like it.'

David Parker stood sipping his Pol Roger and watching the room. It was full of well-known Vegas faces and the real movers and shakers. Jack knew how to throw a party, but they were only here because of Jimmy. Jimmy was back and he had helped him get there. Seven years since he had first got to know him. He was just a washed-up mess back then, but David could see through the mask Jimmy had hidden behind. See the nice guy beneath the drunk. Hear the talent that was drowning in booze and self-pity. For all the things David had achieved in his life, rescuing Jimmy gave him the most satisfaction. From the Desert bar in the Riviera in third rate Blackjack to Carpenters on the Strip in Vegas. What a story. He sipped his champagne.

'We did it David.'

David turned to see his old friend Michael smiling back at him and raising a glass. 'Here's to Jimmy Wayne and the Second Chance.'

'I'll drink to that!'

On a walkway above the room, a lone figure stood observing. He wore a brown suit topped with a brown trilby. He smiled to himself. All the pieces were dropping into place.

As the clock slowly ticked towards 7.30 p.m., Kid smiled at Jimmy.

'This is it Jimmy, after this there is no going back, you're going to be famous.'

Jimmy turned to Kid and put his arm around him. '*We* are going to be famous. Even No Relation and Doug will be famous. This is a band, and we are sticking together.'

'That's great, Jimmy. I'm just saying, now is the last chance to walk out that back door.'

Jimmy looked at Kid as if he was mad. 'Why would I do that?'

'There's a price to fame Jimmy. Look what Ron Blazer did to you in the first interview. Found a son you never knew you had. After this you are going to be public property. Privacy will be a thing of the past, and secrets will have a way of being found out. Walk away now and none of that will happen. Thanks to Aksel you got money.' Kid looked at him waiting for his reply.

'I ain't going nowhere.'

Kid nodded and then a huge smile spread across his face. 'I'm glad you said that buddy because me and the boys are looking forward to taking this ride!'

Just then David came into the dressing room. 'Two minutes, boys. A full house awaits!'

'What's it look like?' asked No Relation.

David shook his head. 'It's not what it looks like, it's how it feels. You could cut the atmosphere with a knife. Feels like the whole town's waiting for you.'

The boys looked at each other like nervous schoolboys.

'It's really going to happen,' No Relation grabbed Doug and hugged him.

'It's really going to happen.'

Jimmy smiled, these boys had been with him through thick and thin – mainly thin – and now they were about to reap their rewards.

'Gather in boys, I got some stuff to say.'

Doug pulled a face. 'Here comes Jimmy's win one for the Gipper speech.'

Jimmy grinned. 'None of that, I just want to thank you boys for sticking with me all these years. I know I wasn't always reliable.'

'You were never reliable,' said No Relation.

'Guilty as charged, but that ain't happening again. Now is our moment. The train's in the station and we are getting on. I dunno where it's taking us but as long as it's going I'm on it till the end.' Jimmy looked at the four faces that looked back at him. Kid, Doug, No Relation and David. He loved these guys, some more than others, but he did love them. 'Let's go be famous.'

They let out a collective, 'Yeah!'

Except for David. 'Absolutely!' He couldn't have been more British if he tried.

Jimmy stood in the wings with Kid, and a familiar face was waiting for them. Steve Cronkite, the velvet toned handyman from the Riviera was there. Jimmy grabbed him and gave him a big hug.

'Steve, what are you doing here?'

Steve grinned. 'David thought you might want the ole velvet voice to announce you one more time.' His voice dripped like melted chocolate.

Jimmy turned to David. 'Thanks buddy, I can't think of anyone better.'

The lights went down in the auditorium and cheering erupted from the 680 people jammed into every seat in the house. Steve waited for the cheering to die down and then stepped up to the mic.

'Ladies and Gentlemen, Carpenters would like you to welcome to the stage Jimmy Wayne and the Second Chance.'

Jimmy was the first onto the stage, followed by Kid, and the cheering and applause hit them like a wave. He glanced at Kid, who was strapping on his Telecaster. Kid winked at him. Jimmy turned to No Relation and gave him the nod.

'One, two, three, four,' and they were off into the first bar of 'Scattered Bodies'.

Floating high in the back of the theatre, Wendy smiled. Good old Jimmy, had to get his most explicit song about killing in first, the boy had no shame!

The band sounded great, and when the song finished Carpenters went crazy. Jimmy waited for the applause to subside; he hadn't forgotten his promise to Wendy.

'Thanks folks, we really appreciate you coming out.'

Another wave of cheering broke out and Jimmy rode it waiting for it to subside. When it did, he spoke.

'I'd like to dedicate this next number to a very special lady called Wendy. She means everything to me and always will.'

Wendy smiled. Jimmy and the boys were on their way, but where they were headed, she could not go. That door had closed forever. A fleeting moment of regret swept over her, a sense of loss at the realisation that in this world she no longer had a place. Their paths had parted, and she had her own journey to make, and it would be without Jimmy. As Jimmy sang, she remembered all the happy times they had shared. They had had their moment and now like the evening sun it had faded and was just a memory, its last rays of light shimmering and illuminating what might have been. She turned her back and floated out through the roof. The stars lit the night sky like sprinkled diamonds caught in moonlight. Somewhere out there was the new world in which she would have to find her way. She took a deep breath and headed for the horizon. Places to go, people to see!

Read an exclusive excerpt from Book 3:

ALL THE WORLD'S A STAGE

Jimmy opened his eyes; he was in the shower in his bathroom at Carpenters Hotel in Vegas. He didn't understand how he had just been at the Song Cemetery with Wendy but he knew he had. She just seemed to be able to tune into his mind whenever she wanted. He walked out of the shower leaving a trail of soapy water in his wake, his soap on a rope hanging provocatively over his groin, he really would have to shorten that rope. He grabbed his phone from the bedside table and pulled up Kid Oscarson's number. He pressed dial. To his surprise Kid answered on the second ring.

'Jesus Jimmy, it's only 10 a.m.! What's the problem?'

'Sheriff Pence has bought a dog.' There was silence on the other end of the line. 'You still there, Kid?'

'Surprisingly, yes.'

'Didn't you hear what I said, Sheriff Pence has bought a dog!' There was no disguising the panic in Jimmy's voice.

'And that should interest me because?'

'It's a Bloodhound.' Kid absorbed this new information.

'That's good to know Jimmy, is that all?'

'He's started walking it.'

'That's nice. Dog like that needs regular walks.'

'He's walking it near the Song Cemetery.' Kid took a deep breath, this changed everything.

'You ever killed a dog before, Jimmy?' Jimmy thought about it for a moment.

'I clipped one once with a pick-up truck but it was only bruised.'

'Well I guess there's a first time for everything.'

'Are you suggesting I go to Blackjack and kill Pence's dog?'

'I guess I am,' said Kid. Jimmy was appalled.

'I can't murder a dog in cold blood.'

'Well, you don't seem to have any problems with killing people.'

'It's not the same.'

'Course it's not, ain't no death penalty for killing a dog.'